Through Lust, We Fell

THE LUST & DESIRE DUET
BOOK 1

KASONDRA FOX

Fox & Flame Press

FOX & FLAME PRESS

Copyright © 2025 by Kasondra Fox

All rights reserved. No part of this book may be reproduced, distributed, or transmitted in any form or by any means—including photocopying, recording, AI use or other electronic or mechanical methods—without the prior written permission of the publisher, except in the case of brief quotations used in reviews or critical articles.

Cover design & internal art by Carly's Bookish Beasts

This is a work of fiction. Names, characters, places, and incidents are either the product of the author's imagination or are used fictitiously. Any resemblance to actual persons, living or dead, events, or locales is purely coincidental.

All brand names and product names mentioned are trademarks, registered trademarks, or trade names of their respective holders. Fox & Flame Press is not affiliated with or endorsed by any product or vendor referenced in this work.

Printed in the United States of America

First Edition: March 2026

ISBN: 979-8-9945012-5-2 (Amazon Paperback) 979-8-9945012-2-1 (E-Book) 979-8-9945012-9-0 (IngramSpark Paperback)

Excerpt(s) from SHADOWFEVER: FEVER SERIES BOOK 5 by Karen Marie Moning, copyright © 2011 by Karen Marie Moning, LLC. Used by permission of Delacorte Press, an imprint of Random House, a division of Penguin Random House LLC. All rights reserved.

Formatted using Lacuna

"Some people bring out the worst in you, others bring out the best, and then there are those remarkably rare, addictive ones who just bring out the most. Of everything.

They make you feel so alive that you'd follow them straight into hell, just to keep getting your fix."

—*Shadowfever*, Karen Marie Moning

For the women who love with fire,
the men who fear the burn,
and the good girls who finally stop apologizing for the smoke.

Author Note

Through Lust, We Fell is a contemporary romance and the first book in *The Lust & Desire Duet*. Their story is one of passion, vulnerability, and self-reckoning—where love isn't always enough, and growth demands honesty. Some moments move quickly on purpose, allowing us to experience Khloe and Waylon's emotional and physical reactions in real time; others sit with them longer, giving us space to understand them more deeply. If you prefer to go in blind, turn the page now... Their journey continues in *Through Desire, We Burn*, where every truth they've avoided finally comes to light.

Reader discretion is advised. This novel contains mature themes, explicit intimacy, and emotional triggers surrounding trauma and mental health. Please take care while reading.

If you're in your healing journey, I hope you remember—your scars are not the full story, and you can be soft without being weak. You are seen. You are worthy. Always.

A list of trigger warnings can be found by scanning the QR code below or visiting **http://authorkasondrafox.com/content-warnings**.

Happy Reading!

Kasondra Fox

P.S. You've been warned. Now, enjoy the chaos.

Good Girl.

Through Lust,

We Fell

Prologue

The Week Before the Fall...

Last night's girl stirs, stretching like a cat before propping herself up on an elbow. Sunlight cuts through the blinds and drapes across the bed. I blink awake, roll to the edge, and plant my feet on the floor. Behind me the sheets rustle.

"Did you have fun last night, Waylon Rhodes?" she asks, voice all sugar and curiosity.

Fuck, what's her name again?

"Sure did... hun," I say, letting the easy lie roll off my tongue. My voice dips naturally into that low, slow drawl women have called "*Southern silk*" more times than I've bothered to count. I never ask for compliments—they come uninvited but always welcome.

She smiles, apparently satisfied, humming as she settles back into the pillows as if she expects the conversation to continue. I stand instead, tug on my boxers, and grab my phone from the dresser. It vibrates with a string of unopened texts from Aaron Brooks—my best friend from the Corps—a man who bleeds for the people he loves. He's moving in across the street today and has been texting me like a disgruntled girlfriend ever since I joked I might forget to pick him up at the airport.

AARON

> You ignoring me again or still buried in someone's daughter?

AARON

> Bet you're balls deep in some bad decisions. Call me anyway.

AARON

> I'm landing in an hour. You ghost me one more time, I'm calling your mama.

I smirk and toss the phone onto the bed.

The woman watches me from under the covers. No request for breakfast. No puckering up for a kiss. Smart girl. She dresses and slips out with a wave and a smile.

The silence that follows settles over the house like an old habit. I cross to the mirror and rake a hand through my hair. Same cocky smirk. Same eyes that pretend they don't need anything. The confidence I've perfected over the years looks effortless, but it's nothing more than armor. A mask I wear until women believe in the illusion like gospel.

I make temporary things feel permanent... at least for a night. My charm always spreads like wildfire. I don't mean to steal hearts, but I never stick around long enough to give 'em back. I wasn't built for staying put. Not after *her*.

I yank on jeans and shoot Aaron a text back.

WAYLON

> On my way. Try not to cry before I get there.

Maybe him moving here will jolt me back to life. God knows chasing tail and outrunning feelings hasn't done it yet. Time to shake shit up.

Prologue

North to South, Heart in Tow

Bubble wrap pops under my knee as I lean onto another cardboard box and shove the last of my clothes inside. Half of my life's already packed in the back of the U-Haul. The other half I sent ahead.

My phone sits on speaker, propped against an old candle jar. Flora's voice crackles through from San Antonio. "Are you sure you didn't forget your stethoscope again?"

"I triple-checked," I mutter, taping the box shut. "I might forget my underwear and whatever's left of my heart, but I'm not starting my new nursing job without the one thing that makes me look official."

In the background, I hear Missy's laugh before she says, "Leave the heartbreak up north, baby. Down here, we only collect men's souls, not emotional damage." She's a fellow nurse whom Flora swears I'll love and occasionally want to strangle.

I roll my eyes. "Not why I'm moving."

"Of course not," Flora coos. "Just a totally normal, not-at-all-trauma-related cross-country relocation for Khloe Navarro."

My throat tightens. *I am trying not to think about those*

things, which is why I'm driving 1,800 miles south.

"I need a fresh start," I say instead, tugging on my jean jacket.

"And I need tacos. Hurry," Missy yells in the background.

Flora laughs. "Text me when you hit the Tennessee line."

"Will do."

I look around my empty house one last time, grabbing the framed photo I purposely left out as the last thing to pack.

I lay it on top of the last box. An old woman I loved more than oxygen smiles up at me, an arm around my photographed shoulders, both of us in matching aprons from the year she taught me how to bake pecan pie. I swipe a thumb across the glass, swallowing the ache, and grab my keys.

Connecticut knows everything I have survived. Texas knows nothing about the wounds I carry with my stethoscope, and that is exactly how I want it. I am not going there to share or bleed. I am going there to begin again.

I lock the door behind me and don't look back.

PART I

Chapter 1

Clean Flannel. Dirty Soul.

...One week later...

I yank my flannel from the dryer, still warm and smelling like detergent instead of last weekend's forgettable fuck. Small victories—I didn't remember her name, but at least I remembered to do laundry.

I catch my reflection in the mirror as my phone buzzes on the counter with a text from a girl I barely remember meeting.

BLUE STAR BAR BRUNETTE

U going out tonight?

I start to answer, then stop. It's like I'm chasing comfort in the dark but waking up empty anyway. There's a knock at the door. "Aaron?" I call, tugging on my flannel.

He steps in, his broad shoulders filling the doorway, the dim light casting deep shadows over his rich brown skin. He's wearing sweats and carrying takeout like he plans on melting into my couch.

"I thought we were staying in," he mutters.

"Hell no. You're not hidin' in my house in pajama bottoms," I say, tossing him one of my nicer shirts.

Aaron rubs his bald head. "I don't know, man. I think I'm jet-lagged or something. I should stay back." His gaze flickers toward the door, as if it's offering him salvation.

"We're goin' out. One drink."

He hesitates. That haunted look sits behind his eyes, one I've seen in my own mirror more than once.

"You sure?" he asks.

"Positive." I smirk because I know that smile works on damn near anyone. "You've earned that much, and you need a distraction."

Aaron nods reluctantly. I clap him on the shoulder and grab my hat off the counter, tugging it low as I herd him toward the door. There's a tension in him that tells me he needs this. Fresh off a tour and discharged from the Marines, he's still figuring out how to live with all he's been carrying.

Tonight's about helping him. Being the responsible one for once. But damn if my bones aren't already wondering what the night has to offer me.

I swing open the Uber door, boots thudding on the pavement. Aaron follows, rolling his shoulders as we step toward the entrance of the River Walk. The city is alive with music, movement, and the low hum of conversation, broken by the occasional burst of drunken laughter. I shove my cap down low, trying to block out the sinking sun and the keyed-up feeling in my chest.

Many shots later, we're leaning against the bar. A half-empty beer in one hand and a relaxed smile on my lips as two women drift toward our end of the bar with bold smiles, flirty eyes, ready for something. I tip my beer to them, then jerk my chin toward Aaron. "He's the single one tonight," I tell them with a wink. One gives me a pout like I just broke her heart, the other drifts toward Aaron. He barely glances up from whatever game's on the TV, and the women take off.

I lean back against the barstool and pretend to be unbothered, even though I can feel his mood dragging mine down. The mission is to get Aaron to loosen up, not me sinking my teeth into some stranger. But, fuck, he's not letting me play wingman. Some ghosts don't take a night off, no matter how much alcohol you pour.

A redhead slides into the empty seat beside me and shoots her shot. "Hey, what's your name?"

"Waylon. And this here is my friend, Aaron."

Aaron barely glances her way, so her attention comes back to me. I flash her a confident smile. "So, what brings you out tonight?"

"Bad day," she says, twirling a strand of hair between her fingers.

I give her a polite chuckle, let her keep talking. It's easy flirting, but I'm not here to chase. Normally, a night out for me is about the hunt, about satisfying a craving that runs deeper than I'd like to admit. A craving only a beautiful woman can fulfill. But tonight is supposed to be different.

So I take an easy exit, turning back to Aaron with some story from basic training. And the redhead gets up and leaves. I drain the rest of my beer, watching her walk off.

Mama always says I'm "close enough to tease, never close enough to keep."

Aaron's sitting with our empty shot glasses, lost to whatever war's playing behind his eyes, one he sure as hell won't let me fight with him. Time to recalibrate. Maybe if I queue him up with someone disarming, he'll snap out of it. I spot a blonde a few stools over, flash her a grin, then tip my gaze toward Aaron. She catches the hint and slides down, touching his arm. I watch her start talking to him as I feel eyes on me.

Across the room, a curly-haired brunette catches my stare; all honeyed skin and guarded eyes. There's something in the way she looks at me. Curious, resigned, like she knows men like me break things.

Perfect. She's pretty enough to make every other girl in the room disappear. Enough to make me want to wreck my whole damn night.

I push off the barstool to make my move, and she snaps her gaze away like she touched a hot stove.

Aaron groans beside me. "I think I'm gonna be sick."

Chapter 2

Choker tight. Grief tighter.

After the third outfit doesn't fit right, I rip my bra off and fling it aside. It lands near the pile of clothes I've already rejected for being too much, too little, too not-me.

Across from me, Flora slides into a flirty blue dress. One that my breasts would burst out of before I made it to the door.

"You're overthinking it," she teases, her messy blonde bun bobbing as she slides on heels. I tuck my black wavy curls behind my ears. They're rebelliously springing back to life after hiding from the rain.

"Nights out aren't my thing," I grumble, searching my suitcase for an outfit that doesn't scream rolled-out-of-bed—or worse, post-shift nurse energy. Anything that doesn't scream I'm on the brink of emotional collapse.

I settle on a loose-fitting white spaghetti-strap blouse and throw it on. The fabric catches the light as it falls against my warm beige skin. Adjusting the straps, I smooth it over my hips, then shrug on my favorite jean jacket.

Turning to my best friend, I lift a brow. "What do you think?"

Flora smirks. "Perfect… if you're auditioning for a '90s sitcom."

I roll my eyes, grab my velvet choker, and fasten it

around my throat. "*J-14* cover model, actually."

She laughs. "You need this. A little fun. A little reminder that you're still alive. You've been through hell these past few years."

The burden of it all settles over me. Alive hurts. The decision to leave and the jarring reality of starting over. Alive remembers too much.

Flora pulls me out of my thoughts. "You okay over there?" she asks, her brightness softening when she notices my silence.

I force a smile, nodding. "Yeah, just... thinking."

Flora gives me that face. Best-friend mode, reading me like a book. She consistently supports me; she understands me completely, flaws and all.

I paste on a smile and nod anyway. "Promise me we'll grab a drink or two and come back. I still have to unpack."

"Pinky promise!" She throws her pinky in my face. I laugh, hooking mine with hers.

Tonight isn't about healing. It's about forgetting. For a few hours, at least.

I adjust my choker, the delicate fabric brushing my skin as Flora and I step out of the cab. The humid air of the River Walk closes around us, thick with earth and algae, cut through by the sharper scent of street food sizzling nearby. Neon lights flicker, reflecting off car windows as the pulse of San Antonio invites us in. A live band thrums in the distance, broken up by the occasional honk of a car weaving through crowded streets.

I glance around and realize I don't know what I'm looking for. Maybe that's the problem.

We settle in at a bar along the water. From across the room, I catch sight of a gorgeous guy's head turning from girl to girl as they approach him and his friend. Half curious, half unimpressed, I watch. I'm not here to flirt, but I can't seem to stop myself from looking.

I turn back to my drink while Flora chats with Missy. Missy's got that all-American kind of pretty—warm ivory skin, sharp jaw, brown hair pulled back like she means business, hazel eyes that look right through the bullshit.

But without meaning to, I glance back. He's the kind of handsome that doesn't ask permission. The kind that wrecks your whole damn life. His eyes catch mine and light up like he's found gold.

I drop my gaze fast, but not fast enough. Flora's already clocked me. She nudges me under the table, grinning. "Checking out Mr. Hat? He looks like trouble, you know."

I arch my brow. "I wasn't checking him out. I was... observing. Ya know, like a scientist studying wildlife."

Flora laughs. "Observing? Sure."

Missy turns and snorts. "Be careful with that one. I've seen him around. Always a new girl, a different day."

I glance back briefly, my lips pressing into a thin line. "Noted."
Figures. Same guys, different city.

Missy takes a sip of her drink before continuing. "I mean, he's hot, but don't expect any rings or flowers, Khloe."

Flora smiles. "I won't let her get swept up in that bullshit."

"What's the actual story, Khloe? Why'd you leave Connecticut? Witness Protection?" Missy teases.

Flora shoots her a look, half warning, half amused. "Missy!"

"It's fine," I say, waving it off, though the reasons are lodged deep in my chest. "It's not exactly a fun story."

Missy leans in, propping her chin on her hand. "C'mon. I'm nosy. Spill."

I hesitate, tapping a twitchy rhythm against my glass. The urge to shrug conflicts with the ache in my chest. Flora gives me a nod that says *you don't have to carry it alone*. I sigh. "It wasn't just one thing. It was... everything." I give her the cliff notes version, enough to make her face freeze between awe, pure rage, and grief for me. And then I end on *him*. I look up at the end of my story to meet Missy's eyes.

Missy stares at me, mouth half-open. She shakes her head. "Motherfucker." Sitting back, she crosses her arms, giving me a look. "He's lucky you left, Khlo. 'Cause if you hadn't, I would've rearranged his dick with a baseball bat."

Flora lets out a choked laugh. I crack a genuine smile.

Missy whispers, "I'm serious. Big ass bat. Not the cute little hollow ones kids use. Like, full-send Texas Rangers home run."

It's ridiculous. It's wildly inappropriate—and exactly what I needed to hear.

She continues. "And I'm sorry about your memaw; mine is my biggest critic. You're lucky to have had a good one." Missy's phone buzzes, rattling her drink. She checks the screen, chuckling. "Alright, I'm out. Going to meet my sister, Lena. Don't wait up unless y'all wanna bail me out."

Flora throws an arm around me. "You'll love Lena, Khloe. She's a hot mess. And even more vulgar than Missy."

Missy tosses us a wink, strutting off. "Talent runs in the family."

Chapter 3

Heat & Hollow Places

I follow Aaron out, the humid air hitting us harder than the tequila. He leans over the tree boxes, heaving. I stand there, patting his back like it'll fix anything. I shake it off with a practiced shrug, but still, something sits too heavy in my chest tonight.

Nights like this used to be enough. The noise, the flirting, and the drinking. It's thinner, though. Like chasing something that slips through your fingers faster every time.

Aaron groans again, and I laugh. Dad's words echo through my mind.

Distract yourself. Laugh it off. Move on.

I grew up hearing that after Uncle Beau died. Grief hollowed my dad out without ever saying a word. Dad took my cousin, Jackman, under his wing, and made sure we were all prepared for a world that didn't hand out second chances. We weren't allowed to talk about it or cry. My sister, Jackman, and I learned early that the good ones leave you. Don't get too attached. Don't count on anybody sticking around. And if you feel too much, bury it deep before it has time to grow roots.

I shake the memory away. I wonder if I looked like Aaron back when PTSD first started creeping in. Before the bad dreams and the short fuse. Before everything inside me got too loud to ignore, and I dragged myself into the Marine Corps shrink's office.

My chest tightens watching Aaron, doubled over and breathing like he's drowning in open air. He needs a distraction. Hell, we both do. I thought I'd found one back in the bar. One second, I was scanning the crowd so I could play wingman. Next thing I knew, my gaze was on the curly-haired brunette across the room. She was pretty as sin, but that wasn't what stuck with me. It was the way she looked at me, like for a heartbeat she *recognized* something in me I didn't even know I'd been hiding. And that's when I feel a weight against my skin, heavier than the humidity.

Eyes.

Chapter 4

The Looks

Flora and I stroll along the River Walk path, sipping daiquiris as the sun casts an orange glow across the water. After a long first week, this is what I needed. Fresh air, a chance to enjoy the night, and a little gossip about work.

"So, you're telling me you turned down the first hot doctor that hit on you?" Flora asks in disbelief.

I shrug. "He wasn't exactly subtle, Flo. Guys like that think they're God's gift to women."

"Maybe he is," Flora teases. "You never know."

My snarky reply is halted when a guttural sound shatters the quiet. A man groans as he throws up. We stop in our tracks, exchanging looks.

"What the...?" Flora says, craning her neck.

Ahead, near a bench, a man's crouched over, clutching his knees, emptying his stomach. Another man stands beside him, one hand on his back, the other braced on the bench.

"Classy," Flora mutters, wrinkling her nose.

The standing man is staring at us. Even from a distance, his sharp features and confident posture are impossible to miss. A sense of recognition dawns as I study his face. Mr.

Hat. He straightens up, flashing a lopsided grin that seems entirely out-of-place given the situation.

"Well, hey there," he drawls, his Southern accent warm and rich. "Didn't mean to interrupt your evenin' stroll."

I pause, unsure whether to keep walking or say something.

Flora, of course, doesn't hesitate. "You guys alright?" she asks, concerned and curious.

The man tips his hat, grin widening. "We're doin' just fine. My buddy here thought he could out-drink me. Spoiler alert: he can't."

"Not my finest moment," the man mumbles, waving a hand weakly.

I sigh, my nursing skills kicking in. "Does he need water? Or I don't know, an ambulance?"

"Nah," the standing man says. His eyes are a little too focused on me. "Aaron'll be fine. He's tougher than he looks. Aren't ya, buddy?" The standing man slaps his friend's back.

Aaron groans in response.

I raise an eyebrow. "Well, he doesn't look fine."

"Darlin', you're sweet to worry, but I've got it handled," he says, smiling. His eyes trace up my body, thick with meaning. "Name's Waylon, by the way. You are?"

I roll my eyes, crossing my arms. "Not interested."

Waylon's grin deepens. "Feisty. I like that."

Flora giggles, stepping closer to them. "Ignore her. I'm Flora. She's Khloe. We're not feisty. Just practical. Big difference."

"Well, Flora and Khloe," Waylon says, his voice wrapping around our names like a song, "y'all made my night a little brighter."

Aaron groans again. "Waylon, for the love of God, stop flirting. Help me up."

"Hold your horses," Waylon mutters, hoisting Aaron to his feet.

Flora nudges me, whispering, "I think the cowboy could

be an excellent distraction for you."

I shoot her a look. "Absolutely not."

Waylon glances our way, while Aaron leans heavily on his shoulder. Flora perks up, her trademark mischievous grin unmistakable as she gives Aaron a slow once-over. "Oh, I have an idea. Why don't we all go for drinks? You can rehydrate your friend while we *supervise*."

"Flora—" I start, but Waylon cuts in, matching Flora's energy.

"Now that sounds like a plan. Aaron could use water. I could use somethin' stronger." He winks.

Aaron sighs. "I'll... rally."

Flora lights up. "You buying?"

Waylon chuckles, shifting Aaron's weight. "Depends. Y'all stickin' around?"

Flora doesn't wait for my response. "Oh, we're in."

I groan but don't argue. Against my better judgment, I follow Flora and Waylon along the River Walk, Aaron staggering along beside him.

We claim a corner table tucked inside the bar. Aaron sips water like it's medicine while Flora keeps the mood light. "So... tequila shots, huh?" Flora leans toward him, her expression mock serious. "Bold move. Any regrets?"

Aaron chuckles weakly. "One or two. But I'm alive, so there's that. It was jet lag."

Flora arches her brow. "I love a man with excuses."

Aaron's eyes narrow as a smirk plays on his lips.

Waylon lounges beside me, beer in hand, grinning at the back and forth, but his gaze keeps drifting to me, like I'm the only thing worth returning to. "Flora, you're relentless. I like it," he says, eyes already back on me.

I sip my cider, pretending not to notice how often he looks.

"So, Khloe." His voice cuts through my thoughts. "What brings you to the River Walk on a Friday night? Waitin' for me to sweep you off your feet?"

I roll my eyes, but the corner of my mouth twitches. "Hardly. Flora dragged me out."

"Well," he says, his grin as confident as ever. "Lucky me, then."

A blush creeps across my cheeks. My eyes dart away before he can see the curiosity in them. "You don't quit, do you?"

"Not when I see somethin' worth chasin'."

How many times has he used that line?

Waylon tips his glass toward me and takes a sip as he removes his hat, laying it on the table. It's then that I really look at him. There's something undeniably naughty about him, as if he's always on the verge of saying something daring. Or meant to make me smile, whether I want to or not.

Sensing my stare, he runs a hand through his hair. Under the dim lights, the dark brown strands shift, revealing how neatly styled they are beneath his cap. The sides are cropped close, fading into a slightly longer top; enough to hint at a rebellious streak. Enough to tousle with his fingers when he's thinking too hard, or to fall out-of-place after a long day. Structured yet undone.

The contrast of his dark hair against his vibrant green eyes makes them glow. They crinkle at the corners when he smiles. A smile that seems permanent, like he doesn't know how to be anything but charming. And his lips: thin and tempting.

The longer I look, the warmer my skin feels. He's all edges and at ease. My fingers tighten around my bottle. I should look away, but I don't. He has these faint freckles across the bridge of his nose, barely there, like the first snowflakes before a storm. They soften him enough to make the sharpness feel inviting rather than dangerous.

My gaze dips lower. His flannel sleeves are rolled to the elbow, freckles scattering across his forearms, practically begging to be traced. Above them, the fabric stretches over large, defined biceps wrapped in plaid. He's distant, but impossible not to want closer.

My eyes dance back up to his. He *sees* me seeing him.

Damn him.

Waylon taps his glass gently against my bottle. A silent

toast. God, he's dangerous. I hesitate, then raise my drink and take a sip. A silent surrender. For the first time, I let myself enjoy his attention. His grin widens like he's won.

"Pardon me," he says, rising to his feet, "I'm off to the little boys' room."

Aaron stands too, but before he can take a step, Flora grins and tilts her head. "Aw, how cute. Boys go in pairs now? Should we expect a bathroom selfie?"

I laugh as the guys walk away. Flora leans in, eyes wide with mischief.

"Are we lucky or what?"

I glance around, pretending to stay neutral, then shrug.

Flora rolls her eyes at me. "Come on, Khloe. Aaron looks like he was carved out of smooth chocolate and good decisions. That shaved head and eyes that smile before his mouth does. Those shoulders look like they're in the gym every morning, but too humble to mention it. And don't even get me started on his jawline—it's unfair."

Khloe laughs. "Sounds like you've been staring."

"Please," Flora says, waving her off. "I've just got eyes. And taste." I chuckle as I take a sip of my drink, but Flora continues. "Prepare your liver, I'm going to get us shots."

I watch her walk off, blonde bun bouncing, and something tugs at my chest.

This week, I signed the mortgage on my little house in Alamo Heights that I'm sharing with Flora—peeling paint, creaky floors, and the first place that feels like mine. A new life, bought with a slice of Grandma's inheritance and more courage than I thought I had.

I swallow the lump in my throat. Grandma would've loved this messy new start, even if I'm not sure I do yet. It was a decision that felt equal parts terrifying and liberating. Flora made it feel possible. She always has.

Our relationship had been forged in the thick of life's challenges, a bond that only grew stronger over the years. From fifth-grade recess until now, she's been the one friend

I never had to question.

When her family moved to Stamford, I was drawn to her infectious laugh and relentless optimism. Flora says she was drawn to me because I always let her talk, but also because of my strength and resilience. I didn't see myself that way—not then.

But maybe now I do. Maybe starting over means finally believing I deserve something good.

Chapter 5

Stall Talk

Aaron leans against the sink in the bathroom, splashing cold water on his face. "Okay, I'll admit it. I may have underestimated the tequila shots."

I bite my tongue, holding back a laugh, adjusting my cap in the mirror. "Yeah? I was startin' to wonder if I'd have to carry you home."

Aaron huffs a laugh, wiping his face with a paper towel. "Not tonight, Romeo." He shoots me a look. "Bro, Flora's been all over me. What about you?"

"She's got a mouth on her, I'll give her that. Quick with the wit."

Aaron raises an eyebrow. "Flora?"

I tilt my head. "Khloe."

Aaron hums. "Ooh. That's why you've been throwing your eyes all night?"

I turn on the faucet, running my hands under the water. "She's fightin' it," I say, shaking off my hands, "but she looks at me like she wants to know what I'd do if she didn't."

Aaron snorts. "Not used to a woman resisting you?"

I grin as I dry my hands. "Can't say I am. But I'm enjoying myself." It's true; most women fold fast for me. They fall in line without me needing to lift more than a smirk. But Khloe's making me work for it. And I like the hell out of that.

I glance at Aaron. "So, you takin' Flora home, or is she playin'?"

Aaron shrugs. "She's got energy for days and looks like trouble in heels. All pale legs, sunshine hair, and that smile she probably uses to get out of speeding tickets and into people's business. Those big blue eyes aren't bad either. I think she just enjoys messing with me."

"Don't let that sweet face fool you. I have a feeling she'd gut someone with ease if they crossed her." I size him up, choosing my next words carefully. "Are you sure you're okay, though? Jetlag's a cute excuse. You don't need to talk to someone?"

"I'm good. I promise. I'm acclimating. That's all. D.C. isn't this humid."

Aaron's always been that commanding man, but he wears confidence like a shield. Like someone who's used to fighting battles on every front. He's always been secure and dependable. But tonight, that shield looks cracked.

I clap his shoulder as we step out. "Good thing you've got me to keep you upright."

Chapter 6

Backwards Hat

Flora returns to the table with a tray of four shots and two more ciders.

I squint at the shot glasses, then at her. "You bought the guys' shots? Aren't you such a gentleman?"

Flora raises a shot glass, with that familiar gleam in her eyes. "First one to finish both shots doesn't have to kiss their admirer."

I frantically grab my glasses. Before I can swallow the second shot, Flora slams both down with a triumphant grin. "Dude, not fair! You had a head start." I cough, grabbing my cider to ease the burn.

Flora grins. "It could be worse. The cowboy could be hideous. Have you seen those eyes? Swoon of the century."

She dramatically pretends to faint in her chair as the guys walk up. We exchange glances before turning to them.

"We thought we lost you." Flora chuckles.

Aaron gestures toward the back. "A pool table opened up. You guys wanna play?"

Flora grabs my hand. "I suck at pool. Let's go!" Laughing, she tugs me toward the tables. Then, shooting me a sly smile, Flora looks back at the guys and calls out, "I need another drink!"

Aaron waves her toward the bar. "Guess it's my turn to buy."

They veer off, leaving Waylon and me behind. I turn to him, arching a brow. "She's so subtle. Wanna sit over here?"

He follows me to a pair of stools beside the empty pool table. I set my drink on the built-out mantel as I sit down. Waylon sets his beer down, taking off his hat again. The two shots hit me at once, along with the sight of him hatless, his messy hair, and that smirk in full view.

Fuck, he's hot.

"What's your name again, cowboy?" I ask, carried by drunken confidence.

He opens his mouth, and in that deep, syrupy drawl, he answers, "Waylon, darlin'."

He reaches up to place his hat back on, and I boldly reach for it, stopping him. "Don't put it back on," I tease, smiling as I slide it out of his hands. "It hides your beauty." Grinning, I flip it backward onto my head.

I often think of myself as unremarkable. A girl who could fade into the background of a crowded room. Next to Flora's striking blue eyes, my dark ones feel ordinary; their warmth blends into the butterscotch hue of my skin. I'm used to the way most guys' eyes drop to my chest before they even bother looking me in the face. But Waylon's gaze doesn't slide down like I expect. It stays on my eyes.

And that leaves more of a mark than any pickup line ever could.

Chapter 7

That Girl Is Poison

I should be thinking about how good she looks wearing my hat, because, damn, she does. But she's telling me some story about Flora, hands moving, mouth quick and animated.

And I'm actually listening. Not just nodding along, waiting for the next opening. Not plotting how easy it'd be to lean in, murmur something smooth, and make sure tonight ends the way it usually does. I'm watching the way her eyes light up when she gets going, the way she bites her lip when she's holding back a laugh.

She's not only sexy. She's intriguing.

And for a man like me, that's dangerous. I don't only see her beauty. I see past the sharp tongue, the quick smiles, and the careful walls she keeps pulling tighter around herself. My eyes trace the honeyed gold buried in the rich brown of hers. The way it flickers when she laughs, the way it catches when the light hits. There's amusement there and something quieter.

Her lashes flutter when she flirts, full and expressive. She's considering letting me in, but hasn't decided whether she should. Like she could disarm and vanish in a blink.

Waves of black curls frame her face, spilling easily over her shoulders.

There's nothing forced about her, not in the way she moves, not in the way she smiles. Her skin glows under the soft lights, smooth and golden. The curve of her cheekbones is highlighted enough to make me stare longer than I should. Her mouth hovers between teasing and tender, and when that dimple shows, it nearly does me in. She's not just a pretty face. She's someone to know.

My questions come in gentle waves, luring her into a rhythm. What makes her happiest? Where is she from? What brought her to San Antonio?

They aren't simple curiosities. They're hooks designed to make her unravel. Khloe, however, has mastered the art of deflection. She turns every inquiry back on me, steering the conversation away from the shadows of her past. But her evasiveness only deepens my curiosity.

From the corner of my eye, I check in on the others and catch Aaron laughing, distracted by Flora's unexpected competitiveness at the pool table. Flora's leaning into the game and Aaron. She tugs at her dress like it'll beckon cleavage she doesn't have. She's the type of woman I'd entertain when I need an uncomplicated escape.

But Khloe isn't like Flora or anyone else. She doesn't demand attention—and that only makes her stand out more. There's something restrained about her, an unspoken storm locked beneath her composed exterior. She's like a caged animal, waiting for a release she probably hasn't named yet. I know what it's like to dull parts of myself for the sake of others, and I wonder how much effort it would take to lure her out.

My eyes drop to the velvet choker snug around her throat. The first time I saw it, something primal stirred within me. It was a whisper of defiance in her regulated demeanor. A quiet rebellion she might not realize she's displaying. That minor detail tells me there's more to Khloe than she lets on. I want to know how deep that mystery runs.

"So, what is it, darlin'?" I murmur, tapping the rim of my beer. "Who broke your heart?"

Khloe freezes for half a heartbeat, barely perceptible, then gives me a dangerous smile and pivots with a question of her own. Deflection perfected.

Chapter 8

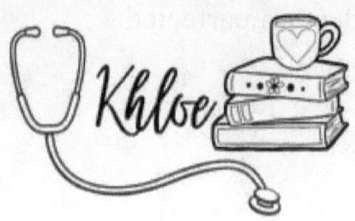

My Head Is Screaming

My drinking slows, but the faint slur in my words betrays me. The warmth from the liquor settles in deep, turning everything a little too smooth around the edges.

The shift between us is subtle. I can feel it humming under my skin.

I turn the tables, asking the questions now. Waylon answers easily. He's twenty-seven. Former Marine, now a U.S. Marshal. Likes the job. Plans to stick with it. No, he's never been married. And he doesn't have kids, but he wants both.

Each answer chips away at the wall I keep dragging back into place. I shift on the barstool, the room tilting slightly. I push off, slow and deliberate, trying to remember how legs are supposed to work.

Waylon doesn't move, but his eyes follow me like a touch I can feel. "Leavin' already?" He's teasing, but he isn't hiding that he doesn't want me to go.

I hesitate. My mouth opens, but no sound comes out. I don't have a clever exit lined up. No half-smirk. No fast pivot. Only this stupid ache I can't name.

I avert my eyes to think more clearly. Flora's still destroying Aaron at pool. I latch onto that for half a second, to pull myself out of whatever this is. But my body betrays me first.

Shit. I lost the shot game. Gotta pay up on my loss.

I lean in, my hand planting on Waylon's chest, solid and warm under my palm. His brows lift, as if he wasn't expecting that.

"Khloe…" His tone is full of warning. "You're gonna be in trouble."

I tilt my head, his hat still backwards on my head, casual and careless for once. Completely at odds with the heat clawing up between us. And I catch a flicker; the split-second crack in the calm confidence he wears like armor.

His jaw tenses. His hands flex open at his sides like he's fighting himself. I feel the tension snap between us. A string pulled tight. The press of my chest against his doesn't help either of us.

His breath stalls before he reels it back in. The moment stretches, so hot, until I stop thinking and move. I kiss him. Soft at first. Hesitant, tasting. Waiting to see if he'll meet me there.

He does, but not all the way. There's a hesitation buried in it, pulling him out of reach. He breaks away, holding me by the hips like he has to physically restrain himself.

"Khloe," he breathes. "You've been drinkin'. I ain't gonna take advantage of you."

I blink at him, surprised. Not because he said no, but because he means it. And God help me, I like that he's fighting the pull we're both feeling.

My mouth curls into a devious smile. I lean in again, this time catching his bottom lip between my teeth, giving a teasing bite.

A dare.

Waylon's whole body jerks with a sharp inhale. His hands tighten on my hips, pulling me closer. No hesitation now. The shift is instantaneous.

"You're definitely gonna be in trouble, Khloe," he mutters, voice like sandpaper and sin, as he leans to meet his lips with mine.

And for once, I don't run.

As we step out of the Uber, my head is screaming. *You just met this man. What if he's a serial killer? You barely know him.*

But, I'm not stopping. I'm walking, my hand in Waylon's, his grip tightening as if he can sense my hesitation. I glance up, meeting his eyes, and the warning bells dull to a whisper.

Flora is right. *Danger can be charming.*

"You'll be fine." His lips curve into a serene smile.

I exhale, letting the indecision slip away, following his lead.

Waylon turns us toward a townhouse, unlocking the door with a smooth flick of his wrist. "Ladies first," he says, holding the door open.

I step inside, expecting manly and messy, but it isn't. Boots are lined up neatly by the door. White walls, black trim. A deep gray leather sectional. Modern and structured. It feels like Waylon. Open and intimate. The scent of cedar and coffee. No mess, but no fluff either. No throw pillows. No fake plants. There's no sign of anyone else living there. Everything has a purpose.

He guides me toward a door off the living room. I slip inside and realize it's his bedroom. Deep, dark gray walls accent the room. His king-size bed is neatly made with a black comforter. An oak-colored desk fills the corner next to a dresser pressed against the wall. It feels like a room someone could disappear into. Not to hide, but to breathe.

I'm still taking it all in when I feel him behind me. So close, I can feel the heat of his breath enticing me. Waylon's arms slip around my waist, pulling me closer. I freeze before meeting the moment head-on, turning in his arms.

Our eyes meet. His steady, mine uncertain. But when he

gives me a sly smile, I can't help but mirror it, even as my heart pounds against my ribs. I know he senses my hesitation, but he doesn't pull away.

His hands slide up my sides, tracing the curve of my arms until they settle at the back of my neck. He cups my face, his touch firm but careful, coaxing me closer. I lean in, chest to chest, soft curves pressing into solid muscle, letting myself fall deeper.

Other one-night stands were a race to get off: clumsy hands, forgettable kisses, thirty seconds of regret. But Waylon moves like he's got all the time in the world. And I'm navigating this with my guard down, half-terrified, half-dizzy with it.

His thumb grazes the corner of my mouth, a whisper of a touch that sends a shiver skimming down my spine. He kisses me deep, full of meaning, like a promise he hasn't spoken out loud yet. Heat coils low in my stomach as our breaths mix. His mouth moves over mine with a patience I don't expect from men. He tastes warm, like whiskey and something I can't explain. It feels dangerously close to home.

I melt into him, unable to fight the pull—a surge of need consumes me. His hands tighten around me, like he feels it too. I gasp against his mouth, panic slamming into me.

Fuck. This is intense.

"Wait," I blurt out.

Waylon freezes, holding my face gently, eyes searching mine like he's trying to figure out what broke.

My lips tingle. My heart's hammering out of control. This isn't supposed to feel like this. Not this fast. "I need to check on Flora," I say, the lie rushing out. "Can we just... make sure she's okay?"

Waylon probably sees straight through the excuse. But he doesn't call me out on it. His hands slide down, settling at my waist.

"Alright," he says reassuringly. "Aaron's house is across the street, two doors down."

I step around him, needing the space. But the ghost of his hands lingers against my skin, making it impossible to breathe normally. As I open the door, I know this isn't over. Not even close.

Minutes later, we're standing on the porch of another townhouse—two stories, pale stucco, almost identical to Waylon's. The porch light flickers faintly overhead, with a worn welcome mat sitting crooked by the door.

I knock hard, urgency pouring into the motion, my stomach still tight.

Beside me, Waylon leans lazily against the doorframe. "Damn, darlin', you're knockin' like you're the cops."

Despite the nerves twisting in my gut, I shoot him a faint smile. "I want to make sure she's okay." He gives a nod. No pressure, like he's in no rush to pull me away if I'm not ready. The tension between us lingers, but it's softened by the same unspoken purpose.

I knock again, harder this time. "Flora? You in there? I need to see you!"

A rustling noise sounds from inside, followed by a soft giggle. Aaron swings the door open and stands there, moving slowly, like we're early for a party he forgot he was throwing.

I don't wait. I push past him without a word, cutting through the kitchen straight toward the couch, my focus narrowing in on Flora sprawled out, too relaxed and too loose-limbed for my liking.

I march over and grab her hand. "Where's your phone?"

Flora giggles, waving a lazy hand toward the corner of the room. "Dead, as usual. It's plugged in, charging."

Only then does she seem to really see me, the tightness in my shoulders, the way I'm probably two seconds away from dragging her out by the elbow. Her face sobers a little. She pushes herself upright, brushing her hair out of her face.

"Everything okay?" she asks, softer now. "C'mon," she adds, reaching for me. "Let's go to the bathroom."

Chapter 9

Forgot How to Leave

I smirk as the girls disappear down the hall. "You're lookin' at Flora like you're already in trouble," I tease.

Aaron scoffs, crossing his arms. "Please. I've dealt with plenty of wild girls."

I chuckle. "Yeah? How many of them made you lose two pool games on purpose, so they'd keep playin' with you?"

Aaron's jaw tightens. "That's not what happened."

I laugh. "Sure. Whatever helps you sleep at night, man."

He shakes his head but grins. "You're one to talk. You've been orbiting Khloe all night."

I tilt my head, unbothered. "I don't orbit."

Aaron snorts. "Right. And you rarely let a girl who's playin' hard to get keep your attention for hours. You haven't let her outta your sight since the River Walk."

Hell, I've spent the last few years learning how not to stay… but when she kissed me, I forgot how to leave.

I rub my jaw, feeling the grit of my stubble. "It's not like that."

Aaron leans against the wall, arms crossed like he's settling in for a long conversation. "Then what's it like?"

I don't answer right away. My gaze drifts toward the

closed bathroom door, pulled like a magnet.

There's something about her. Those guarded, beautiful eyes. That sharp tongue. The way she lets herself be soft for a second before snapping back into control. She's got me hooked. Like she's daring me to break first. I've stared down worse, but hell, if I don't wanna fold here.

And now she ain't running to be chased; she's holding her ground. And for the first time in a long damn while, I don't wanna walk away. That unsettles me more than I'd like to admit.

"I don't know yet," I finally say. "But maybe this is... not just for one night."

Aaron raises a brow. "Careful, Rhodes. You've got that look, like she could be a blessing... or another woman that'll have you apologizing for the rest of your life."

I huff out a short laugh, rubbing the back of my neck. "Yeah. That about sums it up."

Chapter 10

Wound Tight

I press myself against the cool surface of the bathroom door, trying to calm my heartbeat. The buzz I felt earlier is gone, replaced by the weight of concern.

Flora fumbles with the buttons on her dress, dragging it down with sluggish hands before sitting on the toilet. Her movements are loose and uncoordinated.

"I can't do this," I mutter firmly. "Flora, we need to go home."

She snorts, waving a dismissive hand and pushing to her feet, barely steady. "Khloe, we are *not* going home," she insists, wobbling slightly before grinning. "We're living any female's dream right now."

I huff, crossing my arms as she washes her hands. "Are you sure you're in the right state of mind to be making that decision?"

Flora spins abruptly and cups my face with damp hands. "I am in the *perfectest* state of mind," she announces with flair. "I'm gonna hang out with what's-his-name, and *you—*" she pokes my forehead "—are gonna hang out with Waylon." She wiggles her brows. "He said he'd sleep on the floor. Tell him what you need."

Before I can argue, she pushes me out of the way and flings the door open with way too much force. I don't move. She turns back and yanks me into the hallway.

The boys are in the middle of a conversation, but they go quiet as we approach. Flora nudges me toward Waylon, who's standing closest to the door.

"See you in the morning, beautiful." She hiccups, then winks at me.

Despite my worry, I smile. "Make sure your phone's on, okay? So I can reach you?"

"Pinky promise." She salutes me lazily before draping herself on Aaron.

Waylon already has the door open, waiting. I glance up at him as we step outside.

"Thank you for helping me track her down," I whisper. "Her impulsiveness always makes me nervous."

His eyes meet mine with grounded intensity as he closes the door. "I understand."

That silky drawl of his works its way through me. For the first time tonight, I feel a little safer. As we walk back to his place, I steal glances at him. His stride is smooth, unhurried, laced with confidence. *Why am I always so tightly wound?*

"If you want, I can stay in the spare bedroom. You can take my bed."

I slow down, eyes dropping to the ground. How does he pick up on my unease before I even say a word? He adjusts to my pace without missing a beat, falling into step beside me like it's nothing. When I finally meet his eyes again, they're... waiting.

A small smile tugs at my lips. "That's not necessary."

His grin widens as he slips his fingers through mine, certain and warm. A comfort, silent but clear. That simple touch sends a soft wave of heat through me and straight to my panties.

When we enter his room again, I take the lead. Our lips crash together, urgent and unrelenting. I push him back until his shoulders hit the wall with a solid thud. Waylon responds instantly, his fingers diving into my hair, tugging to tilt my head. Then, his teeth sink into the curve of my neck, the sharp bite pulling a gasp from me.

I pull back, breathless, grinning up at him.

Chapter 11

One Word

My mouth leaves her neck reluctantly as I slide off her jean jacket and tug her shirt over her head. Her clothes hit the floor in scattered, forgotten heaps. Then I see her, no bra, her breasts rising before settling with a mesmerizing bounce. I suck in air through my teeth, my chest tightening. A groan rumbles low in my throat before I can stop it.

She starts to cover her breasts. Her hands look small next to those perfect curves.

"Breathe," I whisper, reaching for her.

She lets out an exhale, her shoulders relaxing. I catch the shift, the surrender, and it hits me straight in the chest. I grab her wrists and guide them down to her waist.

Leaning down, I whisper, "Do you trust me?" Chills ripple across her skin. I see them, feel them.

"Yes," she says.

There's no hesitation this time, and fuck, that does something to me. I guide her to the center of the room, never breaking eye contact. She's breathtaking. Standing there, open and vulnerable, it nearly levels me. I take a step back. It's not only lust pumping through my veins. It's something I don't quite have words for yet.

"Then close your eyes," I say. There's an edge beneath it—a command wrapped in care.

She obeys immediately, her eyes fluttering shut. Her breathing picks up. She's in this with me. I open the dresser drawer, the quiet slide echoing louder in the silence. The faint clink of metal follows as I reach for the cuffs. Her breath catches.

I stand in front of her, gathering her wrists together. The cool leather wraps around her skin. The buckle clicks into place, and I feel her pulse pounding. So close to the surface. I love knowing every sound, every touch is magnified now. I circle her slowly, like a predator closing in. But there's reverence in every step. Every move calculated, not to trap but to worship.

"Khloe." Her name falls from my lips, thick and slow. "We are going to explore you. Take off your pants and panties."

She obeys blindly, her hands bound. I watch her fingers fumble at the buttons of her jeans. The tiny clicks echo in the quiet. She slides them and her panties down over her hips. They pool at her feet. She steps out and nudges them aside with her foot.

She stills. The silence stretches before I break it. "Kneel," I command. "And open your eyes."

She sinks to her knees, hands bound in her lap, and when her eyes meet mine, I see something that makes my throat tighten. She should look scared. Instead, she looks straight at me, unflinching. Brave as hell.

I drop into my desk chair, leaning back with ease. My shirt's open at the top, exposing the hard lines of my chest, but her eyes are locked on mine.

And my eyes are devouring her.

"Khloe, tell me what you want."

She looks down for a second, like she's searching for the right words. When her eyes rise again, they're focused.

"You."

One word—but fuck, it hits like a punch.

She swallows, then continues, stronger now. "I want all of you."

The moment she says it, it hits a place I didn't know still existed. I stand and stalk toward her, my eyes locked on hers.

"Stand, Khloe."

She reaches up, takes my hand, and lets me pull her to her feet. Her fingers curl around mine like it's instinct. I turn away for a moment, opening the drawer again. When I face her, her gaze drops for a split second. She sees what she's done to me. The thick line straining against my jeans. Her lips part, and I catch the way her thighs tense.

"I'm going to blindfold you, Khloe."

The words are a promise and a test. She smiles. One that tells me she's *ready*. I've never had anyone smile in these moments. And God, it burns through me. Not just in my cock, but somewhere I didn't know anyone could reach anymore.

I move in close, soft fabric in hand. I circle her, teasing the blindfold through my fingers before gliding it over her cheeks. She shivers.

I knot it gently at the back of her head, careful with her hair. Then I step back again. And take her in. Thick thighs. Curves that beg to be touched. Power in her posture, even now. Especially now.

Then I see ink. A tattoo on her upper thigh, detailed and unexpected. I step forward, fingers reaching before I can stop myself. I trace the lines, slow and deliberate. She inhales as I linger, memorizing the design. My hand stays like it's listening. Like her body is telling stories only I can hear.

"Khloe." I soften. "Listen carefully. If this becomes too much, say 'Stop.' Say it clearly. I'll stop. No hesitation. I don't want to hurt you. I want to please you. Do you understand?"

She nods too fast. I shake my head, chuckling. "Use your words, darlin'."

"Yes," she says, firm and certain.

My smile returns. "Good girl."

I come full circle to face her again. Her smile is playful. Bold. A little defiant. God, I'll live for that face. I cup her jaw in my hand, drawing her closer until our breaths mingle.

"Kiss me," I growl.

And she does. Sightless and trusting, she lets me guide her. Our lips meet. Exploring at first, tasting. I feel her surrender, the slight hitch in her breath, the way her mouth moves with mine like we've done this a hundred times.

She doesn't know this yet, but I don't kiss during play. Not like this. Kisses are personal. Intimate. A line I don't cross. And yet, here I am.

Chapter 12

Is This Really Happening?

I feel the shift, the intensity of it, pressing deeper than his touch ever could. For a moment, it feels like he still holds all the power. Until I take it back.

I bite his lower lip. A playful nip.

Waylon inhales sharply, his grip on me tightening. His reaction sends a thrill through me, and I can almost hear the smirk in his tone when he murmurs, pulling back, "Oh, you are trouble. Stay still."

I obey—waiting.

"Khloe, you need a spankin'."

My eyebrows shoot up. *Is this really happening? What am I doing? Why does it feel right?* My brain screams danger, but my body is already begging for more.

Before I can process it, I hear the quiet slide of the drawer opening again. A moment later, something thin and smooth traces up the inside of my thigh.

The sensation is unfamiliar. Smooth but edged, cool against my skin. Not metal. Not fingers. Something else. It glides between my thighs, pausing at my clit like it's testing me. My breath snags while my thighs tremble with the effort to stay still. He lingers just shy of where I need him most, pulling back. Teasing me.

Crack.

The strike is sharp, precise, landing exactly where I'm most sensitive. Heat spreads in ripples from the strike, crawling across my skin until every nerve feels raw and alive. My whole body jolts as my knees buckle and a helpless moan tears from my throat.

Waylon chuckles, satisfied. "I'm going to place you at the edge of the bed," he murmurs smoothly. "Bend over when you feel it." He guides me forward, his touch firm.

My thighs meet the soft bedding, and I lean forward, my stomach pressing down as my bound arms stretch out onto the mattress. He steps in behind me, his presence overwhelming—radiating heat despite the barrier of his pants. There's a quiet shuffle. His foot nudges between mine, spreading my legs apart. Warm hands grip my waist, pulling me back toward him. I arch instinctively, pushing my ass closer to the thick, rigid bulge straining against his jeans.

"Slow down, Khloe," he warns, voice thick with control. "I set the pace."

But I'm greedy. I arch further, shamelessly seeking more contact.

"Khloe," Waylon growls darkly with promise. "I need you to understand that your defiance is an invitation."

I laugh, breathless. "Prove it, Waylon."

A crack splits the air, followed by a sharp sting across my ass. The impact steals my breath, a jarring burst of fire that burns hotter than I expect. My jaw falls open around a moan I didn't mean to give him. Shame collides with desire so fast I can't tell which wins.

And I fucking smile.

Chapter 13

Good Girl

"Fuck." I exhale, tight with something raw clawing up my chest. "Why the hell are you smilin', Khloe?"

She turns her head, flashing a wicked, breathless smile. "Do it again." The words tremble with need. "*Please*."

I should tease her—make her wait, but I can't. She arches into me again, offering herself up, but instead of another slap, I slide my hand between her legs. And her body snaps to attention.

God, she's soaked.

My fingers circle her clit with purpose. She whimpers. I slide two fingers deep inside her as she grips me in tight, fluttering waves. It shoots straight to my cock. With my other hand, I rub the cheek I punished, feeling the warmth still blooming there. The contrast sends a shiver down her spine.

She's unraveling fast—and I fucking love it. Her legs quiver; she's holding on by a thread.

"Good girl, Khloe," I murmur, keeping the rhythm controlled but unrelenting. "Feel it. Enjoy it."

I push deeper, stretching her, letting her feel every inch of my control. She comes undone, trembling, panting, and completely overwhelmed. She tightens around my fingers, and suddenly there's a rush of wetness against my palm. She gasps, her head flying back.

"Waylon! Fuck!"

Her entire body shakes, her orgasm tearing through her like a storm. Warmth splashes against my palm, unexpected. She shudders beneath me, her whole body wrung out, trembling. I pull my fingers out, soaked, dripping. I stare down at her, more stunned than smug.

"Well, goddamn," I mutter, eyes tracing the mess we've made.

She's breathless. "I didn't... know I could... do that."

I chuckle, thick with pride. "I figured as much," I murmur. "But I'm not done with you yet. Get on the bed... on all fours."

She shivers, obeying without question. Following my instructions, she arches her back, shooting her ass up into the air. Goddamn, she's beautiful like this. Bare, cuffed, my submissive.

"Khloe," I say as I step behind her, "I need you to count."

She turns her head, confused. "Count what, Way—"

The first slap lands hard. Her breath punches out, and the sound of it echoes between us.

"One," she gasps.

"Good girl." I rub over the mark, soothing. Then, I do it again. Another slap. Then another.

Her voice gains confidence with each number, even as her legs shake. I hear the strength in the way she breathes. In. Out. Measured, trying to stay in control, but control doesn't belong to her right now.

When she reaches twenty, her body's trembling beneath me. The skin beneath my hand is flushed a perfect red. She's panting, her knees barely holding her weight. She's a mess under my control, and I've never seen anything more perfect.

I let the silence stretch. She braces for more, shoulders tight. But I don't give her twenty-one.

I lean in close. "I'm gonna take your blindfold off. Lie

flat on your stomach after."

She nods, still catching her breath. I loosen the tie and slide it off gently, watching her blink as the light hits her eyes. She looks dazed, in the best way.

I step off the bed, moving to the dresser. I toss the blindfold inside, then grab the bottle of lotion from the top. When I turn back, she's watching me, confused, still hovering between afterglow and clarity. I squeeze a generous amount into my hands and exhale a warm breath between them. I rub them together, working the warmth through my palms.

She narrows her eyes slightly, like she doesn't know what comes next.

I kneel beside her, my tone softer now. "We're doin' your aftercare." I brush my knuckle across her cheek. "How are you feelin'?"

Her lips twitch, a ghost of a smile. "I've read *Fifty Shades*, but I've never tried anything like this."

My face drops. "Khloe..." I say flatly. "You're kiddin' me, right?"

She hesitates, like that wasn't the response she expected. I clear my throat and focus on her skin, gently smoothing the lotion into the red marks I left. My fingers move with purpose, soothing her inch by inch.

That damn choker had me assuming. I figured she knew what it'd do to someone like me, but she's never done any of this. Despite that, she gave it to me like it was second nature.

"You were such a good girl for me. Did you enjoy it?"

She meets my gaze, more sure of herself now. "I loved it." Then she smiles. "Can we do it again?"

My hands move up her spine. I should be grinning, teasing her, but intimacy with her feels off script. I don't say it out loud. Hell, I don't even fully let myself think about it, but a feeling lingers, pressing in at the edges. This isn't just another scene.

"We will... but not tonight. Your body needs a break."

She rolls her eyes. "I'm not made of glass, you know. I've

been spanked before." She lifts her cuffed wrists slightly. "The blindfold and cuffs, though? That's unfamiliar territory for me." She bites her lip. "And... whatever else you were using... that was definitely new."

I smirk as I reach for the cuffs, slowly unlocking them. My fingers knead into her wrists, rubbing lotion in with care.

"You'll learn in time," I murmur. Another promise.

She chuckles. "You think there's gonna be a next time?"

I meet her eyes. "Oh, there'll be a next time, Khloe."

Chapter 14

A Circuit Closes

"You sound pretty confident," I tease, eyeing him as he stands tall, his hands sliding to his waistband.

His eyes lock with mine. "I am confident," he says simply. There's no arrogance in it, only certainty. "But we're takin' this part slow."

I bite my lip as he unbuttons his jeans, eyes flicking between his hands and his face. A grin threatens to spread across my lips. I try to stop it and fail.

"Slow, huh?" I toss back, light and playful, but everything in me is buzzing.

His lips twitch into that damn smirk. "Slow doesn't mean easy, darlin'." He lets the words settle between us like a dare, then pushes his jeans and boxers down in one flowing motion.

I swallow hard.

He steps out of them with an ease that should be illegal. Confidence rolls off him, quiet but absolute. My eyes dip lower.

He catches me, grinning. "Like what you see, darlin'?"

I fight back a laugh. "You're alright, I guess."

He laughs and steps closer until his face is inches from mine. "Alright?" he echoes, pure amusement in his tone.

"I'll make you take that back soon enough."

His lips hover near mine, teasing, but he doesn't kiss me. "Spread your legs."

I obey, anticipation humming through me. His hands find my hips, guiding me to the edge of the bed like he already knows exactly how I'll move. And the second our bodies connect, it's like a circuit closes.

A soft sigh slips from my lips, and from his, too. It's instinctual, like our bodies remember each other, even if our heads are still trying to catch up.

He moves with purpose. Deliberate thrusts that build a rhythm. I can feel it in every inch of me.

My body responds before I even think, matching his pace, falling into it like it's natural. Like it's always been this way.

The intensity starts to climb, sharp and consuming.

"Khloe, I want you to come."

The command hits me like a lightning strike. My back arches. I pull him closer, my nails digging into him. I'm desperate now. Everything turns hot and urgent, movements shifting from steady to frantic.

I break, pleasure tearing through me, my body shaking as I convulse around him.

"Waylon!" I cry, gripping onto him like I might fall apart otherwise.

"Khloe," he groans, hips thrusting deep one final time as he follows, his release crashing into him with the same intensity. His whole-body locks before shuddering with the aftershock, breath ragged against my skin.

Silence follows, thick and heated. Our breathing slows, the air heavy with something we don't say out loud.

I blink up at him, lazy and sated, with a smile I can't stop. As I stare into his eyes, I realize this isn't only sex. There's a connection. Heat.

Something alive between us I can't shake. Like a thread has been tied between us, invisible and unbreakable.

And the way his eyes lock onto mine tells me neither of

us is ready to let this go.

Chapter 15

Do I Care?

The sun pushes through the slight break in my curtains. Khloe stirs. She's curled up on top of me, arm across my waist, legs tangled with mine. Her cheek rests against my chest, soaking in the rise and fall. For a moment, she's calm. Then her body stiffens, like she forgot for a second who I am and what we did.

But she's wrapped around me like we've done this a hundred times. And our bodies fit like we already know how to find each other in the dark.

I keep my eyes shut and wait.

She lifts her head. I don't have to look at her to know what's happening. Flashes are hitting her. My hands. Her moans. The way she gave in. Again and again. The things I did to her. The things she let me do.

"Woah," she mutters under her breath.

I almost smile. Then I feel her go rigid beside me. She freezes, face probably flushed, mind racing.

Embarrassment. Cute.

She sits up fast. I crack one eye open to watch her; the blanket slides down, exposing her bare skin. She moves carefully, like waking me would make it real. She won't look at me, as if avoiding my eyes might erase the entire night.

Heat rises in her face. She looks at the blanket, staring at the faint white streaks on the dark bedding. The stains we left behind. Proof.

She eases out of bed and tiptoes to the door before slipping into the hall. Her bare ass disappears, skin still red from last night. I exhale, smirk slipping off my face. She's gonna overthink this. The thought settles heavily in my chest. I stare at the ceiling.

Do I care? *More than I should.*

It wasn't only how she moved with me, though. She fits so well in my hands. I can still feel the shape of her thighs around my waist. She was vulnerable and defiant. She tested me even as she surrendered, aching for control but willing to give it up—to me—in ways I'm not sure she even understands. And I didn't only take it. I handled her, protected her. Made her come so hard she forgot who she was for a minute. Now she's out there trying to make sense of it.

So yeah. I care.

I don't do this with everyone. And I don't always understand the need myself. Back in Cedar Ridge, I remember my friends bragging about losing their virginities in cheesy, awkward teenage ways. When it finally happened to me at fifteen with Stacy, it changed me. She was a friend of my older sister, Loretta. Stacy asked me to spank her, and the moment I did, something inside me clicked. It was like waking up a part of myself I didn't even know existed. I couldn't stop thinking about it. I spent hours researching to understand why that moment, that feeling, made me feel so alive. And why it scared me just as much.

Boys in town didn't talk about shit like that yet. You baled hay, fed cattle, married your high school sweetheart, and kept your hands clean; even when they weren't. Caroline tried. We both did, but I came back from the Marines with parts of myself missing.

No amount of love could fix what war took from me. And here I am.

I should've known better than to let myself feel again. Khloe had crawled into my bed like she belonged here. On a regular morning, I'd be halfway dressed by now—another woman on her way, another week, another blank slate in the rearview. No cuddling. Not looking too long. Nothing to make it feel real. I've spent years making damn sure no one ever did.

And the worst part? I don't want Khloe to leave.

Chapter 16

Bruised & Smiling

I barely breathe as I crack the door open, peeking into the hallway. My bladder protests with a sharp ache, and my body—God, my body is sore in places I've never been sore before.

Bathroom. I need a bathroom.

I spot a door near a large vanity mirror and nudge it open, exhaling with relief. The moment I settle on the toilet, a sting flares across my ass, and I wince. My body remembers, even if my brain is still catching up. Curious, I glance over my shoulder.

I'm marked.

Red blooms across my ass, with faint purplish edges beginning to surface. I bite my lip to stop from smiling.

Why does this make me happy?

Heat curls low, pulsing quietly. I should be horrified. I should question everything. Instead, I let myself grin. I don't feel shame. This feeling's addictive, intoxicating even.

This isn't normal. And yet it feels like the most honest I've been with myself in a long time. Shaking my head, I refocus as I stare into the bathroom mirror. I run my fingers over the velvet choker still wrapped around my neck.

Who broke your heart?

Waylon's question whispers back to me like he left it here on purpose. I *chose* not to answer it. Not because I didn't know what to say, but because I do. I adjust the velvet band, pretending that's enough to keep the truth tucked under my skin where it belongs.

After washing up, I tiptoe back into his room. Everything feels different now, but looks the same. Our chaos is still sprawled across the space. A riding crop at the edge of the bed.

That's the leathery culprit that stung.

My bra, panties, and pants are scattered across the floor. Looking around, feeling excited and scared, it all means something more. Every piece of clothing and scuff in the sheets is evidence of what we did—everything I let happen.

I scan the room for my phone. Nothing. Anxiety prickles beneath my skin. I move fast, reaching for my panties like putting them on will somehow bring me back to myself. My hands fumble as Waylon clears his throat.

I meet his eyes and manage an awkward smirk. "Oh… Hi," I say before looking away.

Chapter 17

Stay a Little Longer

I smile, stretching lazily. Still bare, the covers kicked down to my feet; I have no problem being on full display. She's the one scrambling like she's late to church.

"What're you doin'?" I ask, clearly entertained.

She keeps pulling her panties up, raising a brow. "What does it look like I'm doing?"

My grin deepens. "Looks like you're puttin' clothes on when I'd rather you leave 'em off."

She turns and smirks, but doesn't stop. "I need to go see Flora."

I lift a brow. "Why? Has she called?"

She frowns. "I'm not sure. I haven't found my phone yet."

I sit up, resting on my elbows. "Come here."

Her body shifts. There's a subtle straightening of her spine. She hears the command, but she's fighting it.

"No, sir," she says, tone teasing but firm. "I have to get dressed."

I study her, milking it. I like this part. The push and pull. The way she's holding her ground when we both know she's already half mine. I don't move, but I pin her with a look and wait. Still playful, but it carries a roughness, the part of me that wants her honesty.

"I'm gonna need you to come here, Khloe."

She hesitates, but I know she's going to give in. She steps closer, and I take her by the waist the second she's within reach. Her skin is warm.

I hadn't expected her to bolt, but I sure as hell hadn't expected her to kiss me, then act like none of it mattered. Now that I've got her in my arms, I'm not sure I can let go.

My hands slide down, catching the waistband of her panties, dragging them down her thighs. She sucks in a breath as the fabric pools at her knees and drops to the floor. I let my fingers skim over her slit, feeling the heat radiating off her. She freezes, still trying to fight it. I look up, locking eyes with her, seeing the war in them. She's wondering if last night was a one-off. But I know better.

Instead of pushing, I reach up and cup her cheek, brushing my thumb along her jaw. "You gettin' shy on me," I murmur, "after everything we shared last night?"

She laughs, the sound easing some of the tension. But I feel the way her knees tremble beneath her. "Maybe a little."

I smirk, trailing my hand down. My fingers slip inside her with purpose. My thumb circles her clit as her lips part. Her head drops, forehead brushing my shoulder. She's already slick. But I'm nowhere near done.

"Good girl," I murmur.

I guide her onto me, our bodies pressing close. Tight and perfect. She shudders, looking down at me, eyes scanning my face like she's seeing it for the first time. Her fingers trace my cheekbone. Her other hand presses right over my heart.

Our eyes lock. This isn't about control right now. It's something neither of us has named yet. She isn't trying to run now, and I'm not letting her go.

She positions herself over me, breath shaky but sure. In one smooth motion, she sinks onto my cock, taking all of me in. A sharp gasp rips out of me. My hands are gripping her hips as she moves, setting a steady rhythm. I give her the reins, and as her confidence builds, she rides me hard, like every thrust is a way of taking the control back I had last night. I lose my breath. The way she moves, the way we meet; this isn't a one and done kinda fuck. There's too much passion between us. Too much fire under every touch.

I won't let this stop.

Chapter 18

Daylight & Goodbyes

I pull my shirt over my head, trying to get dressed before the temptation to go another round wins out. My body is tender in the best way, but I can't handle more—not now, at least.

Waylon stands in front of his closet, pulling out a pair of shorts and a white tee. His back is lightly freckled, and the skin there is a warm pale that reminds me of slightly toasted tortillas. The thought makes me chuckle, and I fail to hold it in.

"Somethin' funny, ma'am?" he drawls, sliding his shirt on and glancing over his shoulder, smiling.

I quickly look down, fumbling to pull my jeans up over my hips as my cheeks flush.

"Nothing," I mutter, though my smirk betrays me.

Waylon takes a couple of steps toward me, closing the space between us. Before I can straighten up, his fingers hook under my chin, tilting my face toward his. The morning light highlights his green eyes. He laces a curl of my hair in his hand and takes a deep breath in.

"Mhm, vanilla shampoo," he teases. "You're even more beautiful in the daylight."

Heat rises in my cheeks, and I try to suppress the flutter

in my stomach. I'm sure he says this to every woman who spends the night in his bed. I roll my eyes, hoping to deflect.

"I could say the same to you, but I wouldn't want to make your head any bigger."

His eyes narrow playfully as his lips twitch into a half-smile. "There's a bit of sass under all that mysteriousness."

I shrug, my smirk growing into a full-blown grin. "Guess you'll have to stick around to find out."

His smile widens. Caught between the pull of his charm and the slow drawl. His voice makes my heart skip a beat, a clear sign I need to get out of here before I lose myself in it. I reach for my shoes as he interrupts my escape plan.

"Khloe," he whispers. "Do you always disappear into your thoughts like that?"

I pause, surprised. It feels like he's looking straight through all the noise I usually hide behind. His playful demeanor giving way to something more genuine. Maybe someone finally sees me.

"I guess I do," I admit, laughing. "Old habits."

"Hmm. Well, don't let 'em take you too far away, darlin'. I like it better when you're here."

His words hold a quiet sincerity laced through the teasing. For a man who probably says all the right things without thinking twice, this feels intentional.

"Noted," I say lightly, resting my hands on my hips. "But don't think that means I'm sticking around to boost your ego all day."

Waylon chuckles, lazy and confident. "You're welcome back anytime, ya'know."

I bite back a smile. Every part of me wants to say *yes, yes, yes.* Instead, I shrug, hoping the casual gesture will mask my racing pulse.

"I'm sorry. I'm not used to this." I motion vaguely between us. The closeness, the proximity of his lips to mine, the magnetic pull of his presence. Shit, the thought of his hands on me again is far too distracting. The understanding in his expression almost makes me stay.

"Have you seen my phone?" I blurt out before I lose the battle with my own wants.

He reaches toward the nightstand, pulling it from under his wallet, and surprises me by double-pressing the power button to open the camera. The screen fills with an image of us in sharp contrast: his softly pale skin against my warm beige tone, his piercing green eyes to my deep brown ones.

I smirk. "What are you doing?"

"Now, aren't you gonna smile for the camera, darlin'?"

Instant goosebumps shiver down my spine. I smile instinctively, glancing toward the camera. He snaps the picture, the image freezing us in time. Two people who probably shouldn't fit together yet somehow do.

Before I can react, he leans in, kisses me—and snaps another photo. I laugh as I grasp for my phone, but he lifts it high above his head, well out of my reach.

"Waylon," I say, laughing as I jump to grab it. My five-foot-six-inch frame is no match for his six-foot height, and he knows it.

The phone vibrates in his hand; the screen lights up with a picture of Flora and me. He raises an eyebrow, answering the call before I can protest.

"Hi, Flora." His smirk grows as he speaks. "Oh, Khloe? Your friend? Oh... I'm not too sure. She got up in the middle of the night and hasn't come back."

"Waylon," I growl, rolling my eyes. "Not funny." I lunge for the phone again.

Chuckling, he finally hands it over, but as I bring it to my ear, he leans into my other—his breath warm against my skin.

"That's five spankin's for rollin' your eyes, Khloe." My cheeks flush instantly. I glare, but my racing heart betrays me. Waylon grins and steps back with a fake-innocent shrug. I try to focus on Flora, ignoring the way his eyes linger on me like he's savoring a meal.

"Khloe," Flora sings. "Hello? My beautiful best friend,

are you there?"

I clear my throat. "Yes, Flora. I'm here. You okay?"

She chuckles. "Oh, just great. I woke up to this guy's mom calling him back-to-back. He's heading out. Can I come over to you guys?"

I glance at Waylon as his hand traces the velvet choker around my neck. He nods, leaning in too close.

"Tell her we'll meet her outside."

Flora's laugh crackles through the speaker. "He must be on top of you because I can hear him loud and clear. I'll see you guys outside."

I tuck my phone into my pocket. Turning toward the bedroom door, I feel Waylon's hands catch mine and pull them behind my back. He closes in behind me, his chest warm against my back. A smirk tugs at my lips before I can stop it.

"Am I under arrest?" I ask, arching into him.

"That depends. How fast can you come?"

A moan escapes me before I can stop it. "Depends on how good you are," I counter, the words trembling.

His hand slips into my pants, fingers gliding across my center with a slowness that makes my knees feel weak. I part my legs as he slips two fingers inside me. His low growl in my ear sends a fresh wave of heat through me.

"Good girl," he murmurs, satisfaction bleeding into each word.

Dammit, why is he so good at this? He multitasks like it's an art form, his fingers pumping rhythmically while his thumb massages my clit. My hips grind into his hand, chasing the release that's already building.

"Waylon," I gasp. "I'm gonna come."

"No, you're not, Khloe."

The words barely register. I grind harder; hungry for the peak that's so close. Until suddenly, I feel empty—he withdraws, leaving me teetering on the edge.

I spin to face him, mouth open in protest. The sight of

him silences me. He lifts wet fingers and inhales before dropping them to his lips. My heart pounds as I watch him lick them clean, eyes closing like he's savoring a delicacy.

He locks eyes with me. "Fuck, you taste good."

I'm still reeling when he turns toward the door.

"Orgasm denial is amazin'," he says over his shoulder. "Next time, you won't take it for granted when I let you come."

I follow him out of his bedroom, completely stunned, my jeans brushing against the ache between my legs. It's maddening. Every step reminds me of how close I was. When we reach the front door, he holds it open with one hand and threads the other through mine.

"Get out of your head, Khloe. Tell me what you're thinkin'."

"World domination," I mutter.

He stops, pulling me in by the waist. "What are you really thinkin' about?"

I narrow my eyes at him, faking anger. "Walking fast so I can come since *you* deprived me."

His head falls back with a genuine laugh. "Khloe, walkin' fast isn't gonna get you off better than I can. And for the record, those eye rolls earned you your punishment."

Before I can fire back, Flora calls out, "Hey, lovebirds!"

I pull away, grateful for the interruption, and spot her walking down Aaron's porch with a wide grin. Her eyes sparkle, looking between us. I know I'm in trouble before she even speaks.

"You're glowing, Khlo. What did he do to you?" Flora's voice carries across the road.

I groan, casting my eyes toward the ground. "She's the worst."

Waylon's hand reaches for my chin, tilting it up.

I flush under his stare. "Are you looking for the glow?"

"Darlin', I don't need to look. It's written all over you."

I'm sitting in the passenger seat of Waylon's truck, head leaning on the window. Flora's stretched out in the back, half-asleep. Waylon keeps glancing at me. I've been quiet since we piled into the truck.

Last night wasn't like me at all. Not the alcohol-fueled sparks or the spanks.

"You okay over there?"

I straighten. "Yeah, just tired."

He nods, turning back to the road. I hope he didn't notice how I shifted closer to the door.

Flora yawns. "Waylon, you've got the softest truck suspension. Almost makes me want to ride with you more often."

He chuckles, glancing at her in the rearview mirror. "Glad to know my truck's got your seal of approval, Flora."

She teases, "It's growing on me, cowboy. Don't let it go to your head."

I don't join in the flirtatious banter. I watch his fingers tighten on the wheel as he pulls up to our place, shifts the truck into park, and glances at us. Flora hops out, mumbling about needing coffee and a nap. I linger, my hand resting on the door handle.

"Hey," Waylon says, leaning toward me.

I turn to face him, cautious but curious.

"Those pictures we took this mornin'," he says with a grin. "The ones on your phone? Mind sendin' it to me?"

I blink, surprised. "Uh, yeah. Sure."

"You know that means I'll have your number, right?"

My cheeks flush instantly. "I. Uh... I guess I didn't think about that."

"Well," he drawls, leaning back in his seat, "now you know."

I hesitate, pulling my phone out of my back pocket. I pull up my photos, feeling his watchful eyes. When I find the two candid shots where we appear to be a couple, I glance at him.

"Okay," I say, quieter now. "What's your number?"

Waylon rattles it off, and I type it, sending the photos without another word. He pulls out his phone, glancing at the screen with a satisfied smirk.

"Got it. Thanks, darlin'."

I roll my eyes, though a faint smile tugs at my lips. "Don't call me that."

"Noted. And don't roll your eyes at me, baby."

I climb out of the truck quickly, avoiding hearing baby pass his lips again.

He leans towards the door. "Hey, Khloe?" I pause. "I'll see you around," he promises.

I nod, my stomach doing an unexpected flip. The picture might've been his excuse, but something inside me hopes he actually reaches out.

As I walk up to my house, I take it in. It's a small two-bedroom bungalow, worn but cared for. The muted steel-blue paint and crisp white trim give it charm. The driveway is cracked, the flower beds slightly overgrown, but the green grass fights through vibrantly. The front porch is modest. A short set of wooden steps, but there's a stillness to it that speaks to me. It's not grand or flashy, but it holds itself together—like I do.

I push the front door open and close it behind me, leaning on it for a second, heart racing. The familiar scent of home settles around me. I walk through the main hallway to Flora sprawled on the couch, coffee in one hand, phone in the other, looking far too relaxed for the chaos echoing in my head.

Flora looks up and smirks. "So? How'd that little goodbye go? You were out there for a while."

I groan, making my way through the open space toward the kitchen. "Oh, just dominance. Nothing new."

Flora arches a brow, following me. "Domination? Now

this I've got to hear."

I fill a glass with water, taking a long sip before turning to face Flora as she leans against the counter with her mischievous grin.

"He asked me to send him pictures he took of us this morning," I say as my cheeks heat.

"Pictures?" Flora prompts, her grin widening.

"Yes. Then he made a point of telling me it means he has my number now," I admit, setting the glass down with a clink.

Flora gasps dramatically, clutching her heart like she'd heard the juiciest news of the year. "He *what*? Waylon's got your number now? Khloe, that's practically a marriage proposal!"

"Oh my God, stop," I say, unable to suppress a small smile.

Flora leans closer, her eyes narrowing playfully. "Wait, wait, wait. You're blushing. What's that about? What else happened between you two last night?"

I hesitate, suddenly very interested in the countertop. "Well..."

Flora's jaw drops. "No way. Khloe! What aren't you telling me?"

I cover my face with my hands, words muffled. "We... we did very, very adult things. Stuff I thought only happened in dark romance books. Like my ass is bruised!"

Flora freezes in pure shock before bursting into laughter. Stepping closer, she grabs my hands, pulling them away from my face.

"*You*? Miss Guarded and Overthink Everything Khloe? You slept with him? Bruises—like you let him spank you? Is that why you were walking funny? Oh, this is better than I could've imagined."

"Stop," I say, half laughing, half groaning. "It's not funny. I don't even know how it happened. One minute we were making out, and the next... well, you know."

Flora's laughter softens into a knowing smile. "And now you're freaking out because he has your number. And because he wants to see you again."

I sigh, leaning against the counter. "I don't know what he wants. I barely know what I want."

"Well," Flora says, crossing her arms, "do you *want* him to call you?"

I bit my lip, my silence answering the question—but wanting something means it can be taken away.

"That's what I thought," Flora says, nudging me with an elbow. "You like him, Khloe. I know you're scared, but this could be something good. You should text him."

I look down at my phone. Waylon's number is now saved, and the pictures I sent are still open on the screen. I type out a quick text and hit send before I change my mind. My stomach flutters, but the familiar hit of doubt lingers in the back of my mind.

"I guess we'll see," I mumble.

Flora grins, raising her coffee cup before setting it back down. "Oh, I bet we will. And let's not forget to toast to you ending your celibacy streak with a *spank*," she claps her hands loudly, "literally!" She bursts out laughing, leaning forward, nearly spilling her coffee.

I groan, covering my face with my hands. "You're the worst, you know that?"

"I prefer to think of myself as the best," Flora shoots back with a wink. She heads back towards the couch and plops down.

I follow her. "So how was your night with Aaron?"

Flora throws her hands up. "Oh, it was amazing! The best 30 seconds of my life. I mean, he's well-endowed, but I think he was a little too excited."

I can't help but laugh. "Aw, just like you."

Flora wrinkles her nose, throwing a pillow at me. "You're awful, Khlo. Hmm, I think we should celebrate properly tonight. We'll grab some hair of the dog to fix this hangover."

I roll my eyes, but I can't help smiling. "Alright, but this is my last night out for a while. Back to the grind Monday morning."

Flora pouts dramatically. "Fine, I'll take what I can get. Don't expect me to let you off the hook this easy next time."

I smile as I walk into my bedroom. Flora has always pulled me out of my shell—she gets that from her mom. Her parents, Mr. and Mrs. Calloway, are both doctors. They are the picture of success and generosity, always kind to me, and stepping in when Grandma couldn't. During the holidays, when Grandma had to work or was too sick from cancer treatments, Flora's family invited me over without hesitation.

I used to joke that they were my favorite movie family. Huge dinners every night, globe-trotting vacations, and a house that looked like it belonged in *Architectural Digest*. But despite all their wealth, they were incredibly grounded. Flora had chores to earn her privileges. I helped, and we'd both end up with an allowance. They valued humanity over status. Their love was obvious, welcoming, and real.

It gave me a glimpse of the love I wanted. My ex hated the way Flora and I stuck together, even though he'd never say it outright. Only once after a fight did he let it slip bitterly. "She makes you think it's okay to stand out." Derrick had sneered, his lips curling as if the words were poison. He never liked that I wanted more. More than him, than Stamford, and more than the predictable, planned-out life he was perfectly content with.

But Flora made that wound feel like a gift. Flora's an only child like me, but that's where the similarities end. Her world was bright, structured, and full of support. Mine was stitched together by survival. But somehow, she's always understood me in a way Derrick never could. She encouraged me to dream bigger, to accomplish my goals, and to be the person I was too scared to become. Derrick despised her for that, or maybe because I was starting to listen.

When we graduated from nursing school, Flora stuck around long enough for us to work a few shifts together.

Then she packed up and moved to Texas. She said the guys were hotter, the tacos better, and she needed a new view. She begged me to come too. But I couldn't leave Grandma. She was the only family I had left.

My visits to Flora were frequent, but never permanent. I had responsibilities. I wanted to find my footing before leaping into something new. Even with two thousand miles between us, our bond didn't waver. And now, we're here—sharing a house, late-night confessions, and bruised-ass aftermaths. The love I grew up watching in her house was soft and consistent. And what happened last night was nothing close to soft. It was fire and risk and something I can't fully articulate at the moment. But I feel like I'd be a fool not to explore it.

Chapter 19

Reflections on the Road

I rest one hand on the wheel, the other drumming against the gearshift as I pull away from Khloe's place. The morning sun is sharp in my rearview, but my mind isn't on the road—it's stuck on the girl I just left.

My phone rattles against the dashboard. I don't have to look to know it was her. I smile, but I don't reach for the phone. Not yet. I let the next red light slow me down, finally flicking my gaze to the screen.

KHLOE

Thanks for last night. I needed it.

Short, but it makes me pause. If I answer right away, it'd be easy. The problem is, I want to answer. I know how this works. I've spent enough time around women who want something from me. The second I make myself predictable, the game shifts. Not answering lets me act as if I'm still in control, but last night shook me loose. I exhale, merging onto the main road. She got under my skin in a way no one has in years. That should scare me; instead, I'm excited and uncomfortable.

Another message. I glance at the phone this time, see another woman's name, and let out a low chuckle. *Figures. Women always reach out first.*

Another buzz. I stare at the screen, watching Mama's name slide across until it fades to black. I don't decline it, but I don't answer. My mind's racing too hard, and she'd hear it. She always does. And I wouldn't know how to tell her I feel off balance. Mama is the heart of the family. She's kind. Resilient. Keeps the books balanced and the house running. She wanted more for me, encouraged me to dream beyond the ranch.

Dad and the ranch taught me discipline, hard work, and how fast life can fall apart. I grew up waking up before dawn to feed the cattle, repair fences, and bale hay under the brutal Texas sun. Our family's cattle ranch had been in the Rhodes family for generations. Dad ran it like a machine, efficient, disciplined, and with no room for softness. He wasn't wealthy, but he was proud and hardworking. And I became a reflection of that.

When I was eighteen, everything changed. A drought hit Cedar Ridge, and the economy tanked. Dad had to sell off most of the cattle to keep the lights on, but it still wasn't enough. College? Forget it. I couldn't stomach the thought of leaving him to shoulder everything while I went off to chase some dream. So, I followed his suggestion and enlisted in the Marines. It felt like the only way to escape the ranch while still sending money back home.

Within weeks of high school graduation, I shipped off to basic training. I left behind the only home I'd ever known. And my new bride, Caroline. She was everything I thought I wanted. But war changes a man—I lost brothers, I lost a part of myself. And no matter how hard she tried, I wasn't the same man she had married. Even with therapy, I couldn't be the boy I was. Caroline tried to hold us together, but eventually, she stopped trying and left.

After four years, I left the Marines with an honorable discharge and returned to Cedar Ridge. I'd saved enough to help Mama and Dad rebuild the ranch, but things weren't the same. My father's health had declined, and the responsibility of running the ranch now fell on my shoulders.

While trying to keep it afloat, I also began volunteering with the local fire department and helping with search and rescue missions. I had a knack for helping people, for staying calm in crisis situations. It gave me a sense of purpose I hadn't felt since leaving the Marines.

A buddy told me the Marshal's office in San Antonio was hiring. At first, I said no. I wasn't eager to dive back into high-stakes work. But the more I thought about it, the more it made sense. Being a Marshal wasn't just a job—it was a way to use the skills I'd honed in the Marines. To protect and serve the people, the country—something that mattered.

I still help Mama and Dad. They are partially retired, doing enough to keep their bones active. I should call Mama back. Instead, I check the rearview like it'll show me something worth going back for. I've done everything right since I left that ranch. I built my life on duty and distance, but Khloe makes both feel like excuses.

Chapter 20

Misunderstandings & Missed Connections

The music at the bar is loud but not deafening, creating a perfect backdrop for the night Flora had insisted on. I adjust my black leather jacket, trying to shake the residual thoughts of the night with Waylon. The way he'd touched me, the way he'd looked at me, still replayed in my mind. The soreness on my ass is an ever-present reminder. I'd left his truck this morning feeling like I was floating, but now I was trying to ground myself since he hadn't answered my text.

I lean back in the booth, a half-empty margarita in front of me. Across from me, my best friend plops down, beaming with drunken excitement. She sets more drinks on the table. The faint chime of a message pulls her gaze to her phone.

"Aaron just texted me!"

I smile. "Of course he did. You two are basically attached at the thumbs now."

She ignores me, fingers flying across the screen as she types back a message. "Wait, listen to this. Aaron moved here a few weeks ago and got a job with the U.S. Marshals."

I raise an eyebrow, sipping my drink. "Oh yeah? Good for him."

"No, you don't get it," Flora says, her eyes sparkling. "He's working with Waylon."

I freeze mid-sip, cheeks warming. "Waylon? Seriously?"

Flora smirks, leaning forward. "Seriously. And oh my God, your face right now is priceless. This deserves a cheers!"

Flora raises her glass. "To our future! To new beginnings, to your amazing new job with me, to Aaron's new job, to our beautiful new home, and... most importantly... to my brilliant best friend!"

I chuckle, clinking my glass with Flora's. "You're ridiculous, but thank you."

She sips and slaps the glass down like a mic drop. "No, seriously, Khlo. This is a big deal. A few months ago, you were... well, not living in San Antonio with me."

I laugh. "I know."

"And now," Flora continues softer, "you're here. You're thriving. You're building something amazing for yourself. Your grandmother would be so proud of you."

My heart tightens at the mention of Grandma. I take a sip of my drink to swallow the lump in my throat. "I wish she were here to see it."

"She is," Flora says, reaching across the table to squeeze my hand. "Every step of the way."

I nod, but the ache behind my smile lingers. It's not just Grandma I miss; it's the version of myself I lost somewhere along the way. I promised her I'd never follow in my mother's footsteps. But that promise came from years of watching Mom drift in and out, high on whatever she could get her hands on. She disappeared for good after my fourteenth birthday, and we only learned she was alive when Grandma read about her conviction for drug trafficking. Fifteen years in prison. Somehow, that was a relief. I'll never forget the look on Grandma's face, exhausted but grateful. At least her daughter was alive. At least she had a semi-safe place to rest her head.

Enrolling in nursing school with Flora right after high school was my way of building a life that wouldn't mirror the chaos I came from. Derrick never understood that. He didn't grow up wondering whether his mom would show up sober, or show up at all. His parents divorced, but they tried to outdo each other with cars, vacations, and constant overindulgence. Grandma used to call him a "spoiled rich white boy," and I'd laugh, reminding her she was half white herself.

"I'm not spoiled. I work hard for what we have," she'd reply. "That's the difference."

Grandma was overjoyed when I ended things with Derrick; I didn't know it would be the last chapter we'd close together. When she was near the end, Flora was on the first flight home. She cried with me, held my hand so tight at the funeral that I had to ask her to loosen her grip. Her words of encouragement pulled me up when I was drowning in grief.

"I couldn't have done any of this without you, Flora," I admit.

"Damn right you couldn't, Navarro," Flora teases, flipping her blonde hair over her shoulder.

"But seriously, Khlo, this is your moment. That's what best friends are for. Besides, you've done more for me than you realize. We've earned this."

I grin, raising my glass again. "To us."

"To us," Flora echoes. "I'm so glad you're here, really. It's been weird being here without you. Like I am me, but not fully me without my partner in crime."

The rest of the night flows easily—Flora drinking, me laughing, and the unease of the last few months finally lifts.

"One day," Flora says, twirling her hair, "we're going to be those old ladies who annoy everyone with stories about the crazy stuff we did when we were young."

I giggle. "Like that time you got us kicked out of that karaoke bar in Nashville?"

"Exactly." Flora grins. "And you're going to have this

amazing career and a family if you decide you want one. But no matter what, we're going to..." Flora freezes mid-sentence, her eyes narrowing at something across the bar.

"What is it?" I ask, turning my head.

"Oh, nothing," Flora says, clipped. "Just your *friend*."

I follow Flora's gaze and spot Waylon instantly. He's leaning casually against the bar, his eyes glinting under the dim lights. But he's not alone. A tall blonde is standing with him, laughing at something he'd said, her hand gliding across his arm. My stomach flips. I tear my gaze away, focusing on the condensation dripping down my barely touched margarita glass.

"Seriously?" Flora snaps. "After last night?"

"It's fine," I murmur. "It's not like we're... anything, Flora."

Flora raises an eyebrow. "Khlo, I saw the look on both of your faces this morning. He looked at you like you were the only woman left on the planet. Don't pretend it didn't mean something to you."

I don't respond. I glance at Waylon again. We make eye contact for a split second, just in time to see him lean in closer to the blonde, his signature smirk firmly in place. The sight sends a wave of irritation through me, followed quickly by a pang of disappointment I don't enjoy feeling. I have no right to be jealous. He's not mine. He never was.

My phone lights up on the table, Waylon's message appearing on the screen.

WAYLON

> Khloe, didn't expect to see you here. You look incredible.

I hover over the screen, hating the butterflies rising in my chest.

"Are you going to answer him?" Flora asks, peering at

my phone.

"Nope," I say, locking the phone and setting it face down on the table. "I'm not playing that game. I guess Missy was right."

"That's my girl," Flora says, raising her glass. I laugh as she says, "Let's finish these drinks and get out of here."

I leave my glass unfinished on the table, and Flora chugs hers. We stand walking towards the exit. As Flora opens the door, the cool night air hits my face, but there's a heat at the nape of my neck. I glance back, my eyes instinctively finding Waylon still at the bar. His eyes are fixed on me, brows wrinkled.

I turn away quickly, my heart pounding as I link arms with Flora. My phone vibrates again.

WAYLON

Khloe, please talk to me.

"You good?"

"Yeah," I say, making myself smile. "Let's go home."

Flora nods, squeezing my arm as we walk down the street together. I will not allow myself to be sad about a one-night stand ending up a one-night stand.

Chapter 21

Regrets

I lean on the bar, cold beer in hand, scanning the crowd when Khloe walks in. She's breathtaking; her presence, the elegant sweep of her hair. She has my attention without even trying, still wearing the glow I gave her.

My phone buzzes in my pocket. A regular's text showing up.

UNSAVED NUMBER

You free tonight, handsome?

Ignoring it, I lock it. The blonde next to me keeps begging for attention. But my eyes are on Khloe as she turns, and our eyes meet for a second. It hits me like a jolt—recognition passes between us, but she looks away, dismissing me. *Why is she avoiding me?*

I text her and let my eyes drift back to her. Flora's talking, all wild hands, and big expressions. Khloe throws her head back, laughing, eyes shining. But her phone stays down. I tense. Had she seen the blonde? I wasn't interested, but I get how it looked.

The minutes drag on, each one amplifying her silence. I watch her stand and leave. But before they're gone, my eyes drag to her ass. Her dress hugs her waist and dips just enough to highlight the flare of her hips. On cue, Khloe glances back. Our eyes meet again. This time, the moment lasts, and I freeze. I want to go to her and say anything that might keep her here. But she turns without a word and disappears through the door.

Later in my truck, my phone glows, lighting up my face. I scroll through our texts, staring at the photos of us. God, she's gorgeous. I re-read her words from this morning. I sigh, rubbing my face. This wasn't how tonight was supposed to go. We had something; I felt it. With most women, I'm done by now. But I don't want this to end. Unless I misread her—like Caroline. I type one last message.

WAYLON

Thanks for last night as well.

I toss the phone onto the seat. It lands with a soft thud on something familiar. Her denim jacket. I grab it and turn it over in my hands, laughing to myself. Guess fate isn't done with us.

A few nights later, I'm sitting at Aaron's kitchen table, watching him laugh like this is the funniest damn thing he's heard in years.

"Rhodes," he says, wiping a tear away, "Flora said you were nearly making out with some blonde with Khloe there? Why not go to her?"

I pick at the peeling label on my water bottle. I could've

done that. Maybe I was still denying what she's done to me. Instead, I observed. The blonde wasn't significant. Of course, Flora turned it into some scandal.

"I was barely flirtin'," I answer. "I don't know, Brooks. I'm not sure how I could take things further with Khloe." Aaron raises an eyebrow, but he says nothing. That's the thing about him. He doesn't push. He waits, giving me the space to unravel my thoughts. I drum my fingers. "I couldn't care less about that blonde. I can't stop thinkin' about *her*, Aaron. What the fuck am I supposed to do?"

Aaron leans back in his chair, giving me his usual *I'm listening* face. He's always been better at handling his feelings than I am. He's had relationships that ended cleanly with women who still send him Christmas cards. Meanwhile, my ex would probably laugh at my funeral.

I rub my face and sigh. "As you know, I have a certain... taste in intimacy. And Khloe let me take things to a level I didn't expect. Some girls bail before we even agree on a safe word. But her?" I shake my head, an ironic smile pulling at my lips. "Khloe waved it off and asked for more. I had to be the one to tell her we needed to let her body recover. Can you believe that?"

Aaron blinks as if I confessed to robbery. "Uh, no. I don't think I can."

I laugh humorlessly. His stare goes wide, a deer in headlights. I've told him bits and pieces before, but he's never really understood.

"Anyway, Khloe's got depth. She gets it in a way I didn't expect. I can't tell if that scares me or makes me want her more."

Aaron raises a brow. "Your life as an adult started with you running toward danger."

I shrug. "Maybe it's the only way I know how to survive."

He leans forward, his gaze steady. "Khloe's dangerous too, just not in the way we're used to."

He's right, of course. She's the danger that gets under

your skin and makes you feel things you'd rather ignore. Makes you question everything you thought you knew about yourself.

"I don't know what she is," I admit quietly. "But I know I can't get her out of my head."

Aaron studies me before he nods. "Sounds like you already know what to do, Rhodes. You need to quit second-guessing yourself."

I chuckle, shaking my head. "Easier said than done."

Aaron smirks. "So's everything that matters. The only thing worse than letting her in and losing her is never letting her in at all."

Hell, Aaron's always right.

But this could mean losing control, and control lives in my bones—primal and unrelenting. Taking someone to my edge; holding them there, trembling, waiting, and trusting me not to let them fall. That's where I come alive. It's more than power. It's intimacy in its rawest form. A conversation spoken in gasps and silence; her body telling me how far she'll go.

Khloe doesn't know all of me yet—not really. I stayed just shy of showing her everything. I gave her glimpses. And the way she looked at me, smiling eagerly, like she was searching for something only I could give. She stirred something dark in me, too. Something I didn't even know I had left to give.

She doesn't realize it yet, but she's made for this; made for me. She leaned into my touch, starving for it. Like she wants to be unraveled and rebuilt. It makes my blood burn.

I want to show her what she's capable of. I want her to see how goddamn beautiful she looks when she's undone.

But it's not only about pain. There's trust, release, and surrender. The flush of her red-streaked skin under my hand. A quiet moan. A sharp intake of breath. That's mine. Her body spoke in ways words never could. She whispered my name, hoarse and wrecked. I was pulling something out of her that no one else ever had. It's a goddamn addiction.

But with Khloe, it wasn't just the thrill. It was the way she trembled, not from fear but from anticipation. The way her lips parted when I drew her toward that edge, like she realized she could take more than she thought.

God help me, I want to take her further; shatter every limit she thinks she has and break it wide open.

I want to claim every gasp, every shiver, every piece of her she's too afraid to give to anyone else. And when she does, when she's lost in that space only I can bring her, I know she'll see it too.

Khloe Navarro is mine.

Chapter 22

Graveyard Whistling

The night hums like a heartbeat—steady, exhausted, too familiar. The monitor beside Room 214 beeps in rhythmic protest as I adjust the IV line, the fluorescent lights bleeding color from everything. The patient, post-op, mid-forties, and barely conscious, mumbles about pain. I whisper back, "I've got you," and press the button to release another slow wave of relief through the line.

As I head into the hallway, the scent of antiseptic and over-brewed coffee fills my nose. Around this hour of overnight shifts, the hospital becomes an echo chamber for thoughts I'd rather forget. I should be thinking about the promotion notice pinned to the nurses' bulletin board—*NP scholarship applications open through January.*

Instead, my mind drifts somewhere it shouldn't. To Waylon. The way his voice rasped my name that night. The weight of his hand when he touched my throat, gentle and commanding at once. How it felt to finally stop thinking, to just feel.

I blink hard and focus on my next patient's vitals. 118/78. Good. Stable.

But stability doesn't last in my head. Not with thoughts of Waylon sneaking in. Seeing him last night and that blonde laughing beside him burned behind my eyes long after I left. I know I promised myself one night—one beautiful, reckless mistake before I started fresh. Yet these reflections are undoing me all over again.

I change a saline bag, hanging it on the pole with practiced ease. My fingers don't tremble until I remember his hands, rough and sure, and how easily I'd trusted them. I can't afford that kind of distraction. Not when I've fought too damn hard to build something steady by leaving behind my world of neglect.

The intercom crackles overhead, calling all available personnel to help with an urgent situation. I move on autopilot, heart pounding with the rhythm of every hallway I've run since nursing school. I'm good at this. I *am* this. The chaos makes sense in a way love never has.

When the subsequent emergency subsides, I catch my reflection in the supply-room glass: curls frizzing, circles under my eyes, exhaustion carved into every line. But there's still fire there, a spark that looks like ambition instead of the heartbreak I always carry.

"Hey, Navarro," Missy calls over her shoulder from the nurses' station. "You ever think about med school? You do so well in emergency situations. You've got the patience for the patients."

I snort, flipping a chart closed. "Please. I barely have patience for you."

She laughs, typing away. "Still, you'd make a great doc. Or NP if you don't wanna drown in debt."

"NP's plenty," I say, but the words hang longer than I expect.

She shrugs. "Less paperwork, better hours, same respect—if you pick the right hospital or join a practice."

I don't answer, but the seed plants, taking root somewhere under the exhaustion. I love what I do, but maybe loving it could mean leveling up, too. Maybe that's what I needed to remember.

Waylon Rhodes fades into the background as I mentally plan.

After three days of overnight shifts, I drag my feet into our home to find Flora perched on the couch. My scrubs still smell like disinfectant and burnt coffee.

She eyes me over a pint of ice cream. "Look at my night shift survivor!"

"Barely," I mumble, collapsing beside her.

She grins. "You look like you wrestled a zombie and lost."

"Two codes, one new admit, and a guy who tried to bite me. So... close."

Flora laughs as she types away on her phone, then tilts her head, her blue eyes gnawing into me. "Sorry, texting Aaron. He's so sweet. You still didn't text Waylon back, did you?"

I groan, dropping my head against the couch. "You keeping tabs on my notifications now? You're the one glowing like someone who's in love."

"Aaron might be in love. He's been texting me the cutest questions; we're getting to know each other. He asked if you planned on ever talking to Waylon again. I left that question alone."

"I'm busy," I say, tugging at the drawstring of my scrub pants.

"Busy *and* ignoring," she teases, spoon halfway to her mouth. "You sure you want to play the mysterious card?"

"I'm not playing anything," I protest. "I just... don't want to rush into another mess. Derrick cured me of impulsive decisions."

Flora's smile softens. "Okay, fair. But you can't ghost someone and claim it's emotional maturity either."

I sigh. "Fine. I'll text him tomorrow. Maybe."

"Good." She nudges me with her elbow. "Just don't overthink it, Khlo. Sometimes the right person shows up when you're finally doing your own thing. Don't scare him off with logic."

I roll my eyes, stealing her spoon. "You done playing therapist?"

"Not even close," she says, laughing.

Her laughter fades as I head into my bedroom and plop onto my bed. My body aches from the shift, but my mind drifts to possibly returning to school, to Waylon's text I still haven't answered, and to the idea that Flora's right. I could reply; I've thought about it every day this week. I wanted to, but between doubles, sleep, and that NP scholarship notice continuously staring at me, the days blurred together. Maybe that's for the best; sometimes, space is safer.

Still, when the quiet hits as I succumb to sleep, I catch myself wondering if he's already moved on. If he's the type to wait—or the type to show up, anyway.

Chapter 23

A Second Chance

I'm standing on Khloe's front steps, her jacket draped over my arm. The house is small, well-kept, sturdy—like her. There's something about it that mirrors her exactly. That same tension between wanting more but settling for what is. It's been six days since she walked into my life and left nothing the same—because that night rewired me. I've thought about returning the jacket a dozen times, but I second-guessed myself like Aaron said I would. Now, I wonder if this was a mistake. I should have mailed it. Maybe she didn't care about it... or us.

The door swings open. Flora stands there, eyebrows lifting in surprise. She glances from the jacket to me. Her eyes light up.

"Well, if it isn't Mr. Cowboy. What's the occasion?"

I shift awkwardly, holding up the jacket. "Khloe left this at my place. Figured she might want it back."

Flora leans on the doorframe, arms crossed, smirk widening. "After *that* night, huh?"

My ears burn as I nod. "Yeah, after that night. I don't think she realized she left it."

Flora tilts her head. "And you decided to hand-deliver it? Bold move, Waylon."

"I wasn't sure if she'd want to see me."

Flora sighs, waving me in. "She'll want to see that jacket—her grandma gave it to her. She's not here, but I can tell you where she is."

I follow Flora in. Their place is open and clean, with soft gray walls, warm wood floors, and enough color to feel like Khloe. Put together without trying too hard—bright and welcoming. A place that makes you wish you could stay a little longer. As I enter the kitchen, the familiar scent of vanilla hits me immediately. A reminder of how badly I wanted to see Khloe.

"Where is she?"

"At the River Walk," Flora says, picking up her coffee from the counter. "She's been going since she moved here. Clears her head, I guess."

I frown, tightening my grip on the jacket. "You think she wants to see me?"

Flora sets her mug down, her expression softening. "Honestly? I think she does. Khloe's not great at asking for what she wants, but that doesn't mean she doesn't want it. She's been in her head a lot, and knowing her, she's probably convinced herself you've moved on and gotten married."

"I haven't."

"Then go tell her." Flora chuckles. "She's special, Waylon. She's been through a lot. It's hard for her to believe someone's gonna stick around. But if you care about her—and I'm hoping you do since you didn't FedEx the jacket—then go give her more of your hell."

I nod slowly, glancing down at the jacket. "Thanks, Flora."

She grins, leaning against the counter. "Anytime, cowboy. Just don't screw it up."

I chuckle and head toward the door. I climb into my truck, pulse quickening at the thought of seeing her.

THROUGH LUST, WE FELL

I spot Khloe sitting on a bench by the edge of the River Walk. The light spring wind teases her wavy curls. My boots crunch on the path, and she turns. The air immediately shifts between us. I walk up and look out at the setting sun rippling across the water. As I turn to her, her expression is unreadable. She's hard to pin down, but that only makes me want to know her more.

"You left this at my place," I break the silence, laying the jacket next to her. "You never texted me back. Guess that means you've been busy?"

Her lips twitch into a small smile. "I have been, actually. Work's been a lot."

I sit beside her. "You never did tell me what you do."

Khloe hesitates, her fingers trailing over the bench. "I'm a registered nurse."

I blink. "Really? That's impressive."

She shrugs. "It's not that big of a deal."

"The hell it's not," I say, leaning back. "That's hard work. I've got friends who've spent time in hospitals. The nurses were always the ones takin' care of 'em. Seems like a damn important job to me."

She laughs lightly. "It's rewarding, but exhausting too. Long shifts, short staff, patients who sometimes don't appreciate you." She pauses, glancing at me. "But then you get moments that make it all worth it."

"Like what?"

She smiles, eyes drifting back to the water. "Like holding someone's hand when they're scared. Or seeing a patient finally go home after weeks in the hospital. It's the little things, you know? Things most people don't think about."

I nod, my respect for her growing with every word. "Sounds like you've got a lotta heart to do what you do.

Most people couldn't handle it."

She shrugs again, though her cheeks flush. "It's not always easy. I've lost patients, too. And those stick with you. You wonder if you did enough, if you could've done something differently."

"Khloe," I say gently. "From what I've seen of you, you've got a way of carryin' the weight of the world, even when it's not yours to carry."

She looks at me, her eyes soft but wary. "It's a heavy world."

"It is. Trust me on that."

She laughs. "Glad we're having this conversation after we've already seen each other naked."

"Shame. I would've offered you a live-in position." I grin. She smiles but doesn't respond.

The silence that follows is comfortable, filled with the sound of water lapping at the River Walk. Khloe turns back to me, meeting my eyes. "So, what about you? How is it being a Marshal? I bet you see a lot."

I chuckle, leaning closer. "You could say that. Some days it's chasin' down bad guys; other days, it's helpin' someone out. Sometimes I'm gone for weeks at a time. It's unpredictable, but that's exactly what I like about it. Makes me feel like I'm doin' somethin' that matters."

She tilts her head. "Doesn't it get... intense? Seeing the worst parts of people all the time?"

"It does. Some days, it feels like all I see is the bad. But then there are moments that remind me why I do it. Catchin' the guy who's hurtin' people, makin' sure someone gets home safe. That's what keeps me goin'. Kinda like you, I guess. It's the little things."

Khloe smiles faintly. "So, fixing broken parts and people for me, maybe the world for you."

I grin at her. "Guess we've got somethin' in common then."

She laughs. "More than you think."

And like that, the tension fades, replaced by an ease I'm unfamiliar with. I'm not the kind of guy to get caught up in sunsets and quiet moments. Or, hell, anything that feels this close to real. But here I am, a foot away from Khloe as the river catches fire in the dying light, and for once, I don't have a damn thing to say. I'd come here to flirt, throw out one of those lines that always gets me that laugh, that look, that invitation.

But when she turns to me, eyes catching the gold of the horizon, it knocks the air clean out of my chest.

"Beautiful, isn't it?" I manage, though I sound strange—almost worshipful. She nods, but instead of looking back at the water, she looks at me. Her eyes hold mine, searching, as if she's seeing through me and finding something beneath. My throat goes dry. Most women notice the charm, the smirk, the usual performance, but Khloe's gaze cuts right through it. Like she's hunting for something I'm not ready to give. I shift my weight, resisting the urge to look away.

"Yeah... it is," she whispers.

I tell myself to keep it together, but sitting here, caught in her gaze, I feel my armor crack a little. "Khloe..." Her name comes out like a confession.

"Yeah?" she asks softly, and damn if the sound doesn't do something to me.

I force a smile. My go-to defense, but this one feels unsteady. "Nothing. Just... I don't usually stick around for stuff like this."

Her brow lifts. "Stuff like what?"

I hesitate, searching for a line to turn this moment back into something I can control. But there's no quick escape.

"Stuff that matters," I say, without thinking. The air between us stretches, and I don't rush to fill it.

Maybe I don't want every woman to stay for the night and leave first thing in the morning.

We sit in silence as the water shimmers with reflections of old stone buildings and swaying palms, each ripple catching the quiet. Khloe stands first, pulling her jacket tight as the breeze picks up.

"It's getting late," she says hesitantly.

I nod and rise, hands sliding into my pockets. "Yeah. I should head home."

"Well," she says, brushing a strand of hair out of her face, "thanks for... you know, last week and tonight—for being here."

I smirk, but I know it lacks its usual sharpness. "Didn't do much."

She turns, takes a step toward the path by the river, then stops. When she looks back, her eyes are serene, but there's something else pulling me in, luring me to follow.

"Sometimes being there is enough."

The usual smooth reply sits on the tip of my tongue, but it feels too shallow to twist this. All I can do is stare at her before I say, "You take care, Khloe."

She tilts her head. "You too, Waylon. Goodnight."

I watch her walk away, the fading light glinting off her dark hair. I don't feel the urge to call her back with some pickup line. I stay rooted where I am, watching until she disappears around the bend. As the heaviness of last week and this afternoon sets in, I realize that whatever just happened was meaningful.

After a restless night, I sit on the edge of my bed. I should get ready for work, but I'm staring at a blank message screen. Friday morning sunlight streams through the half-closed blinds, warming the room, but not my usual confidence. I don't overthink texts. Hell, I don't text first at all. But something about Khloe stuck with me, like a song I couldn't get out of my head. My dream last night proved that. Her body weaved with mine like we were the morning after. I never dream of specific females, just motions, and movements of the satisfaction of having one, and even that's rare.

Finally, I type:

WAYLON

> You always hang out by rivers or was last night special?

I stare at the message and tap *Send* and toss the phone onto the bed like a grenade. Each second drags slower than the last. When my phone goes off, I snatch it up fast.

KHLOE

I don't make a habit of it. Why, thinking of starting a tradition?

I smirk, her reply hitting the right balance of teasing and seriousness.

WAYLON

> Maybe. You free later? I could use another deep, philosophical riverside moment. 😌

KHLOE

Philosophical, huh? Didn't take you for the type.

WAYLON

> I'm full of surprises.

I wait, watching the three little dots dance on the screen before her reply pops up.

KHLOE

Same spot, 5?

A flicker of excitement stirs within me.

WAYLON

I'll bring the philosophy. You bring those dangerous eyes.

KHLOE

See you then. ☺

I set the phone down and lean back against the pillows. It's not a big deal. Just another girl, another day. But deep down, I know I'm not walking away from this one clean.

I arrive first at the same weathered bench by the River Walk, a half-empty coffee cup in my hand. The breeze is lighter today. I hear her footsteps before I see her. Turning, I catch sight of Khloe walking towards me in a pink sleeveless blouse, a nice contrast to her sun-kissed skin, her hair pulled back, showing off her high cheekbones. She gives me a smile, and oddly, it feels like the sun just got a little warmer.

"Didn't think you'd show," I tease.

"Why's that?"

I shrug, taking a sip of my coffee. "Figured you'd be too busy doing whatever mysterious people do."

Khloe's shoulders lift in a small laugh. "Mysterious, huh?"

I study her for a moment, my usual smart-aleck responses coming slower today. "Yeah. You've got that whole quiet, thoughtful thing going on. Keeps people guessing."

She tilts her head. "And what about you?"

I give her my boyish grin. "Oh, I'm an open book. No mysteries here."

"Mm," she says, sitting down on the bench. "I'm not so sure about that."

"Oh yeah? What do you think you know about me?"

Khloe looks out at the water. "I think you're good at pretending. You make jokes, keep things light. Spank girls, but you don't really let people in."

Her words weren't what I expected. I chuckle, biting my lip before I say, "You got all that from one night?"

She turns to me. "I'm guessing." She shrugs.

I don't say anything. Damn, she sees right through me. I sit down beside her, the usual cockiness slipping away. "You're not wrong," I admit, surprising myself.

Khloe doesn't push. She nods in understanding. The rustle of trees and distant tourists fills the silence

"You know," she says, glancing at me, "I don't usually stick around for things like this." She smiles widely. "Ya know, things that matter?"

I chuckle, shaking my head. "You don't let up, do you?"

"Nope."

The sun dips lower on the horizon, casting long shadows across the water. Khloe shifts beside me, rubbing her arms. Goosebumps rise along her skin, and I shrug off my jacket, draping it over her shoulders before she can protest.

"Can't have you freezing on me." I flash a quick grin.

Khloe pulls the jacket closer. "Chivalry from Waylon? Didn't think you had it in you."

"Don't get used to it," I tease, standing and stretching. "Come on, I'll walk you back to your car."

She hesitates, then stands, following me along the walkway that winds through the cypress trees. The serenity fades, replaced by city traffic and the distant sound of a mariachi band.

"So," I say, shoving my hands in my pockets. "Back to the mysterious life tonight?"

Khloe laughs. "Maybe a book, some tea. Wild, I know."

"Sounds excitin'," I exaggerate, then add with a smirk, "but I've got a better idea."

"Oh?"

"My truck's parked up the street," I say. "There's a spot in town that makes a decent old-fashioned or whatever it is you drink. Call it a nightcap."

"You sure it's not an excuse to spend more time with me?"

"What can I say? I'm full of good ideas," I say shamelessly.

She shakes her head. "Alright, but one drink. Don't think I'm letting you talk me into karaoke or anything."

"Karaoke?" I pretend to be offended, grabbing my chest as I finish. "I'll have you know I'm a legend at karaoke night."

"Oh, I'm sure." Her response drips with sarcasm.

As we reach my black truck, a weathered but well-kept pickup, I open the passenger door. It creaks as she climbs in, the smell of worn leather and pine filling the cab. I slide into the driver's seat and start the engine, its low rumble breaking the silence. I glance at her, one hand on the wheel, the other resting on the console.

"Ready?"

She nods. "Ready."

As I pull onto the road, the easy banter between us resumes, but beneath it something quieter simmers. It feels like the start of more.

The bar isn't much. Dim lights, scratched wooden tables, finger foods, and a jukebox playing old country tunes in the corner. It has character—a place I feel at home in.

I hold the door open for Khloe, tipping an imaginary hat as she steps inside. "Welcome to the finest establishment this side of the Mississippi," I drawl. My accent thickened just enough to make her roll her eyes and laugh.

"Wow, a real gentleman tonight," she teases.

"Always am," I say, winking as I guide her to a booth near the back. "You just don't know it yet."

Khloe slides into the booth as it gives a soft groan. "Sure, Waylon. I'll believe it when I see it."

I sit across from her, leaning back like I own the place. The regular waitress approaches, a pen tucked behind her ear. "Hi, Waylon, what can I get y'all?"

I give her a crooked smile. "I'll take an old-fashioned, heavy on the old, light on the fashioned."

The waitress smirks, used to my antics by now, then turns to Khloe. "And for you, sweetheart?"

"A whiskey sour," Khloe says. She looks at me. "No theatrics needed."

"Boring," I mutter, shaking my head.

The waitress walks away as Khloe rests her elbows on the table. "So, is this what you do? Charm every woman into a drink at a dive bar?"

"Darlin', I don't need to charm anyone. It just comes naturally."

She raises her brow. "Is that so? Wasn't that what you were doing with the blonde the other night?"

"Mhm..." I watch her for a moment. "She was no one, Khlo. Just someone makin' small talk."

Khloe nods. "Not that it's any of my business, but... I was curious."

"If you think this is my usual routine, you're wrong. You're special."

Khloe rolls her eyes again, but there's a faint smile on her lips. "You must've said that a hundred times."

"Nope," I say, giving her a crooked grin. "First time. Honest. Don't think I didn't catch that eye roll."

A blush creeps across her face. "My bruises have finally faded."

The waitress interrupts my carnal thoughts, delivering our drinks.

When she leaves, I raise my glass. "To the mysterious,

beautiful woman I was destined to meet, who makes sunsets feel more interestin'."

She goes quiet, eyes softening like she's not used to men meaning what they say. We clink glasses.

"And to charming men who might not be as shallow as they seem."

"Ouch." I fake a hurt face. "I'm gonna need a second drink to recover from that one."

"You'll survive." Khloe's smile softens as she asks, "So, how did you and Aaron meet? You guys seem so close."

I lean back, looking past her as I swirl my glass. The hum of the jukebox in the background fades.

"I met Aaron in the Corps. We were both young and stupid. Thinkin' we were invincible. We didn't hit it off right away. He thought I was too much of a cowboy, and I thought he was too much of a smartass."

Khloe smiles faintly, resting her chin on her hand, watching me. "So, what changed?"

I set my glass on the table and look at my hands; the memory pulls me far away. "It was our second deployment. We were stationed in this desert village, a place so godforsaken it barely had a name. Intel came in about a high-value target holed up in one of the houses. Me and Aaron were part of the team sent to clear it." I pause, rubbing the back of my neck. "It was supposed to be straightforward. We were trained for this kinda thing. But the place was rigged, IED's hidden in every corner. We didn't know until it was too late."

Khloe's breath catches, but she doesn't interrupt.

"I was sweepin' the second floor, clearing rooms," I continue, quieter now. "Aaron was downstairs with the rest of the squad. I tripped over a pressure plate. And this loud beep echoed through the walls. Aaron started shoutin' through the comms, tellin' me to get the fuck outta there."

My lips press into a thin line, the sound still fresh in my mind. "But I couldn't move. My foot was caught on somethin', and I couldn't think straight. That damn beeping was gettin' faster. Next thing I know, Aaron's in the room, grabbin' me by the vest and yanking me so hard I thought my ribs would snap. He didn't even hesitate." I meet Khloe's stare. The intensity in her gaze pushes me through. "We barely made it out. The second we hit the stairs, the whole place went up behind us. The heat, the blast... it knocked us both flat on our asses. But we were alive. Barely, but alive."

"He saved your life."

"Yeah. And he'll tell you I saved his ass a few times after that, but nothin' I ever did compares to what he did for me that day. He could've left me there, Khlo. Nobody would've blamed him."

Khloe reaches out, her fingers brushing against mine. "That explains a lot. You guys are incredible."

I smile. "Yeah, he is. Man's been through as much as me, even more. And he's still the guy everyone wants in their corner."

Khloe tilts her head. "You two must've stood out together in the Marines. You're so opposite."

I chuckle, taking a sip of my drink. "That's an understatement. Him, a Black guy from D.C. whose parents are civil rights lawyers who love debating politics—and me, a white boy and a rancher's son from Cedar Ridge, where football and rodeo are life. But none of that mattered when the bullets started flying. He had my back, and I had his."

Khloe's lips curved into a soft smile. "Sounds like he's family."

I nod. "He is. Blood don't mean a damn thing when you've been through what we have. Aaron's more my brother than some of my kinfolk ever will be... But enough about me already. What about you? You never answered why you were in San Antonio, or even where you're from."

Her smile falters for a second. She clears her throat, fingers slowly tracing the rim of her glass. "Well, I am here for a few reasons. One is Flora. The second is my grandmother, and the last is my ex, Derrick," she says, eyes fixed on the table. "He was... he was my first real relationship. We were together for years, throughout high school and after... I thought he was the one."

I nod, watching her closely. I've heard people talk about their pasts before, but there's something in the way she's telling hers. Each word feels careful, like she's balancing on a wire, trying not to feel too much as she says it.

"Turns out," she continues, sharper now, "he was everything I thought he couldn't be. A cheater, a liar. And when I started nursing school, he told me I was selfish for wanting more than him—that I was leaving him behind."

"Sounds like an asshole. Any man who tries to hold a woman back like you doesn't deserve her."

She smiles, but it doesn't reach her eyes. "He was. But I didn't see it back then. I thought if I loved him enough, he'd change. Spoiler: he didn't."

I lean forward. "So that's who broke your heart?"

She laughs, then takes a sip of her drink and sets the glass down a little too carefully, like her hands might betray her if she isn't precise.

"A few people, but the most recent? Ha." She pauses, looking down at her lap, then meets my eyes. "You ever smell cucumber melon perfume and want to punch a wall?" she asks suddenly.

I raise a brow. "Can't say I have." Her eyes flicker, and there's a wry twist to her lips, but it doesn't reach her eyes. I lean in. "Why?"

Khloe exhales a laugh that sounds scraped raw. "That's the perfume the girl wore that my ex had in our bed." The words hang between us. My spine goes rigid. I want to ask a hundred things at once, who, when, where the hell is he now, but I keep my mouth shut and let her keep going.

"I heard them first," she says quietly, staring at the rim of her glass. "Her giggle—my headboard hitting the wall." She swallows hard. "He didn't even stop when I walked in. Just looked at me like I was the problem."

My jaw clenches as the image burns through me: her

standing there, catching him in the act, and him not stopping. My hand tightens around the neck of my beer.

"She left swearing at me," Khloe continues, voice steadier now, cutting the memory down to size. "We threw words like knives and... then I finally said the one thing I knew would piss him off. 'Hopefully you could at least make her come,' and I laughed. And then... he slapped me."

Every muscle in me goes taut. I can feel the blood roaring in my ears. If Derrick were here, I'd put him through the wall. My hands clench instinctively.

"Khloe..."

But she doesn't flinch. She tips her chin up, a spark of defiance there that shouldn't make me proud, but it does.

"It's okay," she says quickly, holding up a hand. "It was almost two years ago. And I had my grandma and Flora. They were the ones who helped me cope. They were both everything to me. And that was it for me," she finishes. "No more excuses. No more trying to fix something broken."

I study her, the way she hides the tremor in her hand by sliding her glass closer to mine. She thinks she's playing it off, making a joke out of perfume and bad men. Her honesty floors me, but I see the invisible scars itching beneath her skin. I don't know what to say. She's laying her soul bare, and all I can think is how damn powerful she is—but so goddamn fragile underneath it all. I want to hold her and tell her she'll never have to feel that way again.

Instead, I exhale, my reaction measured. "That's a lot to carry."

She nods. "It is."

"Khloe, you've been through hell, and somehow, you're still here, still standin'. That says a hell of a lot about you." I throw on the charm, but I actually mean it when I say: "Sounds like no man has ever given you what you truly deserve."

She smiles, and this time it's filled with genuine warmth, like sunlight breaking through a storm. "Thanks, Waylon."

I can't help but smile back, even as my chest aches with the urge to protect her from everything she's faced and is still afraid of. I don't know how to say all of that, so instead, I reach across the table and cover her hand with mine. "I'm not gonna lie to you and say I understand everything you've been through. But I'm here, Khloe. And I'm not goin' anywhere."

Her eyes soften, the guarded edge fading. "That's what they all say," she murmurs.

"Maybe, but I'm not them," I admit, squeezing her hand gently. "You don't get to choose your destiny, Khloe." I wink at her, watching a blush slowly spread across her cheeks. Her phone screen lights up, interrupting our moment. I glance down and nod toward it. "If it's work, don't worry. I know how it is."

Khloe opens the text on the table and reads it.

DR. MITCHELL

Hey Khloe, I wanted to check if you reconsidered my offer. Dinner this time?

DR. MITCHELL

I promise it'll be worth your while.

My easy smile fades as I read the message with her. "Who's Dr. Mitchell?" I ask, my tone carefully neutral.

She follows my gaze to her phone, and her face scrunches. "Oh, he's a doctor I work with."

I smirk, eyes searching hers. "That text seems a bit familiar for 'just a doctor.' Has he done this before?"

She hesitates. "He's made comments. Nothing overt... just hints. I always brush them off."

"Do you want me to talk to him?"

She chuckles. "No, I can handle it. But knowing you

have my back means a lot."

"As long as I'm around, you'll always have someone in your corner, Khloe."

Sure, it's charm, but I mean it.

We talk long into the evening, the chatter light but the looks growing heavier. I keep up my usual flirting, but there is a softness to it. A warmth that even surprises me.

When the check comes, I grab it quickly. "Southern manners," I say with a wink. "Can't help myself."

As we walk out into the cool night air, Khloe pulls my jacket tighter around her shoulders. "Well, I guess I'll give you this." She looks at me. "You're not completely full of it."

I laugh. "High praise coming from you."

When we reach my truck, I lean against the door. "So, how'd I do? Impressed yet?"

She smirks, stepping close to me. "You're alright."

"Good enough for me, darlin'."

As we slip into my truck, the twang of classic '90s country fills the cab, setting a quiet rhythm for the drive. I glance over at her every so often, catching the way her fingers tap against her knee in time with the music. She's wearing a faint smile, lost in her own world. It's a good look on her.

When we pull up to her car, she doesn't open the door right away. She leans her body towards me. "Thanks for another night of things you don't normally do."

I reach over to tilt her chin toward me. "You're a gorgeous woman. Anytime, Khlo. I haven't felt this connected to someone in a long time." She smiles, showing that dimple. "We'd be fools if we didn't give this a chance," I add as I lean in, letting a lingering kiss show her how serious I am.

When I pull back, she's sliding out of the truck. The warmth of her lips burned into me like a brand. I watch as she walks to her car, her shoulders loose, her movements easy. She gets in her white SUV and starts the car. After a quick glance in my direction, she drives off into the night.

I sit there for a moment. The game I've played so many

times before feels distant now, irrelevant. My time with Khloe feels real. Vanilla still lingers in the cab. I think back to our first night, that smile, her reddened ass. The memory of her moaning as she squirted. My bulge is unbearable, begging me to release the pent-up aggression I've been holding in. I haven't been with anyone since Khloe. I rarely have to take care of my own needs, but I have no choice. I unzip, feeling relief and embarrassment that her scent has made me rock hard.

I fist myself in tight, unforgiving strokes, picturing her legs spread by my command. Sweet and soaked, her wetness coating the bed and her thighs. The memory coils inside me, burning hot. Her riding me the next morning, hips slamming into my thighs, eyes wild with need. That's all it takes —I spill onto my stomach, the pressure unraveling instantly.

What the fuck has she done to me? She could destroy me without trying. I've been wrecked before, and I know how that story ends. But I'm not scared to sit with my feelings now.

Chapter 24

Lies, Lies, Lies

As I drive away from the parking lot, the cool night air drifts in through the cracked window, but it does little to quiet the warmth spreading through my chest. Waylon's jacket still hangs around my shoulders, smelling faintly of leather and something woodsy. I can't stop smiling. I shake my head. *Don't overthink this, Khloe. He's a smooth-talking charmer. You've seen his type a million times.*

But Waylon hadn't felt like a type tonight. My phone rings in the cupholder. I glance down, seeing Flora's name. My best friend can always sense when I need someone to talk to.

"Hey, Flo."

"Khloe! Finally!" Flora bursts with energy. "Where have you been all day? You ghosting me?"

I laugh. "No, never that. I was... out."

Flora gasps dramatically. "Out? With who? Spill."

I bite my lip. "Waylon."

"Wait... Waylon? Player? Cowboy Waylon?"

"The very one," I admit.

"Okay, okay. Details. Did he say something stupid? Or

did he impress you?"

"He's more... raw than I thought."

"How?" she begs.

"He's still got that cocky, southern-charm thing going, but tonight, he felt real. Like he wasn't trying so hard to play a part."

Flora hums knowingly. "Sounds like someone got under your skin."

"Maybe."

"And did you get under *his*?"

"I think I did," I admit. "He made a comment that stuck with me." I clear my throat to mimic his accent. "'You don't get to choose your destiny, Khloe.'"

Flora bursts out laughing. "Wow. Khloe, the heartbreaker. Look at you."

"It's not like that," I say quickly, shaking my head. "He surprised me, that's all. I don't even know if it's anything."

Flora softens. "Well, it doesn't have to be anything yet. But if he's showing you something real, give him a chance. Worst case, you call me for an emergency rescue."

"Deal. I'll be inside in a minute."

I pull into our driveway and cut the engine. I sit there for a moment, the night quiet around me.

"Don't get your hopes up."

The next day feels like a setup. Flora drags me out for a shopping trip on the River Walk, insisting we need to stay out a little longer right before we 'coincidentally' run into Waylon and Aaron.

Hours later, I'm beside Waylon, my leg draped over his thigh, his hand resting on the booth back behind me. Our shoulders touch as he leans in, like this has always been our spot.

Flora and Aaron are mingling near the bar.

Waylon nurses his whiskey, watching me. "You're layered, you know that?"

"How?"

"Most folks I meet try too hard. You don't seem to care what anyone thinks. And that first night, there was too much damn passion in you for me to ever forget. I tried to play it off, but the truth is, I've been burnin' for you ever since."

A blush creeps up my cheeks, but before I can respond, my phone buzzes on the table. Flora's name lights up the screen with a text.

FLORA

Girl, Aaron let something slip about Waylon.
Guess what? Apparently, he's divorced?

FLORA

Did he tell you? You didn't tell me if he did!

I blink hard, wishing the message away as my stomach drops. Divorced? Waylon said nothing about that. When I joked earlier about his past relationships, he brushed it off. I look up, keeping my expression neutral while my emotions shift through confusion, disbelief, and something sharper underneath. I pull my leg back.

"Waylon, can I ask you something?"

He cocks his head, his grin faltering. "Of course."

"Have you ever been married?"

The question hangs in the air between us.

"Why're you askin' that?"

I cross my arms. "Answer the question."

Waylon rubs the back of his neck. "Alright, fine. I was married. A long time ago. Barely counts, honestly."

I stare at him. "You've had ample opportunities to come clean. Were you gonna leave that part out?"

"It was a fib, not a lie," he says, sitting up straighter. "I didn't think it mattered. It was a mistake. We were young and stupid, and it didn't last. When you and I first met, I didn't expect it to go this way."

I let out a manic laugh, shaking my head. "Not a lie? That sure sounds like avoiding the truth to me."

Waylon leans towards me. "Khloe, I wasn't tryin' to hide it to hurt you. It's not somethin' I bring up unless I have to—it's ancient history."

I stare at him in disbelief. "If you're lying about something as big as that, what else are you hiding?"

"Please, I'm not tryin' to squirm out of what I've done," he says quickly, the words tumbling out. "This is still a good thing. The feelings are genuine. I just... I didn't want it to ruin this."

My jaw locks, emotions warring within me. Part of me wants to give him the benefit of the doubt, to believe that his omission wasn't malicious. But the part that has been let down too many times before is screaming at me to walk away.

"You don't get to decide what ruins this," I say, standing. "That's my call."

Waylon stands too, reaching for my arm but stopping short. "Khloe, wait. I—"

"No," I interrupt, holding up a hand. "I need to think." I walk away, heart pounding.

Flora catches up with me moments later, immediately wrapping an arm around my shoulders. Her presence is grounding, but my thoughts are spinning too fast to settle.

"You okay?"

I exhale shakily. "He lied, Flora. About being married. He didn't tell me."

Flora frowns, pulling me toward a bench to sit. "That's a big thing to leave out. But do you think he was hiding it to be shady?"

I shake my head. "That's the problem. I don't know. If he kept this from me, what else is there?"

Flora exhales, squeezing my shoulder. "I get it. But Waylon doesn't seem like the kind of guy who lies to be an ass. Maybe when he first met you, he didn't think it mattered. He probably thought he'd never see you again."

I face her, my brows furrowed. "So that makes it okay?"

"No," she says simply, "but it might make it *different.*"

I chew my lip, frustration still bubbling beneath my skin.

"I, ugh..." I drag my hand through my hair. "If he's hiding this, what else? My mom lied about being sober. Derrick lied about everything. And now, Waylon?"

Flora's expression softens. "Khlo, not everyone's like your mom. Or Derrick. This isn't proof he'll hurt you. It's proof you're still scared."

I blink. "Scared?"

She shrugs. "Of letting him in. You're looking for a reason to push him away."

Shit. That might be true. I stare at the path ahead on the River Walk. I want to believe that his omission wasn't malicious. But how do you trust someone when honesty feels like an afterthought?

Flora pulls me closer, resting her head on my shoulder. "Whatever you decide, I'm here. Always."

Her words soothe me, but the lump in my throat stays. I glance back at the bar. Waylon's in there, probably wondering if I'll come back. Part of me wants to let him explain, to forgive him. But the part built on years of disappointment and abandonment whispers that it's safer to walk away.

The night stretches ahead, heavy with doubt. Flora tightens her grip on my arm. "You'll figure it out, Khlo."

I nod. *What if I never do?* The question sticks with me as we disappear into the night.

Chapter 25

The Weight of Omission

I know the moment she looks at me that something is wrong. One second, she's flushed from our teasing. Next, she's shutting down right in front of me. Her fingers tighten around her phone; her body pulls away, going rigid. She looks at me as if she's trying to figure me out all over again. Then she asks a question I dread.

Have you ever been married?

Fuck.

I knew this would come up eventually. A part of me had hoped it wouldn't matter. That I'd never have to say it. I play it off, try to find an escape route, but she's not letting this go. I never lied, not exactly. I'd left things out. I hadn't expected her or these feelings. I laid this trap myself; now I'm the one caught in it.

The excuses feel weak. She doesn't believe me. I see her walls are back up before she even speaks. My explanation is too defensive. Her shoulders stiffen. She stands, and I know I've lost her. I reach for her, but my hands falter midair before dropping, fists clenching with everything I don't know how to say.

"Khloe, wait. I—"

She cuts me off and disappears into the night. I want to chase her and make her understand this doesn't change a damn thing. But the damage is done. I was fooling myself.

I sit down, dragging a hand over my face. Eyes fixed on the spot Khloe occupied, my jaw clenched painfully tight. The murmur of the bar fades around me, the low flicker of candlelight doing nothing to ease the pit in my stomach.

Shit.

Flora rushes past me, throwing a sharp look over her shoulder, eyes blazing with disappointment. "Nice job, Waylon. Real fucking smooth."

Then she's off to chase Khloe, calling her name as her heels click hard. Leaving me alone with my mistake. I barely process everything before Aaron slides in across from me, exhaling as he runs a hand across his bald head. His shoulders are tense, eyes flicking down, then back up to meet mine.

"Shit, man," he mutters. "I didn't mean for that to come out the way it did. It kinda slipped out."

I inhale, trying to tamp down the irritation clawing at my chest. "Yeah? Well, it sure as hell *came out* like a goddamn bomb, Aaron."

"I get it. But c'mon, Waylon. You didn't think she was gonna find out eventually?"

I glare at him. I'd known this was going to come up one day, but I'd pushed it aside, convinced it wasn't worth digging up. Hell, I never tell women I've been married. There's never been a reason to. But Khloe isn't just another night I'll forget by the morning. I could *be* with Khloe. Now she's probably halfway across the city, questioning every damn thing I've ever said to her.

Aaron sighs, leaning back. "I know it's not my business, but why didn't you tell her?"

I scoff. "What was I supposed to do? Bring it up between dinner and drinks? 'Hey, Khlo, pass the salt, and oh, by the way, I was married once.'"

Aaron huffs. "No, man, but you *should* have told her before she heard it from someone else."

I drag a hand down my face, fingers digging into my jaw before I drop it. "It was years ago. Hell, it barely happened. What does it have to do with us?"

Aaron gives me a look. "It's not about the marriage, Waylon. It's about the fact that you *chose* not to tell her."

I lean forward, hands clasped at my mouth. I hate how fucking wrong I was.

Aaron sighs again. "Look, Khloe's tough; Flora says she's cautious. You've seen that, right?"

"Yeah," I mutter. "I know. She's got her reasons. She's been burned before. Probably more than she lets on. And whether I meant to or not, I confirmed every doubt she's ever had about trustin' someone."

Aaron studies me for a moment. "You really like her, huh?"

I don't hesitate. "Yeah."

"Then fix it. You're one stubborn son of a bitch, Waylon. And it seems she is, too. You gonna let this be the thing that ends it?"

He shrugs like it's simple, like it's not a fucking mess I made worse. I don't answer because I don't fucking know. Khloe's already literally out the door. I saw the finality in her eyes before she walked away.

Aaron shakes his head when I don't respond. "Don't wait too long, man. If you let her sit in her head about this, she's gonna convince herself you're not worth the risk."

If she did, she might be right. But I have to fix it. She makes me restless with need, not only for her body, but for something I've never let myself want after Caroline. Something that lasts.

She's danger and safety in a way I can't explain. Like stepping into a fight and knowing before the first punch is thrown that you're going to win. That no matter how hard the hit, you'll come out on the other side because she's there.

The office is crowded with chatter, case files flipping, radios crackling, and boots scuffing against the tile floor. I should be focused on work, yet my thoughts are consumed by my damn phone. It's been almost a week since Khloe found out about my ex, and she hasn't said a word to me since.

I texted. I called, hoping she'd at least listen to me. Her response is silence. I rub my hand over my face, sighing as I scroll through our last messages. Every day this week, I've sent something. Something honest and something desperate.

WAYLON

> I'm sorry I wasn't truthful. I know I was wrong. I had no idea you were going to make me feel this way.

WAYLON

> Khloe, I can almost feel you against me. Like when I pull you close, kiss your neck and feel you gasp for air as my muscles tighten around you.

WAYLON

> I can't stop thinking about you. I feel fucking dumb. You're seriously the best thing I've had going for me in forever.

WAYLON

> I am sorry. I was going to tell you. I didn't know that this was going to develop like it has. I know now, and I'm kicking myself for it.

WAYLON

> You know you feel like I do. I hurt you, and in turn, hurt myself. But no matter what's gone wrong, how we feel hasn't changed. I fucked up. Everyone does eventually. All I know is I fuckin love everything about you. The way you smile at me, the way you talk to me, the feeling of your kiss, and your hair on my face. I feel something I haven't felt in forever, and you do, too. We can't let this go.

I exhale hard, locking my phone and tossing it onto my desk. She read them all but hasn't answered a single one.

"Damn, man," Ramirez cuts through my brooding. "You keep staring at that phone like it's gonna grow legs and run."

I grunt in response, shaking my head. Ramirez strides over and leans on my desk like he's got all the time in the world, dark eyes sharp but calm. Skin the color of coffee with too much sun in it, jaw always set like he's still back in the Corps. He doesn't talk much, but when he does, it's usually the thing I don't wanna hear but need to.

Aaron leans back in his chair. "Still nothing?"

"Nothin'," I mutter, rubbing the back of my neck.

Ramirez shakes his head. "That woman is stubborn."

Aaron smirks. "Takes one to love one."

I shoot him a glare. "I fucked up, but who tells a one-night stand you've been married?"

Aaron arches a brow. "Really, bro? This has been going on longer than one night. When you realized she was more than that, you should've been honest, Rhodes."

Ramirez chimes in, "My abuela used to say, 'The one who runs from truth trips over pride.' Sounds about right, huh?" I tense at his words. Ramirez crosses his arms. "Look, man, women don't just shut down unless they're protecting themselves. You sure this is just about the ex, or is it about something bigger?"

I roll my jaw. "From what I know of Khloe, her walls aren't just about me lying. It's about her past. About all her hurt she hasn't worked through. I was supposed to be someone she could trust."

Aaron sighs. "Give her time, but don't stop trying. If she didn't care, she wouldn't be ignoring you this hard."

I nod. Time's the one thing I don't want to give when it comes to her.

Chapter 26

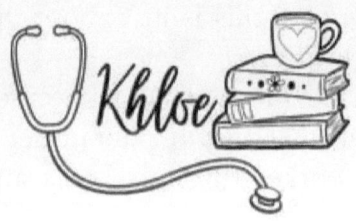

Lingering Doubts

I move down the corridor of the emergency room, my sneakers squeaking against the polished floor. It's been a hectic shift. Codes called, patients admitted, and the paperwork keeps piling on. I glance at my watch, hoping time has moved a few more hours, but only a couple of minutes have passed.

As I round a corner, Dr. Mitchell falls into step beside me. Tall and confident, like Waylon. He is well-liked by the staff. Handsome, but his arrogant demeanor overshadows his looks, leaving me uninterested. His fiery red hair is always artfully tousled, like he knows it sets him apart. A subtle beard and neatly trimmed sideburns frame his sharp jawline. Every time he walks into a room, his pride declares, 'I own this space.'

"Long day, huh?" He's sporting his usual smug look.

"You could say that," I answer politely, eyes ahead. I appreciate friendly colleagues, but something about Dr. Mitchell always put me on edge after he hit on me the first week of work.

"You always handle it so well. I don't know how you do it."

I offer an obligatory smile. "Just part of the job."

When we reach the nurses' station, I sort through charts, hoping he takes the hint. Instead, he leans against the counter, watching me. His shit-eating grin makes my skin crawl, but I keep my expression neutral.

"You know, I was thinking we could grab a coffee sometime. Talk about something other than work for once."

I pause, my hands tightening on the charts I picked up. "I appreciate the offer, Dr. Mitchell, but I don't think that's a good idea."

He raises an eyebrow, undeterred. "Come on, it's just coffee. Promise I won't bite. Unless you want me to." He finishes with a wink.

I hold his gaze firmly. "I'm seeing someone." I haven't seen Waylon since that night, but whatever.

Dr. Mitchell tilts his head like a puppy, his eyes on my chest. "Well, he doesn't have to know, does he?"

"I'm not interested. Respect that."

Dr. Mitchell holds up his hands. "Alright, alright. Can't blame a guy for trying."

I glare at him until he looks away and turn back to my work. "If you'll excuse me, I have patients to attend to."

"Sure thing," he says lightly, but as I walk away, I can't shake the feeling of his eyes lingering on me.

Chapter 27

Confrontation and Reckoning

The bar is loud, the bass from the speakers thrumming against my ribs as I take a sip of my whiskey. It's my first drink, but I feel like I need three more. Aaron had dragged me out, said I'd been acting like a ghost. He wasn't wrong. I still haven't heard from Khloe. I've tried more calls, more texting, and apologizing.

WAYLON

> I'm lonely when you don't talk to me. I promise I can make this better. I can't let this go away. You made me feel things again that I haven't felt in forever. I can't forget you.

WAYLON

> I'm fucking sorry, Khloe. I can't say it enough. You deserve honesty, happiness, and everything.

> **WAYLON**
> You need a spankin…

I can't stop checking my phone, like a hopeless idiot. Aaron's laughing with Ramirez and our other co-worker, Donald. My heart stops when my phone goes off.

KHLOE

I can't stand you. But I also want to roll my eyes directly in your face, so you'll spank me.

I blink. Good girl. I smirk, reading it twice.

> **WAYLON**
> Careful what you wish for, darlin. Where are you?

I watch the screen as if it might say more than her words.

KHLOE

None of your business.

> **WAYLON**
> Too bad. I'm making it my business.

I stand, not knowing where I'm going. Aaron notices, giving me a questioning look as his phone lights up with a text from Flora.

"Is this what has you in a tizzy? They're at the bar down

the block, off of Lexington Ave."

"I need to go handle something."

Aaron exchanges a look with Ramirez before turning back to me. "Waylon, man—"

If she thinks she can toy with me, she's about to find out I know how to play harder.

The drive to the bar feels longer than it should, every red light dragging. My fingers tap restlessly against the steering wheel as her message replays in my head. Frustration and anticipation build as I approach.

And then I see Khloe.

She's at a table, phone in hand, legs swinging in a tiny skirt. All soft curves and golden skin. I need her to know what that does to me. Flora speaks, and Khloe tips her head back in a laugh that doesn't reach her eyes. She doesn't have a damn care in the world, while I've been losing my mind over her silence.

That's when I notice an asshole beside her. My stomach turns when he leans in and she shifts away. My teeth grind together.

Then he kisses her.

My body moves before my mind catches up. I'm standing over them, clearing my throat, blood boiling. Khloe jerks back, eyes wide when she sees me.

"Waylon," she breathes.

I don't look at her. My focus is on the dick, smiling like he didn't cross a line he's gonna regret.

"Didn't realize she was spoken for," he says casually.

I swing before I can stop myself. My fist connects with his face, and he goes down hard, face wiped clean by the blood spilling from his nose.

Khloe gasps, reaching for me. "Waylon, it wasn't—"

"Goodbye, Khloe."

I turn and head for the door. I can't fucking have feelings for her.

Chapter 28

Reconciliation

On one of Flora's forced nights out, the bar is full of energy. Laughter, music, and clinking glasses fill the air. I'm at a high-top table with Flora and Missy. A few other nurses and Missy's sister, Lena, joined us. They're dancing to the music the DJ is mixing effortlessly.

Drinks are flowing, courtesy of Missy, who claims she's celebrating her "survival" of the week. I lost count after the third cocktail Flora slid my way, but the warmth in my cheeks and loose laughter bubbling out of me says it was enough.

"You're more fun when you're tipsy," Flora teases, nudging me. "We should do this more often."

I scoff. "We do this a lot. You just want someone around who can drink like you."

Flora grins, unashamed. "Guilty. But seriously, you're not allowed to overthink tonight. Promise?"

"I'll try."

But my thoughts have already drifted. The pulse of my phone pulls my attention. I unlock it out of habit, but it's just an email. My thumbs hover over the messaging app, finding Waylon's thread. A week has passed since I found out about his marriage. *Ex-marriage*, I remind myself. But the sting hasn't faded. I'd been giving him the cold shoulder, ignoring his attempts to explain. He's called several times. I send him straight to voicemail. I typed several replies but never sent them. I couldn't bring myself to admit my feelings.

Yet here I am, tipsy and restless, staring at his name and rereading his messages for the hundredth time.

Seven days. Seven texts.

They all made me feel separate emotions. Anger at his dishonesty. Temptation because I still crave him. Frustration that he's mixing real apologies with a sexual pull. Sadness because I know he means it. But is it enough? The last message replays in my head.

WAYLON

You need a spankin...

Flora leans over. "Are you seriously thinking about him right now? It's girls' night, Khlo."

I sigh, setting the phone down. "He drives me crazy."

Missy sips her margarita. "You've been talking about him all week, so we gathered that. What'd he do this time?"

"Nothing. He's trying. That's the problem."

Flora smirks. "You miss him."

I pick up the phone again, alcohol lowering my inhibitions. My thumbs move before I can stop myself. I entice him with something that'll piss him off on purpose, hitting *Send*.

"Oh, fuck."

"What?" Flora yanks my phone away, eyes widening as she reads the message out loud, then bursts into laughter. "Oh my God, Khlo. You did *not* just send that."

Missy nearly chokes on her drink. "Who's spanking who? Waylon, the Marshal? He spanks you?"

"Shut up!" My cheeks burn as I snatch my phone back.

"You're not gonna regret that at all tomorrow," Flora teases.

"I already regret it."

On cue, a message flashes across my screen. I stop breathing. I hadn't expected him to reply so quickly, if at all.

"Don't leave him hanging," Flora warns.

I hesitate, continuing to push his buttons. But he pushes back. *I'm making it my business.*

"Fuckkkk," I groan, letting my phone clatter to the table as Flora starts typing.

"What are you doing?" I peek at her screen, seeing Aaron's name.

"Floraaaa. No!"

She grins, pressing *Send*, leaning back in her chair. "I guess we'll find out."

I stare at her, horrified. "Flora! You didn't."

She feigns innocence. "What? You're clearly dying to see him. I'm just giving fate a little express shipping. You're welcome."

I don't have time to argue before Dr. Mitchell appears beside me, making the hair on the back of my neck rise.

"Khloe, this is a surprise."

I sit up, my buzz fading. "Dr. Mitchell—what are you doing here?"

"Call me Ryan," he corrects. "Just out for a drink with some of the other staff. Lucky me, running into you."

Leaning in, Flora speaks loudly enough to attract attention. "Oh my God! Is this the doctor who won't take a hint?"

I laugh nervously, shoot her a glare. "Flora, don't."

He chuckles, unfazed. "Persistence pays off."

I shift, smiling uncomfortably. "Ryan, this isn't the place for—"

Before I can finish, he leans in and presses his lips to mine. I freeze in place as a sharp cough cuts through the moment. I whip around, my stomach dropping as I see Waylon standing too close. His expression, full of disbelief, hurt, and a simmering anger, tightens his jaw, making the vein in his forehead stand out. His fists are clenched at his sides, eyes set on Ryan.

I slide off the stool, stepping toward him. When his eyes meet mine, I know he won't listen. I try to explain, to stop this from sinking.

Then he snaps.

Waylon's fist collides with Ryan's face so fast I barely register it before Ryan is on the ground, blood spilling from his nose. I reach for Waylon, but his words cut through me like a blade.

Goodbye, Khloe.

He stomps toward the exit, leaving me standing there, breathless. I chase after him, heart hammering.

Outside, the night air is cool, but my skin burns with frustration. I finally catch up to him, grabbing his sleeve. "Wait."

When he reaches his truck, he stops but doesn't turn. When he speaks, it's lethal.

"What the hell was that, Khloe?"

I hold my ground. "I didn't mean for it to happen. I wasn't expecting it."

He turns. "You let him kiss you."

"I didn't *let* him," I say quickly.

Waylon drags a hand through his hair. "Khloe, I get that trust doesn't come easy for you. But you've got to see how that looked, right?"

My jaw clenches. "I didn't want him to kiss me. He's been bothering me, and I thought I could handle it on my own."

His eyes flash with darkness, something bordering on betrayal. "That was the doctor who kept textin' you? You didn't think to tell me it was still happenin'?"

I fold my arms, standing firm. "We weren't exactly on speaking terms. I didn't see the point of dragging you into it."

He exhales hard. "Khloe, I don't care how messy things get. You don't have to handle anything alone. But I can't do this if you're gonna keep shutting me out."

I square my shoulders. "I'm not shutting you out. I can handle my shit."

He reaches out and opens his passenger door. "Your silence said otherwise."

I bark out a laugh, bitter enough to sting my throat. "All I've ever done is handle my shit. My grandma is gone. My dad walked out before I even knew his face. My mom picked drugs over me. Everyone I've ever cared for has left, Waylon. Why the hell would you be different?"

The words taste like blood and regret the second they're out. I hadn't meant to say that much, but it's too late.

Waylon freezes, one hand braced on the door. His jaw works like he's chewing on every word. Then his eyes snap to mine, almost daring me not to believe him.

"Because I'm not goin' anywhere. I'm going to keep you."

My chest lurches. He's promising to defeat my fears, and I hate how much I want to believe it. I chuckle. "Yeah, well, people say a lot of shit they don't mean."

His eyes blaze into me like he's daring me to call his bluff. Only it doesn't feel like a bluff; it feels like a vow. His voice drops low, into a dangerous command. "Get in."

"Where are we going?"

"For a ride." His expression is unreadable. "We need to talk."

This might be the start of something, or the end of everything. Either way, I climb into the truck.

Chapter 29

Truths in the Dark

The truck rumbles quietly beneath us, the dark country road stretching endlessly ahead. We're just outside San Antonio, where the city lights fade, and the sky opens wide.

The silence between us is thick with everything we haven't said in a week. My hands grip the steering wheel, knuckles tightening each time I look at her. She's sitting stiffly in the passenger seat, her arms crossed, staring out the window like the stars might offer her an escape.

I pull off onto a dirt road and kill the engine. The sudden quiet is deafening.

"Khloe," I growl. "Are you goin' to talk?"

She turns, her eyes flashing with anger. "I don't think so. After ignoring you for a week, now isn't the time I want to talk."

I clench my jaw. She opens her mouth to argue, but the intensity in my gaze stops her short.

"Why didn't you tell me he'd been botherin' you more?"

Her breathing slows, and she leans back, her hands gripping her legs. "I thought I could handle it," she breathes, not meeting my eyes. "I didn't want to make a big deal out of it. And honestly… I was embarrassed."

"Embarrassed?"

"Yes. And I'm not weak. I can stand up for myself. But when he kissed me tonight, I froze."

I exhale sharply. My gaze locked on her when she finally looks at me. "Khloe, I get that you've been through a lot. I know trustin' people is hard. But you don't have to carry everythin' alone. Let me in. Let me have your back when you need it."

"I didn't want you to think less of me. I didn't want you to think I couldn't handle my life."

I shake my head, my voice rough. "Khloe, I don't think less of you. I think you've carried more than anyone ever should. But stop punishin' me for the people who walked away." Moving closer, my expression softens. "Khloe, listen to me. Everything you've told me tonight means you're stronger than you think. Stop shuttin' me out. I'm here because I care about you. You think I'd walk out like everyone else? That's what you don't get, Khloe. I'm not your ex. I'm not them. But I can't stay if you won't let me."

Her eyes flutter, the tension in her face easing. "I'm sorry, Waylon."

I reach out, cupping her face. "Don't be sorry, Khloe. I'm upset, but not at you. I'm mad at that asshole. But I need to know..." I look between her eyes. "Can you trust me enough to let me be part of your life? Even the messy parts?"

"I can."

"Good. Because I'm not goin' anywhere. But you need to promise me somethin'."

"What?"

"If that bastard bothers you again, you tell me. We'll deal with it together. Unless this isn't what you want—"

"You don't get to decide what I want, Waylon."

I lift the middle console and slide over, my hand reaching for her knee. She stills for a second.

"I don't," I admit, "but I know what I want." My hand slides up her thigh an inch. Her lips part as her gaze softens.

I missed how she looked at me like I matter.

"Then show me," she whispers.

I grab her seatbelt, the click of the buckle releasing, breaking the heavy silence.

"What are you doing?"

"Gettin' creative, darlin'." I smirk. Holding the seat belt taut, I take her wrists and wrap the fabric around them with care. Her pulse races beneath my fingers as I tighten it to hold her in place.

"Waylon." It's half warning, half plea.

My lips brush against her ear as I lean closer, buckling the belt. "Trust me?"

A soft shiver runs through her. "I do."

I pull her hands gently toward me, the restraint forcing her body to follow. My mouth finds hers, the kiss deep and urgent, the week of longing spilling out.

My movements are conscious as I lean across her, reaching for the seat shifter. I slide her back as far as it will go. I reach forward and glide her skirt down. Her breath stops as my hands roam her waist. She reaches for me, but the seat belt tightens.

I settle on the truck's floor. Tugging her panties down, the fabric slides over her thighs, landing at her ankles. I ease her sandals off and toss everything to the side, clearing the path for what's coming next. I guide her legs over my shoulders, gripping her naked hips as I yank her body toward me. She gasps as the seatbelt pulls tighter.

"Easy, darlin'."

My hands smooth over the curve of her hips. She reaches for my hair, pulling as I lower my head. My mouth finds her clit, teasing it with torturously slow strokes of my tongue. I nibble lightly, just enough to make her squirm. Each movement unravels her piece by piece. Her breaths come faster, the air thick with her soft moans. My hands slide under her bare ass to pull her closer to my mouth. She yelps as the seatbelt fights my movements. I'm insatiable. She's by far the best thing I've ever tasted.

I trace her opening with my tongue. Her hips buck against me. The sound of her whimpering my name sends a surge of fire through my veins. I pull one hand forward, sliding two fingers into her, shallow at first, then deeper, matching the rhythm of my mouth.

"Waylon," she cries as her pussy jerks forward, pressing closer to my mouth. A sweet rush of her fluids coats my tongue, and I hold her steady, letting her ride out every wave of her release on my face. The tension of the past week melts away. Replaced by heated breaths, and this moment between us.

When I pull back, I watch her chest rise and fall. Her head tilted back against the seat. Her flushed skin and trembling thighs fuel the satisfaction coursing through me.

"Next time," I murmur, leaning up to capture her lips with mine, my voice husky, "don't make me wait so damn long."

She laughs, her head falling forward onto my shoulder as her body relaxes. "Only if you promise not to lie again," she whispers.

I cup her cheek, tilting her face up until her eyes meet mine. There's no hesitation as I speak. "I will never lie to you again."

Her eyes search mine. I know she's weighing my words against everything we've been through so far. I press my forehead to hers, silently sealing the promise between us.

"Can you tell me the truth about your marriage?"

I sigh, unbuckling her. "I'll tell you anythin' you want to know, darlin'. Let's talk about this at my place. Deal?"

She gives me a small wink. "Deal."

I help her dress, purposely tracing my fingers up her thick thighs. I don't usually help the woman I ravish get dressed afterwards. This moment strikes me as I get back in my seat, start the truck, and get us on our way.

When we get inside my place, I grab her a glass of water and a neat whiskey for me. She's comfortable on the couch as I hand her the glass and sit beside her. She stares at me with lust and longing. The intimacy of the moment feels heavy with everything I'm waiting to say.

"I've got a lot of things I don't talk about, Khloe," I begin. "Not 'cause I'm tryin' to hide 'em, but because it's easier to keep 'em locked away. But you..." I glance at her. "You deserve more than that."

I take a deep breath in and out as I start. "Caroline and I grew up together. Same schools, same friends. She was my everything. We thought we had it all figured out, ya know?" Khloe's eyes drop to her lap, where her fingers toy with the edge of her skirt. "When I enlisted," I go on, "I thought I was doin' the right thing. For us, my family. The ranch was strugglin', and I needed to make somethin' of myself. I joined the Marines not long after we got hitched, thinkin' it'd give us a better start. Caroline said she'd wait. Said we'd make it work, no matter what." I let out a bitter laugh.

"I should've known it wouldn't be that simple. The first deployment wasn't too bad. Letters, phone calls, whenever I could. But when I came back, I wasn't the same. I didn't see it at the time, but she did. Said I was distant, that I wasn't the guy she fell in love with." I pause, rubbing the back of my neck. "She wasn't wrong. I'd seen things... lost people. It changes you, making it hard to open up. But I wanted to believe we could get through it.

"The second deployment was harder. When I came back, she was changed. I didn't blame her, not really. It's hard being married to someone who's always got one foot out the door, always somewhere else. But it hurt, Khloe. God, it hurt to come home and see the look in her eyes. She was already gone."

Khloe reaches out, placing a hand on my arm. I glance at her briefly, with the smallest flicker of gratitude inside me, before I look away. "We separated, and she asked for a divorce a year later. Told me she loved the boy she married, but she didn't know how to love the man I'd become."

Khloe's grip tightens. "Waylon... I'm so sorry."

"It is what it is. I signed the papers, I watched her pack

her things, and that was it. She moved to Austin. I stayed in the Marines for a while longer, thinkin' it'd give me purpose. But all it did was pile on more ghosts." My eyes meet hers. "I don't talk about her much because... it makes me feel like I failed. Not just her, but myself. If I'd been better, stronger, maybe things would've been better. The shrink I saw always told me to stop thinkin' that way."

Khloe shakes her head. "You didn't fail, Waylon. It sounds like you did everything you could with what you had at the time—maybe she wasn't meant to be the one who could handle all of you. But that doesn't mean no one can."

I clear my throat quietly. "You think you can?"

Khloe smiles faintly. "I know I can. If you'll let me."

Her words are caught somewhere between my heart and mouth. I reach for her hand, threading my fingers through hers. "I've never met anyone like you, Khloe. You don't just see the good parts; you see the messy ones too. Please don't run again."

"I'm not running. You're stuck with me."

I shake my head, a self-deprecating laugh escaping me. "I'm not tellin' you this for pity or sympathy. Khloe... I need you to know who I am. The good, the bad, and the parts I'm still tryin' to figure out. It's takin' a lot for me to open up like this, to lay myself out there."

"I appreciate it, and I don't care about the mistakes," she says with sincerity. "We all have things we're not proud of. What matters is who you are now, and that you're being honest."

I look at her, my jaw clenched, trying to keep my emotions in check. "And who do you think I am?"

She gives me a tender smile. "Someone who's trying. And that means more than you think."

I let out a slow breath, shoulders finally easing. "You've got a way of makin' a man feel like there's hope, you know that?"

Khloe's smile widens, and it breaks open a part of my chest that I'd been holding shut for so long. As she grabs my hand and leads me straight to my bedroom, I ask, "What're you doin'?"

"I'd like to return the favor," she says, backing me toward the bed.

Fuck.

She works my belt open, her fingers deliberate as they unbutton my jeans and tug them down, before dropping to her knees. Her lips part as she takes me into her mouth, tongue gliding along my length, drawing taunting circles, coaxing.

Her hand cups my balls, massaging gently as she works me over, her mouth determined to pull me into full, aching readiness. With every pulse of my heart, I get harder and harder. Until I'm reaching down the back of her throat. She's swallowing me whole like she *needs* this and needs me.

I almost protest when she takes me out of her mouth. She spits on my cock, stroking it with slow, firm pulls of her hand, watching me with dark, heated eyes that tell me she knows what she's doing. Knows she's unraveling me. And then she takes me back into her mouth, sucking me deep as she pulls me forward. My hips meet the wet heat of her throat over and over. There's no hesitation. Just pure, seamless control as drool slicks down my thighs. As if she won't finish until my veins become imprinted on the lining of her throat.

I want to take her right here. My God, I might fucking come already, and she *knows it.* She releases me with a wicked gleam in her eyes, standing up like she hasn't just wrecked my fucking soul.

"I'm not done with you yet," she whispers, pressing a hand to my chest and pushing me back until I fall onto the bed.

I prop up on my elbows to watch her work. She climbs onto me, straddling my legs as she wraps her hands around my cock and spits on it again—intentionally dragging out the moment until I'm damn near shaking with the need to feel her mouth again.

And thankfully, she gives it to me, lips wrapping around me, sucking deep, taking me to the edge and pulling me back, playing me like a fucking instrument. Her mouth feels better than most of the pussies I've been in, and fuck, she knows exactly what I want. But it's more than that—I realize with a tight, breathless curse she has control of me. *Total* control. I don't know how much more of this I can take.

"Fuck, Khloe. I'm gonna..."

She hums around my cock, swallowing me down harder, and that's it. I let go, thrusting into the depths of her mouth as she takes everything I give her. But she's not done. She keeps sucking, working me through the aftershocks like she's starving for every last drop, until I'm limp and spent and fucking wrecked beneath her. I collapse, heart pounding, body still trembling from the way she just took me apart.

Fuck, I'm hers.

The next night, I decide it's time for a proper date. To show her this is more than lust, more than the heat that seems to simmer between us. When I show up at her door, she answers wearing this yellow dress that gives her golden skin a glow.

Dammit, I have to fight every primal instinct to pin her against the porch and forget the world exists. The way the fabric hugs her curves makes me want to skip dinner altogether, go straight to dessert, and fucking her through the night. But I keep my cool.

On the drive, I grip the steering wheel tighter than I need to, trying not to let my thoughts run wild. As we walk into the restaurant, I rest my hand lightly on the small of her back to remind myself she is real. Mine. The dim lighting of the restaurant casts a warm glow over the room, but none of it compares to her. She sits across from me, flipping through the menu like it holds the secrets of the universe. I don't even pretend to read mine. My eyes stay on her, tracing the curve of her jaw, the way her lips purse in concentration, the faint furrow in her brow when she's deep in thought. She is utterly captivating, every little movement impossible to ignore.

God help me.

Leaning back, I let the moment settle over me. She has no idea what she's doing to me, sitting there in that damn dress, lost in her own world. And for once, I don't want to rush it. I want to take it all in, to savor every second of this night.

She catches me staring. "You're not even figuring out what to eat," she says, smiling, setting the menu down.

"Already decided. You look torn."

"Maybe I like options," she says, rolling her eyes in that playful way that makes me want to toss her across the table and take her now.

"Sometimes options are overrated." She raises her eyebrows, but I don't stop there. "Once you know what you want, there's no sense in hesitating."

Her smile shifts, cheeks flushing. She closes her menu, the tension between us thick enough to feel. "Is this your way of saying you're impatient?"

I chuckle, leaning forward. "Not always. But when it comes to what I need, I'm pretty damn clear about it."

Her lips part, and I see the hesitation in her eyes. She's curious, but cautious—that makes sense. We're treading new ground, both of us feeling it out.

"So, is this where you tell me I need to call you 'Sir' or something?" she asks with a smile.

A real, unfiltered laugh rolls out of me. "Only if you want to," I say, my grin softening. "But it's not about that."

"Then what's it about?"

My laughter fades. "Control. Trust. And vulnerability. It's about letting go in ways most people don't even realize they're holding on. Sometimes it's about pushing limits, yours and mine. But it's not only about me, Khloe. It's about what we can build together."

I watch her take that in. She sips her wine to buy herself a moment. "I've started reading about it. BDSM, I mean," she says after a beat. "But reading and doing are two very different things."

"I know. That's why I didn't push too hard the first night. I needed you to feel safe. That's the most important part."

"Have you always needed this... dynamic?"

I hesitate, the question bringing up memories I don't always dig up. But she deserves honesty.

"I don't do it with everyone. But after I lost my virginity, I realized structure like that made sense to me. The clarity of it—learning, knowing where the boundaries were. It keeps me grounded. My life was chaotic for a long time. This helped me take control. I usually keep this part of me tucked away, but you're lookin' right at it."

"And your ex-wife?" she asks gently. "Was she into it?"

"She tried. But it wasn't her thing. I didn't want to force it. That was part of the problem. We weren't right for each other in a lot of ways. But I don't want you to think this is all I am. It's a part of me, but not the whole picture."

I run a hand over my jaw. "For me, it's about instinct. I've always been a protector. It's who I am. But it's not just that. It's... sovereignty. In how it lets me take all the chaos in my head and turn it into somethin' that makes sense. It's not just about dominance, though it helps. It's about connection and trust. Knowin' I can take care of you in a way no one else can."

Her lips part, eyes searching mine. I can see the questions she isn't asking. So, I keep going. "There's a part of me that's primal. Always has been. I was born an animal, Khlo, and I'll always be one. But that doesn't mean I don't know how to use it. When I'm with you, and get to let that part of me out, but it's better than wild; it's focused. For you."

Her chest rises and falls slowly, absorbing my words. "You make it sound beautiful."

"It is. Because it's not just about what I want, it's about what we both need."

Khloe's fingers brush against my hand. "I think that's

why I like it too," she admits. "I've spent so much of my life trying to control everything. My emotions, my surroundings, the people around me. I had to, or everything would fall apart. But with you... I can let go and be safe."

I close my hand over hers. "You don't have to do anythin' alone anymore, Khlo. Not with me."

"I'm not sure what I can handle, Waylon. But I know I trust you."

"That's all I need to hear, Khloe. We'll take it slow."

"I'm willing to learn with you," she says, her tone laced with vulnerability. "But you have to promise me something."

"Anythin'," I say without hesitation.

"Be patient with me. I've been through a lot, but I'm ready to dive into something I barely understand."

I take her other hand. "You have my word," I whisper. "It's about giving you the freedom to let go. You're safe with me, no matter what." Her fingers tighten around mine. And in that moment, I realize I'm exactly where I'm meant to be, with the person I'm meant to be with.

Chapter 30

Settling in, Walls Coming Down

It's strange, the way someone can slip into your life and make every day feel like something worth cherishing. Waylon spent the next two months doing just that. He made the ordinary feel extraordinary. Not with grand gestures or poetic declarations, but in the constant, grounding way he simply existed.

The first time we stayed in, he showed up with a stack of DVDs, after making fun of me for having a DVD player, and a ridiculous amount of snacks. Everything from popcorn to chocolate-covered pretzels. "You pick the movie," he said, plopping down on my couch like he'd been there a hundred times before.

I picked something light, a rom-com he pretended to grumble about, but I caught the way he laughed at the stupid jokes. Halfway through, he pulled me against him, his arm draped over my shoulder, fingers lazily tracing patterns on my arm. That intimate touch reassured me I wasn't alone. When the credits rolled, he kissed me, not hungry or rushed, as if he was savoring the moment.

"Good pick," he murmured against my lips, and I

laughed, filling the space between us.

He texted me one random Tuesday afternoon, and in the middle of our conversation, he sent me the lyrics to "A Whole New World" from the Aladdin movie. I laughed so hard and called him an idiot, but secretly, I loved it.

When the lock on our front door broke, he insisted on installing a new keypad. He smiled as he tapped in the code. "Don't worry. I'll always have a way in." Then, saying nothing, he held out a key to his place, letting it dangle between us. I raised a brow as I took it. "Is this your way of claiming me fully?"

He laughed and gave me a gentle smile. "You'll always be mine, no matter what."

He'd show up unannounced, arms full of my favorites. Wine, takeout, Reese's peanut butter cups, and himself. He became a reliable presence I'd stopped believing existed, a stark contrast to the charming, handsome player I'd assumed him to be that first night. Now, he's my boyfriend or, as he puts it, *"I'm yours."* He's tearing down all my walls.

One Sunday, while helping me with laundry, he found an old photo album tucked in my nightstand. "Can I look?" he asked, holding it up. I nodded, watching as he flipped through the pages, his expression softening as he studied the pictures of me as a kid, of my grandmother, of the life I'd left behind.

"She looks kind." He pauses on a picture of my grandmother holding me in her lap.

"She was," I reminisce. "She'd have liked you."

His lips curved into a small smile, and he set the album aside, pulling me into his lap without a word. A silent tear slid down my face, and he caught it with a kiss. It was a moment where words would've felt out of place—his presence was enough. Most days I believe in us, but there's still a part of me that pulls back. I know how fast things can fall apart. I know the pain of letting someone in, only to watch them leave.

Growing up, Grandma was a diehard Dallas Mavericks

fan. I'd cheer alongside her, not understanding the game but loving how excited she got. Eventually, Flora and I joined the cheerleading squad in high school, and that's when I actually learned more about the sport. Grandma was so impressed, I think it made her even prouder than my good grades.

When Waylon found out about my cheerleading days, he couldn't help but tease me. He joked that he'd cheer for the opposing team to provoke me into angry sex. I warned him that it wouldn't end well; I told him how aggressive I get. He laughed, but I could tell he didn't think I was serious.

Before I knew it, we were watching games together. True to his word, he rooted for the other team, grinning like a fool every time I shot him a death glare. When I finally snapped and told him to knock it off, things escalated fast. One minute, I was threatening him; the next, we were tangled and sweaty on the couch. His face between my legs, covered in my cum. I couldn't stop laughing. He had this sheepish grin, like he knew exactly what he'd done, but didn't regret a second of it. He really was perfect, maddeningly so.

Later, as the credits of some random cop show roll, the room falls into a comfortable quiet. Waylon shifts again, his arm sliding around my shoulders. I should move. I should stand up, clean the table, do something, anything to create space between us. But I don't. I let him pull me closer. My cheek rested against his chest. His scent is always clean, woodsy, and undeniably *him*. It fills my senses, and I let myself sink into the warmth of him.

"You're thinkin' again," he murmured, his lips brushing lightly against my hair.

"Am not," I mumbled, muffled against his shirt.

"Liar," he said, his tone laced with amusement. There's no judgment, just a quiet tenderness that makes me feel more for him, in the best and worst way.

I closed my eyes, trying to quiet the thoughts that kept telling me to pull away—because I don't want to. I stayed in his arms, pretending this wasn't terrifying. Pretending that I'm not falling.

One Sunday, we wandered through the River Walk. The day was warm with a humidity that felt heavy against my skin. Waylon held my hand the entire time, his thumb occasionally brushing against mine like he was reassuring himself I was there.

We stopped at a cafe near the water, sipping iced coffee while watching people. He leaned over at one point, his lips brushing against my ear.

"That couple over there has been arguing for at least ten minutes. I bet they're fightin' about where to eat like we do." I burst out laughing, earning a satisfied grin from him. He liked making me laugh. I enjoyed letting him.

For all the times Waylon was open, he was never the type to give anything away easily. His words are measured, his face placid and voice steady. He's sometimes selfish with his thoughts and feelings. But lately, something's shifted. The little things I never expected from him are adding up— it's getting harder to keep my guard up.

Then there were the moments that took my breath away, where he blurred the line between sensual and tender. Like the night we went to a rooftop bar. The city lights stretched out around us, casting a soft glow that made everything feel surreal. He leaned in, his hand resting on the small of my back, his lips brushing my neck as he murmured how gorgeous I looked.

It wasn't just the words; it was the way his touch lingered, the way his presence wrapped around me like a safety net. When his lips finally found mine, it wasn't rushed or wild. It was like he was pouring every unspoken thought into me. When he slipped a few fingers up my dress, I forgot about the crowd, the noise, and the world beyond the two of us.

Sometimes we'd stay in and cook together, though 'cooking' might be a generous way to put it. He was far better at chopping vegetables than I was, and he liked to tease me about my overuse of garlic.

Other times, we'd just lie in bed, the silence between us comfortable. We didn't need to fill it with words. His hand would rest on my hip, his thumb brushing lazy circles against my skin. It wasn't about sex, though most times that's where it led. He made me feel seen, like I was worth slowing down for.

Just over a month into whatever this is, Waylon shifted closer, his hand sliding up from my ankle to rest on my shin. The warmth of his touch spread through me. I curled my toes, trying to ground myself, but it's useless. He's like gravity, pulling me in even when I try to fight it.

"You're quiet tonight."

I shrugged, avoiding his gaze. "Just thinking, I guess."

"Uh-huh." He sighed. "You've been thinkin' a lot lately. What's on your mind?"

I glanced at him. My defenses snapped into place. "Nothing at all."

His eyes narrowed, studying me with that perceptive look. "You sure about that?"

"Positive," I said, forcing a smile. "Why? Are you trying to psychoanalyze me now?"

He chuckled, leaning back against the couch, but his hand didn't move. "Nah. Just tryin' to figure out what's goin' on in that beautiful head of yours. You've got this look like you're tryin' to solve a damn puzzle."

"Well, maybe I am," I whispered, looking away again. He can be a riddle. Am I trying to understand him? Yes, but also myself. Why can't I stop falling for a man who has the power to break me if I give in?

It wasn't huge things that made me fall for him; it's mostly the little things. He always made sure I was on the inside of the sidewalk when we walked. He remembered how I took my coffee. And he'd rush to open my car door every time. I didn't know where this was going, and I was scared to ask. I stayed hooked because, with Waylon, the moment was more than enough.

The changes started small. He texted little things like, *How's your day?* or *Missed you today.* It wasn't the type of attention I expected from him. I'd prepared myself for him to disappear for days and reappear as if nothing had happened, like Derrick did. But he's present in a way I didn't know he was capable of.

Then there are the looks. I catch him staring at me all the time. When I ask if he's got a staring problem, he gives me that stern look and repeats. "You're gorgeous." I'd roll my eyes, half-hoping he'll spank me for it. He sets my heart on fire, and that scares the hell out of me.

After one long work week of doubles, I made my way to Waylon's. I settled down next to him on his couch, relaxed. His phone buzzed. I caught a glimpse of the screen before he quickly flipped it over.

UNSAVED NUMBER

Miss having you control me and your dick inside me, Waylon.

I saw it clearly before he hid it. My stomach twisted. It was too easy for him to brush it off. I didn't let it show, even if it burned. He was mine now. But deep down, I still wondered if it fed his ego; knowing they wanted what I had.

He showed up with takeout late one evening after his long day trip. I was tired, and everything felt a little more exposed because of it. Waylon was leaning back on the couch, shirtless after I spilled my drink on him. His long legs stretched out, showcasing the muscles in his quads, one arm draped casually over the backrest. When he moved, his arm muscles flexed subtly. His body was beautifully sculpted.

The TV murmured in the background. We were barely paying attention to it. I watched him from my side of the couch, the flicker of light from the screen catching the freckles on his face. I tucked my knees under me.

"Can I ask you something?" My fingers played with the edge of the throw pillow in my lap.

His eyes shifted to me, serene as they always were. "Course you can, darlin'. What's on your mind?"

"It's just... I've noticed something."

Waylon raised an eyebrow, a hint of a smirk tugging at his lips. "Noticed what?"

I bit my lip, the words tumbling out. "Why haven't we done anything rough in a while?"

"Does it bother you we haven't?"

"I don't know," I admitted, shrugging. "I... Uh. Yes, I think it does. Isn't it something you need?"

"It is. But it's not the only part of me, Khlo. And it's not all I want from you."

I blinked, sitting up a little straighter. "What do you mean?"

Waylon leaned forward, his gaze locking onto mine. "It's not just about that with you. This. Me and you. It's unique. You're rare."

A flush crept into my cheeks, a mix of warmth and disbelief. "How?"

"You make me feel like I'm not just that guy... the one who takes what he wants and walks away." He ran a hand through his hair, and his usual confidence gave way to vulnerability. "With you, I don't want it to be transactional, Khlo. I don't want to risk you thinkin' this is all about some kink."

My heart squeezed at the honesty in his tone, but I couldn't stop the little laugh that escaped me. "So, what you're saying is you're actually trying to take this seriously?"

His prize-winning grin appeared, but his eyes remained serious. "Yeah. I am."

I stared at him. The meaning behind his words washed over me. Waylon, who practically oozed charm and confidence and had a reputation for never getting too attached, was trying—for me.

"Khlo," he said, pulling me from my thoughts. "I didn't want to scare you off or make you think sex was all I wanted, 'cause it's not. You're not just some game to me."

I swallowed hard, my fingers tightening around the pillow. "I didn't think that."

His eyes narrowed as if he didn't believe me. "You sure? 'Cause if you did, I'd want to know. I don't want you thinkin' you're just another chapter in some story I've told a hundred times before."

I shook my head. "No, Waylon. I don't think that."

He relaxed, leaning back on the couch. "Good. 'Cause with you, I'm playin' for keeps, Khlo. We were made for each other."

The room fell still. His words settled over me. I hadn't realized how much I'd needed to hear that. How much I'd wanted to believe he wasn't the man people thought he was.

"Well," I said, breaking the silence, "if you ever want to bring that side of you back into this... I wouldn't be mad, just so you know."

Waylon's grin returned, and he reached over to brush a curl away from my face. "Noted, darlin'. But right now, I'm happy just being here with you."

After all the peaceful weeks we've spent together, the walls I'd been holding up cracked, piece by piece. Tonight, his words were a sledgehammer.

Chapter 31

Falling Deeper

Every moment with Khloe these past few months has been good. Too good, if I'm being honest. Her laugh alone could bring a man to his knees. And the look she gives me when she's mad but won't say it out loud; I live for it. But it's the quiet times with her that feel significant.

One Saturday, we wandered the River Walk just as the sun dipped, casting a golden haze over everything. The cobblestone path beneath our feet was warm and uneven in a way that made Khloe grip my hand a little tighter every few steps. Restaurants spilled onto the walkway, their small bistro tables set close together as waiters wove between couples and clinking glasses. The scents of grilled steak, garlic, and fresh vegetables drifted through the air, mingling with a sweet aroma from the bakery across the water.

She wore this flowy white sundress that swayed with every step, and I couldn't help but glance at her ass every few seconds, a stupid grin plastered on my face.

"You're staring," she said, her dimple sneaking out with that smile.

"Can't help it," I admit. "You're too damn pretty not to

be stared at."

She rolled her eyes but didn't let go of my hand. "You're insufferable."

"Yet, here you are," I teased, pulling her closer so I could kiss the top of her head.

We stopped at one of those little stands selling churros. She took a bite, and her eyes lit up as the powdered sugar dusted her lips. She laughed when I licked it off. For a second, I forgot about everything else, my job, the women before her, all of it. It's just us.

When I replaced her front door lock with one of those fancy new keypads, the code locked into my memory. Only four digits, but knowing the code felt like more. I held out the spare key to my place without a word. She looked at it, then at me, amused. She didn't need my answer. She already had it.

We spent so many days at her place. Sometimes sprawled out on the couch, with her feet in my lap as we binged some ridiculous reality show she swore was her "guilty pleasure." She kept glancing at me to see if I was paying attention, and when I didn't react to the drama on the screen, she narrowed her eyes at me.

"You're not even watching," she accused, throwing a piece of popcorn at me. I caught it midair and popped it into my mouth.

"I'm watchin'," I lied.

"Name one thing that happened," she said, sitting up as she crossed her arms.

I grinned, leaning forward to kiss her forehead. "Somebody cheated on somebody, and now someone's mad."

Her jaw dropped. "You're impossible."

"But you love it," I said as I grabbed her hand and pulled her into my lap.

She tried to keep the annoyed look on her face, but it crumbled as I kissed her, her laughter melting into my lips. Moments like this, when it's just us, everything feels right.

Another night, we were sprawled out on my couch when my phone went off with a random text from an old hookup. I glanced at the screen and flipped it over the moment I realized what it was. I felt a brief flicker of amusement. It's no big deal—women miss me all the time. Khloe caught my quick move and watched as I turned the phone. Her eyes flickered with discomfort, but I shrugged it off. The text was a weak echo of a past I'd already outgrown. Living in someone else's nostalgia didn't interest me. It was noise. The message was nothing more than an old flame trying to stir up feelings for fucking. Feelings I didn't have anymore—my former submissive's mean nothing now.

I belong to Khloe, my future.

I'd randomly show up some mornings and make her breakfast. She'd stumble out of her room in an oversized hoodie and messy hair. Yawning while rubbing her eyes. I swear she's the cutest damn thing I've ever seen.

"Coffee," she mumbled, raspy from sleep. I gave her a mug without a word, and she gave me this little smile that makes getting up early worth it.

"Thanks," she murmured, sipping it as she leaned against the counter.

We spent mornings like that: me flipping pancakes and her stealing bits of bacon off the plate when she thinks I'm not looking. When I catch her, she just shrugs.

"I'm quality control."

Without trying I became someone I didn't immediately recognize, but Khloe made this version of me feel natural. I'd always show up bringing her favorites. Reese's at the top of the list, and me next. She became my need—I never expected it, not from the guarded woman I first met. But somewhere along the way, she turned into something more. A passion, a love that's mine in every sense of the word. And I was hers.

I'd find myself pulling out my phone more often at work. Typing out a quick check-in or reminding her I'm thinking of her. This need to stay connected wasn't like me, but with her, it felt effortless. I wanted her to know she was on my mind, even if I couldn't always be there. She probably didn't even notice, or maybe she thought it was just me playing some angle. Hell, I thought it was too, in the beginning. But now I look forward to the way she replies. The way her words soften my edges, even when she doesn't realize she's doing it.

The other night, it knocked the air out of me. She was cooking, curls falling loose around her face, moving with an ease that made my heart tighten. I leaned against the counter, watching her like a fool. She didn't notice at first, which gave me time to take her in. Her delicate movements, the way she scrunched her nose when she tasted the sauce, the way she hummed under her breath like she didn't have a care in the world. And damn if that didn't do something to me.

"What?" she asked, catching me staring. The blush that crept up her cheeks, I'd commit to memory for the rest of my life.

"Nothing," I said, letting my smile answer, even though the truth was sitting heavy in my chest. "Just like watchin' you—you're flawless." She rolled her eyes and laughed like she thought I was full of shit. But that laugh, hmm, it made me want to grab her, spin her around, and tell her I wasn't kidding. She was the kind of beautiful that sneaks up on a man and breaks him when he least expects it.

She didn't know what she was doing to me, and I wasn't ready to say it out loud yet. But standing there watching her as she went back to cooking like I hadn't just bared a piece of my soul, I knew I was in trouble. It scared the hell out of me. This wasn't like before with Caroline. This wasn't just a fling or a temporary connection to pass the time. Khloe made me want to stay.

The first time Khloe mentioned she'd been a cheerleader during basketball season, I couldn't help myself.

"A cheerleader, huh? All those pom-poms and high

kicks? Can't believe I didn't know this sooner." I grinned, leaning back against her couch, waiting for the blush I knew was coming.

Sure enough, it crept in. She rolled her eyes, muttering something under her breath about me being hopeless. "It's not that big of a deal."

"Oh, it's a big deal," I teased, leaning closer. "Bet you were one of those peppy ones, cheering your heart out. You like Grandma's basketball team, Dallas Mavericks, right?"

She paused, her lips twitching, trying not to smile. "Yeah. Grandma was obsessed with the Mavericks. When I joined the basketball cheer squad in high school, she acted like it was the best thing I'd ever done."

"Even better than nursing school?" I asked, raising a brow.

"Way better," she said, laughing. "She used to make me watch games with her when I was little, and I didn't understand a thing. But cheering with her was fun."

The more she talked about it, the more I knew I was about to push my luck. "Ya know, if we ever watch a game together, I'm cheerin' for the opponent. Might get you mad enough for some angry sex."

Her jaw dropped, but the way her eyes narrowed told me she wasn't entirely offended. "That would end badly for you, Rhodes. I've punched a guy at a game before."

I blinked. "You punched someone, Navarro?"

"When the Mavericks were playing the New York Knicks," she said, shrugging. "He was talking trash, and I wasn't in the mood."

"You're full of surprises, Khlo." I couldn't stop laughing.

A few days later, we were on her couch watching a game. Mavericks versus whoever. Didn't matter because, naturally, I'd picked the other team. Every time the Mavericks scored, she'd light up. That competitive streak in her eyes practically daring me to say something.

"Looks like your team's gettin' lucky tonight," I drawled, grinning as her head whipped toward me.

"Lucky? They're crushing it, and you know it."

"Guess we'll see. Your boy can't carry the entire team." I shrugged.

The death glare she gave me was worth every second of what came next. She told me to knock it off, and before I could even get a word in, she was in my lap, her hands on my chest, looking like she was ready to strangle me.

Things escalated fast from there. One minute, she was threatening me. The next, my mouth was on hers, her nails digging into my shoulders. Suddenly, we weren't watching the game anymore.

By the time we were done, both of us were sweaty, her sweet sex covering my face. She burst out laughing, and I couldn't help the sheepish grin on my face. I wiped my chin and leaned back, catching my breath.

"Guess I won that round."

"Won? You're ridiculous."

"But you love me," I teased, pulling her back into my arms. God help me, I think she really did. Hell, I was starting to feel the same way.

Another night, we were on my couch, something playing in the background we weren't really watching. She was overthinking something. I could always tell. She asked me a question; it seemed like she'd been holding in for a while.

Her words stirred something in me I'm not used to—equal parts guilt and longing. Guilt because I haven't explained myself. Longing because she's sitting here, trusting me enough to ask. Her question isn't just about sex, and we both know it. She's testing the waters, looking for reassurance I didn't realize she needed.

I give myself a moment before answering, leaning forward to really look at her. I tell her what I can. What we have is special. How she's rare. It's hard to put into words, but I try. I don't want her to think I've been holding back because I'm losing interest. It's the opposite. I've been holding back because she means more to me than I've let myself admit.

"We were made for each other." The way she looked at me when I told her my truth. Hell, that look's been stuck in my head ever since. It wasn't smooth or planned, just honest.

When I tell her she's not just some game to me, it hits me hard. There's relief on her face, sure, but also something deeper. She didn't expect this from me; didn't think I was capable of it. She laughed, and it caught me off guard. The knot in my chest loosened. I didn't realize how much I needed to let her see the parts of me I've kept locked away.

When she tells me she wouldn't mind if that side of me came back—the dominant side—that brought us together. My mind goes back to that night. How it sealed my fate with her and made me want more than I ever did with random women. I can't help but grin. Because someone finally *sees* all of me. The parts I've always thought were too much for most people. And she's still here. I'm done chasing the next escape, the next distraction.

With Khloe, everything shifts. She's the exception. She wasn't a coincidence. She was placed on my path to be worshipped. And if I have to fight every damn instinct I've lived by to keep her, I'll do it.

Every time.

Chapter 32

A Call from the Past and Present

As I step out of the hospital, the evening humid air hits my face. My feet ache from twelve hours of movement. My scrubs cling to my skin. All I want is to get home, shower, and let the day slip away. Digging my phone out to check my notifications, I'm startled when it rings in my hand and it's not Waylon. The number on the screen stops me cold. My body tenses. For a moment, I stand there staring at it. The urge to hit decline is overwhelming, but before I can think it through, my thumb swipes to accept.

"Hello?" I say steadier than I feel.

"This is a collect call from an inmate at Bridgeport Correctional Center. This call is subject to monitoring and recording. To accept this call, press one. To refuse this call, hang up or press two."

Even though I should know better. I press one.

"Khloe, it's me." Her voice is all smoke and regret. My stomach goes queasy.

"Mom?" The word tastes foreign. Almost bitter. I can't remember the last time I called her that.

"Yeah… I heard about your grandmother." There's a

crack, barely noticeable. I wonder if it's from emotion or the years of drug-use tearing her vocal cords.

"I'm sorry, baby."

The words slam into a wound that never fully healed. My hand tightens around the phone.

"You're sorry?" My sharpness surprises me. "That's all you have to say?"

There's a pause; I think she's hung up.

"I didn't know she had passed until I got a letter from one of my old friends," she finally says. "Nobody told me. I should've been there."

I laugh bitterly, walking to my car. "Been there? When were you ever there, Mom? You weren't there when she was alive. Why would her funeral be any different?"

"Khloe," she whispers in a pleading tone that hits my nerves. "I know I messed up, alright? But I'm still your mother."

I stop, gripping my keys so tightly the metal digs into my palm. "You're right. You are my mother, but you should've been better. To Grandma, me, and to yourself. But you weren't."

She groans. "You think I don't know that? I had my demons, Khloe. I still do. But I'm trying. I've been trying."

"Trying?" I echo, my laugh hollow. I unlock my car and slide into the driver's seat, closing the door with a thud. "Trying doesn't erase years of absence. It doesn't change the fact that Grandma had to pick up your pieces while I watched her work herself to death just to keep us afloat."

"I know. I know I can't fix the past," she whispers.

I press my forehead against the steering wheel, the exhaustion from my shift mixing with the anger only she can ignite. "Then what do you want, Mom? Why are you calling me now?"

Her pause is suffocating. "I heard you got the house. And... I know there was some money—from Grandma's estate."

There it is. She's twisting the knife she's already planted. I lift my head, shaking with disbelief. A small part of me hoped this call was different. I shouldn't be surprised that I don't matter more than a check she never earned.

"Are you serious right now? You're calling me after all these years to ask for money?"

"It's not like that," she blurts out, her words cracking with desperation. "I'm trying, Khloe, but I'm struggling. I've worked with the counselors, doing the steps. But it's hard, and—"

"And what?" I cut in, my anger spilling over. "You think I owe you because we share blood? Grandma left that money to me because she knew I'd use it for something real. Something good. Not to bail you out of the mess you've been making since I was a kid."

There's a long silence. When she finally speaks, she sounds defeated. "You're right. I don't deserve it. But I'm still your mom, Khloe—that doesn't just go away."

My eyes burn, but I refuse to let the tears fall. "No, it doesn't go away. But it doesn't mean I have to forgive you either. Grandma was my actual family. She was the one who raised me, who showed me what love was supposed to look like. Now she's gone, and you want to take the only thing she left me? You don't get to do that, Mom. Not anymore."

Her breathing is heavy on the other end. I brace myself for her to lash out like she used to or hang up. Instead, she softens.

"I'm sorry, baby. For all of it. I don't expect you to forgive me, but... I wanted you to know."

"I've heard that before. Maybe this time, say it to yourself." I force the lump down that's formed in my throat.

There's a pause, then the line goes dead. I stare at the phone, the weight of the conversation pressing down on me.

As I pull into the driveway, the tears I've been holding back fall, carving quiet paths down my cheeks. Grandma's absence feels sharper than ever. Her enduring love is a void no one can fill—not even my mother.

Inside, the sound of Flora humming in the kitchen cuts through the fog in my mind. I shrug off my jean jacket and collapse onto the couch. Flora walks over, a dish towel slung over her shoulder.

"Hey, you're home." Her face shifts when she sees me. "You look terrible. Long shift?"

"That's not even half of it." I laugh weakly.

Flora frowns, sitting next to me. "Okay, spill. What happened?"

I hesitate, my hands gripping the edge of my scrubs. I hadn't planned to say anything, but the words spill out. "My mom called from prison."

Flora's face softens immediately, her hand reaching for mine. "Oh, Khlo... what did she say?"

"She said she was sorry," I say, trembling right along with the words. "Sorry for everything. And then she asked for money. Grandma's money."

Flora's mouth falls open. "You're kidding."

"Nope." I lean my head back against the couch, staring at the ceiling. "And the worst part? I actually felt bad. For a second, I thought maybe I should help her."

"Khloe—no! You don't owe her anything. Not after everything she put you and Grandma through."

"I know," I whisper. "But it's hard, you know? She's still my mom. And no matter how much I try to move on, she's always there, like a shadow I can't get rid of."

Flora squeezes my hand tightly. "You're allowed to protect yourself. Blood doesn't mean they're allowed to hurt you. You've worked so hard to build this life, Khlo. Don't let her take any more from you."

My eyes mist over. "Thanks, Flo."

"Always," Flora says, pulling me into a tight hug. "Now, let me pour you a drink, and we can binge something stupid. You need it."

A few nights later, we're at a lively Italian spot, packed with

Friday night life. The air is rich with garlic and basil, layered over the sound of clinking silverware. Laughter rises from crowded tables, servers weave between chairs, and soft music drifts from the speakers.

I lean against the high-top table, half-listening to Missy complain about a patient from her last shift. Flora is sipping her cocktail, her sharp eyes scanning the crowd. She's been doing this since the Dr. Marshall incident. I've seen him around the hospital, but the moment he sees me, he leaves the vicinity as quickly as possible—which I am perfectly fine with.

"You need to get out more, Khlo," Missy says, nudging me with her elbow. "You're not even looking around. What's the point of girls' night if you're glued to your water?"

I laugh lightly, swirling the ice in my glass. "I'm here, aren't I? Isn't that enough?"

"Barely. You've been a ghost since Waylon and you got serious." Flora grins.

My cheeks warm as I roll my eyes. "You have too with Aaron, Flora."

Missy snorts. "Both of you have it bad, leaving me to fend for myself."

Flora gasps. "Well, Aaron is marriage material. I'm gonna make him put a ring on it." She waves her hand in my face as my phone rings on the table. I glance at the screen. Waylon. I hit ignore. Flora notices immediately. "Ohhh, speak of the devil."

"Leave me alone," I say quickly. But then it rings again. And again. My stomach twists as I pick it up. Three missed calls in less than five minutes.

Missy raises an eyebrow. "Is he okay? That's... a lot of calls."

"I don't know," I mutter, my skin prickling under their stares as I silence the phone again. "He does this sometimes."

Flora gives me a look. "He calls you like this a lot?"

I shrug, trying to play it off, but my smile betrays me. "Sometimes."

Missy leans forward. "Khlo, that's not normal. Is he mad about something?"

"No," I say quickly. "He just likes to talk. He likes to know where I am."

When he calls once more, Flora grabs it before I can stop her. "Four calls in a row? What is he, your babysitter?"

She holds the phone out of my reach, her expression turning serious. "Khlo, this isn't cute. It's love bombing."

"Give it back, Flora," I snap, reaching for it.

"Not until you admit this is a red flag," she says, her tone laced with concern. "He's really laying it on thick."

"It's sweet. He just wants to talk to me as much as possible. I feel the same way; I just don't want you guys to get mad if I take the call," I admit shamefully.

"So, you're both love bombing," Flora says, giving me a pointed look.

I sit up straighter. "No, we're just into each other. It's not a bad thing." I sigh, grabbing my phone from her hand.

Flora crosses her arms. "It's bad, and it will suffocate you both."

Missy chimes in, "We're not ganging up on you, but you deserve space to live your life. A guy who can't handle you having a night out with friends is a problem."

I look down at my phone. Three texts and another missed call. Waylon's name sits there, heavier than it should.

"I'll talk to him," I say.

Flora leans in gently. "Just think about it, Khlo. You've been through too much to let someone else take over your life like this."

I slip the phone into my pocket, trying to shake the unease that's settled over me. I know Waylon's being protective—it's coming from a caring place.

Chapter 33

Need for Connection

Sitting on my couch, I stare at the screen of my phone, my thumb hovering over Khloe's name in my contacts. I sent her a text five minutes ago, something simple.

WAYLON

Missing you, darlin. Hope your day's going good.

She hasn't replied yet. I know she's out with her friends, but I miss her. I type another message.

WAYLON

Wish I were with you, spankin you.

Hitting send feels like a win. She deserves to know she's on my mind. It's not clingy; it's how I am when I care about someone. I show it. I've seen what happens when you don't. Relationships fall apart; trust disappears. I don't want that with Khloe. I want her to feel how invested I am in us. But I don't enjoy feeling out of control. I've never been the man to sit back and wait for things to happen. If I want something, I go after it.

And I want her.

I glance back at my phone. Still no reply. I don't think; I dial. It rings twice before going to voicemail, and I hang up before leaving a message. She'll see the missed call.

I try to focus on something else, anything else, but it's useless. I dial again. Straight to voicemail this time. Frustration prickles under my skin, but I push it down. She's busy. That's all.

Khloe's a woman you don't meet twice. She's strong, stubborn, but softer than she lets on. I'm not trying to overwhelm her. I want her to feel secure. To know I'm not going anywhere. That's not a bad thing, is it? I've seen what it's like to lose people, to have them slip through your fingers because you didn't do enough. I'm not letting that happen again. I grab my phone again, typing one last message.

WAYLON

> Can't wait to see you and have you meet my family soon.

Satisfied, I toss my phone. She'll answer when she sees it.

I'd been stuck in the office for so many months recently, I'd lost count. The work wasn't always great. Office time meant processing case files, writing detailed reports for arrests and extraditions, updating warrants, and coordinating with local law enforcement on ongoing investigations. Piles of paperwork and backlogged tasks seemed to grow faster than we could clear them lately. This particular day had worn me down; the shift took more out of me than usual.

Khloe must've heard my exhaustion when she called after work. Without me even asking, she showed up at my door with a few bottles in hand. She doesn't need to say much. She gets it.

The whiskey burns as it goes down, but I welcome it. It blurs the edges just enough to dull the weight I carry without erasing it completely. We talk about the day, about life, and then about us. Always us.

Khloe's sitting on one end of the couch, her legs tucked under her, wavy curls spilling over her shoulders like they've got a mind of their own. She looks so damn comfortable—so at home in my home, and it messes with my head in ways I don't know how to explain.

When she leans in, brows lifted in suggestion, it flips a switch. The alcohol stirs it up, dragging my animal to the surface, the part of me she always craves. She catches me staring and tilts her head, releasing the smile that undoes me every damn time.

"What?" she teases.

I shake my head, trying to downplay it, but the words are already fighting their way to the surface. "Nothin'. Just thinkin' about how dangerous you are."

She sets her glass down on the coffee table. "Dangerous? Me?"

I nod, leaning back on my end, letting the whiskey settle in my chest. "Yeah, you. Look at you, sittin' there, lookin' all innocent while you've got me wrapped around your little finger. You have power over me."

Her laugh brushes the air between us. There's a flicker of something in her eyes, maybe curiosity, or hesitation.

"Waylon, are you drunk?"

"Not drunk enough to lie," I shoot back, grinning. "Drunk enough to tell you the truth, though."

She rolls her eyes, and it hits me like a challenge, the way she always does. She doesn't even know what she's doing to me half the time. Or maybe she does, and that's what makes her so damn threatening.

"Come here," I command.

She hesitates, her smile fading enough to make me wonder if I've pushed too far. But then she stands, walking over to me with that soft sway of hers that drives me wild. She stops short of my knees, her arms crossed over her chest.

"What are you up to, Rhodes?"

I look up at her, taking her in. The way her tank top clings to her curves, the way her lips twitch like she's fighting a smile.

"I'm fallin' for you, Khloe," I say, the words spilling out before I can stop them. "Faster than I know what to do with." Her eyes widen. But she says nothing, and her silence kills me. But I don't back down—I can't. "I mean it. I've been tryin' to keep this simple, but it's not. Not with you. It scares the hell outta me," I confess.

Her lips part like she's about to speak, but I don't let her. Reaching out, I gently grab her wrist and guide her to sit on my lap. She's tense, but as I wrap her in a warm embrace, I feel her body gradually easing up, melting into mine. "Waylon..." she starts, but I shake my head, cutting her off.

"Shh. Just let me talk, Khlo," I murmur, my lips brushing against her temple. "I need you to hear this." She nods, her breath warm against my neck. "I don't wanna scare you off, but I can't keep this part of me bottled up, either. You said you trusted me. You meant it, didn't you?"

"Yes," she whispers, even as her heart races against my chest.

"Good," I say, my hand sliding up her back, tangling gently in her curls. "Trust me now."

The whiskey makes my head swim, but my desires are clear. I know what I want, what we want. With a rough grip on her throat, my fingers caress her neck. Her eyes widen, and the tension hangs intensely in the air.

"Do you remember what I said? About control?" She nods, her breath shallow. "I want to show you, Khloe. I'll make you feel somethin' you've never felt before."

In one swift motion, I pull her closer, her legs straddling me as my hands grip her waist. She gasps, but it turns into a laugh, soft, teasing, and laced with anticipation. I press my lips to hers hard, swallowing her sounds as my hands move to the hem of her shirt.

"Waylon," she murmurs, a mix of breathlessness and warning.

I pull back enough to look at her, my eyes locking onto hers. "What's the safe word, Khloe?"

She blinks, surprised by the question. "S*top*."

"Good girl. Don't forget it."

Her smile fades, replaced by something more serious. I guide her arms above her head, holding them there with one hand as the other slides up her side. Her skin is warm under my touch, her breaths coming faster. I tilt her head back, trailing kisses down her neck.

"Still missin' the dark side?" I whisper against her skin, rough and teasing. Her eyes flutter shut.

"I do."

"Then let me remind you," I say, my hands tightening on her hips. "I'm not just here to keep you safe, Khlo. I'm here to make sure you know exactly who you belong to."

She doesn't say a word. There's a flicker of uncertainty behind her eyes. Not fear… it's curiosity, maybe even anticipation. It's all the permission I need. My fingers tighten around her waist as I weigh my next move.

"Khlo," I say in a whisper, despite the way my heart's racing, "If at any point you want me to stop, you say it. No questions. Say the word, and I will."

"Okay."

"Say it, Khloe. I need to hear you say it."

"I'll tell you, I promise."

My free hand brushes her cheek before sliding into her curls, pulling them from her scalp as an anchor. Her lips part as my fingers tangle further, tilting her head back gently to meet my gaze. "Close your eyes," I murmur. She obeys; her confidence in me is palpable. I take my time, pulling her shirt up and off. Fuck, she's braless. I reach up and take her nipple between my lips and bite.

She's wearing a small belt to hold up her blue jeans. I remove it from her waist and tie it around her wrists. Not too tight, but enough to block her movements and heighten her senses. Her chest rises and falls in a rhythm I quickly match with my own. I lean closer, my lips grazing her ear.

"How do you feel?"

"Nervous," she whispers. "But good. I feel good."

"There's a good girl. Stand." I feel her shiver, body responding to the praise. I guide her to the corner of the couch, my hands firm but gentle on her shoulders. "Sit," I instruct, and she lowers herself, hands resting on her thighs. Her vulnerability in this moment stirs something deeper than just desire.

Pride.

She's offering me this part of her that's never belonged to anyone but me. I kneel in front of her, my hands sliding up her thighs, stopping before they reach the hem of her jeans.

"Every touch is for you, Khlo. Do you understand?"

"Yes," she breathes.

"Good girl," I reply, letting my hands trail back down her thighs. "Open your eyes and stand. Let me take care of you."

Sliding her jeans and panties down, I take my time, savoring every reaction. Her breath stops as I run my hands along the soft curve of her hips. I ease her back onto the couch to lay her down. Her body arches in anticipation as I unfasten my belt, the sound of the leather slipping through the loops filling the quiet room.

Our eyes lock as I fold the belt in my hands, testing its weight before letting the first slap land across her breasts. She moans, back arching off the couch. The streaks spreading across her tan skin fuel me as I strike again. The leather kisses her breasts, leaving behind a fresh trail of pink that deepens to red.

I continue, each slap harder than the last, watching the stripes blossom. Her moans grow louder, her body twisting. When the belt lands lower—grazing her clit—her whole-body goes rigid. I swing the belt again with more force. She winces but doesn't stop me, her hips shifting up as if inviting more.

Pausing, I lean down, cupping one of her breasts as I catch her nipple between my fingers. I roll it gently at first, then tighten my grip, watching her expression twist with pleasure and pain. Dropping the belt to the floor, I slide my free hand down between her legs, pressing two fingers firmly against her opening—she's slick, dripping in a way that makes my pulse race.

"Look at you. You're so damn perfect."

Her face is tense, lips parted as moans spill out. She doesn't say a word, but her body tells me everything I need to know. I bring my fingers to my mouth, tasting her arousal before sliding them back inside her, curling them to hit that spot that makes her cry out. With my other hand, I retrieve the belt, letting the edge tease her nipples in stinging snaps. She's completely undone, and it's a sight I'll never tire of.

Her surrender. Her sovereignty.

Every sound she makes is music, every shift of her body a silent plea for more. Her breaths grow shallow as I lower myself and press my lips to the inside of her thigh, trailing soft kisses up her leg until I reach her core. She gasps when I stop short of where she wants me; her bound hands reaching out to correct me.

"Waylon," she pleads.

"Patience, darlin'," I say with a grin. "You'll learn that's part of the fun." I guide her hands back to the armrest of the couch, pressing them there lightly. "Keep them here."

Her fingers curl around the couch's armrest.

"Turn over and count, Khloe," I order.

She responds without hesitation, rotating her body gracefully. Her arms still draped over the armrest, her confidence evident in every movement. The soft glow of the room highlights the curve of her bare ass, supple and inviting, practically begging to feel the snap of the belt. I grip the leather tightly, letting it fall across her skin with precision.

The first strike lands with a sharp crack, breaking the silence.

"One," she calls out, her voice rich with desire.

I strike again, watching her body arch in response.

"Two," she says, stronger this time.

Each swing is measured, the sound of the belt meeting her skin, matched by the heat of her tone. Her breathy numbers roll off her tongue and hit me low—it tightens everything. My grip on the belt, my jaw, and the need crawling beneath my skin. I'm already hard, but now I'm aching. Straining. It's not just the way she submits. It's how she sounds doing it.

When I pause, the marks on her skin are a testament to her resilience. She's radiant, every inch of her glowing with passion and power. She's letting herself go, piece by piece, letting me hold her together. It's at this moment that I know I've never felt this way about anyone before.

"Khlo," I say, releasing her arms. "I need you to know you're mine."

She smiles. "Waylon, I was yours before I even realized it."

I lower myself onto her, and against every thread of carnal rage I carry, I make love to her. The rest of the world fades away, leaving only us and the depth of everything that's led us here.

The drive to Cedar Ridge stretches long, the sun blazing down as my truck eats up the dusty road. Khloe sits quietly in the passenger seat, her hands resting on her lap. She's been quieter than usual since we hit the highway, and I can feel the nerves radiating off her. But I've got plans. We've only got two nights, and I'm going to make them count.

"You okay, darlin'?"

She nods. "Yeah... just nervous. What... if they... don't like me?"

I reach over, squeezing her hand. "They'll love you, believe me."

She doesn't look convinced, but she squeezes me back. I don't let go until the ranch comes into view, sprawling fields dotted with cattle. The old red barn stands tall despite its age. Our log cabin sits in the center, its wraparound porch lined with rocking chairs and flower baskets swaying in the breeze. That old tin roof has weathered more than just storms. It's held the weight of every season I've lived through. It's nothing fancy, but it's home.

As I pull up, the cedar front door swings open, and Loretta jogs out, drying her hands on a dishtowel. Her honey-blonde braid bounces with each step, and her grin widens when she sees me.

"Hey, little brother!" She waves.

I hop out of the truck and walk around to Khloe's side, opening the door. I offer her my hand. Her grip is firm despite her nerves. Loretta's crooked smile falters for a split second when she sees Khloe. She carries Mom's sharp blue eyes that don't miss a damn thing, but she recovers fast, walking toward us in greeting.

"You must be Khloe," Loretta says, hand outstretched. Her turquoise belt buckle and spunky attitude say it all. Ranch-tough, with effortless charm.

"That's me," Khloe replies, shaking her hand. "It's nice to meet you."

"Same here. I've heard a lot about you." Loretta smiles.

"All good things, I hope."

"Mostly." Loretta chuckles.

I keep contact with the small of Khloe's back as we walk toward the porch, where Mom and Dad are waiting. Dad stands tall in worn jeans, a red-and-black flannel. His silver belt buckle catches the sun, his black cowboy hat shading his weathered, unreadable face. Aaron often reminds me that I'm my dad's less grumpy younger twin. But he's always got his scuffed boots to show he's rugged and all cowboy.

Mom greets with a kind smile and open arms, her soft blonde hair framing a fair face touched by time but not worn by it—every line a reminder of laughter. She wears a breezy floral-print dress that brushes her calves—simple and classic. I remember why everyone in town loves her. Why I do, too.

"This is Khloe," I say, guiding her in the last few steps. "Khloe, these are my parents."

"Nice to meet you, Mr. and Mrs. Rhodes."

Mom steps forward, just about Khloe's height, and pulls her into a hug. "Call me Martha, honey. And this is Jack." Dad nods, his eyes lingering on Khloe a beat longer than necessary. There's a flicker in his expression I've seen before with Aaron. With my shoulders square, instinct kicks in.

"She's lovely." Mom shoots Dad a quick glance before taking Khloe's arm. "Come on in. Dinner's almost ready."

The walls are made of thick logs, their dark wood broken up by pale chinking that catches the light from iron-framed lanterns hung like old memories. Mom's fried chicken is delicious as always. The cedar table is loaded with biscuits, green beans, and mashed potatoes.

Conversation flows easily at first. Loretta asks Khloe about working as a nurse, and I throw in the occasional teasing comment to lighten the mood that my dad has soured. Khloe handles it like a pro, laughing at my jabs and answering Loretta's questions with confidence.

But then Dad speaks up. "So, Khloe, where's your family from?"

"Stamford, Connecticut." She smiles.

"Where are you really from?" The words come out slowly, like he's waiting for the punchline. My eyes shoot daggers at him.

I glance back at Khloe, watching her set her fork down slowly. "My mom is biracial... white and black, and my dad's side is Puerto Rican. I grew up with my grandmother, who is also biracial."

The room goes quiet for a moment that feels too long. Dad raises an eyebrow, his face unreadable. Mom shoots him a warning look. He nods stiffly.

"That's interesting."

"Dad." I meet his eyes as my fingers slide into Khloe's under the table, and she squeezes.

Mom jumps in quickly. "It's a beautiful mix. Your grandmother must've been so proud of you."

"She was. She raised me after my parents... weren't around."

Mom's eyes soften. "She did a wonderful job. You're a remarkable young woman."

Dad stays quiet for the rest of the meal, but the tension hangs heavy. I keep my focus on Khloe, making sure she knows I'm right there with her.

After dinner, I step out onto the porch and spot Khloe leaning against the railing, a glass of sweet tea in her hand. Mom stands beside her, stroking Khloe's arm as they talk quietly. Mom winces as she says, "I hope you didn't take Jack's reaction the wrong way. He's not used to... people outside our little world."

Khloe nods. "I figured. It's not the first time I've been in a situation like this."

Mom rubs Khloe's arm. "I'm so sorry, honey. He'll come around. He needs time to see what I already see—you're good for Waylon. And that you belong here, no matter what anyone else thinks."

"Thank you, Martha. That means a lot." I can tell from the way Khloe's shoulders relax that Mom's done her thing, making her feel at home.

When Mom spots me, she pats Khloe's arm and steps back. "She's a keeper, Waylon," she says as she passes me. "Don't let your daddy mess this up."

I nod, stepping onto the porch. "Everything alright?"

She holds up her tea with a faint smile. "Better now."

I close the distance between us, my arms wrapping around her shoulders and pulling her close. "You know you don't have to prove anything to them, right? You're not here to fit in. You're here because you matter—to me."

She leans into me. "You make it easier to believe."

I kiss the top of her head, tightening my hold on her. "You're stuck with me, darlin'. No one's changin' that."

At the crack of dawn, the barn smells like hay and old wood, a scent that's been burned into my memory since I was a kid. Dad's there, leaning against a stall with his dented thermos, brushing down one of the horses. His strokes are even and methodical, like he doesn't have a care in the world—but I know better. His silence has always said more than his words ever could.

My boots crunch against the hay-strewn floor as I step inside. "Mornin'."

"Mornin'," he replies, not looking up. I watch him for a moment, hands on my hips, trying to rein in my frustration. He doesn't stop brushing the horse. The sound of the bristles fills the quiet space between us. He's stalling. That's fine. I'm not letting this slide.

"We need to talk, Dad," I say finally.

His hand stills on the horse, and his shoulders stiffen. "'Bout what?"

"You know damn well what. Khloe."

He sets the brush down, meeting my eyes. His face is unreadable, but I see the tension in his jaw.

"What about her?"

"Don't play dumb. I saw the way you looked at her last night. Heard it in your tone when you asked about her family. You made her feel like she didn't belong here."

He sighs, dragging a hand over his wrinkled face. "Waylon, it's not that I don't like her. She's just... different."

"Different?" The word stings as it leaves my mouth. I step closer, using the inch I've got on him as my temper flares. "That's what you're goin' with? What the hell does that even mean, Dad?"

He shifts uncomfortably, setting his thermos down on a nearby post. "You know what I mean. We're from a small town. People here have a certain way of doin' things."

I take another step forward, my boots heavy against the wooden floor. "And that way includes judgin' someone because of the color of their skin or where their family comes from? That's what you're standin' by?"

"Now, hold on," he says defensively. "I didn't say that."

"You didn't have to," I fire back. "It was written all over your face. You didn't even give her a chance, Dad. Khloe's one of the strongest, kindest people I've ever met, and you treated her like she wasn't good enough to sit at your table."

His face flushes, and he crosses his arms. "You're makin' this into somethin' it's not, Waylon."

"No, I'm callin' it what it is—racism. You don't get to hide behind excuses like 'small town' or 'tradition.' That's bullshit, and you know it." His face reddens, and for a moment, I think he's going to argue. But he just stares at me, jaw tight. I keep going, frustration and emotion spilling over. "You taught me to be a good man, Dad. To treat people with respect, to stand up for what's right. I won't sit back and let you disrespect the woman I love because she doesn't look like the people you're used to. You didn't act like this with Aaron. There was no problem with me being friends with a Black man?"

Dad's face twists slightly. "Well, Waylon," he begins, hesitating. "Aaron saved your life. He pulled my boy out of hell and brought you back home. How could I hold anything against him when he made sure you got to become the man you are today?"

His words hang in the air for a moment, heavy with meaning. "So that's it?" I shoot back, almost yelling. "Aaron had to save my life to earn your respect? That's the bar? What's Khloe supposed to do, Dad? Rescue me from a burning building?"

Dad's eyes narrow. He's not used to being called out like this. "It's not the same, Waylon," he says gruffly, but there's a hesitation now. A crack in his defenses. "Aaron helped you find your way after Caroline. He got you to stop drinkin' so much, to stop actin' like an ass, and I'll always be grateful to him for that."

I stare at him, a mix of disbelief and anger swirling in my chest. "And you don't think Khloe's done the same? She's made me feel again, Dad... For the first time in years, I'm not just going through the motions. I've been burying myself in work and meaningless hook-ups, and she's the one who pulled me out of that."

Dad shifts. "I didn't say she hasn't had an impact on you, Waylon. I can see it clear as day. You've changed. But—"

"But what?" I cut him off, my jaw tight. "But she doesn't look like the woman you're used to? She doesn't fit into your neat little idea of who I should be with? She's not Caroline."

"That's not fair," he mutters, not meeting my eyes.

"No," I snap. "What's not fair is you judgin' Khloe without even giving her a chance. She's good for me, Dad. And if you can't see that, then maybe you're not the man I thought you were."

I see the way my words hit him as his shoulders sag. "I'm sorry, Waylon," he says quietly. "Maybe I've been too set in my ways. Maybe I... maybe I didn't think about how it all came across."

"You didn't. But it's not too late to fix it. She's not going anywhere, Dad. You need to figure out how to accept that."

He nods slowly, his gaze dropping to the floor. "I'll try—for you and for her."

"And for yourself," I add. "Because if you saw her the way I do, you'd understand what an incredible woman she is."

Dad looks up at me, a faint flicker of understanding in his eyes. "You love her, don't you?"

"Yeah, I think I do."

There's a long pause, the barn's silent except for the faint sounds of the horses shifting in their stalls. Dad straightens, his expression purposeful.

"Alright. I'll do better. You've got my word."

I nod, the tension easing. "That's all I ask." As I turn to leave, his response stops me.

"She's a strong woman," he says gruffly. "And from the sound of it, she's makin' you stronger, too. Don't let me screw that up for you."

I glance back at him. "Damn right I won't."

He exhales. "I didn't mean to make her feel unwelcome. I'm sorry, I was wrong."

"You were, but it's not me you need to say that to."

He nods, picking up his thermos like it's some kind of shield. "I'll talk to her—apologize."

"You better mean it," I warn, stepping back. "She deserves better than half-assed words, Dad."

He meets my eyes, his expression serious. "I will. You're right. I need to do better."

I nod, the tension in my chest loosening slightly. "Good. Start with her."

"She's lucky to have you," he says sincerely. "And maybe we're lucky to have her, too."

I glance back at him, smiling. "We are."

Chapter 34

Facing the Family

I'm in the kitchen, wiping bacon grease off the knotty wood counters, the scent of it still hanging thick in the warm air. I told Martha to go relax, figured I'd take care of the mess. Above the farmhouse sink, a narrow window frames the tree line. Morning light shining in across the weathered butcher block. I'm mid-swipe when the hardwood creaks under a pair of boots, the sound echoing in the wide, open space.

Turning, I see Jack standing in the doorway, hat in hand. His jaw shifts like he's biting back words, eyes skimming the floor before they land on me. The lines on his face look deeper, etched by more than time. It's the first time since I arrived that he seemed less sure of himself.

"Khloe, can we talk for a minute?"

I pause, gripping the rag in my hand a little tighter. "Of course, Mr. Rhodes."

"Jack," he corrects softly, stepping further into the room. "Call me Jack."

I drop the rag and lean back against the counter. "Alright. What's on your mind?"

He shuffles his feet, the familiar, weathered green of his eyes, like Waylon's, catching mine before darting away. "I owe you an apology. The way I acted when you first got here, the questions I asked… it wasn't right. And it damn sure wasn't fair." I blink. "I guess I let my ignorance get in the way," he continues, finally making eye contact with me. "You're not what I'm used to. That's on me, not you. You didn't deserve to feel unwelcome. I'm sorry for that."

I study his face, searching for any cracks in his sincerity, but I don't find any. Derrick's dad would never. My shoulders ease slightly. "Thank you, Jack. I truly appreciate it."

He nods, his grip tightening on the brim of his hat. "Waylon told me I needed to do better. He's right. I can see how much he cares about you, and I'd be a damn fool to stand in the way of that."

The lump in my throat swells. "I care about him, too. A lot."

"I can see that," Jack says, his tone growing stronger. "And for what it's worth, I'm glad he has someone like you in his life. I reckon you're good for him."

I exhale, letting my shoulders drop. Warmth spreads through my chest, loosening the tension that was wound so tight. "Thank you, Jack. That really means a lot."

He places his hat back on his head and tips it slightly, his eyes holding mine. "Welcome to the family, Khloe."

The late afternoon sun casts golden streaks through the slats of the horse barn, filtering dust swirls lazily in the quiet air. The scent of hay and leather fills my lungs as Waylon leads me inside, his large hand wrapped firmly around mine. It's cooler here, shaded and still.

"You know," I say, breaking the comfortable silence, "your dad came to apologize."

Waylon's body stills before I feel him nod. "Yeah?

What'd he say?"

Pulling back, I look up at him. "He admitted he was wrong. Said he was glad you had someone like me in your corner." I pause. "It caught me off guard, but... it felt real."

A flicker crosses his eyes, softening his stare. His shoulders drop a fraction as he lets out a slow exhale. "It was real."

My brows knit together. "Did you say something to him?"

"I might've had a talk with him this morning." He shrugs.

I raise an eyebrow. "A talk?"

"Yes, one that makes it clear I'm not gonna stand by and let anyone disrespect you," he says simply. "I told him he was wrong. That I wasn't gonna let anyone, not even him, make you feel you don't belong."

"Waylon ... You said all of that to your dad?" He releases me and steps away, boots crunching on the hay-scattered floor. He stops, the faintest grin pulling at the corner of his mouth, but those predatory eyes lock onto mine with an intensity that makes my pussy tighten.

"Of course I did," he says as he returns to my side, brushing a piece of hair from my face. His touch is gentle, but his words are firm. "You're worth fightin' for, Khloe. Always."

The air thickens. My spine straightens as tension hums between us, sharp and electric. His gaze drags over me with that dark intensity I know too well. It's not sweet. It's not safe. It's the part of him that ruins me.

"You're thinkin' too much again, Khloe." He reaches out, his fingers tracing along my collarbone. His touch leaves a trail of fire in its wake. "Do I need to remind you that you're mine?"

"Waylon..." I start, but I falter when he cups my chin, tipping my head back, so I'm forced to meet his gaze. Anticipation blooms low in my belly.

His eyes pin me in place. "You trust me?"

"Yes."

"Good." His thumb grazes my bottom lip. "Then turn

around." The command settles over me. I turn slowly, my heartbeat thudding in my ears as I face the sturdy wooden beam in front of me.

Waylon steps up behind me. His breath brushes my back, raising goosebumps. "Hands on the beam. Spread your feet."

I comply—the rough wood cool against my palms. Waylon moves behind me, his fingers hooking into the waistband of my jeans and panties. He takes his time sliding them down, knuckles skimming my skin, tracing over the tattoo he knows so well. He removes my boots, and I step out of my clothes. When I think he's done, he leans down, pressing soft kisses against my ass, before his teeth catch my skin in a playful bite. I yelp and giggle, the sound betraying how much I'm yearning for this. He stands, delivering a sharp slap to my ass that sends a jolt of warmth through me.

I follow his every move as he saunters over to the wall of horse tack—my breath catching as he runs his hand over the equipment. When he picks up a horse collar, inspecting it with a glance, my pulse picks up. His gaze shifts to me, and he winks. An enticing gesture that sends a thrill racing down my spine. I can't help the smile that forms, even as the heat coils low. My body is already feverish for what comes next.

He finally decides on a riding crop, his fingers curling around it like it belongs in his hand. Coming back to me, his strides slow, speaking with a smoothness that borders on sinful.

"For old times' sake. Look forward, baby."

The memory lights a fire in me as I yield to him. Slickness dripping on instinct. I'm ready for him. There's a brief pause before I feel the cutting sting of the riding crop grazing the back of my thighs.

A warning.

I inhale sharply, my body humming with the familiar mix of nerves and excitement.

"You've been needin' this, haven't you?" I moan, my body angling towards him. "Tell me."

"Yes, I need you."

The next slap of the crop lands sharply across the curve of my ass. I gasp, the sound echoing in the barn. I curve further, needing more.

"That's it," Waylon says, his tone dark with approval. "Good girl."

The crop lands again, harder this time, and blooms into a dull ache that lingers long enough to make me hungrier. Each strike is reasoned, building on the last—coordinated domination. When Waylon swings—he *studies* me, listens to my body as it answers to him. There's no rush. Composure clings to him, even when the edges fray.

"Count," he orders.

The word sends a tremor through me. "One." The next strike comes, and I bite my lip to suppress the whimper threatening to spill out. "Two." He doesn't ease until I've counted to ten in shaky moans. My skin burns, thighs quivering. But the pressures of the world, the doubts, the insecurities, have fallen away. There's only this.

Him and I.

Waylon steps closer, caressing the marks he's created, soothing the sting. "You okay, baby?" he asks tenderly.

"Yes," I whisper, my body sagging in relief. "More than okay."

He presses a kiss to the back of my neck, his other hand sliding up my side until it rests on my stomach, pulling me to him.

"I know what you can take. I know what you need," he says, lips sweeping against my ear. "Remember somethin', Khloe?"

"Yes?"

"You're mine. You're safe with me. Always." The words are a stark contrast to the intensity that unfolded. "I'm not goin' anywhere."

I close my eyes and smile. Waylon spins me around to face him, cradling my face in his rough hands. Our lips collide in a kiss filled with hunger and emotion. This moment feels dangerously close to love.

He pulls back, that rare softness in his eyes saying everything; I'm his, and he'll never stop choosing me. His hands move to my thighs, and in one swift motion, he lifts me effortlessly and presses my back against the beam. My legs wrap around him on instinct, my body trusting his strength. His denim jeans do little to hide how hard he is.

With one arm bracing me, he frees himself. In a deliberate thrust, he's inside me. My gasp echoes through the barn, swallowed by wood and heat. His depth and stretch border on pain, but I don't want him to stop. It's all-consuming.

"Waylon," I moan, digging my nails into his shoulders.

He growls, burying his face in my neck as he pounds into me, like he's trying to claim me from the inside out. I'm lost in the way he's intense and tender all at once. The world outside the barn fades. There's only this moment, this man, and the way he's tearing down every barrier between us. And I let him.

I press my face into his shoulder, my body moving to the rhythm we've found. The one that no man except him has ever matched. My teeth sink gently into his skin, muffling the moans that escape as I come undone around him, my body trembling with release.

"There's my good girl," Waylon murmurs, rough and full of praise. The words send a fresh shiver through me. He grips my ass tighter, his movements quickening as he finds his own release, a low moan escaping him as he lets go.

This is Waylon. Raw, unguarded, and completely mine.

Tonight's our last night. We're surrounded by bonfire warmth and an open sky full of stars, a quiet reminder of how small we all are. I trace slow circles on Waylon's knee, his presence grounding me. Across from us, Martha and Jack share a wooden loveseat. Their bodies relaxed, but their eyes sharp. Loretta is curled up in an Adirondack chair, with a blanket draped over her shoulders.

"You sure you don't want another s'more?" Waylon asks.

I laugh, shaking my head. "I've already had two. Any more, and you'll have to roll me back to San Antonio."

Martha chuckles. "San Antonio must feel so big compared to here. What made you decide to move there?"

The question lands softly, but it brings more to the surface than I'm ready for. I twist my hands together, taking a steadying breath before speaking. "I moved there after my grandmother passed," I say, the ache barely hidden beneath. The fire crackles, filling the silence as their awareness shifts to me. Waylon's hand finds mine, his fingers curling around mine. "She raised me after my parents..." The words catch, but I keep going. "Well, they weren't in the picture. My dad left when I was little, and my mom..."

I glance at Waylon, his expression urging me but still supportive. "She struggles with addiction. She's in prison now. My grandmother took me in when I was four. She was everything to me. My mother, my father, my best friend."

Martha leans forward slightly, eyes full of empathy. "She sounds like a remarkable woman."

"She was," I say, a smile tugging at my lips, even as her memory stings. "She taught me strength. And how to love fiercely, even when it felt impossible. She passed away from cancer when I was twenty-four." Loretta discreetly wipes at her eyes, and even Jack's gruff demeanor has softened. "Losing her was tough. I felt... lost. I still do sometimes. I stayed in Connecticut for a while, but it wasn't home anymore. So, I moved to San Antonio to be with my friend Flora. A fresh start, and a place to figure out who I was without Grandma."

The silence that follows is heavy, but it's not uncomfortable. There's no pity in their eyes, but understanding.

"That's a lot for one girl to go through, honey," Martha says in a motherly tone. "But you've built a life for yourself as a woman, and that takes real power."

I nod, the tightness in my chest loosening slightly. "I'm trying. Being a nurse helps. It makes me feel like I can give back and be there for people the way she was always there for me."

Jack clears his throat. "Sounds like your grandmother raised one hell of a woman."

The compliment catches me off guard. I blink, feeling a swell of gratitude. "Thank you, Jack."

Waylon shifts, his arm wrapping around my shoulders. "She'd be damn proud of you, Khloe," he says tenderly. "I know I am." I lean into him, letting his strength and warmth support me.

Martha smiles warmly, her eyes sweeping over us. "Well, it's clear you've found a home here, too. Anytime you need a reminder that you've got people in your corner, you know where to find us."

Tears prick at my eyes, but I smile through them. "Thank you. That means more than I can say."

The fire crackles on, its glow wrapping around us like a promise. I feel like I belong. Not only with Waylon, but with a family that sees me, accepts me, and embraces every part of my story.

The next morning, I'm alone with Loretta on the porch, cradling a warm cup of coffee as the sun climbs into the sky. The ranch is waking up. Cattle lowing in the distance, and the hum of work starting. It's peaceful. We sit in silence, the occasional clink of a mug against the railing the only sound.

Loretta shifts beside me. "Can I ask you somethin'? About Waylon?"

"Sure."

"You know about his ex-wife, right?"

I hesitate. "He's mentioned her. Said they married young, but it didn't work out."

Loretta sighs. "Yeah, but there's more to it."

"What do you mean?"

She leans forward, eyes on the horizon. "Everyone thought they'd make it. But once Waylon enlisted, things changed. She tried to be supportive, but she hated him being gone."

I set my coffee aside, giving her my full attention. "He said that."

"When he came back from his first deployment, she was already pulling away. And after the second... he wasn't the same. He'd seen things no one should. Caroline couldn't handle it. She said he wasn't Waylon anymore." Loretta's voice softens, the bitterness still there. "Said she couldn't live with someone so closed off. But she didn't want to carry any of what he was carryin'. The sleepless nights, the panic outta nowhere. He fought like hell to get through it. Therapy, talking, tryin'... but she didn't want the man who came back."

My chest tightens. "And she walked away."

"She asked for the divorce a year after he really started working on himself. He tried, but she was already gone. She moved away, and far as I know, she's never looked back."

I sink deeper into the chair. "Why are you telling me this?"

Loretta gives a quiet smile. "He doesn't like to talk about it—thinks it makes him look weak. But it doesn't. It makes him real. And you... you've seen the cracks, and you haven't run. That matters."

"I just want him to feel safe enough to let me in. I'm not going anywhere."

Her smile grows. "You're only the second girl he's brought around, Khloe. And I think you're good for him. I really do."

My chest swells with gratitude, love, and a growing understanding of the man I'm falling for. We sit in silence again, the morning light wrapping around us like a quiet truth.

The sun is setting over the Rhodes Ranch, casting a golden glow across the fields. I'm helping Waylon load our bags into the back of his truck. I glance back at the house, a pang of reluctance settling in. The screen door creaks, and Martha steps out, her cardigan pulled tight around her shoulders. She crosses the porch with a sweet smile that reminds me I belong here, even if the weekend has been a rollercoaster of emotions.

"Come here, sweetheart," she says, arms open wide. Her hug is warm, the kind you sink into when you need to feel safe. It reminds me of my grandmother.

"Thank you for everything," I murmur into her shoulder. "Your kindness means so much."

Martha pulls back. "You're family now, honey. Don't you forget that. And don't be a stranger, ya hear?"

I blink against the sting in my eyes. "I won't."

Jack steps out of the house, hat perched low, and boots scuffing the porch steps. He stops in front of me; I brace myself. Instead, he surprises me. He holds out his hand, eyes softer than they'd been all weekend. I hesitate for a second, then take his hand.

He clears his throat. "Khloe, thank you for puttin' up with me. And for makin' my boy happy. That means more to us than you know."

"Thank you for having me, Jack. It's been special." He smiles. Then, without warning, he pulls me in for a quick hug. "You take care of yourself. And take care of my boy, too."

I glance at Waylon, leaning against the truck, watching the exchange with a smile full of warmth and pride. "I will."

Loretta bounds out next, a flash of energy breaking the quiet as she carries a blanket in her arms. "You're not leaving without this," she declares, shoving it into my hands.

I unfold it to see a beautifully handmade quilt, the warm tones and intricate stitching. "Loretta! This is gorgeous. I can't take this."

"Yes, you will. Consider it a thank you for being awesome and for dealin' with my brother's cranky ass."

Waylon laughs. "Real nice, Loretta."

I hug her tightly, overwhelmed by her generosity. "Thank you. For everything."

She steps back, grinning. "Don't make it too long before you come back, okay? We're just gettin' used to havin' you around."

"I won't," I promise.

Waylon opens the truck door for me, and I take one last look at the house and the people still standing on the porch. Jack gives me a nod. Martha waves. Loretta grins like she already misses me. I slide into the seat, a fullness settling in my chest, warm and heavy all at once. Waylon climbs in beside me, brushing my knee before starting the engine.

As we pull away, the ranch fades in the rearview, but the feeling it gave me doesn't. A sense of belonging and being seen. I haven't felt that since Flora's family opened their arms to me.

For a second, I believe I could have this. That I could fit in Waylon's world and he might not disappear. But then, like always, doubt creeps in.

Don't get comfortable, Khloe.

It always starts this way. That voice, louder than calm. Will they still care a year from now? Can Waylon really handle the part of me that freezes when things get too close? That doubts everything good?

I already need him more than I should. And the hope, the aching, terrifying hope, makes me feel like I'm standing on the edge of something that could break me. He doesn't know what it means to love someone like me. The fear doesn't vanish just because he's kind. People leave—even the ones who promised they never would.

I lean against the window, forcing a breath. He isn't Derrick. He isn't my mother or father. He's not leaving. He stood up for me. Stayed stable when I wasn't. Keeps showing me I belong here.

I want to believe in us. But it's hard to trust when your entire life has been proof that love leaves.

I glance at him, steady hands on the wheel, focus unwavering. What if this time is different and someone finally stays?

I breathe in slowly, trying to quiet the storm inside me.

One day at a time, Khloe.

Chapter 35

Drunk Mind, Sober Heart

Garlic and roasted herbs fill the air as we step through Aaron's door. I fight back a laugh when I see my best friend in an apron, stirring a pot with the determined focus of a man on a mission. Flora's by his side, wine glass in hand, looking right at home. She leans into him like they've been doing this for decades, not just a couple of months.

"There they are!" Flora calls out. "Finally. Thought y'all might've skipped dinner and eloped."

I smirk. "Traffic was a pain."

Khloe slides into a seat at the table, watching Aaron and Flora. She's plating food while he stirs, exchanging little touches and grins as if no one else is around. "They're like a sit-com couple," Khloe whispers.

I chuckle. "They're either rehearsin' for a Hallmark special or tryin' to make us look bad."

She snorts, elbowing me lightly. "Definitely the second one."

The table is set neatly, something Flora probably insists on. Once they sit down, Aaron clinks his glass with a spoon, wearing a grin that makes me suspicious. "Alright, big news!"

Flora lights up, squeezing his hand. "We've decided to

move in together!"

Khloe freezes before forcing a smile. "Move in together?" she echoes, a little too sharply.

Aaron smiles. "Yep. It feels right. No point in waiting when you know, right?"

Khloe's body stiffens, her fork hovering in midair. "That's... fast."

Flora shrugs, swirling her wine. "When you know, you know. Isn't that right, Waylon?"

I can spot a trap from miles away, and I wasn't about to fall for it. "Everyone's got their own pace," I answer carefully. I glance at Khloe, but her eyes are fixed on her plate.

"Come on, Khloe. You and Waylon have been spending so much time together. What's holding you back?"

Khloe's cheeks flush. "Not everyone's in a rush," she says, stabbing at her salad like it offended her.

Flora holds up her hands in surrender. "Hey, no judgment. You do you."

Aaron wisely steers the conversation back to safer territory. Khloe stays quiet for most of the meal. I don't push her, knowing better than to pry in front of an audience.

The cool night air feels good after the charged dinner. I walk Khloe to her car, the gravel crunching under our boots. She hasn't said much since we left. I lean against the passenger door of her car.

"Alright, out with it."

She crosses her arms, brow furrowing. "It's just... I don't get it. How can they be so sure? It's been, what, three months?"

I study her for a moment. Her shoulders are tense, nose scrunched into her full lips.

"They've got their way of doin' things. Doesn't mean we've gotta do the same."

Her eyes drop to the ground. "Do you think we're moving too slow?"

I step closer, tilting her chin up gently. "I think we're doin' what works for us," I say quietly. "I'm not goin' anywhere, Khloe. You just met my family. Whether we take it slow or jump in headfirst, I'm here. The only pace that matters is the one we decide on together."

She meets my eyes. The doubt lingers, then she lets it go; inviting me back in with soft eyes and that smile that guts me. "Together," she repeats, testing the word.

I reach out, brushing a stray curl away from her face. "There's my good girl."

The next day, my first Monday back at work after the ranch and that whole move-in dinner mess, I get sent on a quick trip miles away. My assignment's done now. I'm settling into the motel room, sitting on the edge of the bed, boots discarded, gun locked up for the night. I scroll through my phone, debating if I should call her when her name lights up on the screen.

Khloe.

I answer, leaning back against the headboard. "Hey, darlin'. What's goin' on?"

"Waylon," she drags out the syllables, testing the way it feels on her tongue. "Hi."

I can't help but smile. "Hi—you okay? You sound loose."

She laughs, the sound warming my chest. "I might've had a drink or two with Flora. But I'm fine. Just wanted to hear your voice."

I love that she needs these moments. I relax, eyes closed. "Well, you've got it. How's your night been?"

She rambles on for a bit about her evening. Flora was trying to teach her a new dance move at the bar, how Missy and her sister joined them halfway through. Missy embarrassed herself by trying to flirt with the gay bartender. I listen, laugh, and tease her until she falls silent.

"Waylon, I miss you. It's stupid, but I do."

I straighten. "It's not stupid, Khlo. I miss you too."

"I love you, Waylon."

My chest tightens. The words knock me sideways, not because I don't feel it. I do. But hearing it out loud makes it too damn real. The words hang there, dangerous. I clear my throat, my grip tightening on the phone. "Khlo, you've been drinkin'. Let's talk about this tomorrow, okay?"

Her laugh is shaky. "Right. Tomorrow. Sure."

"Get some sleep. We'll talk in the morning." I reassure her gently.

"Goodnight, Waylon," she murmurs, and I hear the hurt she's trying to hide before the call disconnects.

I sit there for a while staring at the ceiling. *I love you, Waylon* plays on repeat in my mind, and regret settles. I haven't said I love you to a woman since Caroline. Saying it back means fully opening that door again. I've always believed a drunk mind speaks a sober heart, but does she really mean it?

The next day, the sun's breaking over the horizon when I pull into her driveway, exhausted but determined. I didn't sleep last night—couldn't stop thinking about her, and how I didn't respond. I need to see her. I want her to know how much she means to me. I like to stay in control of my emotions, actions, and life. My instinct has always been to pull back and regain footing when I'm unsure. I should have said it last night. But I have to do it on my terms.

She answers the door in sweats and an oversized hoodie, her hair a mess, eyes puffy from sleep.

"Waylon?" she rasps, confused. "What are you doing here?"

"We need to talk." I step inside before she can shut the door.

She crosses her arms. "Look, I was drunk last night. You don't have to—"

"I'm not here to lecture you. But you need to know something."

Her gaze sharpens. "What?"

I step closer, untangling her arms so I can take her

hands. "I love you, too, Khloe."

Her breath hitches. "You... what?"

"I didn't say it last night because I didn't want the heat of the moment to take away from the meaning, but I do. I've been trying not to. Been telling myself I shouldn't. But I can't help it."

She stares at me, lips parted, but no words come. Her arms slide around my waist, and she buries her face in my chest.

"I thought you didn't feel the same," she murmurs.

I tilt her chin up. "You think I'd be here if I didn't? You're everything, Khlo. Scares the hell outta me, but it's true."

She smiles, eyes glistening. "I love you, too."

I kiss her, letting her feel every word I should've said last night.

Hours later, her bedroom is quiet except for the hum of the ceiling fan. The toll of the day, the drive, the words I finally said, all hang over me as I stare at the shadows on the wall. Khloe is curled beside me, breathing softly but unevenly. I turn my head, watching her silhouette in the dim light. Her hair spills across the pillow, messy and perfect. I'd thought that saying the words would make things easier, that it would hush the storm inside me. But her silence is drowning me.

"Khlo?"

She shifts, tilting her head enough for me to see her profile. "Hmm?"

"You all right?"

She pauses, making me worry. She sighs, rolling onto her back. Her eyes find mine.

"Do you really love me, Waylon?"

I frown, propping myself on one elbow. "Of course I do. Why would you think I don't?"

She hesitates, fingers twisting the sheets. "I don't know. Maybe because it feels... too fast. Or maybe because I don't understand why you would."

I sit up fully, turning to face her. "Khlo, what kind of question is that?"

She gives a humorless laugh. "Because I'm a mess. I overthink everything. I have baggage most people would run from. I'm not easy to love."

I rest my hand over hers, stilling her fidgeting fingers. "You think love is supposed to be easy? It's not. But you're worth every damn bit of it."

She looks away. "I don't want you to regret this. Or me."

I shake my head, frustration bubbling up. "Regret you? Khlo, I've been through shit most people can't imagine. I know what it means to fight for something that matters. You matter. Don't you dare think I don't know exactly what I'm signing up for."

Her lips tremble. I move closer, brushing a strand of hair from her face. "Stop thinkin' so little of yourself." She lowers her head. "Look at me." She does. "I love you. Not because you're perfect, but because you're you. Yeah, you've got baggage. So do I, but that doesn't scare me. Every day we find something new we have in common or love about each other."

She blinks, tears slipping free. "You make it sound so simple."

"It is," I admit, cupping her cheek. "You're makin' it complicated."

She laughs, shaking her head. "You're impossible."

"And you're stubborn," I counter, grinning. "Guess we're a good match."

She sighs, curling her fingers around mine. "I'm scared, Waylon. I don't want to lose you."

"You won't," I promise. "Stop thinkin' you're not enough."

She watches me for a long moment before saying, "Okay."

I press a kiss to her forehead before settling beside her. She tucks herself into me, and for the first time in weeks, I feel like we're on solid ground. As her breathing evens out and sleep takes her, I stare at the ceiling. She's scared of losing me. But I'm scared too. Scared that I can't be the one to quiet the doubts she carries. But I'll be damned if I let that fear stop me. All I can do is hold her tighter.

Guys' weekend's in full swing, the fire crackling, the lake stretches out black beyond it. We're slinging stories, beers in hand, each one getting more exaggerated with every round. I lean back, sip my beer, half-listening to Aaron and Ramirez argue over who caught the biggest fish today.

My cousin, Jackman, is here too. He's been close with Aaron and Ramirez since our Corps days. He's not officially on the team, but he might as well be. He keeps watching me like he's still figuring out what Khloe did to me. Jackman's a man you don't have to look at twice to know he can handle himself. Broad through the chest, forearms cut with old strength, tattoos creeping out from under his sleeves like stories he doesn't tell. His sandy-blond buzzed hair and trimmed beard give him that squared-away look, but it's the eyes that stick—cool, steady, always watching. He doesn't say much, but when he does, the room listens. Same as the Corps.

"Bullshit," Aaron scoffs, flicking a bottle cap into the fire. "That thing wasn't over four pounds."

Ramirez tips his beer. "Jealousy's ugly, man. I saw the way you were starin' at it."

Donald lumbers past the fire pit, all shoulders and attitude, tossing a log like it weighs nothing as he huffs. Red crew cut, beer gut slipping out from under his shirt, and a face that looks like it's seen every sunrise and regretted none of them.

"It was a catfish, and you looked proud as hell. Like it was a damn trophy."

Jackman smirks. "That's 'cause Ramirez thinks a trophy's the only thing loyal to him."

Ramirez flips him off. "Better than sittin' there with an empty hook all day."

The laughter rolls through the group, easy and familiar. It's a good night. Reminds me of simpler times before everything got tangled up in things that keep me awake at night. Before relationships—before her.

As if my thoughts summon it, my phone vibrates in my pocket. I ignore the way my chest tightens at seeing her name as I slide my phone out.

KHLOE

Hey, how's the weekend going?

I grin as I dial. She answers fast. "Hey." Even with the shitty reception out here, she settles something deep in me. I lean forward, resting my elbows on my knees.

"Khloe," I drawl, letting her name stretch. "Checkin' in on me, huh? You sound like my mom."

Her laugh floats through the speaker, making my smirk widen. "You've been quiet. Just making sure you haven't gotten into trouble."

"Trouble? You think I can't survive a weekend away without you worryin' about me?"

Her response comes through, teasing and just the tiniest bit too honest. "Maybe I don't want you to survive without me."

Something shifts in my chest, unexpected and a little too sharp. I roll my shoulders, ignoring the pull it has on me, and lean back in my chair.

"You're somethin' else, you know that? Checkin' in on me like a crazy girlfriend."

Aaron turns his head, raising an eyebrow.

Her tone is playful, but I hear the bite underneath. "Crazy, huh? That's rich coming from the guy who calls me five times in a row just because I don't text back fast enough."

"Shit. Alright, alright. You got me."

"Damn right, I do. If I'm crazy, you're right there with me." There's a sternness in her I'm not used to.

I hum. "Maybe I am. But I don't mind. Keeps things interestin'."

I can hear a smile. "Well, as long as you're okay. What've you been up to?"

"Went fishin' this mornin'. Caught nothin' worth braggin' about. Been sittin' out by the fire ever since." I picture her then, curled up in my oversized hoodie she always wears, probably sipping on tea. The thought makes me miss her too much. It's only been two damn days.

"Sounds nice. I'll let you get back to it."

The thought of her hanging up settles wrong. "You don't have to go. I don't mind talkin' to you." Aaron snorts beside me, mumbling something under his breath about being whipped. I flip him off.

Khloe chuckles. "Alright, but only if you promise not to call me crazy again."

"Promise. But I'm crazy about you, darlin'. I figure that's allowed."

"You're impossible, Waylon."

I grin. "And you love it, baby."

"I'll talk to you later, Waylon."

I nod. "Count on it. I love you."

"I love you, handsome." She hangs up. I sit there for a second, holding my phone. Aaron nudges me with his beer bottle.

"You got it *bad*, man. But never call a woman *crazy*."

I shake my head, slipping my phone back into my pocket. "Yeah. I know." The fire crackles and the surrounding conversation picks back up, but my mind is still on her.

The next morning, the scent of bacon and coffee cuts through the heated morning air as I stretch, rolling out the stiffness in my shoulders. The fire's burned down to embers, and Aaron is hunched over the makeshift grill, flipping eggs with a focus he usually saves for work.

"Man, this is the best part of campin'," Ramirez says, kicking back in his chair, arms behind his head. "Wakin' up to the smell of bacon and somebody else cookin' it."

Donald tosses a piece of firewood into the pit as he humphs. "Yeah, 'cause we all know your lazy ass ain't gettin' up first to do it."

Ramirez grins. "Damn right. Why would I when y'all do it for me?"

I shake my head, grabbing a tin mug and pouring myself some of the thick, black coffee from the percolator. Settling onto a cooler, I stretch my legs out as the conversation shifts. Aaron flips a piece of bacon onto a plate, glancing up. "So, I finally got the house all ready for Flora to move in."

Ramirez lets out a low whistle. "Damn. You two are doin' this, huh?"

Aaron nods, excitement flickers in his eyes. "Yeah. Feels right."

Donald scoffs. "Jesus. You *sound* like a man about to propose."

Aaron shrugs. "Would that be such a bad thing?"

The guys go quiet for a beat before Ramirez groans. "Shit, man. Not you too. One minute you're livin' the good life. Next, you're buyin' matchin' pajamas for Christmas cards."

Aaron shrugs. "Yeah, well, when you got the right one, it doesn't feel like settling—feels like the next step." He stays silent for a moment as his dark eyes reflect. "I think I'm close to proposing if living together works. My dad called last week. We talked about it. I think I'm ready."

Ramirez shakes his head. "That's what they all say in the beginnin'. Then before you know it, you're sneakin' cigars in the garage and pretendin' you don't hear your wife yellin' about the dishes."

Jackman speaks up, low but certain. "It ain't about avoidin' the hard stuff. It's about choosin' the right person to do the hard stuff with." That shuts everyone up for a second. Jackman doesn't speak often, but when he does, it's usually worth listening to.

I chuckle, sipping my coffee. "Ramirez, you wouldn't trade it for anythin', huh?"

Ramirez's grin softens a little. "Nah. Not a damn thing." He picks up his mug, swirling the last bit of coffee. "Marriage ain't easy, but if you got the right woman, you figure it out."

Aaron hums in agreement. "Yeah. That's what I want with Flora."

I watch him for a second, taking in the ease of his words. He knows what he wants, and he's not afraid to go after it—I envy that. With Khloe, certainty is the one thing I can't seem to hold on to. She's always on my mind, even when I try to push her out. Last night, hearing her made everything settle—made me feel anchored to something real. But I also heard the hesitation, the doubt she won't say out loud. I get it. I really do. I can't express myself. I keep my emotions in check before I give them all away.

I've never been the guy to give a woman reasons to believe I'll stick around. Hell, I was the one who never stayed. Besides Caroline, my life afterwards was built on this reputation of being the guy who didn't belong to anyone. And now, I belong to *her*.

Then there's our third. Any guy would like a third in their relationship, but her abandonment issue is ours. Maybe I haven't done enough to reassure her, but it's not my thing. She's just too damn used to people leaving.

Aaron flips another strip of bacon and glances at me. "Waylon, what about you? You and Khloe ever talked about the future like that?"

I take a slow sip of coffee. "You really think I'd tell *you* before I told her?"

Ramirez chuckles. "Smart man."

Aaron shakes his head, amused. "Yeah, yeah. Keep your secrets, ya selfish bastard."

Jackman glances over, his tone casual but pointed. "She sounds like she calms you down." I say nothing, finishing my coffee. Jackman just nods. "Don't mess that up."

I chuckle, but I still don't speak. I'll be home soon, and I'll have time to remind her who she belongs to.

Chapter 36

Doubts Linger

The ER is its usual chaotic mess, but after all this time in the trenches, the noise and rush barely faze us. The fluorescent lights hum faintly overhead as I push a cart of supplies down the hall. Missy falls into step beside me, a clipboard tucked under her arm.

"Sooooo," Missy says, adjusting her ponytail. "How's Mr. Cowboy doing? Still blowing up your phone every five minutes?"

I shake my head. "Funny you should ask. He called me yesterday... after I sent him one text to check in."

Missy raises an eyebrow. "One text?"

"Yes, one," I say, parking the cart by the supply closet. "And then he says, 'You're like a crazy girlfriend.'"

Missy bursts out laughing, leaning against the wall as I dig through the cart for gloves. "Oh no, he didn't."

"Oh, he did. Remember that night he called like five times in a row? Yet *I'm* the crazy one?"

Missy laughs harder, clutching her side. "The audacity of men, honestly. So, what'd you say?"

"I called him out," I reply, standing up and crossing my

arms. "Told him if I'm crazy, he is too."

Missy snickers, shaking her head. "Good for you. Did he back down?"

"He laughed it off," I say, smiling despite myself. "Said he didn't mind because…" I clear my throat, copying his drawl. "It keeps things interestin'."

Missy pretends to swoon. "Oh, of course. Classic smooth-talker move. How did *you* feel about it, though?"

I hesitate, leaning on the cart. "I don't know. Sometimes it's sweet, you know? Like he really cares, and it's nice to feel that… attention. But other times, it's overwhelming."

Missy nods. "Sounds like he's a lot."

"We both are. He's not trying to be overbearing. That's just… how he is. But sometimes I know we both need space, and I don't know how to tell him that."

Missy tilts her head. "Have you tried just… telling him?"

I snort, shaking my head. "Oh, sure. 'Hey, Waylon, stop calling me so much!' That's gonna go over great."

"It might," Missy says with a shrug. "If he cares about you, he'll listen. And if he doesn't, well… maybe that's something to think about."

I sigh, staring at the cart but not really seeing it. "You're right. I just… I don't want to screw this up. He's a good guy—a little intense."

Missy pats my arm as a patient's monitor beeps in the distance, pulling her attention. "You'll figure it out, Khlo. Just remember, relationships are supposed to make you feel supported, not smothered."

As we head to separate duties, her words stick with me, settling in the back of my mind like a pebble in my shoe. She's right; I need to say something. The question is whether I have the balls to do it.

Chapter 37

Impending Separation

Conversations and clicking of keyboards fill the Marshal's office as I lean back in my chair, rolling a pen between my fingers. It's been another quiet week, mostly paperwork and following up on details from my last case. I've been using the home time to catch up on sleep and spend as much time with Khloe as I can.

I glance at the clock, debating whether I have time to grab a coffee before the next briefing. My boss, Deputy Chief Marshal Jones, steps into the bullpen. A broad-shouldered, big bald man with a presence that quiets a room without a word.

"Rhodes," he calls, nodding toward his office. "Need a minute."

I follow him to his office, closing the door behind me. He motions for me to take a seat while he leans on his desk with a file in hand.

"We've got a situation," he starts, flipping open the file. "Task force out in Nevada requested backup. They're hunting down a fugitive tied to some cartel activity—real nasty piece of shit."

"Alright," I say, leaning forward. "What's the plan?"

Jones' eyes meet mine. "You're going with Brooks. It's gonna be a long one. Could be weeks, maybe longer."

This is the first extended assignment since I started seeing Khloe. Her face flashes in my mind, and the way she holds onto me a little tighter lately.

"When do I leave?"

"End of the week," he answers. "I know it's short notice, but you and Brooks are some of the best we've got for this kind of operation. They need you."

I nod, standing. "Got it. I'll start preppin'."

Jones claps a hand on my shoulder as I head for the door. "Keep your head on straight out there, Rhodes."

That evening, I pull into Khloe's driveway; the news sits heavy on my chest. She opens the door before I even knock. Her face lights up when she sees me.

"Hey," she says, stepping aside. "I wasn't expecting you tonight."

"Needed to see you." I press a kiss to her temple as I walk past her into the living room.

She follows, her brows knitting together as she picks up on my mood. "What's wrong?" she asks, sitting on the couch beside me.

I take a deep breath, combing my fingers through my hair. "Got called in by my boss today. I'm headin' out on an assignment at the end of the week. Could be gone for a while."

Her face falls, and I hate the way her shoulders tense and her smile fades. "How long is a while?"

"Could be a few weeks. Maybe more." I reach for her hand, holding it tight. "It's a big case, Khlo. They need me."

She nods slowly, her eyes fixed on our joined hands. "I get it. It's your job. It's just…"

"What?" I ask gently.

She looks up. "This sounds harsh, Waylon. When you mentioned in the beginning that you might be sent away for periods of time, I wondered if that was something I could handle. If I'm strong enough to... to wait."

I slide closer, cupping her face. "Khlo, listen to me. You're the strongest person I know. I'm not askin' you to wait for nothin'. I'm askin' because I don't want to do this without you."

"What if one day you don't come back?"

"I will. Every time. I don't care how far they send me or how long it takes. I'll always come back to you."

We sit there for a moment, silence stretching between us. Finally, she nods, her hand reaching up to cover mine. "You're perfect."

"Perfect for you," I reply, my warm boyish smile filling my face.

"Promise me you'll call or text when you can. Even if it's just a word or two," she insists. A crease forms between her brows as her mouth opens, then closes again.

Damn it, Khloe.

I get that life hasn't exactly been kind. But I'm not like those other people. Haven't I proven that I'm not the man who cuts and runs? Every time we take a step forward, her insecurities yank us two steps back.

I hate that I'm even annoyed right now because I know where this comes from. I'm fighting a losing battle against the ghosts in her head. I pull her into my arms, hoping she feels the truth in the way I hold her, even if her mind keeps trying to sabotage it.

"I promise, Khlo. You mean so much to me already. I love you. Never forget that."

"I love you, too."

Chapter 38

Echoes of Abandonment

The sound of brakes squeaking makes my stomach flip. I already know it's him—can feel him before I see him. When I open the door, Waylon's standing there, face shadowed by the dim porch light. I smile automatically, warmth rising in my chest. His movements are cautious. Something's wrong. I follow him into the living room, watching the way his shoulders seem heavier than usual, like he's carrying something he's not sure how to put down.

His job is sending him away. *They need him.* And what about me? I pause, suddenly hearing Flora seep into my thoughts. *Say it, Khloe. Tell him what you need.* But the words stick to the roof of my mouth, tangled with every other fear I've swallowed down. I can see it in his face, the way my words land harder than I mean them to. His words should feel like an anchor, but all I can think about is how many times I've heard promises before. Promises that people never kept.

I'll always come back to you.

I want to believe him, but history tells me otherwise. And here I am, still waiting for proof that I won't be left behind again.

But I have to be better for him. I can feel his eyes on me, waiting for me to let this be enough. And I want to. But the war inside me isn't so easily won.

I have to stop being so afraid. He pulls me into his arms, holding me tight like he's trying to fuse himself into my bones. I breathe him in, trying to remind myself that he means every word he says. But as I rest my head against his chest, listening to the thrum of his heartbeat, that stupid voice in the back of my mind whispers, *What if he doesn't?*

I squeeze my eyes shut and will the thought away.

The frequent rhythm of beeping monitors and the smell of blood fill the room as I adjust the bandage on my patient's arm. I catch sight of Flora across the room as she is expertly wheeling a patient back into their room. I walk over to her as she exits the other room.

"God, I'm ready to clock out," Flora groans, pushing a stray hair from her face. "And just in time for drinks with the boys tonight and for them to leave us."

"Yeah, I'm trying not to think about it—a few weeks will feel like a lifetime."

Flora looks over at me, her normal teasing smile sitting on her lips. "You're really gonna miss him, huh?"

I roll my eyes. "I mean, yeah. The second he's gone, I'll imagine every worst-case scenario."

Flora places a reassuring arm around my shoulder as we walk back to the nurse's station. "They'll be fine. Aaron's got Waylon, and Waylon's... well, Waylon. He could probably handle the whole thing solo if he had to."

Before I can respond, a young aide named Ella walks by, balancing a stack of linens. She pauses mid-step, her brows knitting together as she glances at us.

"Wait," Ella says curiously. "Did you just say *Waylon*?"

I level a flat stare at her, lips pressed into a hard line. "Uh, yeah. Why?"

Ella smirks. "Waylon Rhodes?"

My heart pounds. "...Yeah. What about him?"

Ella shifts her weight. "Wow. Small world. My sister used to hang out with him a lot back in the day. Actually, she and her friend."

"Hang out?"

Ella shrugs, her smile widening. "You know. *Hang out*. They both had their turns. He's kind of a... *legend*, if you didn't know."

The air tastes stale as I take a deep breath in. Flora steps in. She doesn't yell, but every word lands like a slap. "Ella, don't you have beds to make?"

Ella blinks, as if only now realizing she crossed a line. "Oh, yeah. Sorry. Just thought it was funny, that's all." She walks off, words hanging in the air like smoke.

I stare at Flora. She grabs my arm and pulls me into the empty break room. "Don't," Flora says, pointing a finger at me. "Don't spiral."

I laugh bitterly, pacing the small space. "Did you hear what she just said? Jesus, Flora. How many more of them are there?"

Flora crosses her arms. "Khlo, you knew Waylon had a past—a laundry list even. He's told you about some of it, but that's *exactly* what it is: his *past*. That guy's head-over-heels for you. You know that."

I sink into a chair, my hands in my hair. "It's not just about the numbers, Flora. Ella just waltzed in and dropped a group of sluts on us. And I have to sit here pretending it doesn't sting."

Flora sits beside me. "I get it. I do. But think about who Waylon is now. He's a changed man with you. Aaron says he's done a one-eighty since you came into the picture."

I look up, feeling small. "What if one day I'm just another story he tells?"

Flora's expression softens as she takes my hand in hers. "Tell him how you're feeling. You lay it all out there. But don't you dare let some gossipy aide's comments ruin what you've got."

I nod. "Yeah. You're right."

"Of course I'm right," Flora says, squeezing my hand. "And next time Ella so much as looks at you funny, I'll trip her with a bedpan full of piss."

I laugh, the tension easing slightly. "Thanks, Flora."

"That's what I'm here for." Flora winks. "Now, let's finish this shift before I lose what's left of my sanity."

As we return to work, Flora's words stuck with me. Maybe it was time to talk to Waylon. Not just about his past, but about the insecurities that moments like this stirred in me. I turn my focus back to finishing our shift and seeing him tonight.

I spot Waylon immediately as we step through the door. His tall frame leans against the bar, head tipped back as he laughs at something the brunette beside him says. My stomach twists into a knot so tight I feel like I might be sick. He doesn't see me.

"Khlo," Flora whispers, tugging at my arm. "Don't jump to conclusions. You—"

"It's fine." I throw my hand up, cutting her off. "It's not like I'm his wife or anything."

Her eyes narrow, but she doesn't speak.

"Don't tell them I was here." I turn, leaving Flora behind. My chest is heavy with memories of that night with Derrick.

When Waylon shows up at my house, I'm sitting on the couch, arms crossed tight over my chest. He freezes when he sees me, the relaxed smile disappearing in an instant.

"Khlo. You're up late. Why didn't you answer my call—"

"Spare me the small talk," I snap, standing abruptly. "I saw you tonight."

His eyes flick back and forth, brows pinched like the words don't quite add up. Genuine confusion flashes across his face. "Saw me what?"

"Flirting with that brunette."

He exhales, rubbing the back of his neck. "Khloe, it wasn't like that—"

"Don't, Waylon. I saw the way she looked at you, the way you looked back."

"I wasn't lookin' at her like anythin'," he mutters. "You're readin' into somethin' that ain't there."

"Maybe I wouldn't have to if you hadn't been with every girl that ever existed," I fire back.

Waylon takes a step closer, eyes narrowing. His words carry sarcasm, not a hint of heat behind them. "Seriously? After every damn thing I've done to prove I'm all in with you, you still don't trust me?"

I hesitate. Shit. "It's not about trust, Waylon," I say. "It's about... feeling like I'm worthy. Like you're not just waiting for someone better to come along." I throw up my hands. "I'm a mess."

He stares at me for a moment. "Khloe, I'm not goin' anywhere. I could have any woman I want, but I am here with you. If you think for one second there's anyone... *anyone*... who could mean more to me than you, then I ain't been doin' my job right."

I shake my head, my emotions bubbling to the surface. "Then why does it feel like this?"

Waylon steps closer, closing the distance between us, grabbing the nape of my neck. "Because you've been hurt before, darlin'. I can't erase that, but I can tell you this: I ain't that guy. I'm not replacin' you. You're it for me, Khloe."

Tears form in my eyes, but I don't look away from him. "I'm scared, Waylon."

"I know. I realize I've treated women as a transaction before. But I ain't with you now. I'd kill for you, Khlo. If you ever doubt that, you tell me, and I'll spend every damn day remindin' you."

I close my eyes, a single tear slipping down my cheek. "It's hard feeling like this."

"I know," he murmurs, brushing the tear away with his thumb. "But you don't have to carry it alone. You've got me, and you always will."

He steps back. "You're mine, Khloe. You know I'm yours, too. Every stubborn, messy, broken piece of me."

A shaky laugh escapes me as I wipe at my face. "You always know what to say, don't you?"

He grins, erasing the pressure in the room, pulling me into his arms. "Only when it comes to you, darlin'." My self-sabotage disappears. I have to remind myself to do better for both of us.

"Khlo, you trust me, don't you?" He dips into that commanding voice that always makes my knees feel weak.

"Yes."

"Say it."

His hand brushes along my jaw, tilting my face up to meet his. "I need to hear it, Khloe."

"I trust you," I whisper.

He smiles. "Good. No matter what doubts are in your head, no matter what fears you've got, we're in this together. Got it?"

"Yes."

"Good girl," he says, his thumb tracing the curve of my bottom lip. His praise awakens my need for him and for us. "Go to the bedroom. Take off your clothes—wait for me. I'll be there in a minute."

I hesitate for a second, but the look in his eyes leaves no room for argument. I turn and walk down the hallway, pulse racing as I enter the room. I strip down, trembling with excitement as I fold my clothes and set them on the chair. I hear the thud of his boots. The vulnerability of standing here, bare and waiting, sends a shudder down my spine.

When he steps into the room, his worn gray T-shirt clings, showing off his broad shoulders. There's something about the way he moves that draws me in every time. He's proud and unhurried.

"On your knees," he instructs.

I lower myself to the floor, the carpet soft beneath me as I sit back on my heels. He approaches slowly. I look up as he hovers above me, his bulge close to my eye level.

"Take off my boots, darlin'."

I reach out, untying them, lace by lace, releasing his feet from each boot and then set them at the edge of the bed. He reaches over to my chair, grabbing my belt from my folded pants, and then he kneels in front of me.

Our eyes meet as dominance fills his face. "Let me take care of you—even when you don't think you need it."

"I will."

He reaches for my hands, wrapping my belt around my wrists with practiced ease. The leather cools my heated skin.

"You're safe with me," he murmurs, his lips brushing my temple. "I need you to remember that."

"I do."

"Stand," he commands.

I move without question. He moves behind me, hands sliding over my shoulders and arms, leaving a trail of heat in their wake. When his fingers skim along my love handles, I can't help the soft gasp that escapes my lips.

"You're beautiful, Khloe. Every piece of you. And you're mine."

"I'm yours," I whisper.

"Good girl," he praises, his hands moving lower to tease my bundle of nerves. I curve into his hand as my core becomes saturated with need. "Hmm," he moans, then leads me to the bed, lowering me onto my stomach, his hands mapping every inch of me. When I think he's done, he reaches for the nightstand where we stashed our new toys.

"On all fours, baby."

I obey. My gaze flicks up just in time to watch him pull the anal plug from its case. He spits on it, fingers brushing between my cheeks, tracing my opening with care.

"Breathe. Don't fight it," he says, guiding the plug to my ass.

I inhale deeply. The plug slips past the tight resistance, and I tense, then melt. The stretch sends heat prickling down my spine as it locks into place, a wholeness blooming inside me. He pauses there, one hand soothing me into relaxation. I shift slightly, adjusting to the weight. My breath comes in jagged bursts. My body is learning the shape of this new submission in real time.

Then comes the flogger. Leather against skin, biting and abrupt. The sting spreads seconds after the strike.

"One," I call out on instinct. The combination of the anal plug and the next swing of the flogger makes my head spin. "Two." My body clinches around the plug, embracing the pleasure.

"Do you feel how much I love you?"

I nod, tears pricking my eyes. "Yes."

"There's a good girl," he continues, his movements slow and calculated, his words a constant reassurance.

Every touch, every kiss feels like a promise, a declaration that cuts through my fears. By the time he finally unbinds my wrists and pulls me into his arms, I feel freer. His touch grounds me in ways I didn't realize I needed, like the weight I've been carrying has been lifted, if only for a little while.

"I'll always come back to you, Khlo," he whispers, his lips brushing against my hair. "Always, baby." I close my eyes, letting his words sink into me as he slides into me with a threatening thrust.

The next morning, I wake to Waylon packing up random things in my room. The realization of him leaving today dawns on me. The ache starts slowly, but I fight it. I can do this—I have to.

His eyes meet mine, and they light up with that familiar warmth. "Good morning, baby," he says softly. "I hope I didn't wake you."

I smile sleepily, doing my best to keep steady. "No, just felt your absence."

He lowers himself onto the bed next to me; the mattress shifts under him. Tracing my face with his finger, he says, "One of these days we're goin' to wake up next to each other every day... for the rest of our lives." My stomach breaks out into instant butterflies as I cover my face with my hands, trying to suppress the nervous laugh bubbling up. "Khloe, stop hiding," he growls. Peeking out from behind my fingers, I find his eyes again. "You have no insecurities now. I put that shit to rest."

I jump up and settle naked in his lap. My hands rest on his chest, his heart pounding. "Why are you so perfect?" I ask, trembling with a mix of awe and disbelief. "I'll always have these issues. Twenty-five years is a long time to just forget."

His hand raises up to my throat and grabs me in his possessive, gentle manner. His stare burns into me, grounding me in this moment. "It won't take me that long. A woman like you deserves to feel like the woman I know you are. You deserve happiness and so much more. Stop lettin' bullshit weigh your mind down."

A shaky laugh comes out as I drop my eyes from the intensity of his stare. "Waylon Rhodes, are you trying to make me a wife or something?"

His hold on my throat tightens. "Why, Khloe Navarro... Yes, I am," he replies smoothly.

My eyes snap up, and I search his face. His tone matches the serious expression etched there. I stop breathing. "You're crazy."

His expression is neutral, but his words are playful. "Yes, I am, especially about you. We're perfect for each other."

His words settle deep into my bones, taking root. I can only stare at him. If this is how he says goodbye every time he leaves for work, I will push him out the door next time.

"Waylon, I love you," I whisper.

"I love you, baby—don't forget it." He pulls me in, his lips brushing against mine in a kiss that sends heat coursing through my veins. "And don't let yourself second-guess while I'm gone. I'm yours, darlin', and you're mine."

Before I can respond, his lips are back on mine, deeper this time—sealing a promise only we can feel. We sink back into the bed, tangled in each other, to say goodbye for just a few weeks.

Chapter 39

Road Trip Reflections

The road ahead to our assignment is long and empty. I lean back in the seat, boots on the dash, eyes hidden behind my sunglasses. Aaron's been quiet for the past half hour, probably waiting for me to crack first. He doesn't have to wait long.

"Khloe was waitin' on the couch when I got home. Arms crossed—didn't even say hi. She saw me at the bar with that brunette."

"Were you flirting?" he asks.

I give him a look. "Come on, man. I was just gettin' a beer. That girl came up to me. I barely looked at her."

Aaron shrugs. "Then what's the problem?"

"She thought I did. I think she thought the chick was a girl I used to have fun with."

Aaron sighs. "Dude, who haven't you been with?"

"Plenty." I chuckle. "The problem is, Khloe doesn't feel worthy. Said maybe I'm just waiting for someone better."

"Damn."

"Yeah." I rub my hand down my face. "Told her I'm not going anywhere. That I want all of her. The messy, scared, overthinkin' parts."

"You think she believed you?"

"Not at first." I lean my head back, eyes on the ceiling. "She was locked in her own head. I had to pull her out."

Aaron smirks. "Let me guess. You didn't use words." I don't answer. He laughs under his breath. "Yeah. That's what I thought."

"It wasn't just about sex," I say quietly. "Not really. I needed her to feel safe. Needed to remind her we're real—that she can believe in us, even when her fear tells her otherwise."

Aaron glances over. The teasing fades. "And now?"

"By morning, she was different. Like she wasn't holding the world up by herself anymore."

I stare out the window, the image of her curled up in bed still fresh. Her eyes heavy and her body full of need.

"She said I love you first a few weeks ago," I murmur. "Caught me off guard."

Aaron's brows lift. "Did you respond?"

"Yeah, eventually... God help me, I'm gone for her."

He nods slowly. "You think she's the real thing?"

I look over at him, dead serious. "She is. I'm going to marry her. Don't care how long it takes. I'll keep reminding her every day, every time I come home, that we're meant to be. That's the whole damn story."

Aaron's face is part surprised, part grinning. "And you're sticking to it. Huh, never in a million years thought I'd hear my boy say shit like this. I'm happy for you, Rhodes."

I smile. "Appreciate it, Brooks. Think Flora's gonna survive six weeks without you?"

He laughs. "She said she's gonna spend the whole time reminding me what I'm missing. The girl has no worries." He falls quiet for a second, eyes back on the road before he says, "Six weeks."

I sigh. "Six too many." Because I already feel the space where Khloe's supposed to be.

Chapter 40

Waiting and Wondering

I curl up on the couch, my legs tucked under me, a steaming mug of coffee warming my hands. Flora paces the kitchen, her phone cradled between her ear and shoulder as she talks to Aaron. Her laughter bounces off the walls, light and carefree.

She is utterly certain that everything will work out. It hits me in a place I don't want to acknowledge. They've only been gone a few days, and it already feels like a century. I've texted Waylon a bit, sent a few photos, but my messages haven't been delivered.

When Flora finally hangs up, she wanders into the living room, plopping down beside me with an energy I can't quite match.

"Waylon told Aaron to say '*Hi darling*' to you," she says with a smile, setting her phone on the coffee table. "God, I miss Aaron already, but he's loving it. You can hear it. I think I'm gonna finally move in when they get back."

I manage a small smile, setting my mug down. "Good, I'm happy for you two. Do you genuinely feel okay about him being away for such a long time?"

Flora shrugs, pulling her knees to her chest. "Yeah, I mean it sucks, but I knew what I was signing up for. Aaron wanted something like this. I won't hold him back."

Her reaction makes me feel like a failure, twisting my stomach in knots. "But doesn't it get lonely? What if something happens to him?"

Flora tilts her head. "Of course it's hard. But I have faith in him, Khlo. And I trust he will be as safe as possible. He'll come home when he can."

I stare at her. It seems so easy for her to say. But I'm standing on a cliff's edge, convincing myself not to look down. "I don't know if I'm built like that," I admit quietly. "With Waylon gone, it's like this pressure in my chest. Like I can't breathe until I know he's okay. I wonder whether I can handle this—I'm not confident like you."

Flora's hand finds mine, giving it a reassuring squeeze. "That's because you're scared. You can handle it. But give yourself a break. You're basically a virgin to this. It's not like there's a handbook."

I shake my head. "It's more than that. I can't shake the feeling that one day he's just... not going to come back."

Flora leans closer, more serious this time. "Khlo, Waylon's not your average Joe."

"I hope so. He insinuated he wanted to marry me. How can I be so sure?"

"Khloe, what! I see the way he looks at you. That man's in deep."

I sigh.

She pushes on. "Men don't just offer marriage for flings, Khloe. But you've got to meet him in the middle, girl. You seriously need a shrink."

Her words linger in the air. Doubt is a stubborn thing. After being damaged, it's a part of who I am.

Chapter 41

Messages from Afar

The desert sun hangs heavy in the sky, the heat radiating off the cracked ground beneath my boots. We've been working on this case for days, holed up in safe houses, tracking leads that take us further into the middle of nowhere. No cell service, no contact with the outside world. Just me, my team, and the constant buzz of adrenaline. I'm jealous Aaron has gone into town for errands and has spoken to Flora.

This situation demands focus, yet Khloe runs through my head nonstop. I've caught myself reaching for my phone more than once, only to remember it's useless out here. The thought of her on the other end, wondering why she hasn't heard from me, twists something deep in my chest.

When we finally wrap things up and I make it back to civilization, the first thing I do is power on my phone. Notifications flood the screen between messages and work updates. I look only for Khloe's name.

KHLOE

> Hey, just thinking about you. Hope you're safe.

KHLOE

> The house feels quieter when you're gone. Miss you.

KHLOE

> Flora and I stayed in last night. We ordered too much takeout, and she said you'd eat all the leftovers in one sitting. She's probably right.

I smile at that one, already picturing the smug grin Flora must've had when she said it. I keep scrolling, the ache of missing her easing with every message. Then, the pictures start. One of her on the couch with a blanket pulled up to her chin, a half-eaten carton of Chinese food on the table. Another of the sunset on the River Walk, the sky painted in dreamlike colors. Then, her in scrubs, holding up a peace sign in the hospital break room.

My favorite, though, is the one of her smiling into the camera wearing my flannel, no makeup, her hair a mess. Just her. Pure beauty. The caption reads: *Miss your face, cowboy.*

I sit there scrolling through every message, every photo, my chest heavy with gratitude.

God, she's trying. She doesn't say it outright, but I can feel it in every word, every image. She's fighting against her fears, against the walls she's built, to let me in. And it's working.

Chapter 42

Reaching out, Spiraling Down

I'm sitting in our small backyard, the sun soaking into my skin. The scent of tamales, fresh-cut grass, and warm pavement drifts through the Alamo neighborhood. My phone is balanced on my knee as I scroll through my reading app. It's been days since I've heard from Waylon. I know he's off the grid, but the silence still gnaws at me. I send the messages anyway, more for myself than for him. Little moments, pieces of my day, to feel like he's part of it somehow.

I tell myself he'll respond when he can. When my phone buzzes late in the evening, my heart leaps and hands shake as I open the message.

WAYLON

Darlin, you have no idea how much I needed this. Thank you for every single one of these.

I smile, relief washing over me.

KHLOE

> You're welcome. I wanted you to feel like you weren't so far away. I felt a little crazy sending them all.

The reply comes fast.

WAYLON

> You did. And Khlo, I miss your face too. More than I can say. I love that you're crazy about me.

I stare at the words, my heart doing that ridiculous little flutter thing it does only for him. When he says what I need to hear without even trying.

A little later, the hum of the TV fills the living room, but I barely notice it as now I sit cross-legged on the floor, flipping through a stack of mail I've neglected all week. The texts from Waylon are still fresh in my mind, lingering like the echo of a song you can't shake. Flora prances in the front door. She plops down on the couch, her legs dangling over the armrest while she scrolls through her phone.

Flora tosses her phone onto the cushion and stretches, her gaze landing on me. "Alright, spill. What's with the dreamy little smile? You look like you're starring in a rom-com."

I laugh, shaking my head. "I don't know what you're talking about."

"Bullshit," she says, sitting up. "Did Mr. Cowboy find time to call, and now you're all heart-eyes over there?"

I roll my eyes, but the heat rising to my cheeks betrays me. "He answered my messages today. He said he loved all of them."

Flora raises an eyebrow, her grin widening. "All of them? How many did you send, Khlo?"

I shrug, focusing a little too hard on the mail in my lap. "A few."

"A few," she repeats, dripping with mockery. "How many is a few? Three? Ten? Fifty?"

"Flora," I groan, but I can't help laughing. "Not that many. Enough to keep him in the loop, you know? To make him feel like he wasn't missing everything while he was gone."

Her teasing expression softens as she sits forward, resting her elbows on her knees. "That's actually really sweet, Khlo, and a big deal for you."

I look up at her, confused. "What do you mean?"

She tilts her head, giving me that knowing look she's mastered over the years. "You opening up, putting yourself out there. It's not exactly your default setting."

I sigh, leaning back against the couch. "It wasn't easy, honestly. Every time I sent something, I kept thinking, *What if he doesn't care?* But I don't know... I guess it felt important. Like even if he didn't see them right away, he'd know I was thinking about him."

"And he clearly appreciated it," Flora points out. "So why the hesitation?"

I bite my lip, staring at the stack of open envelopes. "Because I'm still scared, Flora. What if he stops appreciating it? What if one day I send those messages, and he doesn't care? Or worse, what if I stop sending them because I'm afraid of that happening?"

"Khlo. You can't live your life waiting for bad things to happen. If you're worrying, you're never gonna enjoy the ride."

I inhale, rubbing my temples. "I know. I'm trying. But it's hard not to think about... everything. It's like every time I let myself depend on someone, they leave."

Flora slides off the couch and sits beside me, her hand resting on my knee. "You need help. Waylon's not your mom or Derrick or anyone else. And he's pretty damn crazy about you."

I smile faintly, looking over at her. "I know he is. And when he said he loved my messages, I felt... safe. Like maybe I don't have to hold everything so close all the time."

"Exactly," Flora says, squeezing my knee. "You deserve to feel that, Khlo. You deserve someone who makes you feel safe, and if that's Waylon, then stop overthinking and just let yourself have it."

I nod slowly, her comfort settling in my chest. "You're right."

Flora grins, leaning back with an exaggerated sigh. "Of course I am. I'm always right."

I laugh, swatting her arm. "Don't push it."

As we settle back into the peaceful rhythm of our friendship, I can't help but feel a little lighter. Flora's right—I can enjoy the ride.

I drag myself into the break room, the exhaustion of back-to-back shifts pressing heavy on my bones. The hospital is always too bright, too loud, too full of people who need things from me. All I want is a moment to breathe. I check my phone. Nothing from Waylon.

I tell myself it's fine. He's busy. He warned me that things would get hectic. But the silence makes my chest feel tight, like I'm bracing for something I can't name. I try to distract myself by checking on the NP scholarship application. I applied last week and haven't heard a word.

Missy is sitting at the table, her feet propped up on the chair next to her, scrolling through her phone. She's half-listening to Flora, who's across from her, grinning at her screen as she taps out a text.

"God, I swear," Flora says with a dreamy sigh. "Aaron says he misses me more times than I can even respond to.

It's like he wants to make sure I know I'm on his mind."

I force a smile. "That's sweet."

"It's how it should be," Missy chimes in, not looking up. "It's easy to send a quick 'I miss you' text."

My eyes cast down just as Flora glances at me, catching the way my smile doesn't quite reach my eyes. "Waylon's just on a separate, connected assignment than Aaron," she says. "It's tricky when they're in the field."

I nod, but it doesn't settle me. Instead, I reread old messages, letting my thumb hover over the text thread. He *always* checks in when he can.

Flora and I drive home together after work. She wanted to watch movies together tonight, but I can't get myself out of bed. It's past midnight, and I'm staring at the ceiling. The sheets feel cold, the space beside me untouched. My phone is on my chest, vibrating with a notification. My heart leaps, but when I check, it's just Flora again.

FLORA

You okay?

KHLOE

Yeah, just tired.

I'm lying. I close our texts and open Waylon's. I scroll through, stopping at an old one.

WAYLON

You're mine, Khlo.

WAYLON

> No matter where I am, you're always on my mind.

I'm foolish waiting for a call that isn't coming. I open our chat, my fingers shaking as I type.

> I miss you. I don't know if I can do this…

I stare at the screen but delete it before I can hit send.

The next day, Flora drags me out for drinks, claiming I need a distraction. The bar is warm and full of conversation and good music. The scent of whiskey reminds me of Waylon. Flora orders us shots, sliding one across the table.

"To our men who will be home before we know it," she says, clinking her glass to mine. I swallow it down, the burn spreading in my chest, but it does nothing to loosen the ache lodged in my ribs. Flora leans forward, resting her chin on her hand. "So, what's going on? And don't say 'nothing.'"

I let out a humorless laugh. "I feel like an idiot."

Her brows furrow. "Why?"

I exhale, setting my drink down. "I sit up at night waiting for his calls like a desperate teenager. Because I read old messages, like they mean something now."

Flora's expression softens. "Khlo, come on."

"This scares the hell out of me. Because what if this is how it's always going to be? Waiting. Me overthinking and wondering if I'm just someone he holds onto when it's convenient."

Flora grabs my hand. "You know that's not true."

I shake my head, my vision blurring. "I know nothing."

After days of overthinking and just quick Waylon check-ins, I make a decision. I sit on my bed, the glow of my phone casting long shadows across the room as I stare at the text I've rewritten at least five times. My thumb hovers over the send button, my mind racing. The words feel oddly fitting, yet flawed.

KHLOE:

> Waylon, I think we need some space. I don't think this is working the way we both hoped.

I bite my lip, my pulse thudding in my ears. His absence pulls at me piece by piece; it terrifies me. I feel guilty doing this, but I have to protect myself. I don't know if I'll survive if he ever leaves and stays gone.

Chapter 43

Confrontation

The night air is thick with humidity, the heat of it setting sweat on my back as I sit in the second row of the SUV, parked off a quiet dirt road. Aaron's in the front seat, scanning the area, while I keep my eyes on the rundown cabin a few yards behind us from the backseat, waiting for the green light to move.

I shouldn't be on my phone. Not out here. But fuck, I miss her. I pull it from my pocket, keeping it low just in case Aaron glances back. I fire off a message before I can think better of it.

WAYLON

> Just finishing up for the night. Missin you, darlin. How's your day been?

My tension eases when I see her name. But her response makes my breath stop. The words blur together, my pulse pounding as I read them again, as if I'm seeing them wrong.

What the hell does she mean by *space*?

My hands tighten around the phone, my jaw clenching so hard it aches. "Fuck," I mutter under my breath.

Aaron glances over. "Problem?"

I shake my head, trying to hold my composure. "Nah, just a text."

Aaron doesn't push, turning his attention back outside. "Are you good to focus?"

No, not even close. "Yeah."

I press the call button. She doesn't answer right away, and I hate the way my stomach twists. An eternity later, the phone stops ringing. She's quiet on the other end, barely audible.

"Hey."

I sit up straighter. "Khloe, what the hell is this?"

Aaron turns towards me with a questioning look.

Khloe hesitates before responding. "I... I think we need to take a step back." Her words are shaky, but she keeps going. "You being gone... it's made me think we moved too fast, and—"

"Too fast?" I snap, my frustration bleeding in. "Khloe, where is this comin' from?"

There's silence. I hate it because I know she's in her own head, letting fear write the script for her. Finally, she exhales. "I think... I need space, Waylon. You have a job to do. I don't know how to handle it."

I pinch the bridge of my nose, fighting the chaos crawling up my spine. "You don't know how to handle it, or you're holding on to fear?"

"What?"

"You're scared, admit it. Because this is *real*, and you don't know what to do with that—so instead of tellin' me, you're tryin' to run."

"That's not fair, Waylon," she snaps.

"Isn't it? You're so afraid of someone leavin' you, Khlo, that you're doin' the leavin' first just so you don't have to feel it. I've been right here, provin' it to you every damn chance I get, and now you wanna throw it all away *in a text*? Khloe, don't do this now. We need to have a conversation in person."

Silence.

I tempt her. "I guarantee I can make all those feelings melt away. I want you. I've owed it to myself to love who I love and want who I want."

"You don't understand what it's like to be abandoned. To always feel you're not enough," she whispers.

The words gut me because she believes them. And because I know that pain. "You think I don't understand?" I ask, softer now, more controlled. "Khloe, I've been left too. I've lost people who meant everything to me. But I don't push away the ones who *stay* because of it."

I hear her breath hitch, like my words finally landed. "I ain't perfect," I admit, passing a hand through my hair. "I know I come on strong, and I know I've got my own shit to work through. But I need you to meet me halfway. You gotta stop runnin' every time it gets hard."

She's quiet for a long time. When she finally speaks, it's barely above a whisper. "I don't know how to do this, Waylon."

"Do what?" I ask, my throat tight. "Be loved?"

Another silence. Then, the softest, most broken, "I'm sorry."

My chest aches for her. "You don't have to be sorry," I murmur. "You just gotta let me in. Let me stay."

She exhales shakily, and I can almost picture her curled up in bed, staring at her phone like it holds all the answers. "I'll try," she whispers.

I nod, even though she can't see me. "Good. 'Cause I'm not givin' up on this. On *us*." The line is quiet for a beat before I soften my tone. "Goodnight, Khloe."

She doesn't say it back. The call ends. I let my head fall back against the seat, staring up at the roof of the SUV. I hope I got through to her. I don't know if she'll wake up tomorrow and regret ever answering. But I know one thing: I love that woman. And no distance, no amount of fear, is gonna make that change.

Aaron, who'd been quiet up front, shifts in his seat. I hear the soft exhale of breath, the slight creak of the leather seat as he turns toward me. I don't look at him. My heart is still hammering, my grip on the phone too damn tight.

"You good?" Aaron finally asks.

I exhale, forcing my jaw to unclench. "Yeah."

Aaron snorts. "That's a lie."

I glance at him, a warning in my eyes, but he just shakes his head. "Man, I'm not trying to push, but I've known you long enough to know when you're at your wit's end. That conversation was some real shit."

I rub a hand over my face, trying to shake the stress of it. "She thinks she's doin' the right thing. Like she's protectin' herself from somethin' that ain't even happenin'."

Aaron nods, considering that. "She's scared, man. Doesn't mean she doesn't love you."

"I *know* she loves me," I snap, then immediately regret it. Aaron raises his brows but says nothing, just waits. I sigh, my chest feeling tight. "She just doesn't trust it. She doesn't trust herself not to fall apart while I'm gone."

Aaron leans back in his seat, tapping his fingers against the steering wheel. "What are you doing to fix that?"

I narrow my eyes. "What the hell does that mean?"

Aaron shrugs, turning fully to face me now. "It means you've spent all this time telling her you're not going anywhere, telling her she needs to trust you. Words aren't what she needs right now. Maybe she needs *proof*."

I scoff. "I've been provin' it."

"Have you?" Aaron counters. "Or have you ignored her needs this whole time? You keep telling her to meet you halfway, but if she's carrying all this mental load, you need to walk a little further than fifty percent." I grind my teeth, hating how much truth is in his words. I've been holding on so damn tight, but I haven't been letting her breathe either. Aaron shakes his head. "I know you love her. But if you want her to believe, you need to stop telling her to 'just trust it.' Show her why she *can*."

I don't answer, my fingers still wrapped around my phone. Thinking about the way her voice cracked when she said, *I don't know how to do this, Waylon.*

Aaron sighs, looking back out the windshield. "I'm not saying you have to fix everything for her. That's not your job. But you either fight *with* her, or you're just fighting to *keep* her. And those aren't the same thing."

I stare at the screen of my phone, Khloe's name still sitting at the top of my messages. I think about saying something that might soothe the storm inside her. But this fight she's internally battling, ain't one I can win with words. I have to let her *see* me still standing when the dust settles.

Chapter 44

Reconnection

After a long twelve-hour shift and ignoring some of my mother's prison phone calls, I've felt better for the last few weeks. I'm sprawled out on my bed, with a wine bottle nearing its end on the nightstand. Flora left for an overnight shift hours ago, leaving me alone with my thoughts. A dangerous thing, especially when I've had too much to drink. I stare at my phone, my fingers hovering over the keyboard. The silence in the house feels like it's pressing down on me, and my thoughts keep circling back to him.

Always Waylon.

The wine makes everything feel sharper, bigger, even cosmic. Like every moment in my life has been leading up to him. The thought feels too big to keep to myself, so I open our chat and start typing.

KHLOE

> Do you ever think about how crazy it is that we met?

> **KHLOE**
>
> Like out of all the people in the world, it's us?

I stare at the message for a second, then hit send before I can overthink it. A laugh bubbles out of me, and I pour another glass of wine. Before I know it, my fingers are moving again, the wine loosening words I'd been too afraid to say before.

> **KHLOE**
>
> It feels cosmic, Waylon. Like the universe was fucking conspiring to bring us together. Sorry, I'm a little drunk.

I let out a breath, my chest tightening as I stare at the screen. My thumb hovers over the keyboard again, and then I type the one thing that feels like it might burst out of me if I don't say it.

> **KHLOE**
>
> I fucking love you.

The euphoria of the moment crashes down around me. "Shit."

I set the phone down and bury my face in my hands. The wine makes the silence louder, the space between us bigger. Even through the haze of alcohol and regret, one thought remains: I meant every damn word.

Chapter 45

Presents

I run a hand through my hair, frustration biting at me. I'm on assignment, deep in hostile territory, where even a single text could be the difference between staying hidden or being compromised. Protocol is strict for a reason, but right now, it feels like a cruel joke.

My phone buzzes in my pocket. I shouldn't risk the glow of the screen, but something tells me it's her. I slip it out carefully, keeping it angled low. My stomach flips when I see Khloe's name. A flood of notifications fills the screen that I hadn't been able to check all day.

I scroll through them, one by one, my breath catching at the words she's sent. But damn it, I can't respond. Not yet. "I'm here," I whisper to myself, as if she could hear it. "I see you, Khlo."

The ache in my stomach spreads, a mix of pride and guilt. I'm so relieved she's letting me have these pieces of her. She's putting herself out there, but I can't let her know I've seen it. I set the phone down, staring at it like I can will it to let her know I'm here and that her words mean everything to me.

When the operation finally wraps the next day, and I'm cleared to check in, I don't waste a second. The first thing I do is open her messages again, letting the words sink in all over again, minus *that one*.

Her texts feel like a lifeline, a connection to something good and pure when I've been surrounded by chaos. Another photo comes in, one of her in the soft glow of natural morning light. Her butterscotch skin is radiant, warm, and glowing against my white and gray flannel draped over her shoulders. Her hair is swept into a messy bun, a few curls framing her face, giving her an effortless beauty. The flannel is only partially buttoned, revealing a torturous glimpse of her breasts.

Her expression is relaxed, her lips curved in a faint, knowing smile that's both coy and confident. It's captioned *I need you, Waylon*, which nearly sends my hand into my pants.

I type out a reply, my fingers shaking from exhaustion and a need for her coursing through my veins.

WAYLON

> Khlo, I need you to know I've been thinking about you every damn second. You're right, it is cosmic. And I fucking love you too, gorgeous.

I hit send, enjoying the thought of her needing me as much as I need her.

Fuck, she's going to be my wife

The second I step through her front door, the familiar scent of Khloe's vanilla shampoo smacks me. Just a few weeks felt like an eternity, but standing here now, seeing her curled up on the couch, scrolling through her phone, I realize just how much I fucking missed her.

She doesn't hear me at first. She's got one of those fluffy blankets wrapped around her, legs tucked under her, looking so damn comfortable in my old T-shirt.

I clear my throat, and her head snaps up. For a second, she just stares, eyes wide, like she's not sure if I'm really standing here. Then her lips part slightly, like she's about to say something, but nothing comes out.

"Hey, darlin'."

She blinks, then slowly sits up, letting the blanket slip down her shoulders. "Waylon?"

I smirk, stepping farther into the room. "In the flesh."

She exhales, shaking her head as if she's trying to clear it. "You... you're back. I thought you wouldn't be back until tomorrow. Why didn't you tell me?"

"Surprise." I smile, kicking off my boots. "Got in a few hours ago, debriefed the boss, then came straight here." She taps the spot next to her on the couch, and I make my way to her. I sit down, dropping a Reese's between us. Her eyes light up. "All of your messages made me so happy. Especially the one in my flannel." I wink.

Her eyes light up. "I played with myself, thinking of us."

"You'll show me that later." The blush reaches her cheeks just as I reach up to kiss her. God, how I missed those lips. "Come home with me," I say, reaching for her hand. "Come to the ranch for Christmas. Spend it with my family."

She stares down at our joined hands, fingers flexing against mine. "Waylon, Flora's going to be so sad."

"Darlin', she's going to have to fight me to get the rights to Christmas," I say, grip tightening. I add in my coy smile for effect.

"Okay."

Relief floods through me so fast it almost knocks me sideways. "Yeah?"

She nods. "Yeah. I'll go."

I exhale, bringing her hand to my lips, pressing a kiss against her knuckles. "Good. Because I wasn't gonna take no for an answer."

She chuckles, shaking her head. "You're impossible."

I grin, tugging her closer. "And you love it." My thumb traces her cheek. "Don't run from me again, Khloe. I'll chase after you like a baby mama lookin' for child support."

Her lips curl into something playful, defiant. "Maybe I will. Maybe I won't."

That little smirk and the challenge in her eyes make something dark curl inside me. My fingers tighten around her throat, applying enough pressure to let her feel the command beneath my touch.

"Don't test me, woman."

She doesn't shrink away. She tilts her head back, baring her neck like she's daring me to take what's already mine. "Who would I be if I didn't?" she breathes, her tone dripping with lust and sarcasm.

The look in her eyes sends blood rushing straight to my cock. "No one. Because it doesn't work." My hand slips beneath the blanket, and my patience is rewarded when I find bare, heated skin. No panties. Fuck.

"It's almost like you knew," I murmur, fingers trailing up the inside of her thigh. "I sure hope Flora isn't comin' home soon." Her only response is to part her legs for me, a willing surrender. "Good girl."

Her smile flickers. I watch, enthralled, as her eyes follow my fingers. She's eager to see what I'll do next. I grip the blanket and yank it aside. When I drive two fingers in, she parts around me, slick and ready. Gliding in with ease, stretching her open, my other hand keeps a possessive hold on her throat, keeping her right where I want her. I apply enough tension to make each moan come out strained and needy; her pulse fluttering against them.

Fuck. She's never looked more beautiful than she does now. Deprived, wild, and mine. I set a deliberate rhythm, pushing in deep before retreating to the edge, watching her body chase after the friction. Her mouth parts, her eyes locked onto mine, pupils blown wide with lust.

"You like that, don't you?" I whisper, my thumb circling her clit in teasing strokes. "The way I control you. How I make you wait for it." She gasps, her hips rolling against my hand, silently begging for more. I tighten my grip on her throat to remind her I decide when she gets what she wants —when she breaks.

"I can feel you're close, baby," I taunt, dragging my thumb over her swollen nub again, watching her body tense. "You wanna come for me?"

"Yes," she gasps.

I smirk, never breaking eye contact. "Then beg."

Her lips part, her breath coming in short, shallow gasps. "Please."

I smirk, my fingers slowing to a maddening pace. "Not good enough, baby."

She squirms. Her hips surging forward, ravenous to take more. "Please, Waylon. Let me come. I need it—need you."

That's what I wanted. I pull my fingers from her and sit back against the couch, my hand still wrapped around her throat as I guide her up. "Turn around."

She obeys, climbing onto my lap, facing away from me, her perfect ass pressing against my cock.

Fuck.

I grip her hips, dragging her back against me as I pull myself free, rubbing the thick head along her wet opening. She shudders, her nails biting into my thighs.

"Take it," I order.

She sinks onto me, gasping as she takes every inch, her thighs trembling from the stretch. My hands grip her waist, guiding her movements as she rides me, slow at first, rolling her hips, giving me a show.

"That's it, Khlo. Show me how bad you want it."

She leans forward, bracing herself on my knees as she moves, and the angle is fucking perfect. The view of her completely open to me, back arching as she chases her own pleasure. Fucking hell. It's a goddamn masterpiece.

I land a sharp slap on her ass. She moans, her pace faltering for a second before she picks it up again.

"You're so fucking perfect like this. You're such a good girl for me." My hand snakes around her waist, fingers finding her center again. The second I touch her, she jolts, grinding harder against me.

"Come for me," I growl. "Now."

She shatters, her body tightening around me, her moans sharp and feral as she falls apart. The way she pulses around me, the way she fucking gives in, has me right there with her.

With a sharp thrust, I bury myself deep and let go, pleasure ripping through me like a goddamn hurricane. Her body goes slack against mine, her head falling back against my shoulder as we both struggle for breath. I press a lingering kiss to her shoulder, my grip still firm on her hips.

"Told you not to test me, baby," I murmur against her skin.

Christmas at the ranch always felt the same. Warm, familiar, like stepping into a memory that never faded. The smell of pine and wood smoke mixed with the scent of Mama's pies cooling on the counter. The old radio played a crackly stream of country Christmas songs, and the soft hum of conversation filled the house. It was home.

This Christmas is too special—because of Khloe.

I haul another bundle of firewood inside, shaking off the cold as I step through the back door. My eyes go straight to her, standing at the kitchen counter with Mama. Her sleeves are rolled up, hands working a pie crust like she's been doing it her whole life. She's focused, her brows furrowed, lips pressed together in concentration as she laughs at something Loretta says. The whole damn house got warmer just hearing it.

"She's somethin' special, that girl," Dad mutters beside me, stacking logs by the fireplace.

I don't look at him; my eyes are stuck on Khloe. "She is."

I step away, shaking off the cold and making my way to the kitchen, where Mama and Loretta are enjoying themselves at my expense.

"He couldn't fold a pie crust to save his life," Loretta says, grinning as she ties a ribbon around a gift. "Khloe's already a natural."

Mama smirks, wiping her hands on a dishtowel. "Took me years to get him to follow a recipe right."

Khloe turns as I come up behind her, and I slip my arms around her waist, pulling her against me. "You makin' me look bad in here, darlin'?" I murmur, my lips close to her ear.

She hums. "I'm just proving I can hang with the Rhodes women."

Mama shakes her head. "More like she's showin' you up."

Khloe grins, tilting her head to look at me. "I hear you're not much of a baker."

I smirk. "Guess I'll just have to keep you around then, huh?"

Her fingers curl against my chest for a second before she pulls away, going back to the pie. But I see the blush creeping up her neck, and hell, if that doesn't make me wanna pull her right back against me.

Loretta clears her throat dramatically. "Y'all done flirtin' in Mama's kitchen, or should we give you a minute?"

Khloe shakes her head, laughing. I grin. This Christmas

is perfect, and the reason is standing right in front of me.

I bask in the fire's warmth that fills the living room with a glow and peace I don't get often. Khloe leans against me on the couch, her fingers lazily tracing the rim of her cider mug as Loretta tears into another present. Dad's laughing, Mama's shaking her head. Everything feels exactly how it should be.

The peace breaks when the sound of tires crunching against gravel cuts through it. A car pulls up the long driveway.

Dad glances toward the window. "Who's that?"

Mama frowns, setting down her cup. "Did we forget someone?"

I stand and step toward the window, the cozy warmth of the room replaced by an unwelcome chill when I recognize the sleek black sedan parked outside.

Caroline.

My jaw tightens. Of all the damn days. I mutter her name under my breath, and beside me, Khloe stills. I don't even have to look at her to know she's studying me.

"What's she doing here?" Loretta asks warily.

I exhale through my nose, jaw tight. "Probably stopping by to say hi to Mom and Dad. She doesn't know I'm here. We drove Khloe's car."

Mama stands, already moving toward the door. "I'll handle it." But before she can get there, there's a soft knock. Caroline steps inside, her eyes scanning the room before landing on me. Surprise etched into every part of her face.

"Waylon."

I cross my arms over my chest. "Caroline."

Khloe stands beside me, the tension rolling off her. I turn my head. Her expression is carefully blank, the same way she gets when she's trying to hide how much something is affecting her.

Caroline notices her immediately. "And you must be Khloe," she says, offering a polite smile. "I've heard about you."

Khloe offers a small nod, her smile cautious but not unfriendly. "Hi. I've heard about you, too."

There's a beat of silence before I cut to the point. "What are you doin' here, Caroline?"

She sighs, shifting slightly. "I was driving through Cedar Ridge and thought I'd stop by to wish your parents a Merry Christmas—I didn't mean to intrude."

Dad steps forward. "Well, you've done that now. Merry Christmas, Caroline."

Caroline hesitates, her gaze flicking between me and Khloe. "I'll go. It's... it's nice to see you, Waylon. You seem... happy."

"I am."

Her lips press together like she wants to say more, but she gives me a faint smile and nods. "Good. You deserve it." She turns and walks out the door, the sound of her car engine fading down the long drive.

The room stays quiet for a beat before Loretta lets out a low whistle. "Well, that was awkward."

Mama shoots her a look before turning to Khloe. "Are you alright, dear?"

Khloe nods, her expression impartial. "Yeah, I'm fine."

But I know better. I step toward her, reaching for her hand. "You sure?"

She looks up at me, her dark eyes searching mine. "It just caught me off guard."

"Yeah. Me too." I give her hand a squeeze, and after a beat, she squeezes mine back.

Chapter 46

Christmas Confessions

Christmas at the Rhodes Ranch is too ideal. It feels like stepping into a Norman Rockwell painting. There's warmth everywhere, from the flickering glow of the fireplace to the scent of pine and cinnamon wafting through the air. What I love most is how Waylon's family makes me feel like I'm home.

But of course, something had to knock me sideways. Caroline showing up unannounced had been like a bucket of cold water to the face. I hadn't even fully processed it at the moment. I kept my reaction neutral. That's what I do—I compartmentalize, storing things away until I can deal with them alone.

The porch creaks beneath me as I shift in the rocking chair, cold biting at my fingertips. I tuck them into my sleeves and glance down at my phone. Deadlines, requirements, and tuition that make my stomach twist. Still, I keep scrolling. The door opens behind me with a soft scrape.

Waylon steps out, leans on the railing with a mug in hand. "What're you lookin' at?"

I hesitate, then sigh. "It's just a program I'm thinking of

applying to—Nurse Practitioner."

He's quiet for a beat, eyes on the field stretching out in front of us. "That's what you want?"

I nod slowly. "Yeah. I do."

He takes a sip from his mug. The stream curls around him, softening the edges of his profile. "You'd be good at that."

I glance over, surprised. "You think so?"

He doesn't look at me. "You already take care of everybody like it's your job."

The chair squeaks as I shift again, unsure what to do with the warmth blooming in my chest.

He pushes off the railing. "Lemme know if you need help with the boring stuff. Applications, essays, whatever. I'm goin' clean up and wash my ass." He disappears back inside, the door closing quieter than usual.

I head up to Waylon's childhood bedroom while he's showering. My mind keeps replaying the way Caroline looked at him. And how she said *I've heard about you*, like she'd been briefed on my entire existence. How the hell did she know?

His room smells faintly of cedar and worn leather, like time never really moved forward in here. A heavy four-poster bed anchors one side of the room. A single lamp rests on a crooked nightstand, its shade stitched with western patterns, and beside it, a carved wooden door, worn smooth from years of hands pushing it open.

The walls are dotted with personal relics: a photo collage in a rustic frame, an antique lantern that looks like it's been there since before Waylon was born. It's a room you don't outgrow, because it was never about trends or style. It was built to last, like the boy who slept in it.

I shift in the bed, tugging Waylon's flannel tighter around me as I pull out my phone. If anyone could talk me off the ledge, it's Flora. I hit her contact as I stretch out, staring at the wooden ceiling beams above me. She answers on the second ring.

"Merry Christmas, ho-ho-ho," she greets, too chipper for my current crisis.

"Yeah, yeah. Merry Christmas," I say, rubbing my temple. "Are you alone?"

"Nope. I'm at Aaron's. He made an atrocious attempt at making cookies for his neighbor's kid, and now we're trying to salvage what's left."

In the background, I hear Aaron scoff. "They're fine!"

"They're rocks," Flora says flatly. "Literal weapons." Aaron grumbles something about ungrateful women before I hear the faint sound of a beer bottle clinking.

I shake my head, laughing. "Put me on speaker."

There's some fumbling before Flora confirms, "Okay, you're on."

I take a deep breath. "Caroline showed up today."

Silence.

"What..." Flora's tone drops, all traces of Christmas cheer evaporating.

Aaron follows a second later, amused. "Oh, this is gonna be good."

I roll my eyes. "Can you not?"

"I could," he replies, "but I won't."

Flora chimes in, "Start from the beginning." So, I do. I walk them through the unexpected car in the driveway. The polite but pointed conversation, the way she knew my name, knew about me. The entire time, Flora stays quiet, which is unnerving because that never happens.

When I finish, there's a beat of silence before she finally speaks. "I don't like it."

"Yeah, no shit," I mutter.

Aaron hums in the background. "She knew your name, huh?"

"Yeah."

"Waylon says he never talked to her about you?" he continues.

"Yeah."

"Then someone else did," Flora states.

I sit up, frowning. "Why?"

"Small towns, babe." Flora sighs. "Everyone knows everyone."

Aaron chuckles. "And now the ex is sniffing around. Classic."

Flora shushes him. "Aaron, not helping."

I rub my forehead. "I don't know how I'm supposed to feel about it."

Flora clicks her tongue. "How do you feel about it? Don't overthink it, just say it."

"I trust Waylon. I do. But something about it unsettles me. It's like… I don't know. I don't like feeling like I'm playing catch-up on parts of his past."

Aaron exhales. "Look, not to be the devil's advocate but—"

"You are the devil's advocate," Flora remarks.

"But if he wanted her, he'd still have her," Aaron continues. "The guy doesn't always think shit through, but that doesn't mean he's hiding anything malicious. You gotta decide if you're looking for a problem or if there actually is one."

I chew on that, staring at the quilt draped over my legs.

Flora sighs. "That's the thing, Khlo. I know why you're panicking, but Caroline isn't some other woman in the way you're scared she might be. She's a ghost from his past. That's all."

I nod, swallowing the lump in my throat. "You're right."

"I know I'm right."

Aaron chuckles. "She lives for that shit, Khlo."

Flora ignores him. "Listen, it's okay to feel uneasy—you're human. But don't let your fears sabotage a good thing. Waylon's got his red flags, sure, but his heart is all in on you. And from what I see, that man would rather set himself on fire than let anything mess this up."

That gets a smile out of me. "Thanks, Flo."

"Always," she says warmly. "Now, go find your man and remind him why he's yours."

Aaron snorts. "Yeah, definitely do that. Preferably not on

speaker."

"Jesus Christ, Aaron," I groan, making Flora laugh.

We say our goodbyes, and as I hang up, I feel relief. At the end of the day, I know who Waylon is. I stare at the bathroom door across the hall, listening to the steady rush of water from the shower. Steam curls out from the gap at the bottom, carrying the scent of his soap, clean, rugged, distinctly him.

Waylon's naked in there, and I'm about to be too.

I take a deep breath, my heart drumming in my ears as I slip out of Waylon's flannel, letting it fall in a soft heap onto the bed.

The house is quiet; his parents are already asleep down the hall. I move carefully, tiptoeing across the space. I step inside, closing the door behind me with a quiet click. The heat wraps around me, damp and heavy. The shower curtain is drawn, but I can see his silhouette shifting behind it. Broad, solid muscles flexing under the pounding spray.

He hasn't heard me. Perfect. I reach for the hem of his T-shirt and pull it over my head. My panties slip down next, pooling at my feet before I step out of them, bare and emboldened by the pulse of desire thrumming through me.

I pull the curtain back. Waylon's head jerks up instantly, body tightening like he's expecting a threat. But the second his gaze locks onto mine, the tension shifts, his eyes darkening as they rake down my body. His grip tightens against the tiled wall. I don't give him time to process.

I step into the shower, and he moans, hands twitching at his sides, like he's waiting for permission—restraining himself.

Pressing my palms against his chest, I feel the rapid beat of his heart beneath my fingertips. My chin tilts up, lips barely brushing against his. "Need some company, sir?" I tease.

Waylon swallows hard, his jaw clenching as his hands finally move, gripping my hips with a hunger that steals my breath. His fingers press into my skin, rough and warm and possessive.

"Darlin', you have no idea what you just started," he rasps.

I grin. "Then shut up and show me."

He does—with a groan that vibrates through his chest, he yanks me closer. One arm curls around my waist as his other hand grips my ass, lifting me onto my toes. His mouth crashes against mine, urgent and claiming, the hot water streaming over us as I melt into him. Between the kiss and the heat, I can barely breathe. But I don't want to. I want him and the weight of his body against mine. He swallows my moan when his fingers slip lower, parting me with ease.

A gasp escapes me as he finds my clit, teasing, testing, drawing a sound from me that's swallowed by the rush of the water. My nails bite into slick skin as pleasure ripples through me. Waylon groans, his forehead pressing against mine.

"Fuck," he mutters against my lips. "You're gonna be the death of me."

I shudder as he strokes harder, my body arching into his touch. "Then die happy."

His exhale turns into a ragged chuckle, but the sound cuts off when I wrap my hands around his cock, stroking him with the perfect amount of pressure. His head drops back, breathing picking up. He grips me tighter, like he's barely holding it together.

"Jesus, Khloe."

I press a kiss to his jaw, feeling the way he tremors beneath me. "Fuck me, Waylon."

When I'm thoroughly wet from more than just the water, he moves. With a firm grip, he turns me, pressing my breasts against the warm tile. My arms brace against the wall, my breath coming in shallow bursts as I anticipate what's coming next.

Waylon's hand slides up my spine before curling into my hair. He wraps it around his fist—once, then twice, tugging hard enough to make me whimper. A possessive growl rumbles from his chest, his lips grazing the back of my neck. Before I can beg, he pushes inside me in one deep, claiming thrust. And then nothing.

He stays still.

I whimper again, shifting my hips, starving for more, but his hold tightens in my hair, keeping me exactly where he wants me. My body clenches around him, needing the friction. He pulls my head back, his breath scorching against my ear.

"Khloe," he whispers, dark and reverent. "Remember, I am madly in love with you." Then, rougher, in almost a growl, he finishes, "Because I'm about to fuck you like I don't."

He does. Rigorously. Devastatingly, like a man worshipping at the altar of the only thing he's ever wanted.

Me.

He moves like a man obsessed. His grip in my hair tightens as he pulls me back against him, his other hand gripping my hip, holding me still as he thrusts deep. My breath shatters, a desperate moan slipping past my lips, swallowed instantly by the rush of the water. Waylon groans, his forehead pressing to the back of my neck for a second before he bites down on my shoulder. Hard. A sharp, claiming bite that sends a violent shudder through me.

"You feel so fucking good," he rasps. "You were made for me."

I can't speak. Can't think. All I feel is him everywhere—consuming me, claiming me. His pace quickens, every movement sending shockwaves of pleasure through me. His name is a breathless chant on my lips. My fingers press against the slick tile, clawing for something to hold on to, but there's nothing.

Nothing but him.

He reaches around, his fingers rubbing in deliberate circles that have me gasping. His other arm wraps around my waist, pulling me impossibly closer. As though he wants to crawl further inside me, like the friction between us isn't enough.

I tilt my head, my cheek pressing against his jaw. "Waylon," I whisper, and that does something to him.

His rhythm stutters, his body shuddering against mine. "Come for me," half command, half plea. His fingers press harder, his thrusts turning erratic and wild. "Let me feel you, baby. Give it to me."

And I burst. Blinding and hot, my body tightening around him as he follows right after, losing himself with a strangled, guttural sound against my skin. He stills, his entire body trembling, arms locked around me like he'll never let go.

For a long moment, neither of us moves, the water pounding around us, our breaths mingling in the damp air. He pulls out and turns me to face him. Pressing my back against the warm tile, his hands cradle my face as he kisses me, like he's in love with me.

"You're mine," he murmurs, forehead pressed to mine, like the thought is so absolute he needs to say it aloud. "You always will be."

Chapter 47

Ghost of Christmas Past

The Texas sky stretches wide above us, stars burning bright against the endless black. The air is crisp, but the blanket wrapped around our shoulders keeps the cold at bay.

"I didn't realize how much seeing her would bother me," Khloe admits. "Not because I'm threatened or anything, but… it made me think about what she meant to you."

I turn my head, studying her. Even in the dim light, I can see the crease between her brows, the way her lips press together like she's trying to keep something in.

"She's my past, Khlo. You're my present and my future. There's no comparison."

She gives me a small, almost shy smile and leans her head against my shoulder. "I know, Waylon. It just caught me off guard."

"Fair enough." I press a kiss to the top of her head, letting my lips linger there. "But I need you to know something. Caroline leaving me was the best thing that could've happened because it led me to you."

She lifts her head, meeting my gaze. "You mean that?"

"Every word."

She takes a deep breath in, and I can feel the tension from earlier melting away. She laces her fingers with mine, squeezing lightly. Leaning her head on my shoulder again, she says, "I should have thanked her. Because if she hadn't left, I might not have found you."

I chuckle, my arm tightening around her. "Funny thing about life, isn't it? Sometimes it takes losin' one thing to find the better."

Khloe looks up at me with a devilish expression. "I'm better, huh?"

"Damn right, darlin'—you are superior."

I kiss her deeply, making sure this is what she remembers about tonight, not Caroline, not whatever insecurity that tried to creep in. Because if there's one thing I've learned, it's that you don't let the past mess with something good.

The next morning, I park my truck in front of the hardware store. The engine cuts off with a low rumble. Cedar Ridge is stuck in time—quiet streets and familiar storefronts feel so small after being away. I grab the list Dad sent me with and hop out. I asked Khloe to join me, but she and Loretta were too busy giggling over my baby pictures.

I step onto the street, tugging my coat tighter against the winter air. And that's when I see Caroline. She's standing outside the general store, talking to our old English teacher. I freeze, the air thinning around me. She looks up, her eyes meeting mine like she felt my presence before she saw me. Neither of us moves.

"Waylon," she says. My name carries over the space between us.

I nod, curt. "Caroline."

Our teacher gives me a smile and walks away, leaving us alone on the sidewalk. She fidgets, pulling her coat closer as if it's some kind of armor. "I didn't expect to see you here."

"Funny," I reply clipped. "I could say the same about you."

She winces, her cheeks flushing. "I guess I deserve that. Look, about the other day... I didn't know you'd be home. I was just stopping by to wish your parents a Merry Christmas."

I arch an eyebrow. "And to check on me?"

Her sigh is visible in the cold air, her breath coming out in a shaky puff. "Maybe. I've heard things, Waylon—people still love to talk."

I cross my arms over my chest. "What've you heard?"

"That you've moved on and you're happy. I needed to see it for myself."

That surprises me, but I leave my face unaffected. "Why, Caroline? What difference does it make now?"

She looks away, shoulders slumping slightly. "Because... I never stopped feeling guilty about how things ended. For leaving the way I did. "

I shake my head. "You made your choice. For a long time, I let it eat at me. Made me think we weren't meant to be, but I've been done carryin' that."

Her eyes glisten, and she nods like she's been waiting for me to say those words. "I'm glad. You deserve to be happy, Waylon. I'm glad you've found someone who makes you feel that way."

"She does," I say firmly. "I'm not about to let anythin' mess that up."

Caroline shifts. "It wasn't just you, you know. It was me. I thought your problems were bigger than me, but the truth is... I couldn't handle the fact that you wouldn't share it with me. You wouldn't let me in."

Her words slide into a barrel and fully load into my brain. For years, I blamed her for leaving and not being able to deal with the man I came back as. Now, she's holding up a mirror, and I don't like what I see. I don't like how it makes me feel.

"I didn't know how to let anyone in," I admit. "I didn't want to taint you. I thought carryin' it alone was safer."

Caroline offers a sad smile. "Maybe it was." She shifts on her feet, her tone dropping lower, but the edge cuts clear through the cold air. "You know, Waylon, it wasn't just the PTSD—it was you. You were so damn selfish. So caught up in your own pain, in proving how strong you were, that you didn't even notice me falling apart right next to you."

Her words are sharp and ruthless. "Selfish?" I ask. Why does a piece of me feel she's not wrong?

"Yes," she says firmly, her gaze unwavering. "You were so wrapped up in yourself, in your need to be this... untouchable man who didn't need help, that you shut me out completely. And then you blamed me when I couldn't carry everything for both of us.

Her opinion hurts and pisses me off, but I don't interrupt. Her face tells me she's not done—her eyebrows are cinched together, fists curled in, even in her gloves. "Do you even realize how impossible it was to love you back then?" she asks, her voice cracking. "You never let me in. You didn't share, didn't trust me enough to even try. You made everything about what you were going through, and you expected me to just... deal with it. Like I wasn't hurting too."

I clench my jaw, swallowing the retort bubbling up in my throat. The worst part is she's right. I can almost taste how bitter her response will be as she laughs.

"And you know what's funny? You had this way of making people feel like they were the ones failing you. But the truth, Waylon? You never gave me the chance to be there for you."

I look down, remembering the past and seeing how I could have been wrong. I can't bring myself to look back up at her eyes. I bring my arms up to my chest to cross them before meeting her eyes as she looks away again.

"I wanted to stay," she says softly. "But you made it impossible to love the *you* that returned. I hate that I still feel guilty about leaving, even when I know it was the only thing I could do to save myself." She returns her eyes to mine. To my surprise, there's no anger there, only acceptance, and a sadness I didn't realize I'd left behind.

"Caroline, I can't change what I was back then. I know I hurt you, and I'm sorry for shuttin' you out."

She nods, her lips pressing into a thin line. "I hope you've figured it out," she says gentler now. "Because if you haven't, you're going to hurt her too. She deserves better than the man I had."

I hold her gaze. "I won't make the same mistakes," I say finally, the promise more to myself than to her. "Not this time."

Caroline offers a smile tinged with sadness. "Good. Because no one deserves to be loved halfway, Waylon—not even you."

I look away, my shoulders sinking under the heaviness of her words. I buried parts of myself so deep; I didn't know how to dig back up. And it wasn't just Caroline. I've been doing it my whole life, pushing down what I didn't want to deal with, hiding behind control and distractions. Dad's words echo: *Distract yourself. Laugh it off. Move on.*

"I'm sorry it took me this long to figure that out," I say.

Her smile doesn't reach her eyes, but there's no malice there. Just understanding. "I hope it works out with her. Really, I do."

"It will," I say, meeting her gaze.

She extends her hand, and after a brief pause, I take it. Her grip is firm but brief.

"Merry Christmas, Waylon."

"Merry Christmas, Caroline."

She turns and walks away, her figure disappearing down the street. I stand there for a moment, watching the frost linger in the air where her breath had been. As I head into the store, the conversation replays in my mind, her words sticking like barbs.

Picking up Dad's items, I head to the candy aisle to get

my girl her silly peanut butter cups. Dropping everything on the counter, I realize that seeing Caroline is probably better kept to myself. I've come a long way since those days, but there's still work to do—work I owe to myself and to Khloe.

Chapter 48

Drifting Apart

The ER is not overwhelmingly busy tonight, but just enough chaos to keep things moving. Flora and I are posted at the nurses' station, waiting for lab results and watching a patient chart load on the screen. I roll my shoulders, glancing at my phone for what feels like the tenth time. Still nothing.

Waylon and Aaron left for an assignment across the state. I told myself I wouldn't overthink because Waylon hasn't answered my last few texts. It means nothing.

I look over and see Flora grinning on her phone, listening intently to Aaron. She tucks her hair behind her ear, smiling.

"Uh-huh. No, you shut up." She laughs, cheeks turning pink.

I try not to feel that sinking feeling in my stomach. I could text again, but I'm tired of being the only one reaching out. Flora glances at me, catching my expression.

"It's Aaron," she says, like I didn't already know. "He was just telling me—" Before she can finish, an aide calls her name from across the ER. She holds up a finger. "One sec," she tells Aaron. Then, she looks at me. "Hold this for me?"

She hands me her phone before hurrying off, blonde

ponytail bouncing as she disappears around the corner. I hesitate, then lift the phone to my ear.

"Hey, Aaron," I say, shifting in my chair. There's a beat of silence before he responds.

"Khloe? Hey. Didn't expect you to be on the other end."

I smile faintly, leaning my elbow against the desk. "Flora got pulled away. Figured I'd keep you company."

"Appreciate it. You keeping my girl out of trouble?"

I smirk. "More like the other way around."

Aaron chuckles, but before he can respond, another voice carries through the line. Low and familiar. Waylon.

"Jones, I don't give a damn what he said. The lead's dried up. We're movin' on tomorrow."

My stomach tightens. There's a muffled noise overlapping in the background. Aaron shifts somewhere quieter.

"Khloe?" Aaron pulls me back.

I blink. "Yeah. I'm here."

I press my fingers against my temple. I could let it go. Pretend it doesn't feel like proof of what I've been dreading. Waylon's leaving for this assignment was one thing. After Christmas, he made me feel so whole and loved. I knew I could handle it. But his silence once he got there was a steady fade of effort.

"Did he—" Aaron pauses, exhaling through his nose like he's piecing something together. "He hasn't been checkin' in, has he?"

I laugh, shaking my head. "No. No, he hasn't."

Aaron doesn't rush to defend him.

I sigh. "He's drifting."

Aaron pauses for a moment before he says, "Yeah. He does that."

I squeeze my eyes shut. "You mean he's done this before?"

Another pause. "I mean... Waylon doesn't know how to hold on to things when he's not standing right in front of them. Distance makes him think it's easier to let go."

I stare at the desk, my nails tapping against the surface.

"He's not a bad guy," Aaron continues. "But he's never had to do this before. He's never had someone who mattered enough to—" He stops himself, clearing his throat. "I'm not making excuses for him, Khloe. You deserve better than that. He... I know him. And I know he doesn't want to hurt you. He's just..."

"A selfish fucker?" I offer.

Aaron huffs. "Something like that."

I let the silence stretch for a second. "You're a good guy, Aaron."

He hesitates, like he doesn't quite believe me. "Yeah?"

"Yeah. I see the way Flora looks at you. She wouldn't give you the time of day if you weren't."

Aaron exhales a soft chuckle. "Guess I'll take that as a compliment."

"You should." I lean back, my lips pressing together. "I mean it. I'm happy for you guys. Flora deserves someone good."

Aaron's quiet for a second before he says, "So do you."

I feel choked up for a moment. Before I can respond, Flora cuts in, slightly breathless. "Alright, I'm back."

I clear my throat, forcing a smile. "I was just telling Aaron how much I adore you."

Flora snorts, taking the phone back. "I'm sure you were."

She presses the speaker back to her ear. "Miss me?"

Aaron answers warmly, "You've been gone a whole two minutes. "

I glance down at my phone again. The screen is still blank. No missed calls. No new messages. Nothing from Waylon. I tell myself I won't reach out again tonight.

But I already know, deep down, that the next time my phone vibrates, I'll be hoping it's him.

The restaurant is all warm lighting and chatter. Flora and I are seated in a cozy corner booth, our plates half-empty, the remains of a shared chocolate cheesecake sitting between us. It's a good night. Great food, amazing company. But all I can think about is my phone.

The last message from Waylon sits unanswered in my texts:

WAYLON

What are you wearing, darlin?

That was two hours ago. It's the most I've heard from him all day. Not a "How's your day?" Not an "I miss you." Just something sexy. Something that doesn't require much from him at all. I told myself I wouldn't let it bother me. It's just his way of keeping me close while he's away.

But then I look at Flora, at the way she's absolutely glowing, her phone propped up against the saltshaker on a video call, and I feel that ache in my chest again. Aaron isn't sending her flirty one-liners. No, he's giving her a damn master class on how to meet his parents.

"Okay, so first off," Aaron's face is serious as hell, "my dad's gonna grill you. It's not personal; he just likes to test people."

Flora rolls her eyes, biting back a smile. "I'm not scared of your dad, Aaron."

"You should be," he deadpans. "Guy's been fighting for civil rights since the '80s. He's taken down entire police departments for misconduct. He enjoys breaking people down to see what they're made of."

I snort into my drink, shaking my head. "Sounds like a fun dinner."

Flora shoots me a look, but Aaron laughs. "Oh, it's a blast. My mom's no better. She's just nicer about it. She'll ask you a bunch of innocent-sounding questions that are actually traps."

"Traps?" Flora raises an eyebrow.

Aaron shifts into an exaggerated high-pitched impression. "Yup, like, 'Where do you see yourself in five years?' Say the wrong thing, and suddenly you're getting a twenty-minute lecture on systemic inequalities in the job market."

Flora laughs, but I can see she's wringing her hands in her lap. "So, what am I supposed to say?"

Aaron exhales. "Alright. Rule number one: whatever you do, do not bring up my high school football career. My dad thinks sports are a distraction from real-world issues."

Flora throws her arms up. "But you were a state champion!"

"Yeah, and he called it a waste of potential," Aaron groans. "Anyway, rule number two…"

I sip my drink, listening as he keeps going, listing off every scenario she might encounter. It's ridiculous. It's over-the-top. It's kind of amazing. Aaron really cares. He wants Flora to walk into that dinner prepared, not just to impress his parents, but to understand them. He's not sending cute texts or making her feel sexually wanted. He's letting her in.

I glance at my phone again, tapping my thumb against the table.

"Alright." Flora sighs, running a hand through her hair. "I think I got it. No football talk. No surface-level answers. If your dad tries to break me, I act unbothered. If your mom asks me about the wage gap, I tell her I'm deeply aware of its impact on marginalized communities and cite my sources."

"Exactly," Aaron says proudly.

Flora smirks. "And what if I wanna charm them?"

Aaron's quiet for a second. "Then just be yourself. They're gonna love you, Flora. I promise."

Her expression flickers, something warm settling in her eyes. I look away.

Aaron sighs. "You still there, Khloe?"

I shift back into the camera's view. "Yeah."

"You okay?" His face is casual, but there's something behind it. Like he knows I'm sitting here comparing.

I smirk. "Yeah. Just, uh… taking notes for when I inevitably meet your parents."

It's a lighthearted deflection, but Flora glances at me.

Aaron hums like he's debating whether to press the issue. Instead, he says, "For what it's worth, I think you'd handle them just fine."

Flora grins. "She'd love your mom."

"Hell yeah, she would," Aaron agrees. "You'd get her riled up, though. She'd be dragging you into political debates all night."

I chuckle, shaking my head. "My kind of woman."

Aaron laughs, and Flora's phone vibrates.

"Alright, babe. I gotta go, but I'll call you later, okay?"

Aaron's features soften, a smile spreading across his face. "Can't wait."

Flora hangs up, a soft smile still playing on her lips as she looks at me. "So?"

I raise an eyebrow.

"So what?" She nudges my foot under the table. "Tell me he's not the best."

I shake my head. "Yeah, yeah. He's alright, I guess."

Flora beams. "That's Khloe for 'I approve.'"

I smile, but it's tight. My phone chimes, and my stomach flips until I see the notification. A stupid meme from Missy, not Waylon. I turn my screen over, not in the mood to look at it anymore.

Flora picks up her drink, studying me. "You wanna talk about it?"

I force a grin. "Nah. Not tonight."

She doesn't push. Just clinks her glass against mine and changes the subject, letting me breathe. Even though deep down, I already know this feeling isn't going away.

I sit at Aaron's kitchen island, lazily scrolling through my phone while Flora wrestles with the dishwasher, cursing under her breath. His house is pleasant, clean, and modern, but the dishwasher has a temper. Every time she tries to close it, it pops back open like it's offended.

"You gotta lift it first," Aaron says through the speakerphone with amusement. "Then push it in at an angle."

Flora glares at the phone like he can see her. "I swear, this thing has it out for me."

Aaron chuckles. "That thing has it out for everyone. Damn near lost a toe fighting it last week."

I smirk, sipping my water. "Should I be concerned about the structural integrity of your kitchen?"

"Nah," Aaron says easily. "Just the appliances. I think they're unionizing."

Flora finally gets the dishwasher shut and throws her hands up in victory. "There. Done. Now, keep my girl company while I go fold laundry."

She winks at me before disappearing down the hall.

I shift, leaning my elbow on the counter. "Guess it's just you and me, Brooks."

Aaron hums, the sound of paper rustling on his end. "Good, Navarro. I've been meaning to ask you something."

I raise an eyebrow. "Oh?"

"I heard you were looking into going to school to be a Nurse Practitioner."

I blink, surprised. "Uh… yeah, I am."

Aaron pauses, then adds, "Waylon told me. He sounded excited for you."

I still. I know Waylon's proud of me, but he hasn't really talked to me about it. Not like this. Pride settles in my chest, knowing he's talking about me at all.

"Wow," I say, and I don't mean to sound so surprised, but I am.

Aaron chuckles. "Yeah, I figured that'd shock you. He doesn't always say things out loud, but he's proud of you, Khloe. Told me he thought it was a smart move."

I exhale, toying with the hem of my sleeve. "Well... thanks. That means a lot."

"Of course," Aaron says, like it's obvious. "You're gonna kill it."

I glance toward the hallway, making sure Flora's still out of earshot before I say. "You and Flora... you guys talk about everything, huh?"

Aaron doesn't hesitate. "Yeah. She's my best friend. Why?"

I chew the inside of my cheek. "I dunno. Just... you two are opposites."

Aaron snorts. "We're very different."

I shake my head. "No, I mean... Waylon."

Aaron is quiet for a second. "In what way?"

I sigh, pressing my forehead into my palm. "Forget it. It's stupid."

"Hey," Aaron says, firm but not unkind. "It's not stupid if it's bothering you."

I huff, shaking my head. "It's just... you tell Flora everything. She doesn't have to wonder how you feel. I know Waylon cares about me, I do. But sometimes it feels like... I don't know. Like I have to drag things out of him. Like I only get the pieces he's willing to give."

Aaron exhales slowly. "That sounds about right."

I look up. "So, it's not just me?"

Aaron laughs, but it's not mean. "No, sweetheart. It's not just you."

I bite the inside of my cheek, discomfort twisting in my gut.

"Waylon..." Aaron starts, then sighs. "He's been through a lot and doesn't enjoy feeling exposed. When he cares about someone, he feels like it makes him weak. So instead of letting people in, he just... holds them at arm's length."

I nod, even though he can't see me. Yeah, that sounds about right.

"But," Aaron continues, "he also doesn't want to lose you. Which is why he's probably sending those unemotional texts. He thinks giving you little breadcrumbs of attention will keep you close while he's away."

I frown. "That's... frustrating."

Aaron chuckles. "Yeah, no shit."

I rub my temple. "So, what do I do? Just accept that he's emotionally constipated?"

Aaron laughs loudly. "I mean, yeah, but also... don't let him get away with it. Waylon needs people who challenge him, Khloe. If you need more from him, tell him."

"And if he can't give it to me?"

Aaron sighs. "Then you have to figure out if that's enough for you."

I don't respond. Aaron thankfully doesn't push. Instead, he clears his throat and shifts the conversation. "Back to your career, though. My parents know someone who went to The University of Texas Health Science Center at San Antonio. I told them about you, and they want to help you get into their fast-track program."

I blink. "Wait! What?"

"My mom and dad. They've got connections," Aaron says like it's nothing. "They'd be happy to put in a word."

I stare at the phone like he just told me I won the lottery. "Aaron. That's... huge."

He shrugs. "You deserve the best shot possible."

"I truly can't thank you enough," I say, leaning forward. "Flora's lucky, you know? You're a good man, Aaron."

He snorts. "You tryna make me blush, Navarro?"

I grin. "Maybe a little, Brooks."

Aaron chuckles, but he says with candor. "For real, though. You're gonna be great, Khloe. You're smart, you're tough, and you give a shit about people. That's rare."

I swallow past the sudden tightness in my throat.

"Thanks, Aaron."

"Anytime."

Flora walks back in, tossing a dish towel over her shoulder. "You two bonding without me?"

Aaron responds, "Little bit."

I wink at Flora. "He's gonna adopt me so I can be in your family."

She scoffs. "Please. You couldn't handle having me as a mom."

Aaron groans. "Alright, on that note, I've gotta go."

Flora picks up the phone. "Love you."

Aaron softens. "Love you too, baby."

She hangs up, then turns to me. "You okay?"

I force a smile. "Yeah."

But as I glance at my phone again, still no new messages from Waylon.

Why do I feel like I'm losing him?

Chapter 49

The Weight of Distance

The air feels heavier now that the job is done. I lean against the hood of the SUV, trying to push down the adrenaline still humming in my veins. Aaron's a few yards away, shooting the shit with one of the locals, his laugh carrying over the empty lot. I stay quiet, letting my mind drift for a second. The mission was a success, but I can't shake the feeling that something else is coming.

My phone buzzes in my pocket. I pull it out and pause when I see Jones's name on the screen.

"Rhodes," I answer, standing straighter.

"Rhodes, good work on the operation." Jones' voice is clipped, but there's a touch of something more serious there. "Knew you and Brooks would handle it."

"Thank you, sir." I glance toward Aaron, whose attention is on me. "What's next?"

There's a pause. I hear Jones rustling papers. "I've got something lined up for you. A solo assignment. Deep cover. It's a syndicate tied to arms trafficking and intimidation. The works. We need someone embedded who can gather intel from the inside."

I smile, happy he trusts me, but realization hits. "How long, sir?"

"Six months is the minimum," Jones announces, as impartial as a weather forecast. "Could stretch longer if it takes time to establish the right connections. It's high stakes, Waylon, but you're the guy for it."

Six months or more. My first thought isn't about the job or the danger, it's about Khloe. But I've worked too hard to throw this away. I grit my teeth. "When do you need me to start?"

"You'll have six to eight weeks to tie things up at home and prepare," Jones replies. "After that, you'll report to D.C. for final briefings. Once you're in, you're in. No loose ends."

"Understood."

Jones softens, catching me off guard. "This won't be easy, Rhodes. Especially if you've got someone waiting back home. But you're the best we've got. I'll need your answer soon."

"It's a yes, sir."

"Good. And Waylon? These assignments... they don't just test your skills. They test everything else. Be sure about what you're leaving behind."

The line goes dead before I can respond.

"Let me guess," Aaron says, walking up. "Jones giving you more homework?"

I shake my head. "Not homework. A six-month assignment. Solo."

Aaron watches me closely, arms crossed. "How are you gonna tell her?"

I shake my head. "No clue."

Aaron exhales sharply, rubbing a hand over his jaw. "Yeah. I figured." Something in his tone makes me glance up. "You know what that's gonna do to her, right?"

"I do," I say, jaw tight. "But it's not like I can turn it down. This isn't just some traffic detail. This gives me a chance to prove myself. To show I am in this for the long haul."

Aaron shakes his head. "Don't act like this is just about the assignment."

I narrow my eyes. "What the hell does that mean?"

He exhales. "You've already been pulling back. This is just gonna make it worse."

I don't make eye contact.

"She feels it, Waylon. You might not see it, but she does. And if you keep this up, she won't be there when you get back."

I run my hand over my jaw. "Caroline called me selfish," I mutter. "Said I always find an excuse to leave."

Aaron doesn't hesitate. "Then change. Get your shit together, Rhodes. Because if you keep waiting for this to be easy, you're gonna end up with nothing."

He turns to the SUV, not waiting for a response. I stare out at the horizon. Six to eight weeks. Deep down, I know she isn't strong enough for this, and maybe neither am I.

The house is quiet when I walk in. Khloe's on the couch. A book in hand, with her legs tucked under a blanket. She looks up, relief flickering in her eyes until she sees my face.

"Hey, darlin'," I say as I drop my bag by the couch.

Her brow knits. "What's wrong?"

I walk over, kneel in front of her, and set a Reese's on the couch beside her. Then I take her hands in mine, warm and familiar. Something I'll miss more than I want to admit.

"I got a call," I start. "Jones is sending me on a long assignment. Six months. Maybe more."

Her fingers twitch in mine before she pulls back, wrapping them in the blanket instead.

"Six months?" she echoes. "Waylon..."

"I know," I say quickly. "I know it sounds like forever. But it's big, Khloe. High stakes. They need someone they can trust."

Her jaw tightens. "And what about us?"

I rest my hand on her knee. "Khloe, I'm not leavin' you.

I'm doing my job. That doesn't mean you're not my priority."

She shakes her head. "I'm always second to your job. I get it, I do. But six months? That's not a little while."

"I am coming back," I say, locking my gaze on hers. "No matter what. No matter where they send me, I'll always come back to you." I lean in. "We're more than time apart. More than a few months on opposite sides of the country."

Her lips part like she wants to argue, but she doesn't. She's thinking, weighing every word. Then finally, she exhales. "How can you be so sure?"

"'Cause I love you." I let that settle into the spaces doubt might creep in. "I know you love me. That's what gets us through this. That's what makes us stronger."

She bites her lip and nods. "Okay. But promise me you'll call. Let me know you're okay."

I press my forehead against hers. "I promise, darlin'. Every chance I get."

"Okay."

She grabs my shirt. I'm certain now she's choosing this. Choosing us.

And since that call and Aaron's push, I know I can handle this. 'Cause I've got her to come home to.

Chapter 50

The Breaking Point

It's so quiet that I can hear everything outside. The rustle of leaves, a car rolling past in the distance, the faint hum of a neighbor's wind chime. I should find it comforting. But it feels like a warning.

Then the door opens. Relief flickers in my chest, but the second I see his face, my stomach drops.

Something's wrong.

I straighten instinctively, dropping my book on the couch. My fingers tighten around the blanket draped across my lap. Waylon crosses the room, kneeling in front of me, his movements measured. I don't move or reach for him.

A Reese's lands beside me on the couch, his usual offering. Normally, I'd roll my eyes, take it with a smirk. But not this time. Not when his expression is already confirming what I don't want to hear.

I can handle this. That's what I tell myself as he takes my hands, his palms warm. But the way he holds me, like he's already memorizing the feel of my skin, makes my stomach twist.

When he says six months, maybe more, the words slice through me. I yank my hands back, wrapping them in the blanket, as if that will stop the ache that's already forming.

This is who he is. I've known it since the beginning.

I hold myself together. I'm strong enough for this. I can handle the distance and the waiting. I almost believe it, but then I remember the past few weeks. The way he's already felt distant. How his texts have been shorter, fewer, and less meaningful.

The space between us started long before this moment. Now, I'm supposed to pretend that six months won't widen that gap. I grip the blanket tighter, my pulse thrumming in my ears. The silence between us stretches. He's still looking at me, waiting.

I don't know if I have anything left to give.

He tells me I'm strong, that his love for me is bigger than the miles or the mission. But love doesn't stop the nightmares and doesn't fill the silence when I'm waiting for a call that doesn't come.

Damn it, I could believe him. I want to hold on to the way he says my name. How his arms feel around me, like they could keep me safe from everything, but I know myself. I know what silence does to me and what waiting feels like.

I nod anyway. Because what else can I do?

I whisper, "Okay."

Waylon breathes like that's all he needed to hear. As if my words alone can fix this. But I wonder if he realizes I'm lying. I should try because he's willing to fight for us. I should fight too.

The phone buzzes on my nightstand. Again. For three days, my mom's been calling. Each time, I've ignored it. Pretending she wasn't clawing her way back into my life after years of nothing.

Except tonight, Waylon's at his house, and Flora's in between Aaron's house and mine. Letting my thoughts spiral in the empty silence of my house, I do something reckless.

I answer.

"This is a collect call from an inmate at Bridgeport Correctional..."

I press one.

"Khloe," my mother says. "Thank God, baby. I was thinking you weren't ever gonna pick up."

"I shouldn't have."

"I deserve that... You're mad at me. I've let you down a lot." She's softer, more careful. "I'm trying to improve, baby. I'm working through my shit. I mean it this time."

I laugh, shaking my head. "You always mean it. Then you disappear again."

"I had to," she argues, desperation creeping in. "Prison... forced me to face myself, Khloe. I didn't have a choice but to get clean."

I scoff. "So, what? You want a gold star for not having easy access to drugs?"

"No. I want a chance to show you I'm better."

Something in me aches at the plea, but I shove it down. "I spent my whole life waiting for you to be better," I say through my teeth. "Waiting for you to choose me over a high. To stay when things got hard, but you never did."

"I know." She sounds so small and broken. It makes her seem human. I don't want that. I want to remember the version of her that walked out of my life too many times to count. Not someone who sounds like she finally regrets it.

I inhale sharply, staring at the ceiling. "Why now? Why are you really calling me?"

"I'm getting out soon," she admits. There's the real reason. "I don't have anywhere to go, Khloe. Can you visit? Send money? Maybe I can stay with you. I heard you sold Grandma's house."

"You have to be fucking kidding me."

"Baby, listen—"

"No," I snap, sitting up in bed, my grip on the phone so tight my fingers ache. "You don't get to call me after years and ask me for a goddamn favor. You don't get to act like this is some fresh start just because you finally ran out of options."

"That's not fair—"

"Oh, now you care about fair?"

"I know I don't deserve it, but I'm asking anyway."

I close my eyes. "Go to a halfway house. Go to a shelter. Call anyone else but me."

"Khloe…"

"I'm not saving you, Mom!" I hang up before she can respond.

I sit there for a long time, staring at my phone, waiting for her to call again. She doesn't. I don't know whether to feel relieved or completely shattered. The silence in my house feels heavier than it did before. My mother's absence somehow fills the space more than her presence ever did. I toss my phone onto the nightstand.

She's getting out and asking me to fix things like I'm still within reach. She doesn't even realize I'm states away. It's pathetic. I run my hands through my hair. I should feel relieved. I didn't let her manipulate me back into the role I spent my entire childhood playing. The fixer, the caretaker, the one who stays even when she doesn't want to, but all I feel is guilt. Maybe she'll stop trying to twist her way back into my life. Every bridge between us is already ash.

My mother only 'loves' me when she needs something. When it's convenient and she has no other choice. Inevitably, my thoughts turn to Waylon. I press the heels of my palms into my eyes, trying to push him out of my head. But it's impossible. Waylon loves me at my worst. When I push. When I shut down. Even in the moments I admit I don't know how to be loved. But what happens when he runs out of patience?

Memories flash behind my eyes like a cruel highlight reel. Waylon tells me repeatedly that he's not leaving. But my life has been spent waiting for the people I love to decide I'm too much and walk away.

And now, he's about to leave for six months. I know he's not abandoning me. He's doing his job. I hate the part of me that still feels like a little girl watching her mother walk out the door, wondering what she did wrong.

Six months of waiting for calls that might never come? I can't do it. I won't sit by the phone, waiting to be left behind. I'll leave first.

The sharp rip of packing tape breaks the silence and announces Flora's back. I walk into her room as she kneels by her dresser, stuffing clothes into a box. Her closet is nearly bare. There are boxes stacked near the door, labeled in her loopy handwriting.

"She called," I say hoarsely.

Flora freezes mid-fold, a sweater bunched in her hands. She looks over her shoulder. "Your mom?"

"Yeah." I walk in and plop on her bed, staring at my hands.

She sighs, tossing the sweater into her bag. "Shit. What did she want?"

I let out a mean laugh, running a hand through my hair. "What do you think? She wants something. Money. A place to stay. A reaction. I don't even know anymore."

Flora watches me carefully, her usual energy subdued. "What did she say?"

"That she's sorry. That she's trying. That she thinks I should visit." My words taste sour. "She made it sound like she cares. But then she mentioned the house, Grandma's money, like she thinks she's entitled to it."

Flora's jaw tightens. "Of course she does."

"She doesn't even realize I'm not in Stamford anymore. You know what's messed up? I almost believed her for a second. For one stupid second, I thought she actually missed me. But no, same old bullshit."

Flora gets up and joins me on the bed. "She doesn't get to do this to you, Khlo. Not anymore. You don't owe her anything."

I bite the inside of my cheek. "I know that. I do. But it still fucks me up." I let out a shaky breath. "And it made me think about Waylon."

Flora frowns. "Waylon? What do you mean?"

"I was going to break up with him, Flora," I whisper, barely audible.

Her eyes widen. "What?! When?"

"A while ago, I felt like I was falling apart. He was gone, and it felt too much like... like her. Like waiting for someone who might never come back." I shake my head.

"So, I wrote a text, sent it, but then he called. It snapped me out of it."

Flora's expression softens. "Khlo..."

"It just made me realize how much of my shit I've been putting on him. How much I push because I'm terrified of needing him too much. If I don't fix myself, I'm going to ruin this."

Flora reaches over, squeezing my knee. "Then don't ruin it. Waylon's stubborn as hell, and he loves you. But you gotta meet him halfway, babe. Do you think you should talk to someone? Like a counselor."

I nod, pressing my lips together. "I'm trying to meet him in the middle. I'm not ready to talk to anyone yet."

She smiles. "Okay, but don't think it makes you weak if you do. Therapy is healthy. It's nice to get someone else's perspective."

I look down, unable to meet her eyes. "Should I break up with him?"

"Khloe, you need to talk to someone, babe." She pulls me into her arms, and we sit like that for a while.

"Now, help me shove another box in my car before I ugly cry again about moving out."

I laugh, grateful for the distraction. "Yeah, yeah. But if I find one of my sweaters in there, I'm stealing it back."

Chapter 51

Silent Break

Khloe's bare back rises and falls beneath the sheets, her curls spilling across the pillow. I should be asleep beside her, but I can't turn my damn brain off.

I sit at the edge of the bed. The room dim and the air thick with her vanilla shampoo, a scent that clings to my skin. I've been taking local assignments with Aaron, staying close. It's easier this way, less of a hassle. Plus, I don't want to leave her yet.

Even in sleep, she burrows into my chest, like I might disappear. We're about to hit a real test. But for now, she's in my house. In my head. Under my damn skin.

I rise carefully and head for the kitchen, not wanting to wake her. I sigh, scrubbing a hand over my face before grabbing a glass of water.

As I open the door, she stirs, rolling to her side. Her hand reaches for the spot where I should be. I smile and down the water, slipping back in bed beside her. She nestles closer instinctively. I wrap an arm around her waist, pressing a kiss to the back of her shoulder.

Aaron says there's something about this case that feels off. He's right. The sun hangs low, bleeding gold through the dusty streets of the Villa neighborhood. Shadows stretch long against cracked pavement. The kind that makes people lock their doors and makes me itch for my gun.

Dispatch pings back: Suspect confirmed. Armed and dangerous. Approach with caution.

Ramon Delgado. A walking pile of poor decisions. Multiple felonies. Cartel ties. A runner. A killer.

I slip my phone back into my pocket. "We go in quietly."

Aaron nods, but quiet doesn't mean safe. We round the corner, and there's Delgado leaning against a rusted chain-link fence, an unlit cigarette dangling from his lips. His body screams casual, but his eyes give him away. I step out of the unmarked SUV, boots crunching against grit. Aaron follows, hand near his holster, reading the air like I am. Delgado knows who we are, and he's already made a choice.

Aaron moves first. "Ramon Delgado? We need to chat."

Delgado doesn't move. His fingers twitch near his waistband. His eyes flick left then right.

"Don't do it."

Gunfire explodes.

Aaron jerks back, a sound punching out of him. I don't think, I react.

Delgado fires again. I dive, hitting the pavement as the shot rips past, missing my head by inches.

Sparks fly from the SUV. Aaron stumbles, gun still in his hands. Still in the fight. I fire back, clipping Delgado's arm. He stumbles, doesn't stop, but ducks behind the fence.

A fresh mag clicks.

I push off the pavement, sprinting for cover behind the SUV. Bullets shred metal. Glass explodes from the back window. We're pinned. I glance at Aaron.

He's hit, leaning hard against the car, blood seeping through his fingers, chest rising fast and shallow. Too much fucking blood. Fucking hell.

"Stay down," I growl.

Aaron ignores me, struggling to lift his gun.

"You cover me," I order. "I'm ending this."

I move before he can argue, darting left. Delgado fires. Too slow. I have him lined up.

One shot, and he drops.

The only sound left is Aaron gasping for air. I whip toward him. His gun slips from his fingers as his body sags against the SUV. His eyes are heavy, mouth already stained red.

Fuck. Fuck. Fuck.

I drop to my knees and rip open his vest. My hands sink into blood. I press hard against the wound. "Brooks," I bark, but he doesn't respond.

His eyelids tremble. No, no, no.

"You stay awake," I snap, shaking him.

His head lolls.

"Hey." I grab his neck. "You hear me? Stay awake, goddamn it!"

He forces his eyes open. "If... I don't... make it... Tell Flora... I was gonna... marry her."

I see red.

"Shut the fuck up." I grit out. "You're gonna tell her your damn self."

Aaron's fingers dig weakly into my sleeve. Siren's wail, but his blood covers my hands, seeping into the cracks of my skin, soaking into the gravel beneath him.

"Stay with me!" I press down harder on the wound. "You hear me, Brooks?"

His eyes flutter unfocused. I need to do more to keep him here. Headlights slash through the darkness in my vision. His grip loosens. His eyes slip shut.

I don't know if I'm screaming his name or praying he

can still hear it.

Backup finally screeches onto the scene. A blur of uniforms rushes in, some securing Delgado's body, and some surrounding us.

My only focus is on Aaron. The ambulance doors fly open. Medics swarm us. Hands shove me back as they lift him onto a gurney. He lets out a choked noise; the movement jarring him.

"He's crashing. Move, move!"

I push forward, but a medic throws out an arm, blocking me. "Throw on your sirens and lead us."

I climb into the SUV, flipping the sirens on the second the door shuts.

In front of the hospital, the ambulance doors swing open. I'm already moving. Boots slamming against pavement. His blood is dry on my skin. I follow the gurney inside, pulse hammering in my ears.

Aaron's barely breathing now, his face slack, dark skin too pale under the fluorescent lights. "Where do I go?" I scream. I don't know who I'm talking to. I can't stand still.

A nurse steps forward, blocking my path. "Sir, you need to wait outside."

"The hell I will," I snap, trying to push past her.

Another person cuts me off, pushing me back. My temper frays, my body wound so tight I might snap, and then I hear *her*.

"Waylon."

My head jerks up. My chest goes tight. Khloe. She's in scrubs, dark hair pulled up, eyes locked on mine. She stands like a wall between me and the rest of the world. I didn't even realize I'd led us to her hospital. Or how much I needed her until right now.

She steps forward, cutting through the chaos. "Let us work."

I shake my head. "He's hurt, Khlo." It comes out more like a plea than a statement.

"I know. Let us do our job."

My jaw could crack. My chest feels like it's being ripped open, torn in two between staying and getting the fuck out of the way. She knows I'm two seconds from losing my grip.

"Please, Waylon. Trust me."

She's steel in the middle of my mess. Everything I'm not. That's what makes me take a step back. The stress doesn't ease, but my feet move anyway.

Flora appears beside me. Face streaked with tears and hands gripping my arm. "Come on, big guy," she pleads. "Let her work. Aaron's tough."

I nod mechanically, dragging a trembling hand through my hair. Flora takes my arm, guiding me away. My eyes stay locked on Khloe as she disappears through a pair of doors with him.

I feel helpless. I fucking hate it.

Chapter 52

The Aftermath

The ER is chaos. The usual harsh voices, shrill beeping of monitors, and hurried footsteps. Flora and I finish stabilizing a car accident patient when the doors slam open.

Two paramedics and a gurney. Urgent screams cutting through the noise: *"GSW to the chest! Unstable! BP dropping!"*

Flora gasps. My body locks up; icy dread sinks into my bones the second I see Aaron. Blood-soaked and barely conscious.

My stomach plummets. Flora screams his name, rushing forward. Waylon barrels in behind them. Blood smears his hands. His shirt is torn, soaked through with red. But it's his face that stops me cold. He's not just pale, but haunted. Like he already lost him.

He shoves forward, fighting everyone in his way, looking for answers and control. I don't hear his words, only the edge of his petition. I see the moment his eyes find mine.

A second of recognition. Something breaks inside him, and then he lets go. Not by choice, but because I asked. He steps back, hands shaking, dragging them through his hair.

Flora pulls him away, whispering.

Aaron is slipping as we wheel him towards surgery. I snap on a pair of gloves and move to his side. My training kicks in even as my chest tightens.

"Aaron, can you hear me?"

A low groan. His eyes barely open.

"Yeah, it's Khloe," I say softly, pressing two fingers to his wrist, checking his pulse. Weak and thready. He tries to speak, chest rising unevenly. Every breath is a fight.

"Don't talk," I murmur. "You're safe here."

His lips part again. I lean closer, straining to hear. As a rasp of breath, his voice is barely a whisper. "... *Waylon... Flora.*"

Their names on his breath choke me. He tries to say more, but his body tenses. Monitors start beeping louder, faster.

"BP's dropping!"

"Get that chest tube in. Now!" I glance at the paramedic. "What happened?"

"Firefight in Villa. Suspect pulled a gun. Officer Rhodes took him down, but not before his partner caught one to the chest."

"Waylon's going to carry this," I whisper.

Dr. Mitchell steps in. "Let's focus on the patient for now."

I bite back the urge to snap. If I lose it, he'll pull me off Aaron's procedure. So I shove it down.

Because right now, Aaron needs me. And later Waylon will, too.

Chapter 53

Clarity

I sit, or I try to. My legs won't stop trembling. My stomach is in knots. It should've been me.

It's been forty-five minutes, and I'm pacing. My hands are still shaking. Still coated in his blood. Flora watches me from her seat, eyes swollen, fingers twisting together in her lap.

"Waylon, you're making me dizzy," she cries.

I stop and turn to her. "I should've seen it coming." My fists clench at my sides. "I should've..."

Flora stands, placing a hand on my arm. Her grip is tight, like she's holding herself together, too. "You can't blame yourself for this. You got the guy. Aaron's..." She breaks. "He's going to be okay. He has to be."

I shake my head. "I should have assessed the situation better." My eyes burn. "He's hurt because of me."

Flora's lips part like she's about to argue, but then Khloe slams into the doorway.

I freeze. Her scrubs are soaked in blood. Flora lets out a broken sob beside me. I rush forward, grabbing Khloe's arms.

"How is he?"

Khloe's breathing hard, like she ran here. She had to

fight for him. Her chest rises and falls in deep, uneven breaths. Her lips part, then nothing. She's struggling to get the words out.

My stomach turns to lead. "Khlo!"

Her fingers dig into my sleeve tightly, and she finally exhales. "He made it."

Flora sobs. A small, broken sound as her hands fly to her mouth, her whole-body trembling. My legs nearly give out.

"The bullet... went clean... through," she continues, still catching her breath. "Some lung... damage. It was..." She presses a shaky hand to her forehead. "It was bad. Touch... and go. We nearly lost him."

Flora grips my arm, like she needs something to hold on to. Her whole body shaking.

I exhale sharply, my shoulders sagging as if the world just dropped off me. "Thank God."

Khloe looks up at me, eyes filled with tears. "He's in recovery now," she adds softly. "Unconscious, but stable. He asked for you guys before surgery."

Flora gasps. She looks up at me, eyes red-rimmed and wet. "He asked for us," she whispers.

I nod, jaw tightening as I look down at Khloe. "Thank you, Khloe. For takin' care of him."

She reaches up, brushing a hand against my cheek. "It's my job," she murmurs. Her eyes lock on mine. "I'll always be here for you, Waylon." My chest tightens. "You too, Flora."

Flora wraps us both in a hug. I reach for Khloe and cover her hand with mine, holding it there for a moment. I could say a lot right now, but I don't.

The next morning, I'm sitting beside Aaron in his hospital room still. I haven't left his side. His dark skin is pale, bandaged, and he's hooked up to machines. As I continue to watch him, his eyes blink open, confused and disoriented. Then his body jerks and his fingers twitch like he's reaching for a gun that isn't there.

"Aaron," I say fast, leaning in. "You're safe. You're in the hospital."

His eyes finally land on me. A groggy grin. "You look like hell," he mutters.

I let out a breath, part relief, part exhaustion. "You're one to talk. You scared the hell outta me."

Aaron chuckles, then winces hard, eyes squeezing shut. I hate seeing him like this.

"Don't get soft on me now, Rhodes."

I drag a hand down my face, swallowing the lump in my throat as I lean forward. "I should've seen it comin'. Should've had your back better."

"Bull," Aaron rasps, gaining strength. "You saved my life. Don't you dare turn this into something it wasn't."

I shrug, rolling the tension away.

He continues, "Jesus, even shot, I'm still prettier than you."

I shake my head, my hands gripping the edge of the chair. "I can't lose you, man."

Aaron breathes out, clutching the blanket tighter. "You're not gonna. I'm fine. Thanks to you."

I sit back, running a hand through my hair as the tension in my chest finally cracks. "Yeah, well. You better be. 'Cause I'm not doin' this without you."

Aaron grins faintly. "Guess I'm stuck with you, then."

The door swings open with a whoosh as Flora steps inside. Aaron brightens immediately.

"Hey there, hot stuff." Flora glides to his side, smiling wide as hell. "You could've brought me coffee. You didn't have to get shot to see me."

Aaron scoffs. "My number one goal was to have you more than role-play my nurse fantasy."

"Smooth," I mutter, laughing for the first time since he's been shot. Flora leans down, kissing Aaron gently, and I take that as my cue.

"I'd say get a room, but I think I'm intrudin' on y'all." I stand, walking to the door. "I'll go find my girl."

I'm not even sure they hear me through their make-out

session. I find Khloe in the break room, sitting at the counter, sipping coffee, looking exhausted. I step inside, closing the door behind me.

"Hey."

She looks up, her drained eyes meeting mine. "Hey."

I cross the room, pulling her into my arms. For a moment, we stand there, holding each other. No words. Just warmth and gratitude.

"You're amazing, you know that?"

Khloe smiles against my chest. "You're not too bad yourself, Rhodes."

I hold her tighter, unable to explain how much she means to me. "I don't know what I'd do without you, Khloe."

She pulls back, looking up at me. "Good thing you don't have to find out."

I lean down, pressing a soft kiss to her forehead. "Damn right."

Chapter 54

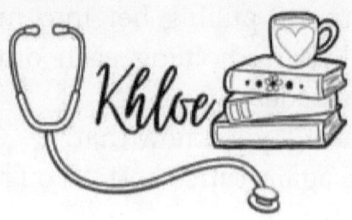

Transitions and Revelations

Flora is five glasses of wine in, sprawled across the couch with her feet in Waylon's lap, giggling in and out of consciousness. Waylon is asleep but saying my name in whispers. They're both drunk but relaxed. They could definitely use the sleep.

Flora's been taking care of Aaron like a personal nurse since he was released from the hospital. Waylon's been putting in double time at work, finishing up loose ends. It's one of the last nights in my house before Flora officially moves in with Aaron. I tell myself I'm fine, but I feel the space she's leaving behind. One by one, the people I love keep shifting away. A part of me wants to tell Flora my feelings, but I decide I won't ruin her happiness.

I make my way from the kitchen into the living room, having refilled my water. Aaron is propped up in the recliner, his injured body resting on a pillow, his good hand nursing a whiskey.

He's sharp and observant, even buzzed, his dark eyes flicking between Waylon and me like he's noting something I'd rather he didn't.

"You've been quiet," Aaron finally says.

I look at him over the rim of my glass. I squeeze onto the couch beside Waylon. "I'm always quiet."

He chuckles. "Nah, you're always thinking."

I arch a brow. "Since when did you get all deep?"

Aaron smirks. "Since a man shot me. The near-death experience earned me some insight."

I roll my eyes. "Well, you're here now, alive. You're welcome!"

Aaron grins, raising his glass in cheers. "That's my girl."

Waylon tenses next to me.

I press my lips together, then glance at Aaron. "You ever think about what would've happened if Waylon hadn't taken that guy out?"

Aaron exhales, his expression softening. "Every day." He shakes his head, knocks back his drink, and leans forward. "But then I remember I'm a bad motherfucker, and I let it go."

I laugh, shaking my head. "How is it you and Waylon are nothing alike, yet exactly the same? You're the perfect best friends."

Aaron hums, stretching his legs out, twitching as he moves. "Honestly? Took me a while to warm up to him. When we met, he was all cocky, country-boy bullshit. A white dude with an attitude who didn't know how to check his mouth."

I smirk. "Sounds about right."

Aaron chuckles, then his smile fades a fraction. "I was skeptical at first, especially 'cause of his dad."

My stomach tightens.

Aaron watches me carefully. "You know how Jack is, don't you?"

I hesitate, swirling my drink. "He's... polite."

Aaron scoffs. "He's polite 'cause you're a woman. I remember the way he looked at me when Waylon introduced us. He was trying to figure out how I fit into his picture of what his son's life should be."

I clench my jaw. "Did he ever say anything to you?"

Aaron shrugs. "Not directly. But you don't gotta say shit to let people know how you feel. It's in the way they talk to you, the way they give you the tight smiles, the awkward pauses." He shakes his head. "Didn't bother me. But it made me wary of Waylon at first. Like, what kind of man does he wanna be? One who sits quiet about that shit or the kind who speaks up?"

I stare at him.

Aaron's face is distant. "Having two lawyers as parents who fight for equal rights for all gives you insight into how to read people. I had to learn to soften myself being around new people in basic training. Especially Waylon." He smirks. "Waylon punched a guy for running his mouth about me being black, while we were in training. So, I figured he was the real deal."

"Waylon never told me that."

Aaron continues, "But it wasn't until I saved Waylon's life that Jack truly showed me respect. Some people are really caught in the old way of doing things. Jack came around, but not without Mama Martha giving him hell."

Aaron exhales and leans back, tilting his head against the chair.

"I get why you're scared, Khloe. But the Waylon I met years ago isn't the same man who's sitting there right now. He's got a ways to go, but he's transformed."

I smile awkwardly. "Really?"

Aaron's gaze flicks to Waylon snoring, then back to me. "Yeah. Because of you."

"That's hard to believe."

Aaron sighs, rolling his glass between his fingers. "When my little brother died, I shut down."

I blink. "You never told me you had a brother."

Aaron gives me a sad smile. "Not many people know about Jermaine. He was nineteen. Just started college and got hit by a drunk driver leaving his campus."

I press a hand to my chest, my breath catching. "Aaron, I'm so sorry."

He waves a hand, but there's emotion on his face. "It's been 10 years. But you know how that shit stays with you?"

He lifts his eyes, and I see him in a new light. Not just as reliable Aaron, but as someone who's carrying things I've never noticed before.

Grandma was right when she used to say, "People are battling things in silence. Don't add to their war."

"I was angry for a long time. Not only at the driver, but at God, at my parents, at myself. I didn't know how to handle it, so I stopped talking about it. Waylon was the first one who saw through that."

I inhale slowly. "What did he do?"

Aaron chuckles. "He didn't let me disappear. He dragged me into his bullshit, made sure I showed up to work, and worked out to clear my mind. He'd piss me off on purpose to make me react. It was his way of saying, *I see you.*"

I look down at my lap, my fingers gripping the fabric of my leggings. Waylon does the same thing with me.

"Look, I know Waylon's got his issues. I know he's stubborn as hell. But he loves you, Khlo. And I don't think he's ever loved anyone the way he loves you."

I let out a shaky breath. "Then why does it feel like he's always halfway out the door?"

Aaron sighs, tapping his fingers against his glass. "Because he's scared. Like you." He lowers his voice. "Flora told me you thought about breaking up with him recently. I need you to ask yourself something, Navarro. Are you thinking of pushing him away because he's leaving? Or because you're scared to let him stay in your heart?"

I can't answer because maybe I don't know the difference. Aaron studies me for a long moment, then nods like he sees the answer on my face. He downs the rest of his drink and slowly pushes to his feet.

"Come on," he says, stretching out slowly. "Let's get

these drunks to bed before Flora spills wine on your damn couch again."

I chuckle and get up.

To celebrate Aaron's recovery, Flora insists on hosting an "I didn't die 2 weeks ago" party. Aaron's back on his feet, though still on light duty. We're having a small gathering at Aaron's house. Waylon and I brought over drinks and take-out. Ramirez, Missy, Jackman, Lena, and Donald show up too, filling the space with their banter. Everything feels normal. Like we had all survived something together, and then the night takes a turn.

Aaron stands, clearing his throat. "Hey, y'all, can I have your attention for a second?"

Flora makes her way back from grabbing more glasses. As she catches sight of Aaron, she raises an eyebrow. "What's going on?"

Aaron reaches into his pocket, pulling out a small velvet box. Flora gasps, dropping the empty glasses on the couch. I suck in a breath, pulse stuttering. Waylon shifts beside me, spine straightening, hands going still in his lap.

"Flora," Aaron begins, taking a step toward her. "These last few weeks, I've been thinking a lot about life. About how fast it can change, how short it is. If I've learned anything, it's that I don't wanna waste another second not making it clear how much you mean to me."

Flora's hands fly to her mouth, eyes wide with shock as Aaron drops to one knee.

"You're my person," he continues, with tears in his eyes. "The one I wanna laugh with, fight with, and come home to for the rest of my life." He opens the box, revealing a simple but elegant diamond ring.

"Flora, will you marry me?"

Tears stream down Flora's cheeks as she nods vigorously. "Yes! Oh. My. God. Yes!"

Cheers erupt around the room. Aaron stands and slides the ring onto her finger. He pulls her into a tight embrace and winces slightly when she jumps up and down in his arms. Flora kisses him, her joy infectious. Everyone is caught in the moment's magic.

I clap, I smile, and I can't believe it. I'm so unbelievably happy for my best friend. Until I look at Waylon. My stomach drops. He's all applause and nothing else.

No spark, no flicker. He's content watching but has no real stake in the moment.

And his eyes never flicker to me. Not even once.

Chapter 55

The Proposal

I should have seen it coming. I didn't have to look at Khloe to know what she was thinking. I could feel it. The way her energy shifted, the way she tensed beside me. I felt her eyes on me, but I didn't dare look at her.

Aaron made it look so damn easy. Saying the right words, promising a forever that felt certain. I wasn't against marriage or commitment. But watching Khloe in my periphery, seeing the way she watched Flora's happiness with longing, I knew I had a problem.

The silence stretches between us as I drive Khloe home. She's quieter than usual, but I'm not stupid. I know she's comparing us to them. I can feel the tension rolling off her. She breaks first.

"Flora and Aaron seem so happy," she says carefully, testing the waters.

"They do." I nod, keeping my eyes on the road.

Khloe hesitates before speaking again. "They're moving so fast, though. I mean, they haven't even been together for a year."

I shrug. "When you know, you know, I guess."

Shit, wrong thing to say.

She turns toward me, her brows furrowed. "We're moving too slow."

My fingers tighten on the steering wheel. I hate these kinds of conversations, but not because I don't care. I'm good at giving her the answers she needs, but not at comparing relationships. But every time talk edges toward forever, my past starts screaming louder than my heart. I've spent years living by one rule: don't give anyone the power that can wreck you. And Khloe already has it.

"I think we're movin' at the pace that works for us," I finally say, choosing my words wisely. "You don't rush somethin' that matters, Khlo."

Her silence is louder than anything she could've said.

I glance at her. She's staring out the window, her profile tense. I know the doubts are creeping in. What the hell do I even say to a woman like Khloe, who's spent her whole damn life watching people walk away?

I know I should say something else to reassure her.

But I don't.

Chapter 56

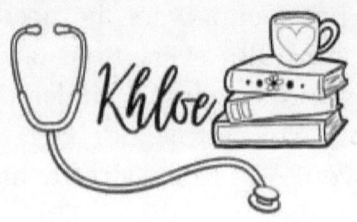

Desires and Fears

His words sit wrong in my chest. I sit there, watching the city lights blur past, reminding me I'm watching everyone else move forward while I stay in place.

After Waylon drops me off, I call Flora to congratulate her again.

"Flora, I'm so happy for you. Aaron's proposal was perfect."

"Thank you!" Flora's voice is bright and full of joy. "I still can't believe it actually happened."

I hesitate. "But... does it ever make you nervous, moving so fast?"

She laughs lightly. "Nope. When you know, you know, right?"

Her words make my saliva taste sour. "What if you don't know yet? Or what if you're with someone who doesn't seem ready to move forward?"

There's a pause. Then Flora asks, "Are we talking about me, or you and Waylon?"

I sigh. "I'm sorry. I'm ruining your night."

"Girl, you could never. Lay it on me, Khlo."

"It's just... seeing you and Aaron take this enormous step

makes me realize Waylon and I aren't there. He said he'd marry me, but now I feel like he's holding back."

Flora's tone softens. "Khlo, you and Waylon are on a separate path from Aaron and me. You've both been through so much. Maybe he's trying to protect what you have, make sure it lasts."

I close my eyes. "I don't want to feel like I'm the only one thinking about the future."

"You're not," Flora reassures me. "You need to talk to him. Waylon loves you, Khloe. That much is obvious."

But is it? Because tonight he didn't look at me once.

Chapter 57

A Looming Choice

I sit in my truck outside my house, staring at the dashboard. Thinking of the look in Khloe's eyes tonight, waiting for something I didn't know how to give. She wanted consoling and certainty. I don't know if I can give her that or if I can give her myself all the way.

I rub a hand over my face, frustration simmering in my chest. I'm not used to real commitment. I've been careful with what I let people see and what I let people have. Khloe already has more of me than anyone ever has. But how much more can I give before there's nothing left that's just mine?

I'm leaving for six months. If I can't make her feel secure now or find the words to keep her from doubting me, what the hell is gonna happen when I'm gone?

I grit my teeth. I should tell her I want this now, before she convinces herself I'm slipping away. But deep down, I know telling her won't be enough. Not if I can't stop holding back. Not if I can't stop being a narcissistic bastard who's never had to let someone in completely.

The air thrums with conversation and bursts of laughter, silverware chiming against plates like background percussion. A server weaves past with a tray balanced high, the scent of salt and steak trailing behind. Flora's laughter carries over it all. Across from me, she sits with her hand on Aaron's, her ring sparkling, mirroring the excitement radiating from her. She stares at him as if she's halfway down the aisle already.

"I'm just saying," Flora says, grinning widely, "this assignment is huge for you, Waylon. Six months? That's career-defining. They don't send just anyone for something like this."

Aaron nods, lifting his beer in a small toast. "She's right. You've earned it."

I sink into the chair. "Yeah, well, it's another job. Someone's gotta do it."

Flora rolls her eyes. "Oh, come on. Don't undersell it. You should be proud."

My eyes flick to Khloe, who's sitting beside me quietly. She's got a smile on her face, but it doesn't reach her eyes. She's pushing her food around on her plate, and I can tell she's only half-listening.

"You okay, darlin'?" I ask, keeping my voice low.

She looks up quickly, as if I've caught her. "Yeah, of course. I'm just... taking it all in."

Flora doesn't miss a beat. "Khloe, you must be so proud. This kind of opportunity doesn't come around every day."

Khloe nods, her smile tightening a fraction. "I am. It's great for him."

There's something in her response. I don't think anyone else notices, but I do. A dread that's been hanging between us since I told her about the assignment.

"Hey," I say, reaching under the table to squeeze her

hand. "You sure you're alright?"

She squeezes back briefly. "I'm fine, Waylon. Really."

Aaron clears his throat, cutting through the moment. "Anyway, six months isn't that long. It'll fly by, Khloe. You'll have us to keep you company while he's gone."

Flora grins, then winks Khloe's way. "Exactly. We'll keep ourselves busy. Girls' and Aaron nights, too much wine, whiskey, and reading. You name it."

Khloe chuckles. Her eyes flick to me, and in that glance, I see everything she's not saying. All her doubts, worries, and fears.

"Sounds like a plan," she says while twisting her napkin in her lap.

The conversation moves on. Flora and Aaron dive into stories about their week, but I can't stop watching Khloe. She smiles and laughs as if she's reading from a script. But I know her too well. I can see the cracks beneath the surface. It's a mask she's wearing.

She's faking it. But I'm the one bleeding for it because I'm the reason she has to.

Hell, I can't be the reason she hurts anymore.

Chapter 58

The Finale

As we say goodbye, Waylon opens my car door, and I slide in, bile rising in my throat. He's downplaying this opportunity because leaving me behind ruins it. I'm ruining it. When he slides into the driver's seat, I glance over at him. I have to say something. If I don't, the words will choke me.

"Waylon," I say, my fists clenching in my lap. "Do you think we're ready for this?" I stare at him, praying for a smile. But he's already gone. His mind is miles away.

"We'll talk at the house, darlin'."

The answer I'm dreading is already written between the lines. At home, he looks tired, shoulders slumping under the weight of his own thoughts. His jaw is tight. There's a frustration that I'm not used to.

"If I'm being honest, Khloe," he says, lingering near the hallway that leads to the exit, fingers raking through his hair. "I don't think you're mentally ready for me to be gone."

The sting of his words spreads through my chest like fire. I sit on the arm of the couch, willing myself to move through it. "I go from certain to panicked in seconds. I need reassurance. I'm not sure you can handle it. That's our issue."

He shuffles on his feet. "Constantly reassuring is not my thing. That's your wound. But I've done nothing to ease it."

I take a deep breath. "Well, if you want me, then it's ours, Waylon."

He mirrors me. "I do love you, but it's something you need to control."

"You're giving up on us because you think I can't handle it?"

"I'm not givin' up," he says, stepping forward. "I'm tryin' to be realistic. I love you, Khlo, but this isn't just about me leavin'. It's about what you're gonna do while I'm gone."

My arms cross defensively. "Do you think I want to feel this way?"

"No. But you're not workin' through it, Khlo. You're lettin' it control you. And I can't leave knowin' you're gonna tear yourself apart the whole time I'm gone."

"Maybe you're right," I whisper. "Maybe I'm not ready."

His eyes are full of regret. "I want you to be okay, Khlo. That's all I've ever wanted."

"I know."

"I had a conversation with Caroline a while ago, and I realized... I'm selfish. I'm not wired to keep offering constant comfort."

I blink at him, confusion and irritation swirling in my chest. "What does your shit with her have to do with me? Fuck you, Waylon."

"You're important, Khloe," he says. His expression is hollow. He's already decided.

"That's redundant. I'm no longer yours to worry about," I snap.

He takes a step closer, like he wants to reach out.

"Goodbye, Waylon."

His jaw tightens. "Don't say that unless you mean it, Khloe."

I hesitate. I've spent my life with the same fate: people always leaving me. "You keep saying you love me, but you don't even tell me all your truths."

He sighs and crosses his arms. "I know. I can't handle giving you everything."

"You've been slowly drifting anyway."

He shakes his head.

I throw my hands up, frustration completely eating at me. "You may love me, but you've been drifting away."

He doesn't answer.

"Goodbye, Waylon. It was nice knowing you."

He nods, face stoic as he walks out. The door clicks shut behind him. I stare at the space he's left behind. I should be used to this by now.

Later that night, my room feels too big as I sit cross-legged on my bed. An empty bottle of wine on the nightstand and my phone clutched in my hands. I stare at the empty message thread, my thoughts racing. I type out a message, my fingers trembling.

KHLOE

> I shouldn't have agreed with you earlier. I let fear speak for me. I don't want to push you away. I want to try Waylon. Please, can we talk?

Minutes stretch on with no response. The wine pushes me to try again.

KHLOE

> I'm sorry for how I acted. I let my insecurities get the better of me.

KHLOE

> I'll do better. The ball is in your court, Waylon. Decide.

Still nothing. His silence is a boulder that grows with every passing moment. I toss my phone onto the bed, fisting my hands to my eyes to keep the tears at bay. Silence is an answer. I curl up under the covers, regret and alcohol pressing down on me.

I wanted to believe we were stronger than this.

The next night, after a shift together, Flora comes over. The exhaustion in my body matches the heaviness in my chest. She hands me a glass of wine, her eyes scanning my face.

"Alright," Flora says, settling beside me. "Spill. What happened with Waylon?"

"We had... a fight, I guess. It wasn't even a fight. We didn't yell. It felt more like... reality slapping me in the face."

Flora's brows furrow. "What do you mean?"

"He said he doesn't think I'm ready for him to be gone. And the worst part is... he's right."

Flora leans in, her face etched with concern. "Khlo, come on. You're one of the strongest people I know. How could he think you're not ready?"

"It's not about strength," I say quietly, my words cracking. "It's about the way I unravel the second I feel like someone's leaving. He's scared I'll fall apart while he's gone. And... I think I will."

Her hand lands on my knee. "And what did you say?"

I laugh bitterly, shaking my head. "I told him maybe he was right and I'm not ready."

Flora's jaw drops. "What? Why would you say that?"

I shrug, trying to keep myself together even though I feel like I'm disintegrating. "Because it felt true. He looked at me like I was broken. I panicked and... agreed."

Flora sighs, a mix of frustration and sympathy crossing her face. "And now?"

My hands tremble. "I texted him. Told him I regret it and that I don't want to lose him. He hasn't answered."

Flora's eyes widen. "At all?"

My eyes burn. "Not a word. It's like... I don't exist anymore."

She sets her glass down with force; her face hardens. "That's not okay, Khlo. He doesn't get to do this to you."

"I keep trying to convince myself he's busy," I say, the tears escaping. "But part of me wonders if this is his way of ending things without having to say the words. Just silence. That's all I get."

Flora leans forward. "Look, I'm not gonna sit here and pretend to understand what's going on in his head. But I know this: you deserve more than silence, Khloe. You always have."

Her words break open my dam. I spill out. "I thought I was worth more than this," I whisper, lip quivering.

Flora pulls me into a tight hug. "You are, Khloe. Do not let his silence make you forget that."

I cling to her, my tears soaking into her scrubs as all the grief I've been holding in comes rushing out. The hurt hits all at once, leaving me gasping.

I am so thankful for our friendship. I would be so lost without her.

Chapter 59

Cowardice

The bar is soaked in dim light, murmurs blurring into background noise; the twang of country music weaving through it all. I sit across from Jackman, nursing a whiskey I don't want, but a man oughta have one on a night like this. Khloe's texts and that damn fight are still sitting heavy, like a stone in my chest.

Jackman leans back, arms crossed. "You been quieter than usual," he says. "That mean you're ready to talk about her?"

I sigh, running a hand over my jaw. "She's in my head, and I can't shake it."

He grunts. "She still sendin' those texts?"

"Yeah." I clear my throat. "Sayin' she regrets it, wants to make it work. I haven't answered."

Jackman raises an eyebrow. "Why the hell not? You love her, don't you?"

"Of course I do," I say. "But what if lovin' her ain't enough? What if I end up makin' her worse?"

Jackman sets his glass down hard. "Boy, you're thinkin' yourself into a grave. You always do this. She's out there fightin' for you, and you're sittin' here actin' like silence is noble."

The bartender, a cute redhead, strolls over. Her smile's warm, her bright blue eyes lingering on me a little too long. "Need another drink?" she asks, eyes lingering longer than necessary.

"No, ma'am," I say it flat. "I'm good."

She hesitates, her smile faltering before she moves on.

Jackman watches her go, then looks back at me. "You could've had her number without even trying. But you didn't bite. That tells me plenty."

I glare at him. "That's the last thing I need. I've got enough of a mess on my hands."

He nods, all sarcasm gone. "So, what are you afraid of? That she'll fall apart while you're gone, or that you will?"

I stare at my glass. "Both," I admit finally. "She thinks I'm gonna leave like everyone else. Maybe she's right to think that, 'cause look at me. I'm out here, halfway across the county, dodgin' her texts."

Jackman leans in slightly, eyes sharp. "You're not leavin' her, Waylon. You're doin' your job. But you leavin' her in the dark like this, and she's got no reason to believe you're ever comin' back for her."

He pauses, his gaze narrowing. "You remember what happened with Caroline? You shut down on her, too. Thought staying quiet was the same as keeping peace. Thought if you just worked harder and kept it all to yourself, it'd be fine. And what happened? She packed her bags and left you wonderin' how the hell it got so bad. Don't act like you don't see the pattern. I ain't watchin' you do that again. Not with Khloe."

He's right. Damn it. "I don't wanna break her."

Jackman shakes his head. "You're already doin' that by not answering. If you want her, fight for her. Even if it's messy. Hell, especially if it is. Otherwise, you're just provin' her fears true."

I drain the rest of my whiskey. "I need to figure out how

to fix this."

He tips his bottle toward me. "Start by pickin' up your damn phone. It's time to stop runnin' and start answerin'. "

Khloe's face, voice, and goddamn texts all loop in my head. Jackman watches me stare at my phone.

"You're torturing yourself," he mutters. "She's not askin' for perfection. She's askin' for you."

I pick up my phone and scroll through her messages. They're all still there, each one tugging at me differently. I've answered almost a hundred times. I'd start typing and stop for no reason other than knowing my absence will be too much.

KHLOE

> I wanted to say a few things. I don't want our last conversation to be the last things we say to each other.

KHLOE

> First & foremost, thank you for coming into my life and being there for me when you didn't have to at all.

KHLOE

> I understand things went really fast and then really crazy. I apologize for my part in that.

KHLOE

> You had an impact on my life, and I do not want you to just be something I try to forget, because clearly forgetting you isn't possible.

KHLOE

I know my overthinking made things worse than they were. If it weren't for you, I wouldn't have recognized some harmful patterns in myself, so once again, thank you.

KHLOE

I have no hard feelings, and I'm sorry if I came across as angry before. I should have appreciated you letting go.

KHLOE

I'm fucking drunk, I fucking miss you. It feels so stupid to say it, but I do.

KHLOE

I loved my name when your mouth spoke it. I loved my eyes when you stared into them. There's this deep need for me to know if my absence has done any damage to you. If it hasn't, please say so.

KHLOE

I fill the void of you by reading things you said to me before & it gives me false hope. Like I still have a chance.

KHLOE

> It's probably unhealthy. It's like a bridge in the rain that gives you a moment of peace, but it never stops the storm. You were my bridge. Now those old messages are my bridge. When I lost you, the downpour swallowed me whole.

And the latest two gut me:

KHLOE

> I love you. Even if you're mad, even if this is over, I need you to know that. But I need you to tell me if this is really over for you, just say it's over. That's literally all I need. My brain can't comprehend that you said the things you've said to me, and you can just give up like that.

KHLOE

> If you don't answer this, I'm just going to take that as I still have an opportunity, and whether it's once a day or once a week, I'm going to keep saying something to you because my heart and my head won't let you go unless I know that you're done with me.

I let out a slow breath, my thumb hovering over the keyboard. My stomach churns as I type:

> Miss you too.

I stare at the words, my finger hovering over the send button. If I answer her now, what the hell am I even saying? I'm ready? That I know how to fix this?

My thumb hesitates before I hit backspace, erasing the message.

Jackman shakes his head. "You're lettin' fear call the shots."

"Maybe," I mutter, setting the phone back down. "I've caught myself scrolling through the texts, rereading her words, lingering on the photos. It's like holdin' onto her without reachin' out. It feels cowardly as hell."

Jackman leans back in his chair. "You don't have to have it all figured out. But don't leave her hangin' forever. Own it or end it."

I nod, shoving my phone into my pocket, ignoring the buzzing in my chest. I push my chair back and stand. "Gonna hit the head," I mumble.

Jackman lifts a brow but doesn't say a word.

I make my way through the bar, my body heavy. My mind is cluttered. The neon light above the bathroom flickers as I push inside, running cold water over my hands and grip the edge of the sink. What the fuck am I doing?

The door swings open, and the cute redhead steps inside. Her blue eyes lock onto mine in the dim light, a knowing smile tugging at her lips.

"Hey, I didn't take you for the shy type."

I let out a scant breath, turning toward her. She's really sexy. A girl I'd normally lean into, play with, let distract me from what's eating me.

She steps closer, fingers brushing lightly against my wrist. "You sure you don't want that drink?"

I watch her tilt her head, inviting me in. Out of instinct,

or maybe out of despair, I let my hands slide to her hips, pulling her closer.

Her lips part slightly in anticipation, hands trailing up my chest. I lean down, and when I kiss her, I expect something. A spark, a rush, or a feeling. But there's nothing. Not even the briefest flicker of heat. She's warm and soft, but she's not Khloe.

I pull back almost immediately, letting her go without explanation.

Her brows pull together in confusion. "What's wrong?"

"I don't fuckin' know." I step past her and push out of the bathroom, pulse roaring in my ears.

Jackman watches me walk back from the bathroom and sees her come out of the bathroom behind me. His jaw tightens as I walk up.

"You lookin' for comfort or punishment?"

I say nothing, but the burn of shame creeps up my neck.

Jackman shakes his head, disappointed but not surprised. "You keep doin' things that make you feel worse and call it copin'. That ain't it, Waylon."

I grab my phone, stare at Khloe's last message one more time, then put it back in my pocket, letting my silence answer her.

I throw myself into work, picking up extra assignments before I leave. It's easier to drown out the memories of Khloe when I'm busy, but the quiet moments are hell. I lie awake at night, replaying our last conversation, wondering if I made the biggest mistake.

Aaron's noticed the change in me. I've been ignoring his attempts to pull me back. "You're not yourself, man," he says one afternoon during a quiet rundown on current assignments.

I shrug, my eyes fixed on the computer screen. Donald and Ramirez round the corner just as I mutter, "I'm fine."

"You don't look fine," Ramirez says. "You look like a guy who let the best thing in his life walk away."

My hands clasp together, jaw tightening. "I didn't let her walk. I pushed her."

"You think that was the right call?" Aaron deadpans.

My silence answers, thick with regret.

The hum of Flora's phone call with Aaron's mom drifts from the kitchen out to the back porch. Aaron and I are planted out here, the Texas night air dense and warm around us. He leans back in his chair, nursing a beer, eyes fixed on me as I work through my thoughts. It's the first time I've really opened up to him about Khloe. I'd avoided it, afraid he'd make me face what I wasn't ready to feel.

"I didn't know what to say to her, man," I admit, running a hand over my face. "She said goodbye, Waylon, and practically kicked me out. I completely shut down. I didn't even push back."

Aaron tilts his head, his dark eyes thoughtful. "Why do you think that is?"

I shrug, but the weight in my chest grows heavier. "Because it's real. She's real. And I'm not sure I'm built to handle it. Every time I let someone get close, I screw it up."

Aaron takes a long sip of his beer. "You're not screwing it up because you let someone in, Waylon. You're screwing it up because you don't."

I stay quiet.

"Look," Aaron says, leaning forward, "I've seen you in worse situations than this. Combat, loss, all of it. You get through it by locking yourself up tighter than a damn vault. But with Khloe, that's not gonna work. She's not looking for a wall. She's looking for the you that you've hidden."

"I don't know if I can give her that," I drawl. "I don't even know how to start."

"By trying," Aaron says simply, "by letting her see what's behind all that armor you're wearing. You think you're protecting her by holding back, but you're protecting yourself."

I open my mouth to argue, but the sound of the sliding screen door interrupts us. Flora steps out, a glass of wine in her hand and a sharp look in her eye.

"Really, Waylon?" she said, her words laced with bitterness. "You're sitting here, feeling sorry for yourself, acting like you're some noble martyr for shutting her out?"

I stiffen, my jaw tightening. "Flora, this is between Aaron and me."

"No, it's not," she shoots back, stepping closer. "You want to act like you're too broken to love someone? Fine. But don't pretend like that's about Khloe. It's about you being too selfish and scared to put in the work."

Aaron raises his eyebrows, but he doesn't intervene.

"Why does everyone keep fuckin' calling me selfish?" I ask.

"You are," Flora says, not missing a beat. "You can't handle the idea of someone actually needing you. You let her feel like she's the one asking for too much when really all she's asking for is for you to be vulnerable. Instead, you ghost her like a coward."

Fuck, that stings.

Flora pushes on. "You don't get to do that to her, Waylon. Not after everything she's been through. If you love her, show her. If you don't... at least have the decency to let her move on."

Aaron chimes in, "She's not wrong, man. Either step up or step out, but don't keep her hanging in the middle. That's not fair to her or to you."

I stare at the ground, the words circling in my head like a storm. I know they're right, but knowing and doing are two separate things.

Flora takes a step back. "You're not a bad guy, Waylon. But you need to decide if you're gonna be the man she deserves. Because if you're not? Let her go."

With that, she turns and walks back inside. Aaron takes another sip of his beer. "She's got a point."

I exhale, the tension in my chest threatening to suffocate me. "Yeah. She always does."

And right on time, a text from Khloe comes through.

KHLOE

Remember that first night, your fingers intertwined with my hair as we walked backwards into your bedroom. Our lips refusing to separate until we met the wall. The pressure of our bodies making me let out a subtle moan that told you I'd be ready for you. Ready to be yours. Ready to submit. The anticipation as you made me get on my knees and cuffed my hands together. You asked me what I wanted, and I said, "You," looking up to meet your eyes. My eyes screaming to tell you I wanted anything you could give me. There was fucking electricity between us, Waylon. The tension built with each spank and each number I called out. When you blindfolded me, and a smile escaped my mouth, and you told me to kiss you.

KHLOE

> I never told you this, but I smiled because not only was I hungry, as you say, but you were fulfilling my every fantasy. Even writing this I'm wet. No man has ever opened me up like that. I fear no man ever will. I know you want freedom, and I don't want to take that from you. But I do want to take your rock-hard cock inside me like it's the first time, one last time. I want to bite my way down your body from your chest 'til I swallow your cock in my mouth. So, let's go to bed...

Fuck.

My hand tightens around the beer bottle. My breathing goes shallow. For the first time since she said "goodbye," I feel fucking *alive*.

I shift in the chair, trying to get comfortable, but there's no hiding it. I'm fucking hard. Her words did that. Sharp, dirty, and soaked in everything I've been trying not to want. I drag a hand over my thigh, keeping myself tucked under the table.

Aaron looks up, eyebrows cinched together. "You good? You look like you're blushing."

I lock my jaw, pretending I'm not one wrong move from giving myself away. I am fucking drowning as a picture of her fully nude pops up. She's on her knees, head tilted back, neck exposed, one arm holding her throat and the other holding her pussy open.

Holy shit. I start to text back, but stop myself.

Shit. I need her.

Fuck it.

> **WAYLON**
> I been trying so hard because I can't give you what you want.

> **WAYLON**
> I think about you every day.

> **WAYLON**
> I need to see you.

I stand quickly; I have to get to her now. "I gotta go. I'll see you tomorrow."

Aaron looks up, confused, and stands, following me to the door. "The hell, man? What's got you moving like that? Where are you going?"

My phone pings.

> **KHLOE**
> Come over.

I was coming whether or not she answered.

Flora is in the kitchen, eyes flickering between us. "Where's the fire, boys? What the hell's got you wound up, Waylon?"

Aaron chuckles. "I'll give you one guess, and it starts with a K."

Flora follows. "Jesus, you look like a man on a mission."

Aaron adds. "Guess we know where he's going."

I don't answer as I throw their front door open. I practically run to my truck as they watch from the front door.

Chapter 60

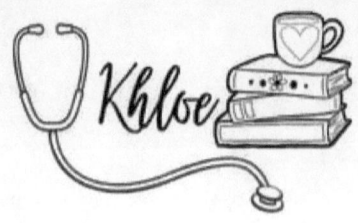

One Last Plea

I spent the night with Missy, drinking, planning for school, thinking about him. Always him. I sent that text, not hoping for tenderness, just wanting to get under his skin. To reach the part that never needed words.

My phone pings. I know which part answered. My fingers hover over the keyboard. It's been weeks since we've spoken. His silence screamed in every empty space. My thumb taps two words before I can stop it.

I don't hesitate when I hear the knock. Waylon stands there with shadows under his eyes, like he's been fighting for sleep and losing. His face is pale in the porch light, and my chest twists.

For weeks, I've convinced myself that my absence didn't touch him. But looking at him now, I realize I was only fooling myself.

"Hey," he mumbles.

"Hey."

I step aside to let him in. We stand in silence, the tension between us palpable. His hand lifts, brushing a strand of hair from my face.

"I missed you, Khlo."

His touch sends a jolt through me, but I clench my jaw, my defenses in place. "What do you want from me, Waylon?"

He exhales, his hand falling to his side. "I need you."

No.

But I nod and go to my room. He follows.

In the dim light of the bedroom, everything feels heavier. His gaze, his touch, the weight of our unspoken feelings hover between us.

He's tender as he slides my shirt over my head. His lips press reverent kisses along my shoulder. "I never wanted to hurt you," he whispers, voice breaking. "Not once."

"Why didn't you answer?" I ask, my fingers trembling as they trail over his chest.

True to his character, he's silent. He pulls me close, his lips meeting mine in a kiss that feels bittersweet, like a promise and a farewell all at once. There's no rush, no edge.

We collapse onto the bed, bare and tangled. It feels like that first night. The way his hand slides along my spine and the quiet sound he makes against my throat pulls at my soul. I close my eyes and wish I could rewind everything. Go back to the version of us that hadn't fallen apart.

He buries his face in my neck, his breath warm against my skin. "I think about you every day, darlin'. I don't know how to stop."

I hold him tighter, tears slipping silently into the pillow. "You don't have to. Don't shut me out."

He doesn't respond.

His touch is too gentle. I want him to slam into me, claim me with a force only he is capable of. Instead, his slow, deliberate strokes pull me in. It feels good, but it's not us. Like he's trying to memorize us, not lose himself in it.

He hasn't met my eye, hasn't kissed me. Fuck. I know exactly what this is.

My body betrays me, reacting like it's another late-night fuck after dinner on the River Walk.

I'm slowly coming undone, my body tensing as I pulse around him.

He finally looks at me. I wish he hadn't. His eyes are so distant. He's already gone.

This isn't a new beginning. It's goodbye.

I know it the second I come.

Chapter 61

Goodbye

She's beneath me, legs wrapped around me, but it doesn't feel the same. I pull her closer, trying to commit the way she feels against me to memory. Her breathing changes when I push deeper. Her fingers dig into my back like she's afraid I'll disappear.

I want to take her rough as I always do, but I move painstakingly slowly. Every stroke is measured, not to claim her, but to remember her. To burn her into me, so when I'm gone, I won't forget the way she feels.

I haven't kissed her. I haven't stared into her eyes. Despite that, she moves with me, like her body refuses to acknowledge what we both know. As she starts to come apart around me, it's then I finally let myself look at her. Her mouth open, brows pinched together, lost in the pleasure I'm giving her. And when her eyes lock with mine, something in her shifts.

She knows.

She knows this isn't another night between us. She knows this is something else entirely. I want to crush my lips to hers and take back the space I've put between us.

But I don't. I can't. Because she'll think this isn't what it is. Me fucking her goodbye.

I hold her until she falls asleep. Once she's out, I slip free of her grasp.

I'm sitting at the edge of her bed, staring at a blank sheet of paper. My grip on the pen aches from the pressure, from holding onto this moment. To her. To what I'm about to let go of. I should walk out and let silence bury what's left.

It's better if I become the villain she can get over.

But Khloe deserves more than that, even if it's the last thing I ever give her.

I set the pen to the paper.

> Khlo, I'm selfish. I can't be that man, no matter how much I want to be.

I grit my teeth, feeling every ounce of truth in the words. Wanting isn't enough. She needs more than a man who shuts down when things get serious. Fuck, I tried.

> I'll always love you. You'll always be mine.

My throat is dry. This is the only thing I'm certain of. She was mine long before I ever had the right to claim her. I knew it the first time she smiled at me like she wasn't afraid of the storm inside me. And I was hers, in every way that mattered. But love doesn't fix everything. It doesn't make me the man she deserves.

> It's better this way. I can't be what you want.
>
> Love, Waylon.

The lie masks all the truths. Or maybe it isn't a lie at all.

Maybe this was what she needed, to be free of me, of waiting for me to leave and to come home. She might hate me for it, but she'll be okay. She's strong.

I sit the pen down, staring at the note for a long time. My teeth grind like I'm trying to crush the words I'll never say. I want to wake her up, kiss her, and tell her something softer than these words. But I won't let her spend her lonely nights listening for footsteps that won't return.

So, I fold the note and set it on the nightstand where she'll find it first thing. I sit there for a long time, watching her sleep. She's more beautiful than anything I ever thought I'd have in this life. She looks so fucking peaceful. And it kills me. Because I know she's going to wake up reaching for me, only to find an empty bed.

I need to leave. But my body won't move. The weight of what I'm about to do presses down on my chest. Then it hits me.

I can't close the door all the way.

I grab the note and stuff it into my back pocket, not daring to look back as I walk out.

Sitting in my truck a few blocks away, I watch the sunrise, my chest heavy with the mess of what I've done. Our last night is burned into me. It'll haunt me for the rest of my life. But I know this is the right thing.

I start the engine, forcing myself to drive away.

For good this time.

Chapter 62

Silent Suffering

I wake up, reaching for him, finding cool sheets. His scent still lingers, faint but unmistakable. I lie there waiting until the silence swallows me whole.

"Waylon?"

My hands start to shake as the truth roots into my stomach, heavy and sharp, like ink in water, impossible to contain.

He's gone.

But I don't cry. I get up and get ready for work. One foot in front of the other. Like I always do when someone leaves.

Like I've done every other time someone has abandoned me.

It's been a week. I'm really trying. I eat, but everything tastes like nothing. I turn on music, but it's just noise; every song reminds me of him.

I'm exhausted but can't sleep, staring at the ceiling at two a.m., feeling like my heart is too massive to stay in my chest.

I sit on the floor of the shower, water burning against my

skin, but I don't feel it. I'm waiting to feel *anything*.

My reflection in the mirror is unrecognizable. Flora says my eyes are hollow. I think I look fine in my new normal.

I text him all the time, asking why he can't have a conversation with me. He never answers. A few times, I've called to see if I'm blocked.

I'm not.

He's getting all my messages and ignoring me. If he hadn't told me he'd never abandon me, I don't think I would feel this bad.

I get drunk with Flora and Aaron, and on the outside, I still appear put together. But secretly, I've texted him probably fifty times.

The latest:

KHLOE

> You can't seriously be this selfish that you can't just tell me to stop & leave you alone. I need fucking closure, Waylon. If I have to be a crazy bitch to get it, then so be it.

I send it and get nothing.

In the days that follow, I go through the motions. Wake. Move. Pretend. Repeat. That's all I've got in me right now. Aaron and his parents secured my acceptance into UT Health. I should be excited and proud. But everything feels washed out, like the world's been drained of color.

Flora keeps trying to get me to open up. But every time I think about him and how he held me that night, I feel like a fucking failure.

What kind of person says the things he said and still leaves? A disappearing asshole. A self-centered, controlling dipshit. Just like all the people before him. But Waylon beat them all at making it feel like love right before the fall.

As the weeks pass, I continue drowning in my schedule. Work. School. No play. No pause. I know it's not healthy, but it's the only thing that keeps me from unraveling.

Flora's been coming over to clean out her old room. She's taking forever. Part of me knows it's her way of checking in without making me say I need her. She's here again tonight, between the kitchen and the hallway that leads to my room. I keep catching her watching me through the open door.

Every time she peeks in, I plaster on a smile, mostly for her. Proof that I haven't completely lost it. I'm studying or pretending to. Reading Waylon's old messages like they hold a secret I missed.

If I reread the words enough times, I'll understand how it all came apart. It's pathetic; I know. But it's the only thing keeping me tethered.

It's been about a week since I texted him, probably because I haven't been drinking. I know it's my weakness. I have relied on alcohol to suppress the pain of abandonment before. But now, sitting in it without numbing the edges, I think Flora was right. I might need to talk to someone.

I'm angry at everything, crying over nothing. I snap. I shut down. I sink. I'm tired of pretending I'm not. I'm ready to talk to a professional.

Waylon's memory has wrapped itself around every part of me, and I let it. I've fed it. I've kept it warm. I'm starting to think I deserve better than a ghost.

Here goes nothing.

The office is warm, the air thick with the faint scent of lavender. Soft earth tones cover the walls, colors meant to put you at ease. But my stomach still twists as I sink into the plush chair, hands wrapped around a cup of tea the receptionist handed me.

Across from me, Dr. Elena Morales sits with a notebook in her lap. She looks calm and confident. A person who sees right through bullshit.

"So, Khloe, what brings you here today?"

I shift. "I've been struggling with relationships and myself."

Dr. Morales nods, her expression encouraging. "Can you tell me more about that? What's been happening?"

I hesitate, but I need to keep going. "I just got out of a relationship. It was... intense. I think I got too attached. When he left, it felt like I couldn't breathe."

Her expression softens. "That sounds painful," she finally says. "How long were you together?"

I chuckle. "A few months." I shake my head, feeling heat rise to my cheeks. "Not that long, really. But it felt... different."

Dr. Morales leans forward. "What about him felt that way to you?"

I exhale, my fingers tracing the rim of the cup. "He... Waylon made me feel safe. Like I didn't have to be in control all the time." I swallow hard. "And we explored... things together."

Her brows lift with curiosity. "When you say 'things,' do you mean sexually? Like BDSM?"

My cheeks burn, but I continue. "Yeah." I glance down, embarrassed.

"It wasn't just about the sex, though. It was about the faith I felt in him. The way he paid attention to every detail.

It made me feel... cared for."

Dr. Morales offers a small smile. "BDSM can be a powerful tool for connection and trust when done consensually and safely. But it can also bring up a lot of deep-seated emotions, especially for someone who has experienced trauma or abandonment. Does that resonate with you?"

I tense. "My mom left when I was a kid. My dad, too. My grandmother raised me, and she was amazing, but... I've always been afraid the people I love will leave. Waylon would leave for long work trips for days and weeks at a time."

She scribbles a note. "That fear is real, Khloe. And it sounds like it might influence the way you attach to people now. When Waylon would leave, did you crave that sense of safety and care more intensely?"

"Yes," I whisper. "When he was on assignment, there was this... ache. He'd be gone for long stretches, sometimes without access to his phone. And even when he *had* it, I'd still be waiting and hoping he'd text or call. When he didn't, or even when he did... it was always sexual. I felt like I was unraveling."

She nods, her expression thoughtful. "It sounds like his absences triggered your PTSD. And the intimacy you shared, particularly in a BDSM dynamic, might have amplified that. Letting someone take control, even in a loving and consensual way, creates a deep emotional bond, sometimes deeper than we realize."

I bite my lip, my mind racing. "So, what does that mean? That I shouldn't have done it?"

Dr. Morales shakes her head. "BDSM isn't the issue. It's how those experiences interacted with the wounds you already had. You gave Waylon a lot of trust, and when he left and would be distant, it felt like a confirmation of the fears you've been carrying for a long time. But that doesn't mean you can't work through it."

I blink, trying to push down tears. "I don't want to feel like this anymore. I don't want to be so... dependent."

Dr. Morales smiles. "That's a great first step. Healing starts with awareness. Right now, the best thing you can do is focus on yourself. Understanding your patterns, where they come from, and how to change them. It might help to take a step back from relationships while you do this work."

"But what if Waylon comes back?" I shift in my seat. "So... I need to stay single?"

"For a while," she says gently. "Not forever. But right now, it's important to build a firm foundation within yourself. That way, when you're ready for a relationship again with anyone, you'll be approaching it from a place of strength and self-awareness. Not fear."

I exhale. "I think I can... I mean, I have to, right?"

She smiles, kind but unwavering. "You don't have to do it alone. Therapy is about giving you the tools to navigate this journey. And Khloe?" She softens. "The fact that you're here, willing to do the work, says a lot about your strength."

I sit with that for a second, the words settling inside me.

Strength. I don't feel strong. I feel raw and unsteady.

But for the first time in weeks, I'm moving forward instead of drowning

Chapter 63

Returning to Regrets

This apartment reeks of perfume and sex. Doesn't smell like her. The tangled sheets are beneath me. Can't tell if it's the ceiling fan or the ceiling that won't stop spinning.

But my chest is *empty*. My dick's satisfied, but my head found no relief. No fucking *anything*.

Khloe's still there.

I turn, and the woman beside me sighs in her sleep, blonde hair fanned across the pillow.

What's her name again? Goddamn it. Here I am again.

I sit up, my stomach twisting. My whole body feels like it's rejecting what just happened.

Instead, it proved what I've been trying to ignore. Khloe isn't just another woman on a long list. She's the one I'll never be able to replace. The thought makes me nauseous. Or is that the whiskey?

I get up, dressing quickly in the dim light from the window. The girl stirs but doesn't wake. Good. I don't say goodbye. Don't leave a note. She'll figure it out.

Outside, the night air is chilly against my skin, but it doesn't clear my drunk head. The guilt clings to me like sweat. I order an Uber and wait. My phone is warm in my hand as the screen glows. And before I can stop, I'm texting her.

WAYLON

no idea how bAd I wan na fuk u.

I stare at the words. It's not what I meant to say, but it's all I can say because if I try to explain, I'll crack open completely.

The Uber pulls up. I climb in, rubbing a hand over my jaw. Waiting, hoping, and dreading a response. But she doesn't answer. She shouldn't.

The next morning, I feel and look like shit. Ramirez notices immediately.

"Damn, Rhodes," he drawls, dropping next to me. "You look like hell."

I grunt, sipping my coffee. It isn't helping.

Ramirez leans forward with his usual cocky smirk. "That bad, huh? Rough night?"

I exhale. "I fucked up."

Ramirez snorts. "Not breaking news."

I glare, but his smirk doesn't waver. "Seriously, though. What happened?"

I roll the coffee cup between my hands. "Went home with someone. Thought it'd help. Thought it'd... I don't know... snap me out of it."

Ramirez hums. "And?"

"I left before she woke up," I mutter. "I'm a goddamn stranger in my skin."

Ramirez watches me for a long moment before letting out a low chuckle. "Yeah, that shit happens when you're in love. Abuela always said tequila doesn't fix heartbreak, but it sure as hell makes it louder."

I scoff. "I'm not in love."

Ramirez tilts his head. "No? Then why do you look like a man who buried his own heart?"

I tense. Is he right?

"Look, man," Ramirez says, his tone losing its teasing edge. "I been where you are. Had my fair share of meaningless fucks before I met Val. But at some point, the high wears off faster than it used to. All you're left with is the same damn hole in your chest."

I grind my teeth. "Love ain't enough."

Ramirez lifts an eyebrow. "Nah, but shutting down sure as hell isn't either."

I shake my head. "You don't get it."

Ramirez crosses his arms. "No, *you* don't get it. You think pushin' her away is protectin' her? But you're hurtin' her in a worse way. And for what? Some bullshit idea that you're bad for her? That she's better off without you?"

I don't answer because he's right. And that's exactly why I *have* to do it. She deserves more than this version of me. More than the man who can't love her without ruining her.

I already destroyed one woman I cared about. I won't do that to Khloe.

Ramirez watches me carefully. "You gonna keep running?"

I exhale. "No, I'm gonna let her go."

Ramirez nods once, his expression neutral. "Your call, man."

My phone pings.

KHLOE

Did you have an unsuccessful night out?

WAYLON

Not unsuccessful.

KHLOE

Too bad she wasn't good enough to erase me from your memory.

KHLOE

Put me out of my misery and tell me we're over.

She deserves better than waiting for me. I love her too much to let her keep holding onto me when I'm selfish and broken. I put my phone down.

Ramirez watches me like he's waiting to see if I'll break.

I won't, but I've made my choice.

If I wasn't leaving, we would still be together.

Doesn't matter now. But I won't fucking tell her we're over.

Fuck it, call me selfish.

Epilogue

Thunder, Not Rain

Some days, I don't even recognize myself. A year ago, Khloe Navarro wouldn't have believed we'd come this far. She couldn't imagine surviving, let alone thriving, without Waylon's hand to hold or his love that swallowed me whole.

But here I am. I'm damn proud of myself. The old version of me was stitched together with fear of abandonment, never being enough, and waking up feeling incomplete. But that isn't the foundation I stand on now. I've done the fucking work.

Therapy has forced me to hold a mirror to the wounds I spent a lifetime trying not to see. Dr. Morales challenged me in ways that felt brutal before they felt healing.

Writing letters to people who had been there for me, Grandma, Flora, and Aaron.

Then, to the ones who broke me. My mother, my father, Derrick, and, of course, Waylon.

It started as an exercise in love. Then it hurt like hell. I peeled open scabbed wounds to make sure they'd heal right this time. Along the way, it became an exercise in freedom. In letting go of the girl who'd lived in those cracks.

There were days when I wanted to quit. When the weight of my past threatened to crush me. But I had learned to sit with it. To let the emotions come and not let them own me. I learned that love wasn't a currency. I didn't have to earn it through silence, proving myself, or enduring absence.

Today's Khloe gave herself the love I once begged for. Because of that, I'm thriving. I'm crushing the UT Health Nurse Practitioner program. I've made the Dean's List and the President's List. I won the hospital's scholarship and a few more through the school. I'm top of my class *and* on track to graduate early.

Last year, I doubted whether I was good enough. Now I know I am without question. But it isn't just about academics. I have confidence in my skin and voice. When I walk into a room, I don't shrink; I take up space. I don't need someone else's validation to feel whole. I've even gone on a few dates and had some hot hookups.

I express my needs without feeling ashamed. I'm not perfect, and I don't pretend to be. Definitely not bombproof, but I have tools now. When stress creeps in, when the past whispers in my ear, I don't drown. I use my coping techniques: grounding exercises, journaling, or even the simple act of calling Flora.

"Hey, I'm in my head. Talk to me about literally anything else."

And tonight, I'm celebrating. Flora and I booked a long-overdue vacation to Virginia Beach. My first actual break from the whirlwind of school, work, and the constant push towards the future. We insisted that Chelsea, our friend from high school, join the party.

After a long day of soaking up the sun, we're three drinks deep in a cozy bar off the boardwalk. I can drink now without my mind instantly going to *him*. Without feeling the pull of his absence like a gash.

But every once in a while, he slips back into my thoughts. Who am I kidding? Some loves are hard to completely forget. Especially when the sex is mind-altering. But it isn't sadness, not anymore. It's just unfinished.

I perk up in the quiet between us girls. "Alright. Screw it. You wanna hear some shit I probably should've deleted months ago?"

I pull out my phone, scrolling through my notes until I land on Waylon's letter. The one Dr. Morales told me to write but not send, unless I really want to. I'd poured everything into it, every jagged piece of hurt, every restless realization, every ounce of closure I never got.

Chelsea stares, wide-eyed, like she's stumbled into the middle of something sacred or slightly unhinged.

Flora snorts, reaching across the bar before I can say anything else wild. "Khloe, babe," she says, gripping my wrist. "That's a fucking eulogy. You have to send it." Her eyes gleam with that perfect mix of drunk bravery and ride-or-die loyalty.

I hesitate, my thumb hovering over the screen. "It's pointless. He won't care."

Flora scoffs. "Who gives a shit if he cares? You care. I know you. If you don't send it, one day you'll wonder what it would feel like to hit send. So, fucking send it."

Chelsea raises her glass. "As a therapist, I say no. As your friend, fucking send it."

I exhale, glancing down at the screen. It's for me, not him.

So, I do it. The second it says *Delivered*, I feel relief. This is the ultimate closure, the final goodbye. What he does with it isn't my problem.

I look up at my friends, a grin covering my face. "Alright," I say, tipping back the rest of my drink. "I *fucking* sent it. Let's get another round."

Flora cheers. Chelsea smiles. This is the final fucking nail in the coffin. I didn't expect it to feel this freeing.

I am succeeding, not just surviving. Alive, and free of the weight I've carried for way too long. It doesn't feel like I'm waiting for anything. No response is necessary.

THROUGH LUST, WE FELL

With our drinks refilled, Flora raises her glass. "Well, that's that. Now you never have to think about him again."

I take a long sip, then swirl the glass. "I barely think about him now."

Flora arches a brow. "Except when you'll see him in a few months."

"At the wedding? Pssh." I toss back my glass. "Please. I've faced worse things than an ex with unresolved issues."

Chelsea laughs under her breath. "Savage."

I shrug, eyes drifting to the other end of the bar. "Anyway. I've got better things to focus on."

There's a flicker of awareness, like heat on my skin. Someone's watching. He's leaning against the bar, tall, light-eyed, and sinfully attractive. Tattoos trace his forearm, and a glass of bourbon rests in his hand. He isn't Waylon. And that's exactly why I let my gaze linger.

Flora catches me and grins like the devil herself. "Oh, *hell yes*, babe. You deserve a little fun."

I raise an eyebrow. "You think?"

Chelsea tips back her drink. "Again, as a therapist? No. As your friend? Fuck yes."

He's still watching me, waiting. I push back from the bar.

Flora's eyes light up. "You're actually going?"

I shoot her a wink. "Yes. Time to celebrate."

I walk straight up to him, hips swaying, as his jaw tightens.

"Hi," I say confidently.

His lips curl, eyes dropping to my mouth before meeting mine again.

"Hi yourself." His voice is deep, edged with something rough and dark. That is the exact thing I need tonight.

I lean in close, letting my lips graze his ear. "You gonna buy me a drink or take me somewhere I won't need one?"

His smirk deepens, full of intent. "I think you already know the answer to that."

It takes only five steps, a quick glance at the back hallway, and a door slamming shut behind us. The bar's single-stall bathroom is small, dark, and discreet enough that I forget the world outside.

God, it feels good to let go.

My back's to the wall, his mouth claiming mine with an edge of hunger. He inches my dress up and rolls a condom on. His strength doesn't surprise me when he hoists me up, hands gripping my hips, and his fingers sliding against bare skin. I gasp. My arms grips his back, while his tongue traces fire down my neck.

The bass from the bar pulses through the walls, a perfect counter to the rhythm of my hips rolling against his. Our inhales turn into breathless moans. His hand curls around my throat, not tight, just there. Enough to make me lose myself completely. I come fast, biting back a moan as pleasure rips through me.

His smile is smug when he pulls back, his thumb sweeping over my bottom lip. "You needed that."

I let out a breathless laugh, running a hand through my hair as I straighten my dress. "You have no fucking idea."

Then I walk out, heels clicking, without a single glance back.

I'm barely back in my seat when Flora's jaw drops. My cheeks are flushed, lips swollen, and legs deliciously shaky.

"Bitch. Did you just—"

I grin, tipping back my drink. "I *did.*"

Chelsea lifts her glass. "I don't even need to know the details. That's some next-level closure."

I lick the taste of bourbon from my lips.

Not exactly closure because I'll see him again. But next time, I won't be the girl standing in the rain. I'll be the *thunder* rolling in behind it.

Epilogue

Mine. Mine. Mine.

I've been back for a few months from the six-month assignment that turned into eight. Aaron came through when things got tough, but he always found ways to get back to Flora when he could.

Since returning home, I've slipped into my old rhythm. The routine before Khloe.

I pour myself a drink, watching the amber liquid settle in the glass. The air in the house is cool and filled with the silence I usually welcome. But tonight, it feels different.

My phone pings with a text I almost ignore. Until I see that name.

Khloe.

I exhale, rolling my shoulders before unlocking the screen. It's fucking long.

I can't even read it in its entirety. Only the parts that jump out at me.

KHLOE

> Sometimes I wonder if we made a mistake. What if we weren't supposed to let each other go? What if it was a test... and we failed? At this point, oh well. You've made up your mind.

My jaw flexes as I skim over the words.

> I'm jealous of you. Jealous you were able to escape the connection we had. But you never were truly serious about us. If you were, you'd be able to love my summer breeze and then my crazy storms.

A knock interrupts me. She's always right on time. I take a sip of whiskey, letting it burn.

"Come in." I run a hand over my jaw, shoving down the tightness in my chest.

She steps inside, always following my commands. Already setting the tone. She knows exactly what I need. And she's not *her*.

She looks me over. "Rough night?" I let out a grunt. She watches me, eyes gleaming with devilry. "I like it when you're in a mood. Means you'll be mean."

I roll my neck. Flex my fingers, not responding. She steps closer, eyes scanning over me like she's sizing up the damage.

"You know what your problem is?" she muses. "You're incapable of love."

I swallow another sip, face blank. She trails a hand down my arm, nails dragging. "And that's what makes you so fucking fun."

My jaw ticks. "You talk too much."

She grins. "You like that about me."

I roll up my sleeves. "I don't like you."

Focus and control take over. I let myself step into the role, into the distraction. The one thing that had always been simple. But even as I move and do exactly what I'm supposed to, her words still claw under the surface.

> Bravo to me for realizing you use sex because you can't connect to people any other way.

I clench my jaw. Shoving them down to concentrate. I don't think about her again. At least not until I'm alone on my couch, legs stretched out, a half-empty drink in my hand.

Aaron walks in, shaking his head at me. "Jesus. You look like hell."

I chuckle, looking at my phone. I tilt my glass in salute. "Always a pleasure, Brooks."

Aaron doesn't buy it. His eyes flick to the phone I haven't touched since the text came in. He doesn't ask, just grabs it, thumb sliding over the screen. I let him. The text is still open. He reads it, lips pressing into a thin line before he lets out a low whistle and tosses the phone into my lap.

"Damn," he mutters. "She nailed your ass to the wall."

I take another sip of my drink.

Aaron stares, arms crossed. "You read that text and went straight to another meaningless hookup, didn't you?"

I sigh, swirling the whiskey in my glass.

Aaron snorts. "Yeah. That's what I thought."

I still don't say a damn thing because there's nothing to say. She's not wrong. And I don't want to admit that. I won't explain my patterns. Not to Aaron. Not to myself. Not to anyone. I barely get another sip in before Aaron rips the glass from my hand, slamming it on the table with a loud clunk.

"The fuck is wrong with you, Rhodes?"

I arch a brow. "Didn't hear any complaints."

"Yeah? That's 'cause you weren't listening, dumbass." Aaron leans forward, eyes blazing. "Let me break it down for you. Khloe called you out for being an emotionally stunted motherfucker, and you proved her right in record time."

My jaw flexes. "I don't need a damn lecture."

He laughs, full of bite. "No? Then why the fuck are you sitting here like this?"

Silence.

"Why wouldn't you block her? Or answer her?"

He looks at me as if I've kicked his puppy. Like I hurt someone *he* cares about. I shrug, voice flat. "I'm too curious to block her. But I won't answer."

Aaron shakes his head. "You're pathetic, man. Pathetic. You spent months chasing that girl, breaking down her walls, making her trust you, and then what? She *needed* you, wanted you and you couldn't handle it, so you backed off? She begged for your attention. Then you left. Instead of holding on, you let her slip right through your fingers."

Aaron's tone drops, more anger edging into it. "Khloe *loved* you, Rhodes. You let her think she was *too much*."

I stare past him, his glare like a loaded gun.

"Guess what? You better get your shit together, because you're gonna have to see her real soon."

My fingers grip the armrest. "What the fuck are you talking about?"

Aaron gives me a shit-eating grin, but there's no humor in it. "Oh, you forgot? Guess you've been too busy drowning in whiskey and mediocre pussy to keep up."

I keep staring, jaw locked.

His smile fades. "Mine and Flora's wedding, Rhodes. You. Khloe. In the same damn place. Hope you're ready for that."

My stomach knots.

He continues. "I swear to God, if you fuck with her, if you pull your usual shit, try to worm your way back in just to leave her hanging again? I'll be the first one to lay your ass out."

"I ain't gonna mess with her."

Aaron's eyes narrow. "Good. Because she's doing just fine without you. Moved on. Happy. And you're sitting here in the dark, reeking of bad decisions, drinking your feelings like a coward."

I grit my teeth. "You done?"

He tilts his head, eyes burning into me. "Nah, you've got a choice, Rhodes. Keep spiraling. Keep pretending you don't feel a damn thing. Keep running from the only woman who ever saw you, the real you, and still wanted you. Or?" He shrugs. "Or you do something about it. But either way? Stay the fuck out of her way unless you've got something real to say."

I stare at the floor. Let his words settle long enough to feel them. Then, I shove them back where all the other regrets live. Locked up tight.

I look up, voice flat. "That it?"

Aaron's lip curls in disgust. He turns to leave. "Yeah. That's it. I'd tell you to think about it, but I know you won't."

I don't stop him when he walks out or flinch when the door slams shut. I glance down and see Khloe's name still lit up on the screen. I reach for my glass. Then my phone.

I pull up another woman's number, a great sub. A diversion. But I can't follow through.

I swipe back to Khloe's name, digging in.

KHLOE

Sometimes I wonder if we made a mistake. What if we weren't supposed to let each other go? What if it was a test... and we failed? At this point, oh well. You've made up your mind. I'm jealous of you. Jealous you were able to escape the connection we had. But you never were truly serious about us. If you were, you'd be able to love my summer breeze and then my crazy storms. Love isn't in the top 5 most important things in your life, but you pursued me anyway. And then made me feel needy when you acted like I was a priority. You're afraid of commitment because that means you may have to give up your need for alone time. You shield your brain from others in fear of them seeing the animal you are. Don't hide your needs next time. I wouldn't have ever threatened your need to be alone. I would have given you all that you needed if you had been upfront.

KHLOE

You told me once no man has ever given me what I deserve. I sure as shit don't think I deserved this. You abandoned me and, in the process, abandoned what you could have had.

KHLOE

I realized after you that I don't need reassurance. It was difficult to gauge what you thought of me or how you felt about me when you would go on your long moments of silence. You gave me false hope because you began things being very attentive and paying more attention to me than I was used to. Then you just stopped. No warning, no explanation, just that you were busy. But ironically, you hadn't been too busy in the beginning to woo me in. I know that was the butterflies on your behalf, but it confused me. You confused me.

KHLOE

Everything that you did in the beginning gave me reassurance, and then you took it away. That's why I slowly became a confused girl when I had started off so strong. You made me a weak bitch, and for that, I almost feel bad for you. If what you did to me is something you regularly do to females, all you'll ever do is create women who will fall apart and not be able to handle you.

KHLOE

Your soul was the most exquisite and devastating creature I've ever crossed paths with. Sad little thing with the power to be beautiful, if only it allowed itself to be loved. You were so loved by me, Waylon. I'm glad you allowed me to do so, even if for such a brief span of time. Love made the danger in you look like safety. Thanks to you, I know now I want a love that's all-consuming. Something fierce, untamed, and a wild ride. A love that pulls me in, shakes me up, and makes me feel alive.

KHLOE

I hope one day I pop into your head & you think, "We shouldn't have stopped trying." By then, I'll have forgotten the taste of your lips and the feel of you on my body. Notice I said MY. My lips, my body, my heart, my soul. Bravo to me for realizing you use sex because you can't connect to people any other way. You'll never have anything that is mine again. Goodbye, Waylon.

My stomach drops, thumb hovering over the screen. I type out three words. Then delete them.
I try,

I'm sorry

but trash that too.

Then nothing. My chest tightens, a knot I refuse to untangle. I lock my phone and down the rest of my drink. Her voice lives in my head, unforgiving and final. That one sentence hangs in the air like smoke.

Over and over, I hear her voice telling me…

You'll never have anything that is mine again.

Mine. Mine. Mine.

Until the word doesn't even sound real anymore.

"We'll see about that."

It's not a challenge, but a truth I cling to in silence. I never completely released her because every part of me believed she was made to be mine.

To Be Continued...

Take a peek at the sequel...

Through Desire, We Burn

Prologue
Aaron and Flora's Wedding Party Roster

Flora

Aaron knows the second I pull out the list that he's screwed. "I don't see why we need to make it even," he says, rubbing the back of his neck.

My eyes lift over the paper in my hands. "Because symmetry is aesthetically pleasing, babe."

Aaron sighs. "I don't think symmetry is the issue."

I'm cross-legged on the couch, twirling my pen. Wedding-planning mode is in full force, which means Aaron has as much say in these decisions as our baby puppy. He takes a sip of beer as I dig in.

"Alright, let's finalize this. Bridesmaids and groomsmen." I tap the notepad.

"Obviously, Khloe," Aaron throws out.

That isn't up for debate. Khloe was my first real best friend. I still remember being teenagers, sitting on Khloe's bedroom floor, an outdated magazine spread between us, talking about all the places we'd escape to one day.

Khloe has been with me through every milestone, every heartbreak, every late-night phone call. When I doubt myself, Khloe reminds me who I am. When I met Aaron and felt the ground shift beneath me in that instant, Khloe was the one to tell me to go for it.

"She was destined to be first on this list," I say.

Aaron smiles. "That's more than obvious."

"Then there's Chelsea. When Khloe was post-breakup, I didn't want to feel like I was shoving our good times in her face," I say, chewing the pen in my mouth. "Chelsea would tell me whether I was rushing into things with you. She was the one who kept me grounded."

Aaron raises a brow. "You thought you were rushing into things with me?"

I raise my eyebrows. "Baby, of course I thought about it. We hadn't been together a year before you put a ring on it. But Chelsea never tried to push me. She just made me sit with my feelings like a true therapist."

Aaron smirks. "Worked out for me."

Chelsea has always been a sounding board. She isn't the friend who tells me what I want to hear. Chelsea isn't the loudest or the most sentimental of my friends, but she is constant. She challenges me and makes me think.

Aaron sighs. "I know she's been good to you. I just—"

"You just don't like that her X-ray eyes see through all your shit," I cut in, grinning.

Aaron scowls. "I don't have that much shit."

"Oh, baby... okay, Marisol—I know you still haven't met her, but she's special. Like I've said, we always promised each other as kids we'd be in each other's weddings. Her smile hasn't changed since we were preteens. All gap-toothed charm turned grown woman."

"You always are one to keep your word. But doesn't she have kids—how's she going to travel for events?"

"She won't come to them all, just the important ones. She's in the middle of a divorce from her husband now. Typical Florida man." I roll my eyes and hum.

"Anyways... Missy." Aaron nods as I add, "Lena."

Aaron groans, "Oh, come on."

"She's my new ride-or-die."

Lena came into my life through Missy, her just-as-spunky younger sister. When I moved to Texas, I met Missy at work, and she insisted on taking me out on the town. And then Lena. We three have been thick as thieves ever since. But now, with Missy happily barefoot, pregnant, and settling down with the bartender of her dreams, Lena is the new life of the party.

"They've both been chaotic, amazing additions," I say simply. "And Lena may be nuts, but she's stepping up now that Missy is plus one."

Aaron sighs. "Fine. But I'm avoiding her at the reception." I laugh as Aaron mutters, not-so-quietly, "She's vulgar."

"That's why I love her."

Aaron

I flip my notepad open. "Alright, my turn."

Flora leans forward in anticipation. "Ramirez." No arguments there. Ramirez was stationed with Waylon and me overseas, and now we work together. He's a blunt, sarcastic asshole, and has a way of pointing out the obvious in the most annoying way possible. But he's also trustworthy and funny.

"He was the one who sat with me after we lost Daniels when Rhodes was on assignment," I say, quieter now. "He didn't try to fix it. He just... sat there. And drank with me."

Flora reaches across the table and squeezes my hand.

I clear my throat and move on. "Jackman."

Flora nods. Even though Jackman is Waylon's older cousin, I've grown close to him. We were stationed together in Afghanistan, not in the same squad, but close enough to trust each other when it mattered. But Jackman's connection to Waylon runs even deeper than blood.

"When Big Jack's brother, Beau, had his first kid, he wanted to honor him," I say. "So, he named his son Jackman. A tribute to his big brother without straight-up naming him after him."

Flora nods, her expression softening. "And Beau passes."

I exhale. "Yeah. Jackman was in his teens when he lost

his dad. Jack, Waylon's father, didn't try to replace him. But he remained a stable presence in Jackman's life. And Jackman's not gonna let Waylon off easy."

"He shouldn't," Flora agrees.

Jackman's family in a way that matters. Shaped by the same roots, the same losses. He and Waylon might not have always been close, but Jackman has seen him spiral before. He sure as hell will not stand by and watch him do it again.

I chuckle. "Speaking of people who won't let anyone off easy. Nolan."

Flora laughs. "I knew you'd put him in."

"If I didn't, you'd stick him in a dress," I mutter.

Flora shrugs. "He'd probably rock it. Nolan's my favorite cousin. He's impossible not to like. He's charming, flirty, and has a natural way of making everyone feel like they are the most interesting person in the room. And he was the first person in my family to flirt with you."

I huff out a small laugh. "And the last."

Flora smiles mischievously. "That you know of. He enjoys seeing you sweat."

"Good luck with that." I tap my pen against the table. "And then there's Kyle."

Flora's expression cools slightly.

"We both know I have to include him," I say. Kyle was in boot camp with Waylon and I. "Despite being an arrogant son of a bitch, I can't deny that Kyle has been there for me, especially after my brother died."

I finish in a more serious tone. "And my other brother in arms and life, Waylon. Hope he keeps his shit together."

Flora scribbles in her notepad. "You know what's crazy?"

"What?"

Flora sighs. "That out of everyone, Khloe and Waylon, means the most to both of us. And they're the ones we have the least control over."

I shift in my seat, not loving where this is going.

"Khloe's been my rock, my safe place, the sister I chose.

And she's finally taken the time to take care of her mental health. To heal. She's grown into the woman I always knew she could be, confident and unfazed. There's nothing I wouldn't do for that woman."

I clear my throat. "Waylon's saved me in more ways than I can describe. He was there for me when therapy was heavy after I was shot. He's not perfect, but he's always had my back... But his selfish, reckless tendencies make it hard to watch him burn his own happiness to the ground. But on the other side, he's family."

"I know," Flora murmurs.

Silence stretches between us. I look down at the list again. "This wedding is going to be a disaster."

Flora grins, leaning back against the couch. "I know."

After the Lust:
Book Club/ Reader Questions

1. When Khloe first meets Waylon, what draws her to him after knowing he's a playboy, and what should've warned her? Do you think attraction rooted in pain can ever be healthy?
2. Waylon talks about control often. Do you think his dominance is about trust, love, or fear? How does that change by the end?
3. Khloe's trauma and Waylon's guilt both drive them to hide behind physical connection. At what point do you think lust turns into something deeper for them?
4. Flora often tells Khloe that she should seek professional help. What does that reveal about Flora's understanding of Khloe's pain and Khloe's resistance to healing? Do you think Khloe would've reached that point on her own without Flora's push?
5. Waylon says, "She was mine long before I ever had the right to claim her." If you agreed, how does your answer shift after finishing the book?
6. The BDSM elements in the story are deeply emotional rather than purely erotic. How does vulnerability play into their scenes? Did any part of that surprise you?
7. Both characters struggle with trust. Who do you think learns to trust first, and why?
8. Family and found family are powerful themes in TLWF. How do Waylon's and Khloe's pasts shape

what they want in love and belonging?
9. If you could give Khloe one piece of advice at the start of the book, what would it be? Would it change by the end?
10. If you could have a whiskey with Waylon, what one question would you ask him after finishing TLWF?

Please send me your answers from your book club!

I would love to answer any questions you may have.

My DMs are always open on Instagram.

TLWF Soundtrack

1. Rent Free (Acoustic)—6LACK
2. Blowin' Smoke—Teddy Swims
3. Body Like a Back Road—Sam Hunt
4. Spin You Around (1/24)—Morgan Wallen
5. You Put a Spell on Me—Austin Giorgio
6. Strawberry Wine (Remastered 2021)—Deana Carter
7. Issues (Acoustic)—Julia Michaels
8. Losin Control—Russ
9. Missing Peace—Pecos & The Rooftops
10. Cowboy Take Me Away—The Chicks
11. River—Leon Bridges
12. 3:15 (Breathe)—Russ
13. Wrong Turns—Old Dominion
14. Tennessee Whiskey—Chris Stapleton
15. Sunrise (Live from Abbey Road Studios)—Morgan Wallen
16. Ruin—Usher
17. The Night We Met—Lord Huron
18. Wine Into Whiskey—Tucker Wetmore
19. Wouldn't Have to Miss You—Pecos & The Rooftops
20. Stay—Rihanna
21. Choosin' Texas—Alanna Iman
22. One Last Time—Ariana Grande
23. This Damn Song—Pecos & The Rooftops
24. If You Want Love—NF

25. Workin On Me—Russ
26. Lose You to Love Me—Selena Gomez
27. Blood Sport—Sleep Token

Acknowledgments

Thank you to my readers who took a chance on this indie author. I hope I didn't hurt too many feelings with that ending. Hehe. But if you made it here, then you deserve your praise, good girl 😉

Please, please, please review. Reviews are so important to us indie authors!

Thank you to my sister, Amanda. For reading all the early excerpts. For being okay with me edging you with details and hints. And always trusting my insane plan, even when you thought you'd hate it.

To Lina, the most inspiring Beta reader. Girl! You are amazing. Your insight took my early draft from subpar to out of this world. You gave me so much confidence to move forward with Khloe and Waylon.

To Kaila, my soul twin. Where do I even start? I guess the beginning with THE CRAFT, who would have thought a GIF would give me my newest light in my life. The transition from stranger to best friend and birthday twin is still astonishing to me. Thank you for always rooting me on. We will be bestsellers soon! AND I CAN NOT wait to see you :-)

To Carly, my AMAZING cover artist, who took all my character dreams and made them real. Your talent is unmatched. Thank you for the 3000 edits on Khloe, perfecting her until we found just the right one. Again, still thinking about taking out that million dollar loan. HAHA! Thank you again and always.

To Ramona, my editor. You truly were there for me for every random question, random should we do this or that, and even just reposting and sharing almost everything I post. Thank you for helping me make TLWF incredible.

Special shoutouts to Jess, my other beta. To Holly & Michelle, my proofreaders. To Haleigh, Kim, Marta, Ciera, & Bonnie for always letting me talk about book nonsense with you. To all of my stories that started by accident and ended in truth, I'm grateful for every page.

To my exes, hahaha—special thanks to every heartbreak that found its way onto these pages. You woke something up, even if you didn't stay long enough to see what it became. I survived. Khloe survived. We're thriving. Thanks for the memories—Fall Out Boy style.

To my husband, thank you for never thinking I was crazy for doing this, even though I am. Thank you for always listening, giving feedback even if I don't like it, and being my ride or die. 🖤

To my daughters, I hope you never read this, lol. But know you are always loved, always cherished, and you're worthy of every dream you aspire to have. Always reach for the stars, babygirls.

About the Author

Kasondra Fox writes romances where raw intimacy, mental health, healing, and modern love collide. Her stories are crafted for readers who crave depth with their heat. When she's not writing or reading, she's probably creating playlists for her characters, obsessing over her dog, traveling, or plotting her next smutty, devastating scene. Kasondra lives in upstate New York with her family, a beautiful pit bull, and an endless supply of Reese's. Her series are published under her indie imprint, Fox & Flame Press.

Visit https://authorkasondrafox.com/ to stay up to date.

www.ingramcontent.com/pod-product-compliance
Lightning Source LLC
LaVergne TN
LVHW091701070526
838199LV00050B/2240